Rose Melikan was born in Detroit, Michigan, and since 1993 she has been a Fellow of St Catharine's College, Cambridge. She lives in Cambridge with her husband, Dr Quentin Stafford-Fraser.

Praise for *The Counterfeit Guest*:

'A period thriller that zips along with elan and excitement'
Easy Living

'[A] confident voice, quirky characters and sparkling period detail' *Publisher's Weekly*

THE
BLACKSTONE
KEY

Rose Melikan

For Quentin, most of all

First published in Great Britain in 2010 by Sphere
This paperback edition published in 2011 by Sphere
Reprinted 2012

Copyright © Rose Melikan

The moral right of the author has been asserted.

*All characters and events in this publication, other
than those clearly in the public domain, are fictitious
and any resemblance to real persons,
living or dead, is purely coincidental.*

A CIP catalogue record for this book
is available from the British Library.

ISBN 978-0-3513-2420-8

Typeset in Garamond by Palimpsest Book Production Limited
Falkirk, Stirlingshire
Printed and bound in Great Britain by
Clays Ltd, St Ives plc

Papers used by Sphere are from well-managed forests
and other responsible sources.

MIX
Paper from
responsible sources
FSC® C104740

Sphere
An imprint of
Little, Brown Book Group
100 Victoria Embankment
London EC4Y 0DY

An Hachette UK Company
www.hachette.co.uk

www.littlebrown.co.uk

Places of interest in
The Blackstone Key

The Wash

Aylsham ○

Norwich ○

St Ives ○

Bury
St Edmunds ○

Cambridge ○   Newmarket ○

Stowmarket ○

Woodbridge ○

Ipswich ○

Landguard Fort

Colchester ○

Chelmsford ○

Waltham Abbey ○

*North
Sea*

LONDON ○

Woolwich ○

River Thames

0   10   20   30 Miles

1

The clock at Great St Mary's Church in Cambridge tolled the half hour on a grey, gloomy, October morning in the year 1795. The rain had stopped, but heavy clouds made further showers likely, while the wind streaming down from the north had a wintry bite. In short, it was the sort of morning that could easily have defeated scholarly enthusiasm and kept the shops on King's Parade dark for at least another hour. And yet traffic was brisk and included more than one gentleman's carriage, while at the Eagle, a prominent coaching inn, such was the noise from the crush of patrons that the bells of the University Church went unheard.

The door of the Eagle opened, unsuccessfully at first, for there was someone standing against it, and a young woman slipped inside. She was dressed in a travelling cloak and a black tricorne. In a less crowded establishment the tricorne might have excited interest. Everything else about its wearer suggested the economy of a woman in genteel poverty. Her cloak was worn and frayed along the bottom, and her boots had been re-soled, while her scarf had been knitted by inexpert fingers, one of which peeked out of a hole in her glove. Against all of this the tricorne was a rebellion, for such a hat could not have been purchased for less than ten shillings. Moreover, when perched jauntily upon auburn curls, it conveyed an independence of spirit that had not yet been overwhelmed by circumstances. Amid the hubbub of the Eagle's parlour, however, none of this attracted much attention.

Only one man was aware of the newcomer's presence, and that was because he knew her. Dr Smithson Nichols was a Fellow of Trinity College, and usually he took notice of few facts apart from that one. The young woman in the doorway, however, looked remarkably like one of the teachers at the school in nearby St Ives where his sister, Miss Nichols, was also employed. Therefore he waved imperturbably in her direction and, as the man sitting beside him was smoking a particularly foul-smelling cigar, even made the effort to cross the room to speak to her.

'Ah, it is *Miss Finch*, is it not?' he intoned, upon reaching her side. 'Greetings and felicitations from the Alma Mater. I see that my dear sister does not accompany you, but I trust that all is well? Mrs Bunbury's academy remains unchallenged in the land as a temple to female learning?'

Mary Finch disliked Dr Nichols *and* his dear sister, but she was feeling sufficiently ill at ease to regard him with more friendliness than she would otherwise have done. She had little experience of a noisy public house, and Dr Nichols at least had the advantage of familiarity – even if he was a pompous windbag. 'Yes,' she replied, endeavouring to smile in appreciation of his witticism, 'We are all well, only . . . I am . . . making a journey.'

'A *journey*?' repeated Dr Nichols. He rolled the word around in his mouth, as if he did not quite like the taste of it. 'I see.'

2

There was no reason why Mary need offer an explanation to Dr Nichols, but there was something in his tone of voice that made her feel as if she ought to do so. Or perhaps she was anxious about the entire scheme and wished to justify herself. At any rate, she answered his unspoken question. 'Yes, to visit my uncle, Mr Edward Finch. He has an estate in Suffolk, and he has invited me to visit him. You may read all about it in Cary's *Atlas* – about his estate, I mean.'

Mary felt foolish as soon as the words were spoken, and the implication that he might be in the habit of perusing such a common publication made Dr Nichols frown. 'Indeed,' he replied, loftily. 'Most gratifying, I am sure, to know that the particulars of one's drainage are perused by readers of Cary's *Atlas*. Whomever they may be,' he added, after a slight pause.

'Yes, well . . .' Mary looked about her, thinking that Dr Nichols was even more unpleasant than his sister. He might be the . . . the *Duke* of Cambridge, the way he talked, whereas in fact he lived in his college rooms and very likely knew nothing whatsoever about drainage. And he would probably go straight back to Trinity and read all about her uncle's estate in Cary, for all his airs and graces.

Fortunately none of this indignation was perceptible in her next remark; at least it was not perceptible to Dr Nichols. 'How very crowded it is,' she observed. 'Do you know, is this usual?'

Perhaps surprisingly, this question caused Dr Nichols to unbend slightly. He liked being asked his opinion – he gave it freely, whether or not it had been requested, but he preferred to be asked. 'No, indeed,' he explained, 'today's unpleasant crush is the result of a horse race.'

'A *horse race*?' Mary cried. 'Here? I mean, in Cambridge?'

3

'No, no, at Newmarket. The contest has long been anticipated, so I am told, in consequence of which anyone with either an equine interest or a desire to rid himself of a large sum of money – which includes a very large proportion of the populace – is hurrying to that locality by any means possible.'

'Oh, dear,' said Mary, 'then I suppose that it may be difficult to book a place on the coach.'

'Nearly impossible, I should say. But *you* can have no interest in witnessing such a gross spectacle, surely. I would certainly not recommend it.'

'Well, I *might* be interested,' countered Mary, if only because she did not want to accept any recommendation from him, 'but I must go to Newmarket regardless. It is on the way to Suffolk, you see.'

'Ah, yes, to be sure.' Dr Nichols had forgotten about Suffolk, or, rather, he had not listened very carefully in the first place. 'Well, this is not the day to travel to Newmarket,' he decreed. 'I would advise putting off the journey until tomorrow, or next week.'

Mary recalled her employer's less than enthusiastic response to the proposed leave of absence. If Mary were to return now it would be ever so much more difficult to get away a second time, and it would look so . . . weak to acknowledge oneself defeated by the first obstacle. 'It would not be quite convenient to put off my departure,' she replied, with as much coolness as she could muster.

Dr Nichols seemed to recall that Miss Finch was a somewhat headstrong young woman – she would undoubtedly please herself whatever prudence (in the person of Dr Nichols) might suggest. He merely shrugged his shoulders, therefore, to acknowledge his helplessness in the face of her shortcomings, and observed that she had better try to book her place.

'Yes, I had better,' she agreed, and, drawing herself up, she edged forward into a gap in the crowd without waiting for a reply. Dr Nichols considered this highly ill mannered, especially as it prevented him from offering a final admonition against young women travelling alone in public coaches. Instead, he pursed his lips and said, 'Good morning,' to the place she had just vacated and took his leave.

Mary threaded her way into the taproom and finally reached the bar, where the landlord confirmed Dr Nichols' prediction: all the places on the Ipswich coach were already booked, at least as far as Newmarket. Then a group of men in long riding coats pressed forward, competing with Mary for the landlord's attention, and her further conversation with him was conducted in a series of shouts.

'Oh!' she exclaimed, as a large man pushed past her.

'Should've booked earlier,' bawled the innkeeper. He served up three foaming tankards and mopped the bar where one had overflowed. 'All right, I heard you – two pints of the Old Reliable.'

'Yes, but what shall I do *now*? When is the next coach?'

'Day after tomorrow!'

'What? I beg your pardon!' This time she pushed back. 'Is there nothing else?'

The landlord wiped his hands and consulted his booking register, running down the page with his finger. 'Sorry, miss, I can't see – no, I tell a lie. I've the one seat left on the Norwich diligence.'

'But I wish to go to *Ipswich*!' Mary reminded him as a man leaned over her shoulder to collect his drink. She steadied herself against the bar, and her hands came away sticky from spilled beer. Why was everyone in such a state, jostling and calling out? Some of the men behind her seemed almost angry, and the race was still some hours away.

'The diligence'll beat the coach to Newmarket. Wait a minute now, sir; I'm dealing with the young lady. You can change there, miss, and carry on to Ipswich!'

'Well, I suppose I must do that. I trust there will be places *after* Newmarket?'

'Bound to be,' agreed the landlord. 'It's only this race has brought the crowds. Hi, Bill! Here's the last for the True Blue! Tell Jeb that all's secure! Better make your way to the yard as soon as you can, miss. Jeb Miller's that particular about setting off to time.'

Mary dug her purse out of her cloak pocket and managed to open it, half expecting that someone would seize it before she could extract the fare, and flung her money down on the bar. Then she struggled back through the crowd to the courtyard, where she encountered an even greater tumult. Conveyances of all kinds were being readied for departure. Saddle horses, whose owners had stepped inside for refreshment before continuing to Newmarket, were being walked up and down to keep them warm. The blast of a horn announced the arrival of the London mail coach. Its four steaming horses stood trembling and tossing their heads, while the coachman demanded instant service in recognition of his valuable cargo. 'The Mail! Make way, the Mail! Horses off!'

'Where's your luggage, miss?' asked Bill, a husky, fair-haired boy.

'I have no idea,' Mary admitted, and she looked about her anxiously. 'When I arrived one of the other boys – with a leather apron – said I could leave my bag with him.'

'Don't you worry, miss,' said Bill, cheerily, 'you did quite right. What sort of bag is it? A leather grip?'

'Yes, with two handles. One is loose – well, broken.'

'I'll see you aboard and then I'll fetch it for you.'

'Thank you very much.'

'That's all right, miss,' smiled Bill. He did not often get the chance to serve such a pretty young lady, and that green feather in her hat just matched her eyes. 'My word, what a day, eh, miss? How'd you like to be the cause of all this?'

'I do not think it a very likely possibility,' Mary laughed. She still felt as if she had been caught up in a rather alarming melee, but she was beginning to see the funny side of it. The Eagle was like an anthill that had been disturbed – it appeared chaotic, but everyone seemed to know his business. She must simply trust that they would send her on her way, and in the right direction.

'Well, all this is Lord Seymour's doing,' Bill continued. 'They say the colonel's been trying to match Swiftsure against the Arabian Prince for months, but Lord Seymour weren't having none. They only came to terms on Monday, and look at the punters! Mind yer step, miss; the yard's in a right old state today.'

Bill steered her toward a neat blue carriage, whose side panel proclaimed itself: *The True Blue. Cambridge. Newmarket. Thetford. Norwich*. A team of glossy black horses stood between the shafts. 'Here you are, miss. This young lady's yer fourth, Jeb,' he announced, nodding to the great-coated figure striding up and down beside the vehicle.

The coachman touched his hat to Mary. 'Will you step aboard, miss? We're ready to start.'

Mary climbed inside, glanced at her three male companions, and slid into the remaining vacant place. Her bag was secured, and then the coach swayed as Jeb Miller ascended to his perch. Almost immediately the servant holding the horses' heads called, 'Horses on!' to which Jeb answered, 'Let 'em go!' The servant stood aside, and the coachman urged his team forward.

Then they were turning into the King's Parade, and she was on her way. *On her way* – what a thrilling expression! *On her way* and not *back to school*. And yet, as she settled into her seat Mary's thoughts turned inexorably to the life she was leaving behind – perhaps forever – and that possibility caused her a pang of distress. She had been three years at Mrs Bunbury's school, and three years was a long time when one was only twenty years of age. The routine of the school, such as it was, she knew by heart: morning and evening prayers led by Mrs Bunbury; lessons – some interesting, some tedious, most indifferent; meals, with the inevitable jam roly-poly for dessert and never enough milk for tea; church on Sunday mornings, and the long Sunday afternoons spent in some 'useful' occupation such as darning one's stockings.

Mary mentally checked off the several components of a typical week at Mrs Bunbury's and smiled ruefully to herself. How could she possibly feel homesick for such a place? There was nothing the least bit exciting about it, and no one interesting ever came to visit. The most that could be expected was some news about Dr Nichols, triumphantly relayed by his dear sister. It was not all bad, of course, and Mary would miss her colleagues – well, some of them – very much.

She glanced out of the window and watched the autumn countryside roll past her. It was rather dull, if she was honest with herself. The ground was flat, and the rain had beaten the leaves from the trees so that they stood stark and bare. If only the sun would shine it might still have been a cheerful morning, but instead the world seemed an unrelieved palate of grey and muddy brown. If viewed from her bedroom window, the scene would have excited little interest – but, of course, she could have seen nothing of this from *any* window in Mrs Bunbury's

8

academy. This view, the diligence, her fellow passengers, even the hurly-burly of the Eagle were all new, and that made all the difference. No pupil, escaping the toils of the schoolroom at the end of term, could have felt a keener sense of freedom.

2

The journey to Newmarket was a largely silent one. Mary had never made conversation with a group of strange men, and she was at a loss how to begin. Her companions knew very well what they wanted to discuss, but felt unable to do so in her presence. They were three middle-aged townsmen who, in a moment of rebellion against the everyday tyranny of home and shop, had decided to attend the big race. Horseracing, they all felt, while capital sport and well worth the sacrifice of a day's wages, was not a fitting subject for a young lady's ears. Thus, only the occasional topical reference was possible, while amusing comments about what one's wife would say about today's adventure were left unuttered.

The remarks of their coachman did occasionally pierce the silence inside the vehicle. He expressed himself in a very forthright manner, and with little toleration for anyone impeding his progress. Nor did he seem much concerned whether there were any young ladies within earshot, although, as it happened, he had rightly judged the situation. Although she could not see the obstructions that provoked his ire, Mary found herself sympathising with him. *He* did not stand for any nonsense from lazy carters or self-important gentlemen who thought they could drive 'and didn't know one end of a horse from t'other'. What were they doing on the road, in any event, when other people had very important business, and did not wish to be delayed by such foolery?

'Get out of the bloody road, would you?'

Mary wished that she could tell someone to get out of the bloody road – Dr Nichols, or even Mrs Bunbury, sometimes. *No,* she frowned, *not 'bloody' – that would be cursing. 'Abominable', perhaps. 'Get out of the abominable road!' That was almost as good.*

The abominable road certainly grew increasingly congested as they approached Newmarket, and Mary began thinking about her connection. What if she missed it, or what if there were no places on the Suffolk coach, despite what the landlord of the Eagle had said? She imagined herself carrying her bag through the deserted streets of Newmarket, all of whose inhabitants had abandoned their homes and businesses to watch Swiftsure and Arabian Prince.

'I beg your pardon,' she said, taking in her three companions with one glance, 'but could any of you tell me the name of the inn where we shall stop in Newmarket? I must change to a Suffolk coach, you see.'

Her words were greeted with amazement; she might have been proposing a journey to the moon. 'Suffolk, miss?' cried one of the men. He had a prominent Adam's apple, and now it worked up and down. 'Why that's where them Frenchies are! They'll have your head straight off, they will.'

Mary stared back at him in shocked silence, while his companions ridiculed him as a darned fool; of course the French weren't in Suffolk – what a thing to say to a young lady, frightening her and all. He ought to be ashamed of himself. They might come any day, of course, with Suffolk being so much closer to France from a geographical point of view. It was a dangerous place; that was for certain, what with the war and all. Was she sure she wanted to go there?

They looked as if they were going to suggest some alternative destination, but when Mary confirmed her intentions, heads were shaken and lips were pursed, and no further warnings were given. (It was the same when a customer insisted on serge when a good quality felt would have done quite as well for half the price. If they were that set on serge, it was better not to argue about it.) In fact, Mary was far less confident than she sounded. Was her journey really so very perilous? She did not know very much about the war, apart from the fact that it had all come about because the French had put their king to death – and that itself was an extremely grisly notion. If Frenchmen of that sort were about to invade, the prospect of a seat on the Suffolk coach was even worse than no seat at all!

She alighted at the White Hart in Newmarket, therefore, in some trepidation, but her fears were soon put to rest. In the cosy parlour she received the reassuring information that the Ipswich coach was not fully booked and was expected shortly. Nor were there further worrying prognostications about imminent French invasions. Indeed, no one seemed to regard the journey as in any way ill-advised, and Mary observed their expressions closely, in case they were trying to conceal the danger in order to obtain her fare. She perceived no such ignoble intention, and the realisation that she could sensibly continue her journey flowed through her like a calming wave. Such was her relief that she recklessly ordered a muffin and a cup of tea.

As had been the case at the Eagle, the White Hart was bustling with patrons. Fortified by her muffin, her seat by the fire and her place on the coach, however, Mary viewed the comings and goings around her with equanimity. Everyone was talking about the day's great event, and she heard quite a lot about the two horses, their respective jockeys, and what would have been the outcome if a third animal, Blue Moon, were competing. A large, white-faced clock on the wall opposite informed her of the time. At a quarter past ten the landlord reported that the race traffic in Cambridge must have delayed the Ipswich coach. 'Never fear, miss,' he assured her, 'you'll be off by half past. This here is nothing. Why, we're often held up for hours when there's a full card.'

'Who do you think will win?' Mary ventured. The racing jargon had piqued her interest, although she did not know whether it was preferable to have 'an easy action' or 'a quick turn of foot'. Both appeared to be highly desirable attributes.

'Well, now,' considered the landlord, his head to one side, 'if I was a gambling man, which I ain't, I don't say I mightn't be tempted by Swiftsure. But on this ground, it's a brave man who bets agin Lord Seymour.'

'Is it true that Arabian Prince is much smaller than Swiftsure? It does not seem fair that he should have to race against a bigger horse – will he be given a head start?'

'Oh, no, miss,' said the landlord, smiling. 'But don't you worry. The Prince may be small, but he's game, don't you see? He's got bags of courage, and he hates losing. And then, of course, he carries less weight, and I've seen horses of his size over nine furlongs—'

But Mary was not interested in furlongs. Her heart warmed to the brave little horse that did not like to lose. 'Oh, I hope he wins,' she cried.

13

A sudden commotion brought the landlord's explanation to a close. 'I'm sure I do too, miss, but that'll be your coach, now, so quick as you can.' He hurried outside, and Mary followed him. In the courtyard they watched as a low-slung coach disgorged three men and a dog, while another eight men descended from the roof of the vehicle.

'That's the way to kill the horses, Sam,' observed the landlord, '*and* have the law down on you.'

The coachman shrugged his shoulders. 'Weren't me that let 'em on board. "I don't turn away extra fares," he says to me in Cambridge, and then tells me to go easy. Couldn't help but go easy, with all this crowd.'

'Well, there's just the one fare, this young lady, and see you don't damage *my* team on the Bury run.'

'You know I ain't no flogger,' complained the coachman. 'Suppose you quit jawing and hitch 'em on.'

Judging by the landlord's remarks and the number of persons who had left the coach, Mary expected that she would be travelling alone to Bury. She was very surprised, therefore, when she opened the door and discovered two prior occupants. The first was a large woman, dressed in an old-fashioned Mantua robe of grey satin, a fur tippet, and with a lace cap tied under her chin. She was so broad that at first Mary thought she must have been wearing a hoop, a fashion that some older ladies still favoured. Closer inspection, however, revealed that she needed no artificial enlargement. Opposite her was a small, prim-looking, elderly man in a suit of brown plush, and they both seemed to have suffered from the confined conditions of the journey from Cambridge. They introduced themselves as Mrs Oldworthy and Mr Treadgill, and while Mr Treadgill straightened his wig and adjusted his coat, Mrs Oldworthy informed Mary of what they had endured.

'Miss Finch, I do assure you it was unbelievable. The

14

crush inside this coach – I thought I must faint – and poor Mr Treadgill! Mr Treadgill has travelled in India. Didn't you say that this crush was worse than any you'd had in India?'

'Oh yes, far worse.'

'I hope neither of you has been hurt,' said Mary, sympathetically. Mr Treadgill made a slight deprecatory gesture, while Mrs Oldworthy carried on in a strong, confident voice. There had been eight men on the roof, which anyone must agree was unsafe. An actual crash had been avoided by a succession of miracles. 'And there was that great monster in here, barking and slavering. I don't know how we weren't all bitten, he was that wild.'

Mr Treadgill explained in an undertone to Mary that the dog, a mild-mannered creature, might have fallen if he had been put on the roof. 'A dog is not a cat, you know. He cannot grip and hold, on account of having the wrong sort of toenails – for gripping, I mean.' He looked as if he were going to offer an anecdote about a dog, but Mrs Oldworthy cut him short.

'Well, they needn't think that I shan't complain,' she announced, 'toenails or no toenails. A regular scandal, that's what it was, and I shall have something to say about it, when we return to Cambridge. Mr Treadgill oughtn't to be made to endure such things.'

'I wish I had known of this race,' piped Mr Treadgill, 'I should have liked to see it. I once won twenty pounds at Epsom, you know, when I was home on leave.'

It transpired that Mr Treadgill had retired to Cambridge after a long career as the senior clerk of Ashton & Howell, a spice business operating under licence from the East India Company. He was making a visit to his sister accompanied by Mrs Oldworthy, his housekeeper. 'I'm a Suffolk man, you know,' he explained. 'My sister, Mrs Perry, lives

15

in Hadley. Mr Perry — he's dead now — was born in Sudbury, but my family has always lived in Hadley. Except myself, of course.'

Mary, in turn, explained something of her own situation, that she was a teacher of History and Drawing at Mrs Bunbury's school in St Ives — perhaps they had heard of it — and that she was on a visit to her uncle. Mr Treadgill did not know the school but thought education a very fine thing, and Mrs Oldworthy wondered why more people did not visit their uncles. It was a pleasure to them all to discover that they would share each other's company as far as Ipswich.

They reached Bury at about half past twelve. Owing to the rain, which had begun to fall shortly after they left Newmarket, and the coachman's desire to make up some of the time lost on the first leg of the journey, their stop was extremely brief. This was a disappointment for Mr Treadgill, who had been hoping to show Mary some of the chief attractions of Bury when they descended from the coach at Angel Hill. He contented himself with opening the windows on both sides of the coach and pointing with his stick, while Mrs Oldworthy consumed a mug of small beer. All too quickly that lady was shutting the windows again, and the fresh horses were being hitched on. Then they were away once more.

The sound of the rain and the motion of the coach, not to mention the small beer, soon sent Mrs Oldworthy to sleep. Mary and Mr Treadgill automatically lowered their voices, although this was quite unnecessary. Not only was Mrs Oldworthy immune to the sounds of those around her, she actually contributed more to the volume inside the coach than both of her companions.

'I wish you would tell me something of India,' Mary

urged. 'It must be very thrilling to live abroad, as you have done.'

Mr Treadgill had gone out to Fort St George as a young man, and had spent most of the next forty-five years inside the offices of Ashton & Howell. He endeavoured, however, to describe things that a young lady – a highly educated young lady – would find interesting. In fact he was not very skilful in this respect, but it hardly mattered. Each word created for Mary a vivid picture. As English rain streamed down the windows of the coach she walked through the bazaars, crowded with people selling everything from monkeys to emeralds, and rode on an elephant beside an Indian prince and princess – the latter dressed in gold silk and fragrant with exotic perfume. She heard the worshippers in a temple chanting to a strange god; some were offering gifts of fruit and incense, and from beyond there was the sound of marching feet and martial calls. She watched them stride past, the brave soldiers of the East India Company, who kept Madras safe from man-eating tigers and almost equally ferocious tribesmen.

'How terribly exciting it all sounds,' breathed Mary, shivering at the thought of tigers. 'What an adventure you have had, seeing all those things.'

'Of course, my life was really very dull, you know,' Mr Treadgill protested, 'spent mostly among the accounts. But occasionally great events may sweep up even mere bookkeepers such as myself. In the year '80, for instance – I suppose you never heard of a fellow called Haidar Ali here in England?'

Mary shook her head. 'We never heard of him at Mrs Bunbury's.'

Mr Treadgill gave a more or less accurate account of how the touchy relations between the East India Company and the ruler of Mysore had broken down, resulting in the latter routing the Company's forces and laying siege to the city of Madras. There he had been resisted by the largely civilian defenders, among them the doughty senior clerk of Ashton & Howell. 'I don't imagine that I hit anyone with my musket, for my eyesight has never been very good, but I fired it several times with great vigour in the direction of the enemy.'

'I am sure you are too modest. But what happened?'

'We held out, much to our surprise – and theirs too, I daresay. And then the governor – Governor Hastings – sent Sir Eyre Coote to take charge of the situation. Well! Sir Eyre had fought the Pretender in '45; he wasn't going to stand for any nonsense from Haidar Ali! He soon had the fellow on the run, *and* the Frenchman he had with him.'

Mary thought it was wonderful, and that Mr Treadgill had been very brave, but he disputed the second point. 'I do not know that bravery had anything to do with it. There was simply nothing else to be done.'

'Well . . . perhaps. Still, it was a very great adventure.'

'Yes, I daresay it was.' Mr Treadgill smiled in recollection, and seeing it Mary admitted that she was having a sort of adventure herself, although nothing to compare with Haidar Ali. 'You see, I have never met my uncle before. In fact, until I received his letter, asking me to visit him, I never had any communication with him in my life.'

'My word,' gaped Mr Treadgill, 'and did you say – I beg your pardon – is he indeed your *only* relation?'

'Yes, my parents died three years ago of the influenza. That is why I came to Mrs Bunbury's.'

Mr Treadgill thought the situation extraordinary – not that anyone should die of the influenza but that close relations should have had so little contact when there was not the excuse of a continent or more between them. 'But perhaps your uncle has been travelling, or engaged in some great work,' he suggested.

'Perhaps he has,' Mary agreed. Her left hand was in the pocket of her cloak, and she crossed her fingers, which undid most of the wickedness of a lie. Not that this *was* strictly a lie. 'In any event, his letter came as a very great surprise.'

'And you accepted the invitation straightaway? I mean, I know nothing of girls' schools, of course, but it occurs to me that . . . taking a leave of absence without due notice must have inconvenienced your employer.'

Mary started to say that if he *had* known anything of a girls' school the very idea of postponing an opportunity to escape would not have occurred to him, but she closed her lips against the words. He was frowning very slightly, and she gathered that such cavalier behaviour as hers was *not* how they had done things at Ashton & Howell. 'Oh, no,' she assured him, crossing her fingers a second time. 'It was not in the least inconvenient, and, naturally, I did not like to seem ungrateful to my uncle.'

'No, of course not.'

Mr Treadgill's expression had resumed its usual benignity, but the reality of the unpleasantness which had accompanied Mary's departure from the school was particularly vivid to her at that moment. She could feel herself blushing, and cast around for something to distract her memory. 'Some people say that the French are going to land in Suffolk. Do you think we shall be in serious danger?'

Mr Treadgill considered this. 'Well, I certainly hope not. We have the Navy between ourselves and France, and that is some comfort in these grave times. Captain

19

Carlisle, who came home with me on the *Queen Charlotte*, was a capital fellow. He said, "You may always rely upon the Navy, Mr Treadgill," and I trust that he was right. There has been some distressing news from the West Indies – about our forces there – but I trust this is just a brief setback, and the Navy will win through as it always has.'

Mary nodded, frowning. She knew nothing about the news from the West Indies, because Mrs Bunbury disapproved of newspapers, but agreed that the British Navy must always come out on top in the end. It soon emerged, however, that the threat was not only a foreign one. Hostile agencies were also at work in England. Mr Treadgill mentioned radicals – Englishmen so devoted to their ideas of democracy and liberty that they would surrender their country to the enemy for the sake of those theories – and smugglers, who cared not whether government consisted of the lawful king and Parliament or a crowd of murdering Frenchmen, so long as they could carry on trading with those same Frenchmen.

'In Hadley, where I come from, the smugglers were a terribly bad lot, and I daresay little has changed. When I was a lad, the gang was led by John Harvey. A killer, no doubt about it, and his word was law. No one dreamed of giving him away to the authorities, though the reward was big enough. Honest men went in fear of what would happen some dark night if they did not keep mum.' Mr Treadgill shook his head . . . 'Where did you say your uncle lives?'

'Near Lindham.'

'Ah well, you ask him about the "freetraders", Miss Finch.'

'*Mr Treadgill!*' exclaimed Mrs Oldworthy, suddenly waking up. 'Miss Finch ask her uncle about *smugglers* – why, I never

20

heard of such a thing. Have I been asleep? Whatever have you been talking about?'

'Frenchmen,' said Mary, 'and radicals, and smugglers, and Mr Treadgill's adventures in India.'

Mrs Oldworthy shivered. 'I hope it hasn't made your blood run cold, my dear; it would mine. I'm not saying aught about *all* foreigners, mind you. Mr Oldworthy knew a Welshman once as was perfectly respectable. But the more Mr Treadgill tells of the goings-on in India, the more I think they're barely human over there. None of them Christian, of course, but praying to idols, the poor things, and up to all sorts of odd capers. Do you know, Miss Finch, Mr Treadgill's house is so full of foreign gewgaws and trinkets that sometimes I think robbers will come to hear of them, and we shall all be murdered. There was a gentleman murdered on the Trumpington Road not six months ago. They say his head was fairly split open. And now these nasty Frenchmen are coming to England to set up their gee-o-teens and their liberty trees, and— My word, is this Stowmarket already?'

It was indeed Stowmarket. Mary half expected that Mr Treadgill would enlighten her on the various delights of the town while the horses were being changed, but he did not do so. Perhaps he felt that his recent observations had not, after all, been quite suitable, or perhaps he was simply no match for Mrs Oldworthy, rejuvenated by her nap and issuing orders to the landlord of the Rose. On the other hand, it may simply have been that Stowmarket on a cold, rainy October afternoon did not inspire eloquence. For whatever reason, therefore, the stop was not an interesting one, its only notable feature being that two different men opened the door to ask whether this was the coach to Bungay.

When they had set off again, Mrs Oldworthy announced

that it was time they had a meal. She produced a large dinner basket from under her seat, and she and Mr Treadgill pressed Mary to join them. As she had eaten nothing all day, apart from the muffin, the invitation was most welcome. Together they made a merry, and extremely fulsome, meal, the climax of which was Mrs Oldworthy's plum duff. 'We call it *plum* duff,' Mr Treadgill confided to Mary, 'but what makes it special is that it contains not merely plums, but also greengages, as well as medlars.'

Mrs Oldworthy acknowledged the compliment with a demure bow of her head. They mustn't expect too much, she warned, for of course it was cold and, lacking sauce, might even be judged dry.

'Never let us stand upon sauce or ceremony,' cried Mr Treadgill, holding out his napkin. 'And Miss Finch, can we tempt you?'

They could indeed. Mary took a tentative bite of the dark, slightly gooey slice, and then a second, more confident one. It *was* very good. Mr Treadgill pronounced it superior, even in its cold, unadorned state, to any ordinary duff served hot.

The remains of the dinner had only just been packed away again when the coach slowed to a stop. 'Hello,' said Mr Treadgill, who had been consulting his watch. 'It is coming on for four. He has certainly made up the time.'

'But we are not in Ipswich,' said Mary, and she looked out of the window. 'We are still on the road. I wonder why we have stopped.'

'Highwaymen,' gasped Mrs Oldworthy, clutching the dinner basket. 'Or the Gidding's burst its banks and flooded the road.'

'It is nothing to be excited about, I am sure,' Mr Treadgill assured them. He let down the window and called to their driver. 'Hello there! What is the trouble?'

22

'Looks like there's been a crash, sir,' shouted the coachman. 'Ned's jumped down to have a look.'

'Dear dear,' murmured Mrs Oldworthy, and she replaced the basket under the seat. 'But these coachmen are such reckless creatures. We should count our blessings that there aren't *more* crashes.'

After a few minutes they heard the two men outside conferring, then the guard opened the door and made his report. He was a big, imposing man, despite his sodden greatcoat, and he spoke in a low, rumbling tone. 'Bad accident just ahead, sir and ladies. Gen'leman's upset himself and gone into the ditch.'

It was not clear what ought to be done. The gentleman seemed to be very seriously injured, so much so that the guard feared to move him. Yet Ipswich, where someone called Dr Truelove could be found, was more than three miles away. The coach could convey the news to Ipswich, but that would mean abandoning the injured man.

'Perhaps if someone waited here, while the rest went for a doctor?' suggested Mary.

'That's what Sam and me thought,' agreed the guard, scratching his chin. 'Maybe, if Sam drives to Ipswich quick as he can, and sends a doctor back to the gen'leman, that'd be best. I'll stay here and have a go at patching up the gig. That way, if the doctor don't come quick, I might bring the gen'leman on, ever so gently.'

'But who will be looking after him while you are mending the gig?' Mary persisted. She glanced at her companions, but no one moved. 'Surely we ought to do something?' And before she was conscious of having made the decision, she had volunteered to stay behind as well.

'Oh, Miss Finch!' exclaimed Mrs Oldworthy.

'This is very noble of you,' said Mr Treadgill, 'but are you sure? Perhaps *I* ought—'

'With your bad chest? Why you'd catch your death of cold, Mr Treadgill.'

'But what about Miss Finch?'

'I will be quite all right,' said Mary, buttoning up her cloak and pulling on her gloves. 'I may be able to do something for him, and even if I cannot . . . well . . .'

Mrs Oldworthy continued to offer objections, but Mary was already climbing down. 'Do not worry,' she urged. 'Mr . . . Ned will be nearby, repairing the gig. Please hurry and send the doctor, won't you?'

'At least take this bottle of cordial. I never travel without it, and it may revive the poor man. Shall I give Miss Finch these spare hankies of yours, Mr Treadgill?'

'Of course, Mrs Oldworthy; I only wish we might do more to assist. We shall certainly send back help as quickly as we can.' Mr Treadgill looked uneasily up at the sky. 'If only it had not grown so gloomy. I wish . . . see that you look after the young lady, now,' he warned Ned.

'I'll do that, sir. Never you fear.'

The bottle and handkerchiefs were handed down to Mary, and then she stepped back as the coach pulled away. 'Goodbye!' she called.

'Goodbye, Miss Finch, and God bless you.'

'This way, miss,' said Ned.

Mary hurried after him, jumping to avoid the worst of the puddles in the road. Already she was half regretting her precipitous decision to leave the coach. Her experience of nursing was confined to stings, splinters, and skinned knees. What could she possibly do for a man with all sorts of grave injuries? He might be bleeding, or even . . . She had to stop herself from conjuring all the gruesome conditions of which her imagination was capable, lest she frighten herself into immobility. She had

24

said she would try to help, and now she must do just that.

Ned stopped where the road curved sharply to the right. In a ditch to the left lay the battered, overturned gig. Further along stood the mare. Her front and hind legs were gashed and bloody on one side, and her creamy coat was splashed with mud. The remains of her harness lay twisted across her shoulders. Ned had hastily tethered her to a tree using a piece of her reins. He pointed now to a man lying in the undergrowth beyond the gig. The grey, louring afternoon was giving way to dusk, and from a distance the crumpled figure was difficult to identify. It might have been anything. 'There he is, miss. He must've took this corner too fast. He tried to pull up, the mare slipped on the wet ground and over they went.'

'Yes, I see,' Mary grimaced, picturing the scene. It had probably happened suddenly; one moment he had been driving along quite happily, and the next . . . 'Can you help me down to him, please?' Clutching Ned's hand, she slid slowly down the wet, grassy slope and then struggled to avoid the tangle of young tree branches and brambles at the bottom. She began to feel sick as she approached the silent, motionless figure, his upturned face looking deathly pale on the sodden ground.

'He was awake when I first seen him,' Ned whispered, 'said his name was William Tracey. I reckon he's pretty bad.'

Mary nodded, forcing herself to breathe deeply. She knelt down beside the stricken man, feeling the cold and wet seep quickly through her cloak and skirt. Ned continued, 'I'll just see to the mare first, and then I'll try to put the gig to rights. Sing out if you need me.'

'Yes.'

William Tracey was a fair-haired man, no longer young

25

but not so elderly as Mr Treadgill. He was decently dressed in a dark-green driving coat and top boots, and his hat, now sadly crushed, had been a fashionable one. If he had not been flung into a muddy ditch, he would probably have been described as good-looking. Mary stripped off one of his leather gloves and felt his hand. It was cold, and she rubbed it gently. How long had he been lying there? After a moment she wiped his face with one of the handkerchiefs. 'Mr Tracey, can you hear me?' she asked.

He opened his eyes. 'What happened?' he murmured.

She explained that he had suffered an accident, unconsciously adopting the slow, deliberate voice reserved for invalids, foreigners, and the hard of hearing. 'We have sent for a doctor, and he is coming as soon as he can.'

'Bad corner.'

'Yes, I believe it was very slippery. Can I . . . do anything to make you more comfortable?' His right leg was bent at an unnatural angle, and she dreaded the idea of trying to straighten it. That she might have to do so made her forget the invalid voice. 'I think that your leg may be broken – does it hurt very badly?'

'No,' he sighed, 'I don't feel it. Who are you?'

'Mary Finch. Our coach stopped when we saw that you had been hurt, and the others have gone ahead to fetch the doctor.'

'What— Where is the other one?'

'Do you mean Ned, the guard from our coach? Shall I fetch him?'

'No,' whispered Tracey, his eyes closing. His lips were parted, and he was breathing in short, light gasps.

He looked as if he were going to faint again. Mary loosened the folds of his neck cloth and undid the buttons of his greatcoat, thinking that this might make him more comfortable. Then she remembered the bottle of cordial.

26

The label said: *Dr Fairweather's Elixir. A natural tonic of minerals, astringents, and aqua-vitae, made by appointment to the Duke of Liguria. For toning, strengthening, and general improvement of the constitution, take one spoonful thrice daily.* Tracey was in need of rather more serious medicine, but surely toning and strengthening his constitution could do no harm. She uncorked the bottle and sniffed the contents. It had a slightly spicy odour, something like mint. Lacking a spoon, she carefully poured a small amount into his mouth.

Almost immediately Tracey opened his eyes and began to cough. Then he stared at Mary. 'Finch?' he gasped. She answered, and he glanced about him vaguely. 'Are— Are we dead?'

'No, sir; we are on the road to Ipswich.'

'How did you— Thank God you found me.' Tracey made a feeble gesture with his hand, and Mary clasped it firmly. 'I've had such strange . . . fancies,' he admitted. 'Ever since . . . but that wasn't my fault, you know.'

'Shh,' Mary urged. 'No one can blame you for an accident. And you are quite safe now.'

'Nothing's safe – not now. But I didn't mean any harm. Do you— Do you believe me?'

'Yes, of course I do. Please do not worry.'

'So tired . . . I'll rest now,' murmured Tracey. 'It's good of you . . . not to mind.'

Mary released his hand and sat back, uncertain what to do next. She had not understood what he was talking about, but supposed it was right to agree with him, if only to ease his mind. But ought she to revive him again? Was it better that he rest, or keep awake? One of the girls at Mrs Bunbury's had suffered from fainting fits, but Mary could not remember how these had been treated – and besides, the girl might have been shamming. There

27

was Ned, moving among the trees – perhaps she should ask him about fashioning a splint.

Then she became aware that Tracey had awakened; he stirred slightly and grimaced. Taking this as a sign that he wished to speak but could not do so unaided, she administered another dose of the cordial.

'Not much longer now, Mr Tracey,' she assured him, trying to sound confident. 'The doctor is on his way.'

'On his way,' he agreed, speaking quickly. 'Maybe, but he's damned late. How much longer should we wait for him? We're taking one hell of a risk.'

Mary urged him to rest, but this only increased his agitation. He flailed his arm impatiently and then made as if he would try to sit up. She restrained him, hands on his shoulders, and he stared up at her for a moment. 'I'd better tell you,' he muttered. 'We may not have much more time.'

May not have much time? Oh dear, thought Mary as she bent over him. *Surely he is not going to die here in this ditch?* 'Please—' Then she hesitated. If he had something he particularly wished to say, it was unkind to discourage him. But he had closed his eyes, and she was not sure that he was still awake. 'Sir, can you hear me? Can you speak?' she cried, rubbing his hand. As soon as she perceived that he was conscious she asked in a loud voice, 'Mr Tracey, do you wish me to do something for you?'

'Everything's inside,' he breathed. 'I have the key. Only I . . . Thank God you're here . . . but we must be careful.'

'Careful of what?' she frowned. 'Your key? Shall I keep it for you?'

He shook his head wildly. 'No! No – I must see to it. You cannot guess what they . . . the risk . . . you don't know . . .'

28

I certainly do not know, thought Mary, but aloud she urged, 'Please, do not talk if it upsets you. I only meant – the doctor will be here soon.'

This information may have reassured him, for he grew quiet. Mary, too, relaxed slightly. Then he asked, in quite a different tone of voice, what had happened. She repeated her original explanation, thinking it best to humour him. 'This road is very dangerous.'

'Dangerous,' he agreed. 'They'll try to stop you, if they find out. But we must stop *them*.'

Again she tried to establish what he meant and what he wanted, but her questions did not reach him, and he continued to follow his own confused train of thought. 'I shall . . . do what I can to help. I'm not afraid. But you must be . . . ready to go.' And then he lost consciousness.

His pallor frightened her, and she administered the cordial without hesitation. The dose revived him, but now his cough produced bloody spittle. Mary wiped it away, and he demanded of her in a shaking, urgent voice, 'Is everything ready? I cannot meet him unless you're sure.'

'Yes, yes. I am sure. You needn't worry,' she answered rather desperately. *Where is the doctor? Surely the others must have reached Ipswich by now?* Mr Treadgill's observation returned to her; it *was* decidedly gloomy. Was that why Mr Tracey's face looked so ghostly? 'I beg your pardon, Mr Tracey,' she continued aloud, 'I must borrow your watch for a moment.'

A gold chain was visible outside his waistcoat, and she pulled it gently. When their coach stopped it had been nearly four o'clock, and Ned had said that they were about three miles from Ipswich. That would mean— She started as the watch emerged from Tracey's waistcoat pocket, and then she stared. It was an elegant device, small for a repeating watch, with delicate hands of blue steel

29

and an arcaded minute ring. Unusual too, with its outer case of gilt and tortoiseshell, and its face, not of plain white enamel, but of a more subtle cream. *Was it possible?* Unbuttoning her cloak she reached inside, fumbling until she found the pocket of her gown. Her fingers identified a handkerchief, a sixpence, and then drew forth a smooth, round object. Turning it over in her hand, she forgot to consider the time or to calculate the coach speed, but gazed first at Mr Tracey's watch, and then at her own. They were exactly alike.

3

'What's all this then, dearie? Had a bit of an accident?'

The low, wheedling voice made Mary start. Crouched at her side was a thin-faced, bedraggled-looking little man, in a long dark coat and battered hat. A thin white scar began under his nose and curved around his mouth almost to his jaw like a cat's whisker. He was close enough that she could see the stubble of his beard, which was black and grey in places, and his small, blood-shot eyes.

'Oh! Y-es,' Mary stammered, trying to regain her composure. She had flinched away from him instinctively, but now she reminded herself that a ragged coat did not make one a criminal, and her own hands were none too clean. 'I am afraid he is very badly hurt. Did you— Have you a vehicle on the road?' she asked, hopefully, although he did not look as if he could afford such a luxury.

'Mm,' the man replied, frowning at Tracey. Then he turned to Mary with a sharp, appraising glance. 'And you're lookin' after him, miss?'

'We . . . we have sent for the doctor.'

'That his blood on yer hankie? It don't look good, him

31

bleeding like that. Reckon he won't last long enough for no doctor. I knows a bit about such things as this, maybe I oughter—'

'No, please,' she protested. 'I do not think—'

'Oy!'

The man snatched back his hand and rose quickly as Ned shouldered his way through the undergrowth. 'What are you doin' there?' he demanded.

'Take it easy, mate. I meant no harm,' the man assured him. 'Only doin' me Christian duty, tryin' to help this young lady and her friend.'

'Christian duty, is it? Well, go and do it somewheres else,' snapped Ned. 'We don't need no help from the likes o' you.' He opened his coat to reveal a sizeable pistol thrust into his belt.

'All right, all right,' agreed the man, holding out his hands and taking a slow step backward, as if retreating before a large, and possibly dangerous animal. He looked smaller when he was standing, his muddy coat flapping against his legs. 'I meant no harm,' he repeated.

'Good,' Ned affirmed. 'And there's no harm done – yet. Clear off, now, before there is some.'

Ned maintained his scowling expression and aggressive posture until the man had wandered away, in the opposite direction from the road. Then he relaxed. 'You all right, miss?'

'Yes, I— Who was he?' breathed Mary.

'Oh, some tramp or other,' Ned shrugged. 'It ain't safe yer talkin' to that sort o' fellow. Where'd he spring from?'

'I hardly know – he was simply *there*. I did not like him,' she admitted, 'but . . . perhaps he might have helped us?'

'Helped himself to Mr Tracey's purse, you mean,' scoffed Ned, 'and yours. Thought he'd got himself a good thing,

32

I reckon, with only you and him.' He gazed uneasily at the injured man. 'He does look poorly.'

'Yes,' Mary nodded, 'I think he is *very* ill.' She chided herself for allowing the tramp to distract her from her task, but when she conferred with Ned on the subject there did not seem anything more to be done for the sufferer. Ned had repaired the gig, but it was too small and too rickety to bear Mr Tracey in his injured state. They must simply wait for the doctor, and when Tracey started coughing bloody spittle again they wondered whether even a doctor could save him.

Then the sound of horses' hooves clattered on the road above them. 'Halloo! Ned Garrow! Halloo!' shouted a voice.

Ned stood up. 'That you, Ned Jenkins?' he called. 'Took yer time, you did. Where's the doctor?'

'There ain't no doctor,' said the other Ned in a crabbed, surly voice, as if inspired by the unhelpful nature of his message. 'Dr Truelove's gone to see a lady that's poorly, up Elmswell way, and 'pothecary says *he* can't come.'

'Old Dimcock? Why can't he?'

'Says he can't drive nor ride since he had the rheumatism so bad. Says fer us to take the gen'leman to the White Horse if he ain't dead, and to Fletcher the undertaker if he is. I've Tom Bamford's wagon here, so it makes no odds.'

'He ain't dead,' said Ned Garrow, 'but pretty near to it.' He paused. 'Well, what're you waitin' for, Ned? Help me fetch this gig onto the road, and then we'll have to bring him up. I can't do it all on my own, you know.'

'All right, I'm coming,' complained Ned Jenkins, as he made his way cautiously down the sloping ground from the road and into the ditch. 'Miserable bugger,' he added, under his breath.

33

'And you mind yer manners,' snapped Ned Garrow. 'There's a young lady here, and she don't care to hear no coarse language.'

'Beg yer pardon, I'm sure, miss,' grumbled the other Ned. 'Didn't see yer there.'

Mary staggered to her feet and shook out her wet skirt. Suddenly she was very cold, and her knees and back ached from kneeling so long over Mr Tracey. Still clutching the bottle of Dr Fairweather's Elixir, she scrambled up the bank and waited for the two Neds. When they had laid Tracey on the floor of the wagon and tied the horse and gig up behind, it was suggested that Mary might climb in beside the injured man, in order to prevent him from moving about during the journey.

'Give him a bit o' cushion,' said Ned Jenkins.

'None o' yer lip, now,' warned Ned Garrow.

Mr Tracey had fainted again during the climb to the wagon, and when she was settled beside him, Mary attempted to revive him with the elixir. This time, however, it had no effect, save that he continued to cough blood. 'All secure, miss?' asked Ned Garrow, from the driver's seat. 'Likely to be a bumpy ride, but I reckon *he* won't mind.'

As the wagon drew its wretched burden slowly toward Ipswich, Mary found that she was giving only half of her attention to Mr Tracey's condition. With the other half she was debating with herself. How ought she to interpret what Tracey had said to her? If only she could ask him a few more questions! *A terrible risk, you said − but what sort of risk? Of discovery, surely, but of what? A murder? Or robbery? Or of a man . . . someone for whom you were waiting, and who means to . . . to help you or hinder you? Someone who . . . knows something about a very grave danger.*

34

It must be grave, for it frightened you, or upset you badly. And there are others – you said that they will try to stop me if they find out – find out what? Who are these others, and what might I possibly do that anyone would want to prevent?

She glanced at Tracey, but his pale, silent countenance gave nothing away. Only the thin pulse under her fingers proved that he was still living. Then the wagon shifted awkwardly as one of the wheels dropped into a rut, and his arm slid toward her, as if he were trying to attract her attention. *What might I do*, she wondered, *or what might I discover that could so upset anyone?* The answer – or some part of the answer – was obvious; she had the evidence, and yet she could hardly believe it.

The grey afternoon had given way to dusk, and Mary was growing very tired. Thub, thub, thub, thub; the wheel of the gig was rubbing where Ned Garrow had repaired it. Its monotonous rhythm forced her thoughts into a kind of chant. *He said it was dangerous – what sort of danger? Something is wrong – the watch proves that. Some kind of trouble, trouble for my uncle? How can I solve any trouble for him?* She repeated the words to herself, again and again, hardly conscious of what they meant. Somehow, with each repetition she felt more comfortable. *Something is wrong – the watch proves that.*

She awoke with a start. Lights, voices, a crowd of people. Then she heard Ned's voice, and she remembered Mr Tracey and the accident. Men were lifting him out of the wagon and placing him on a stretcher. Someone helped Mary to her feet; she climbed down, still feeling dazed and stupid.

'Here she is, Mrs Bamford, here's the young lady,' said a voice, and then a large, comfortable woman was embracing Mary and calling her 'a real heroine'. Awake now to her responsibilities, Mary called out, 'Mr Tracey—' but the woman said, 'You leave him to the medical men, my dear. They'll look after him, poor gentleman.' And she led Mary inside.

'This is a right sorry welcome for you at the White Horse,' she continued, guiding Mary into a crowded parlour, 'but we're that glad to see you.' The other patrons stepped aside to let them through. 'Come and sit by the fire – *do* let the young lady have that chair, ma'am – and I'll fetch you something hot.'

'White horse?' asked Mary, thinking confusedly about Mr Tracey's mare.

'That's right, miss,' said the woman. 'This here's the Great White Horse hotel, and I'm Mrs Bamford. Sit down and rest yourself, and don't worry about a thing. Your bag is upstairs, and when you've had a bite of supper, I'll take you to your room.'

Mary sank onto the chair. *Her bag* – she had forgotten all about it, and yet, that morning, how she had worried that it might have been misplaced! The morning and its problems seemed very remote and unimportant. And had she really begun the day in her room at Mrs Bunbury's? She smiled vaguely to herself, and Mrs Bamford admonished her not to move. 'You're that done in, and I don't wonder, with all you've been through.'

The landlady bustled back and forth, producing first a glass of hot milk and then a bowl of steaming, fragrant soup, while in between she explained how news of the calamity had reached them. Mrs Oldworthy had been the chief informant, and Mrs Bamford was full of praise for Mary's valour and kindness. How they had fretted about her! Not but what Ned Garrow was a very steady man, but a young lady on that lonely stretch of road . . . why, it didn't bear thinking of!

Mary received her accolades politely, but she could not

36

really appreciate them. She was exhausted and troubled by what had happened on the Stowmarket road, and now conversations swirled around her that were far from re-assuring. The crash seemed to have awakened in the patrons of the Great White Horse a wider interest in death and violent injury, and they were indulging it to the full. Near the bar a knot of men listened enthralled as one of their number related how he had seen a gypsy trampled by a mad bull. In a corner an elderly midwife claimed to have delivered a two-headed baby, while two sailors almost came to blows over whether the drowned invariably kept their eyes open in death.

The rapt, eager faces filled Mary with dismay. In the dim light they looked ghoulish, and their loud, contentious voices were making her head ache. Not one of them seemed capable of understanding what had happened, and Mr Treadgill and Mrs Oldworthy, although delayed by the latter's account of the crash, were now long gone. Mary did consider, briefly, whether she might confide in Mrs Bamford, but that lady's stentorian announcement, that the surgeon proposed to take off Mr Tracey's leg if he survived till morning, dissuaded her. She was terribly alone.

Gradually, however, the soup and hot drink had their effect; she began to feel comfortable, and while she was still confused about the future, her immediate situation seemed less bleak. Moreover, the parlour conversation drifted to more general topics: the war, taxes, and the price of corn. Pipes were lit, another round of beer was ordered, and a chaise departed for Somersham. By the time the nine o'clock coach arrived from Felixstowe, the room had settled back into the usual smoky torpor of an autumn evening.

The Felixstowe coach set down a solitary passenger.

His entry was preceded by a bellow from one of the younger Bamfords that an 'officer chap wants to know has he missed the Norwich mail?' followed by, 'Mother says you ain't missed it, and will you step inside, please, as we've fish pie, mutton pie, or bread-and-cheese,' at a comparable volume. A tall, dark man in a blue coat walked into the parlour and sat down in a chair before the fire. He stretched out his long legs and nodded in her direction. 'Evening, miss.'

Mary murmured a reply. The word 'officer' had attracted her attention, and now she tried to examine him unobtrusively. He had what she supposed was a military bearing – brusque and matter-of-fact. Now that he was sitting near her she took in other details. Although neat, his coat was worn and faded. There was no lace at his cuffs, no adornment of any kind, and his hands were chapped and barked across the knuckles. Yet these things did not detract from his essential air of authority. Her father had always considered soldiers loud, vulgar, and disorderly, and yet this man seemed none of those things. Then she remembered what Mr Treadgill had said about the Navy – of course, *Naval* officers would be a different set altogether.

She stole a glance at his face. He was not good-looking, she decided, and certainly his expression was neither warm nor inviting. And she could not simply begin a conversation in any case. A perfect stranger, and what possible reason could she give for speaking to him?

'Well then, what's your advice about supper?'

Mary started at the sound of his voice. '*Me?* I mean, I beg your pardon?'

He repeated his question. 'I don't like fish pie,' he warned. 'Too many bones.'

Such was her surprise that she answered without

thinking. 'And sometimes it has gone off. Oh! I did not mean *here*, of course, only I *did* have fish pie, once, somewhere else, and it had . . . gone off. But the *soup* is very good,' she added hurriedly. 'I thought it was very good.' She stared at him for a moment and then dropped her eyes. Could she possibly have said anything more ridiculous?

Amazingly, he did not seem to have noticed and, when Mrs Bamford appeared a few moments later, he merely said that he would have soup, on the young lady's advice. Mrs Bamford nodded approvingly and widened the conversation to include beer, bread and cheese, and accommodation for the night. He approved of them all, especially when she informed him that the next coach for Norwich was not until five o'clock in the morning, but he wondered whether there *were* any available rooms. The yard had looked very full when he arrived.

'Oh, yes, sir,' beamed Mrs Bamford, 'I've a perfectly lovely room near the back. The old place *is* in a bit of a stir tonight,' she confided, 'on account of the calamity, but it's only the one room, and I doubt the poor gentleman needs it long.' She sniffed, and rolled her eyes sympathetically at Mary.

'The calamity?'

'Yes, sir, a terrible crash on the Stowmarket road. This poor young lady,' with a further nod to Mary, 'was a— an angel of mercy to the poor gentleman as was hurt. Waiting beside him, all alone, and him fainting and crying out. Oh, it was pitiful. You ought to have seen the blood, sir, and his poor leg. Why, when they carried him in—'

'Hold up,' frowned the officer, glancing in Mary's direction, 'the . . . young lady won't want to hear all that.'

'Oh,' said Mrs Bamford, as if this were a rather odd suggestion. 'Though I daresay *you've* seen all manner of dyin' in your work, sir. Men cut down in their prime, and—'

'So I have, but not before supper.'

'And the *most*— eh?' She paused again, uncertain how to continue. 'Well, sir, it was a terrible calamity, and no mistake. I'll . . . see to your room, now, shall I?'

'Much obliged to you. And don't forget the soup.'

'Right you are, sir,' answered Mrs Bamforth, with an affected brightness. But as she departed she could not suppress a critical shake of her head. He was a strange one.

Mary had resolutely averted her gaze throughout this exchange, but she had listened with a marked attention. When it concluded, she could not resist another glance at her neighbour, and he intercepted it. 'I expect your friend's not so bad as she says.'

'Thank you,' said Mary, blushing. 'I fear his injuries *are* very grievous, although I can claim no particular acquaintance with him – with Mr Tracey. I mean, he *spoke* to me, but it might have been anyone.'

'But weren't you there when it happened?'

'No, not until afterwards. You see, our coach stopped because of the accident, and I got down to help.'

He nodded as a bowl of soup was placed before him and continued, 'You went to help a stranger – all on your own?'

Mary was tempted by a sudden desire to embellish her actions, but she felt obliged to acknowledge the contribution of Ned the guard. It was gratifying to hear that the officer was not very interested in Ned. 'Oh, well . . .' she floundered, but his obvious approval encouraged her to continue. 'I wonder,' she said in a low voice, 'whether I might – would it be very rude of me to ask for your advice in this matter?'

40

'*My advice?* But I don't— I mean, yes, all right. Fire away.'

She drew her chair closer to his. 'Thank you, is it *Captain?*' she ventured.

'It is, miss, and the name's Holland. Robert Holland.' He extended his hand. Not quite sure of how she ought to reply, she shook it. Or rather, she submitted to his enveloping grip, which wrung her hand like a wet rag.

'Captain Holland,' she said as the feeling returned to her fingers. 'I am Miss Mary Finch. I do apologise, and I hope you will not think me strange, but you see I believe that there is an important *mystery* touching Mr Tracey.'

Mary leaned forward urgently as she made her announcement, but Captain Holland frowned at her, as if he did not believe that there were such things as mysteries, and she must be mistaken about this one. 'But I thought you didn't know this . . . Tracey.'

'Yes, *before* the crash,' she reminded him, 'but in his injured state he said things – warned of grave dangers – which may affect my uncle.'

Captain Holland continued to frown dubiously. 'Your uncle?'

'Perhaps I ought to start at the beginning.'

'If you like. Do you . . . mind if I carry on with my supper?'

'Oh, yes, please,' said Mary. 'I mean, please do so.'

As the captain's bread disappeared into his soup Mary plunged into her account, but her task was not so straightforward as his. Of course, when she said 'start at the beginning' she had not really meant the beginning of *everything*, which would have necessitated starting with her own birth, or even before, but it was no good simply saying that she had departed from St Ives that morning

41

and carrying on from there! Why, that would not even begin to set out the facts of the case, and she had the feeling that Captain Holland was not likely to be of much help without them. So she explained that when she was young she had not had many near relations; there had been only her parents, and together they had run a sort of boys' school.

Holland smiled that the girl opposite him should imply that her youth was long passed, but he merely asked what she meant by a 'sort of school'.

'Well, the boys were very little, you see, and we were not so much teaching them scholarly things as how to use their handkerchiefs, and not to spend their pocket money all in one go. They would be moving to schools when they were a bit older, most of them, but they had to learn how to be away from their mothers first.'

'And you helped with that?'

'Yes, when I was old enough to *be* a help and not cause a riot by fighting with them. The boys minded me very well, but then, three years ago we had a very bad winter, and Mother and Father died of the influenza. I could not very well run the school on my own, and I took a job as a teacher at Mrs Bunbury's school, in St Ives.'

'St Ives in Cornwall?'

'No, in Huntingdonshire. It was . . . well, I oughtn't to complain, for I was very fortunate to find a situation of any kind, and I daresay there are far worse places than Mrs Bunbury's, but . . .' Mary frowned slightly. 'I had better not say any more, or I *will* sound ungrateful. However, the day before yesterday I received a letter from my uncle asking me to visit him, which was very exciting because he had never had anything to do with us before.'

'How did he know where you were?' asked Holland.

42

'He did not know; the letter had been posted to our school in Bath, and someone had sent it on – not very promptly – to Mrs Bunbury's.'

'Mm.'

'My uncle lives near a place called Lindham, in Suffolk. He has an estate, which is called White Ladies – I read about it in Cary's *Atlas*, and it sounds very grand. Naturally I wanted to accept his offer straightaway.'

'It sounds as if you took a whole day to decide.'

Mary smiled impulsively. 'No, I needed a day to gather the courage to tell Mrs Bunbury! And indeed,' she shrugged, 'I— I might have written to him, only his letter had been delayed more than a month, and I did not wish to seem ungrateful. And Mrs Bunbury understood that . . . in the end.'

'Hammer and tongs, was it?' laughed Holland.

'No, no,' Mary insisted, 'although she does have a rather carrying voice. And I told her— I mean, she quite saw that I *ought* to go, and so I set out this morning. Unfortunately the coach was delayed at Newmarket, because of a race, but everything was all right in the end, and I set off for Ipswich. However, this afternoon we stopped on the road when our coachman saw that there had been a crash, and that was Mr Tracey.'

Captain Holland sat back in his chair. 'He was in a bad way?'

'Yes, quite bad, and while we were waiting for someone to come – I thought it might be a doctor, but it was only a man named Ned with a wagon – Mr Tracey said the most disturbing things.' Mary described as much as she could remember of Tracey's strange remarks, leaning forward again as the recollection of his anxious, restless mood impressed itself upon her.

Holland, however, seemed strangely unmoved by her

story, and his expression even became impassive as it drew to a conclusion. Stung and surprised, Mary repeated her account in a more emphatic tone, but Captain Holland remained cool. Even more annoyingly, he had an explanation for even the strangest facts. Mr Tracey's knowledge of her name was not uncanny – she had volunteered it, after all. Nor were his vague warnings inexplicable – they were simply the result of shock or great pain. And his message to her was not mysterious – very likely he had no message to convey. 'If you sit beside a sick man, you hear his ranting, but the ranting comes from the fever or the knock on the head he's taken, and has nothing to do with you.'

Ranting – could that have been what it was? The meaningless remarks of a man in pain? Mary did not think so, but she admitted that she *had* been obliged to revive Tracey several times with the cordial, and produced it solemnly. The bottle was nearly empty now, but Holland opened it and smelled the contents; then he smiled. 'No wonder the poor devil spoke all manner of nonsense if you doused him with this. It's gin.'

'*Gin,*' she gasped, and sat back in her chair. 'Oh, I did not know . . .'

'Never mind, miss. Sounds like he needed it.'

This interpretation of the injured man's conduct took Mary aback. Might everything he said have simply been the result of his injuries and . . . intoxication? She glanced at Captain Holland, wishing he would stop grinning at her in that superior way. Then she remembered the watch, and her confidence rose. She leaned forward again. 'Wait,' she said, and rummaged in her cloak pocket. 'I ought to have said . . . please look at this watch he was carrying,' and producing the timepiece she slid it across the table.

'His— Damn it, miss!' cried Holland, and immediately

44

lowered his voice. '*You've stolen his bloody watch!*' He glanced around the room, but no one seemed to be paying attention to them.

'It is *not* his watch. Look inside.' When he did not immediately comply, she frowned and carefully removed the tortoiseshell case to reveal a pierced and engraved inner case. Turning this over she held it out to him; nestling there in her palm was what looked like a small mound of silver. 'How many men carry a watch bearing another man's initials? Do you see, by the maker's name? *E.S.F.* And my uncle is Edward Strongman Finch.'

'It's odd,' he admitted, 'but . . . you're not saying that your uncle is the only man in England with these initials, are you? And you've taken one hell of a— I mean, you shouldn't have done it.'

'Will *this* convince you?' persisted Mary, diving this time into the pocket of her gown. 'Look at *this watch* – no, wait a moment.' She snatched back the second watch and removed its outer case. Then she handed it across. 'What do you think of *that*?'

Captain Holland compared the two watches – two small, silver repeaters with cream faces and tortoiseshell cases. The second was rather more battered than the first, with marks where the key had been inserted, and a long, deep scratch in the tortoiseshell, and the hands said a quarter past three. 'This one's run down.'

Mary sighed and thought him a very dull fellow. Was that all he could say? 'It is *broken*, not run down. I do not use it as a timepiece, only . . . it was my father's watch, you see.' She frowned again. 'He was Richard Abernethy Finch – do you see the *R.A.F.*?'

'Yes.'

R.A.F. and *E.S.F.* Even the style of engraving looked identical. Mary explained that her father's had been a

45

present from *his* father, and very likely her uncle had received his from the same source. How, then, had it come to be in Mr Tracey's possession?

'Well . . .' said Holland, slowly, 'if this *was* your uncle's, maybe he gave it away, or sold it.'

'Rubbish,' scoffed Mary. 'I mean, that is not very likely. *I* believe that Mr Tracey stole it from my uncle.'

'Rubbish yourself,' Holland laughingly replied. 'Is it very likely that he stole your uncle's watch and then warned you of danger? And why shouldn't your uncle have sold it? People sell all sorts of things, when they need the tin.'

'Yes, but my uncle is very wealthy; he is not in need of . . . tin. Perhaps— Oh, I do not know,' admitted Mary in exasperation. 'Perhaps Mr Tracey . . . recovered the watch, after it was stolen from my uncle. Yes. Perhaps the true thieves were chasing him – perhaps they *caught* him. They may even have caused the crash . . .' She nodded significantly.

'For the sake of a watch?' demanded Holland, incredulously. 'It isn't solid gold, you know.'

'No, but if they were desperate . . .' Mary sat back in her chair and crossed her arms defiantly. 'That all this should happen on the very day that I am travelling to my uncle . . . it must mean *something*. And, of course, there is his name.'

'Whose name?'

'*William Tracey* – that was the name of the man who killed the archbishop of Canterbury.'

'*The archbishop is dead?*' demanded Holland. 'When? What happened?'

'No, no,' she assured him, 'not Dr Moore. I meant Thomas Becket – the archbishop who was murdered in Canterbury Cathedral.'

46

'Murdered in the . . . and you think Tracey had something to do with it?'

'No – of course, he could not have done.'

'But you said—'

'No, I only meant—' She frowned, her expression a combination of impatience and chagrin. Then she continued more slowly. 'William Tracey was the man – one of the men – who killed Archbishop Becket at the behest of King Henry II. You know . . . *in history.*'

Holland regarded her blankly. 'In history. You mean a long time ago.'

'Oh, yes – hundreds of years ago.' Mary perceived that the conversation was becoming absurd, although *really* it was not her fault, but his. If he had not been so unsympathetic she would never have been tempted to speak of Henry II. She might have known that he would not understand. 'I oughtn't to have mentioned it, perhaps. I only meant that . . . well, that it was odd that they should have the same name, and the *first* William Tracey a notorious criminal. Of course I did not think that *this* Mr Tracey – only, along with everything else . . . But I am certain something is wrong. Perhaps he had a guilty conscience, and the . . . cordial brought it out. The watch proves something, only . . . I am not quite sure *what.*'

Holland sighed and rubbed the bridge of his nose. 'You know, you've had a bad time of it today. When did you say that you left St Ives this morning?'

'Half past five.'

'And now it's coming on for ten. That makes a long march, and I guess you don't see something like that crash every day. It must have— You must be tired.'

His tone was suspiciously compassionate, and she lifted her chin in defiance. She much preferred his scepticism.

47

'Yes, I am tired, but . . . do you believe I am *imagining* things?'

'No, but I bet you'll see 'em different in the morning.' He was silent for a moment. 'You've never met your uncle, and he doesn't know what's happened to you, or even that you're coming.'

'No, but—'

'Why not write to him and stop here till you get a reply? This is a respectable place; they'll look after you, and once you're sure everything is all right, you can carry on.' Having delivered his judgement, he handed the watches to Mary and folded his arms again.

Mary opened her mouth to argue with him, but closed it again without saying a word. His flat, although eminently sensible, advice was unanswerable. She thought that a Naval officer might have suggested something more interesting than a letter, and yet, if she *had* written to her uncle before departing St Ives, she would not have got herself into this pickle. Indeed, if only she had not made the journey today, she would have missed Mr Tracey altogether.

It seemed important to say something, especially with Captain Holland sitting there as though he were Solomon and had just advocated infant-division. But before she could gather her thoughts Mrs Bamford reappeared, as if summoned by the mention of sleep. She too felt that Mary ought to retire for the night, and she repeated her earlier pronouncement that the young lady was 'done in'. Further private conversation with Captain Holland thus became impossible, and Mary had to let him have the last word. Under Mrs Bamford's watchful eye she merely thanked him for his assistance and wished him good night.

Captain Holland remained alone before the fire, as gradually the other patrons made their way home or up

48

to their rooms. His thoughts ranged over a number of subjects, but they frequently returned to Miss Mary Finch. If she hadn't been so damned pretty, blushing and floundering about a rancid fish pie, he might never have heard her story, and her story was worth hearing. What to do about it, though, that was the question. It certainly complicated things.

After some time Mr Bamford joined him and asked whether he would care for a glass of port.

'No brandy?' asked Holland, smiling. 'A quick dash across the Channel for the genuine article?'

'Not in this house,' replied Mr Bamford, piously, and then smiled in his turn. Although uncommunicative himself, Holland had a knack for obtaining information from others, and over his glass of port he learned that the Revenue officers had grown so crafty that it was not worth Mr Bamford's while trying to cross them, not for the sake of a small profit and the dubious pleasure of dealing with the freetraders. And then there had been two men hanged for smuggling at the Assizes a year ago, and that had put the fear of God into folks sure enough. There was nothing like a hanging to make people take stock of things. It was different, of course, along the coast. There the freetraders did not fear the Revenue nor anyone else. The Navy could not intercept every boat, and the nearest soldiers were at the Landguard fort, not close enough to cause a serious check to the trade.

'Well, good luck to 'em,' said Holland, but he did not indicate whether he meant the smugglers or the authorities.

'That's what I says, sir, live and let live.'

Neither was able to improve on this broad-minded sentiment, and conversation lapsed. Then Holland swallowed the last of his port and remarked casually upon the hotel's most notable guest. 'I hear the injured man's in a bad way.'

'Aye, sir, that's a sad business. *Tracey*, I believe, is his name.'

'He's not from around here?'

'No, sir, never said where he was from.'

'But you know him?'

'Why, in a manner o' speaking, I do, sir,' said Mr Bamford. 'He sat in that chair, just where you're sitting, these last four days. Every day, he does the same thing. Sits down, orders one glass, nurses it the afternoon and leaves. Civil enough gent, but quiet.'

'Didn't say if he was waiting for someone, did he?'

'No, sir, he didn't, though I figured as much, after the second day.' Before he could relate the events of the second day more particularly, however, Mr Bamford was distracted by the unexpected sound of the parlour door opening. Glancing over his shoulder, he frowned at the ineligible figure standing in the doorway – a slight, thin-faced man, dressed in a worn, greasy-looking overcoat that was much too large for him. Bamford's frown deepened when the newcomer surveyed the nearly empty parlour yet slid onto a chair well away from the fire.

'Evening,' called Mr Bamford, in a voice that was not quite hospitable, and when this produced no audible response, continued, 'it's a cold night, for them as lacks bread and board, or the money to pay for 'em.'

'I ain't no beggar,' grumbled the other, hunching his shoulders and squirming irritably in his chair. 'Just wanted a bit o' peace, is all. Can't a man have a bit o' peace and quiet, without being got at?'

'I hope he can,' replied Mr Bamford, 'and soon as you tell me whether it's a drink, or a bite of supper, or a room for the night you're after, you can have all the peace and quiet you like.' He crossed the parlour and stood over his diffident customer, arms folded uncompromisingly across his broad chest.

The little man's glance flashed upward. 'I'll have a glass o' beer, then.'

'All right,' said Mr Bamford, 'now let's see the colour of your money.'

There was a brief delay, during which pockets were searched and Mr Bamford's expression became increasingly grim. At last the requisite coins were placed on his large, open palm. He jingled them for a moment and pursed his lips, apparently considering something. Then he stumped off to the kitchens. When he returned, a few moments later, he set down not only a large glass of beer, but also a plate of bread and cheese.

The sullen demeanour vanished as the little man gazed hungrily at the unexpected feast – but only for a moment. 'Much obliged to you, mister,' he muttered, around an enormous bite.

'That's all right,' answered Mr Bamford with a shrug before turning away. 'Found we had a bit extra, is all. Don't think you can make a habit of it, now.'

'Live and let live,' Holland observed, when his host had resumed his station beside the fireplace.

'Aye, well,' acknowledged Mr Bamford, shaking his head. 'Tramps and raggedy men; we see a lot of 'em nowadays. Most no better than they ought to be, of course. And if this damned war carries on it'll only get worse.' Then remembering to whom he was speaking, he added, apologetically, 'War makes hard times, you know, sir. Sets many a good man on a bad road, and makes those as is already gone to the bad that much worse.'

Holland agreed and, after a decent pause, reminded the

51

landlord about Tracey. 'You guessed he was waiting for someone?'

Mr Bamford *had* guessed it, and now he wondered whether the object of Tracey's vigil might have been Miss Finch. She was known to be visiting an elderly relation, after all; perhaps he had sent Tracey to meet her. Mr Bamford grew solemn as he pondered the mysterious Providence that could have brought the two of them together in such tragic circumstances. Holland did not feel competent to offer an opinion on Providence, but he agreed that there might be something in Mr Bamford's interpretation.

'Say, mister, is that right?' came a voice from behind them. 'He's dying?' Having finished his supper the tramp had crept forward, and now he occupied a chair just out of the firelight. 'Him as had the crash?'

'That's right,' began Mr Bamford, but he quickly frowned. 'What do *you* know about that?'

'Nothing,' protested the other, his voice assuming the aggrieved tone of the professional ne'er do well. 'Only what folks been saying. Your chaps – out in the yard – they told me; fellow upset his gig and was hurt mortal bad.'

'Well,' allowed Mr Bamford, 'so he was.' And then, with a touch of pride, he added, 'He's upstairs now, in my best set of rooms.'

'Do you reckon he's gonna die?'

'So the apothecary says. But you needn't gloat over the poor gentleman's misfortunes.'

'I ain't gloating, only interested, like. I'm sorry for him, same as the next man.'

Mr Bamford uttered a sceptical grunt and shrugged his shoulders. 'That's as may be. And what are you creeping about for? Listening in on private conversations?'

'No I ain't, mister, honest!'

'I reckon that's true, any road,' chuckled Mr Bamford. 'Well, we've had enough of you, honest or no, and I'm fixing to close up for the night. You've had your supper, so off you get. You can sleep in the stables, if you've a mind to.'

'Say, that's right kind of you, mister,' pronounced the tramp.

'I know it is. Go on, now. And if I find so much as a bit o' straw missing come the morning, you'll be sorry.'

'Oh, you can trust me, mister, never fear.'

'I *don't* fear,' agreed Mr Bamford, ushering him outside, 'I lock my doors and sleep like a lamb.'

Although she was very tired, Mary did not fall asleep immediately. Her bedroom was cold, and she lay for some time curled up in the centre of the bed, unwilling to risk its more glacial foot. As she shivered she thought about Captain Holland's advice. Perhaps she *had* been wrong about Mr Tracey. His warnings had been very confused, and if he were intoxicated, as well as in pain, that might explain a great deal. She was not an innocent, after all; she had seen drunken men, or heard them, making their noisy way home at night. They liked to sing, generally, or call out, and they did not care a jot for the annoyance this caused their more abstemious neighbours. She was glad she had recovered her uncle's watch, however, whatever Captain Holland said. That watch . . . She would discover from her uncle precisely how it had come to be in Mr Tracey's keeping. Perhaps there *was* a simple explanation.

And perhaps there was some merit – prudence, even – in halting her journey until she could communicate with her uncle. It would certainly be reassuring to know that all was well, and it might even place their relationship on a more secure foundation. On the other hand, having started a thing with a certain degree of dash, she liked to finish it in the same way, and hanging about in Ipswich waiting for a letter seemed so . . . unenterprising, not to mention expensive. She certainly did not want to meet her uncle and immediately present him with a large bill for her travelling expenses.

And then there was White Ladies; how could a mere inn compare with that prospect? For Mary was certain that such a splendid, romantic name must be attached to an equally superb residence. Very likely it had an interesting history, and a succession of beautiful women had lived there. Or, there were the Cistercian nuns; they had been called the white ladies in medieval times on account of their robes. Perhaps the house had once been a convent, or priory, and been confiscated by Henry VIII. *What a nasty person he was, marrying people and then chopping off their heads*, thought Mary. *Like the French, although they do not marry their victims first. The nuns or beautiful ladies may even haunt White Ladies, for 'white' could refer to ghosts. How exciting to live in a haunted castle – or convent, rather.*

Gradually Mary uncurled to a more comfortable position, and as she did so weariness overcame her. Even in sleep, however, her mind remained active, and she dreamed that she had arrived at White Ladies. It was a beautiful, even magnificent building, with towers and battlements from which one might look down onto rough cliffs and the ocean crashing below. Inside, a company of nuns baked quantities of fragrant plum duff, while outside Captain Holland and Dr Nichols sat upon gilt armchairs and drank Dr Fairweather's Elixir on the lawn, basking in perfect spring sunshine.

So deep was her sleep and so engaging her dream that

she was not disturbed by doors opening and closing, or muffled conversations, or traffic along the corridors, or any of the noises that were inevitable at a busy establishment like the Great White Horse, whatever the hour. Nor did she notice when stealthy footsteps halted outside her door, or when the latch clicked against the bolt and prevented the door from opening. And whoever it was – for no lighted candle revealed his features – went away again, with no one any the wiser.

4

Mary was awakened the following morning by a maid-servant, a pale girl with lank, fair hair, who brought two messages along with the hot water. The first was that Mr Tracey had died shortly before dawn, and the second was that Captain Holland sent his compliments and would like to speak with Miss when convenient. Both messages were extremely interesting, and the girl stared at Mary in hopeful anticipation. She already considered Mary a person of considerable importance, by virtue of a much-embellished account of the adventure on the Stowmarket road, and this was her opportunity to produce something equally dramatic for the staff downstairs.

In this respect Mary proved a disappointment. She reacted soberly to the news of Tracey's death – not even the hint of a swoon – and the message from the military gentleman failed to raise a blush. Appearances, however, were deceptive, for the maidservant's communication actually sent Mary's thoughts into a disturbing spiral. As she dressed she wondered whether a new set of difficulties awaited her – difficulties that might prove both awkward and dangerous.

Mr Tracey, after all, had been fatally injured in highly mysterious circumstances, and she had been a witness – or almost a witness. Certainly she was closely connected with the affair, and now perhaps she would be caught up in the resulting legal proceedings. That prospect would not trouble her, were it not for the watch. Having it on her person now seemed a good deal less reasonable than it had on the previous evening, in spite of the letters *E.S.F.* Was it against the law to steal something from a thief? She imagined what the coroner might have to say about it, and even heard Captain Holland testifying in his curt, unfeeling way that he had seen the watch, and that *Miss Finch* had admitted removing it from the body of the deceased. She supposed that Captain Holland would have to testify against her. It was undoubtedly his duty, and besides, he had been very sceptical about the watch and everything else she had said. Doubtless the coroner would feel the same; one probably became very hard and unsympathetic, having to do with dead bodies all of the time. And then she would be arrested . . . taken up by the Watch on account of a watch. *Yes*, she reflected, *a very amusing phrase. You will probably laugh about it frequently when you are in prison.*

She cautiously descended the stairs and made her way to the kitchen parlour, where breakfast was served to guests at the Great White Horse. Captain Holland saw her straightaway and motioned for her to join him. As he was the only other person in the room she could not easily ignore this, however much she might have wished to, and therefore advanced with as confident an air as she could manage. He looked even more imposing than she remembered, but when she glanced at him he did not appear to be the bearer of bad news. On the contrary, his expression was cheerful. He had, she noticed, blue eyes, which did not have the same capacity for gloominess as brown eyes, and she sat down opposite him, hoping for the best.

Despite her anticipation of a variety of unpleasant remarks, his first words surprised her. What had she decided to do? Would she remain in Ipswich or push on to her uncle's?

She stared at him for less than a moment. 'Yes, I— I *shall* go to White Ladies. I . . . He *did* invite me, after all, and, and that is where I am going. That is what I have decided. Stopping here and writing would be, I mean, it would *seem.* . . . and I have come so far already.'

The raised chin and the flurry of words made Holland smile privately, but when he was sure she had finished he merely added with an assumed offhandedness, 'Well then, I could come along, if you like.'

This time Mary's stare was of a longer duration. The unexpected magnanimity of his suggestion, coupled with its *not* touching in any way upon the watch or possible legal complications, was both amazing and overwhelming. She almost clasped his hand. 'Come *with me* – really? Oh, *thank you*, Captain; that would be— But are you sure? It would not be too much trouble for you?'

He shook his head, and now he admitted the smile. 'A coach for Woodbridge leaves this morning, and I expect we can hire something for the rest of the way.'

'Yes, of course. I am sure we can.' She smiled back at him, thinking that really, he *was* rather handsome, in a rough, hard sort of way, and why had she not realised this before? Perhaps she had been wrong about his lack of sympathy – yes, very probably she had. Then she had another, darker thought. 'You think it likely, then, that there *is* some mystery, or some trouble?'

'No, I don't, exactly, but . . . it doesn't hurt to be careful.'

Mary was all for rushing upstairs immediately to pack her belongings, but Holland thought that she could probably spare a few minutes for breakfast. 'Have you heard about Tracey?' he asked, in a low voice. 'The landlady is sure to give you chapter and verse on the subject, and you want to be ready for it.'

The mention of Tracey dampened her spirits like a sudden shower, and her mood altered swiftly from enthusiasm to guilt. How could she have been thinking of herself, of her own adventure, when poor Mr Tracey was lying upstairs dead? If he *was* poor Mr Tracey, of course, and not a criminal. No, that was ungenerous. She really knew nothing about him, after all, and he *had* died alone in a strange place. All these thoughts tumbled, one after the other, through her brain, and she murmured, 'Yes, I had heard. I hope he did not suffer.'

'Don't ask,' urged Holland, 'that's my advice.'

Mary nodded and glanced down into her tea. Against her will Tracey's wan features appeared on the surface of the liquid, and she stirred it resolutely. 'I had not realised how interested people were in *wounds*, and . . . injuries; last night they spoke of little else. But that reminds me, do you suppose that I shall be wanted at the coroner's inquest?'

'The what? Oh. I— I don't think so.'

In fact, Holland had no idea, and merely nodded when Mary pointed out that she had not, after all, found the body, and the apothecary would be able to explain why Tracey had died. If she left her uncle's address with Mrs Bamford, they could contact her if she was wanted for anything. Surely that would suffice?

He shrugged non-committally. 'Well, I wouldn't worry about . . . inquests, but what about *the watch*?' He whispered the last two words. 'They're bound to wonder about *that*, when they see the empty chain. It will look—'

'As if he had been robbed? Yes; that is why I removed the chain as well.'

'You *what*? But—'

'Without the chain, there is no evidence that he even *had* a watch.'

'*Evidence*,' repeated Holland, frowning. 'How do you know about evidence?'

'My father once explained it to me, and the burden of proof. Without sufficient evidence by the party who bears the burden of proof – that is the Crown in a criminal case – there can be no conviction.'

She looked at him attentively. It all seemed perfectly clear to her, but every comment seemed to increase his exasperation. 'I thought your father was a *schoolmaster*,' he complained.

'He *was* a schoolmaster. But he was meant for the law, you see, and naturally, he explained things to me, when I asked him.'

'But why did you ask him?' Holland shook his head. He had never met a girl who said and did such odd things – and not just occasionally but one right after the other.

'I do not remember,' Mary admitted. 'I daresay I was curious. And the law is very interesting, you know, in places.'

'Well I'm damned. Maybe *you* ought to be looking out for *me* on this trip, Miss Finch.'

The departure for Woodbridge took place in a somewhat morose atmosphere, with only Mary's evident cheerfulness to lighten the scene. Mr Dimcock, the apothecary who had attended Mr Tracey, had dolefully agreed that

Mary need not trouble herself about the coroner's inquest. If she *would* be so kind as to leave an address where she might be found if needed, that would be most satisfactory. Mr Dimcock was rather disappointed to find Mary apparently so little troubled by the recent tragedy as not to require any medical assistance herself. Of course, it was not *his* place to comment on such a lack of feeling, but privately he considered it very hard, and not what one expected in a young lady. Mrs Bamford likewise bade the travellers only a subdued farewell, the Great White Horse having gone into a kind of mourning out of respect for Mr Tracey. For his part, Holland was still suffering the effects of the discussion of evidence and burdens of proof, and he entered the coach without a word.

Mrs Bamford waved her handkerchief as the coach pulled away and sighed feelingly. Under other circumstances she might have commented on how lovely it was for Miss Finch to have such a gallant escort as the Captain, but today her heart was simply not in it. Instead she turned to Mr Dimcock, intending to ask when poor Mr Tracey might be removed – for it would not do the White Horse any good to get a reputation for being a place where dead bodies were to be found, and he was in one of her best rooms, poor gentleman. As she opened her mouth to speak, however, she started, for it was not Mr Dimcock standing beside her, but an altogether less pleasant-looking man, small, with a thin, white face and dressed in a long, greasy overcoat.

'Oh, you did give me a turn,' she cried, drawing herself back from him with an instinctive, housewifely distaste. 'What do you mean by it, creeping up on a person like that?'

'I don't mean nothing,' complained the little man, 'nothing but wanting to see the young lady what helped the poor chap in the crash. That was her, weren't it? I heard she was like an angel, a regular angel, holding his hand and comforting him in his last hours. I take that very kindly, I do.'

Mrs Bamford's expression softened with those words. 'That's what I said,' she agreed, 'a regular angel, and such a pretty thing, too. She's gone away now, on a visit to her uncle. Came all the way from Cambridge, they say, and the uncle very well-to-do. I wonder he didn't send his carriage for her.'

'And who was t'other chap?' This with a nod in the direction that the coach had taken. 'A friend of hers?'

'I hardly like to say, I'm sure,' sniffed the innkeeper, as the mood of commiseration faded, 'but Captain Holland – that's his name – has stayed with us more than once, and I've never had no complaints. No late night capers or outstaying his purse, and always civil.' She glanced down at her questioner, but decided not to mention the captain's lack of interest in the crash; she was no gossip, after all. 'Always civil,' she repeated sturdily.

'Civil is as civil does,' replied the little man. 'And there's none as can say that *I* don't pay me shout – when asked – or that I tries to take somthin' what's not owed me. So, when I hand you this letter, missus,' and he suited the action to the words, 'it don't mean that I'm trying to cadge no favour, for I'll pay fer it fair and square.'

'What's this, then?' demanded Mrs Bamford, squinting at the folded paper thus presented to her.

'It's a letter, of course, what just needs a bit o' wax to seal it up proper, and then to be put in the bag for the London mail.'

'And who is *Mr Jonathan Hicks, Esquire, The Old Bell, Holborn*?'

'Never you mind, but I daresay he's as civil a gent as

anyone hereabouts ever seen, and he's waiting on this letter. So how's about telling me the price? They don't send letters for free, these days, I don't think.'

Mrs Bamford's sceptical glance passed from the letter to its author. 'And you want a bit of wax, you say?'

'I do say.'

'Well, you'd best come inside, then, for I've no wax out here.' She sighed again, as one for whom the sealing and posting of letters was merely the first in a long day of burdensome tasks. 'It'll have to be weighed, and *if* you can pay for it, it will go in the postbag for tonight.'

Mary and Holland were the only passengers in the Woodbridge coach, and her ebullient mood soon conflicted with her sense of propriety. She mustn't be giddy, after all. Mrs Bunbury was always warning the girls not to be giddy. Mary too had issued similar warnings, particularly when she wanted to establish her authority with new students. Now she eyed Holland speculatively as he stared out of the window, apparently oblivious to her presence and whether she was on the brink of giddiness or no. Perhaps he was contemplating important military affairs, and it would be impolite to bother him. On the other hand, she could not treat him like a stranger all the way to White Ladies, and conversation would only become more difficult the longer she put it off. 'I hope that your own affairs will not be badly upset by this delay, Captain Holland.' The coach was rocking to and fro, and Mary had to raise her voice to be heard above the creaking joints and rumbling wheels.

'What?' He started, as if her query had surprised him. 'Oh, no.'

'But now I fear I am disturbing you.'

'No, no, not at all.' He turned away from the window

63

and took a deep breath. 'Sometimes I don't—' and exhaled. 'I'm . . . on leave at present. I was thinking about that.'

Mary nodded, thinking that he seemed tense, uneasy. Could it be that *he* was shy? That seemed unlikely; he used too many bad words to be shy. 'Coarse language', as Ned the guard would say. 'It must be difficult – taking a leave of absence, I mean, in your profession.'

'It's not so bad. And I'm away fairly often on jobs.'

This seemed an odd description of his duties, but she was willing to be instructed and asked, 'What sort of jobs, if you do not mind my asking?'

He shrugged, still looking as if he did not particularly wish to continue speaking about anything. 'This and that. I'm stationed at Woolwich, of course. The arsenal at Woolwich,' he continued, in answer to Mary's enquiring glance. 'It's called "the Warren".'

'Is that where they keep . . . cannons?' she asked, even more mystified.

'Cannons, mortars, shot, all sorts of ordnance.'

This was becoming extremely odd. 'Ordinances?' asked Mary. 'Do you mean *laws*?'

'*Ordnance*,' he corrected, 'leave out the "i". It means weapons; different kinds of weapons.'

'Yes, I see. And they keep them at the Woolwich . . . Warren. Do you have much to do with arsenals? I thought it was more *ships*.'

'Well, there's a bit of that,' Holland allowed, 'but it's specialist work. Firepower is harder to manage at sea, on account of weight distribution, and damp, and teaching the dam – the sailors to fire the guns properly.'

Her continued frown of puzzlement finally provoked a response. 'I *am* a gunner, you know, Miss Finch; an artilleryman.'

Mary blushed, but such was her mood that she laughed

at her own expense – how foolish to have assumed that because his uniform was navy blue he must be a sailor!

Holland found the manner of her admission very attractive, and he assured her that her mistake was perfectly reasonable. Most soldiers did indeed wear red rather than blue. There were exceptions, such as the Light Dragoons and the Yorkshire Blues, as well as the artillery, and the Highlanders had their kilts.

'I am afraid I know nothing about dragoons,' Mary confided. 'Are they men or weapons? They sound more like a kind of mythical creature. Leave out the "o".'

'Well,' he laughed, 'sometimes they're left out altogether, when they've charged over the bloody hill and don't come back till the fighting's over. They're part of the cavalry, so they go about as they please and don't think much of the rest of us.'

'Oh. And the Navy?'

'The officers are all blue in the Navy – except for the marines, but then they're soldiers, really, and the sailors . . . in the ships I've seen they hardly had uniforms. A regular Bartholomew's Fair, not like the Army at all, or the artillery.'

'It is very complicated,' said Mary, gravely, 'for an outsider such as myself. My grandfather was a sea captain, but a merchant, not in the Navy. I suppose that is very different again?'

Holland nodded. 'The one takes all the risk and the other gets all the tin – or that's how the Navy officers see it.'

'Well, the Navy is certainly heroic,' Mary affirmed, 'and my grandfather became very rich, so I suppose it is true. That is why I said that my uncle would never have sold his watch, for he was the eldest son, and naturally *he* became very rich when my grandfather died.'

'Oh.'

The single syllable caused Mary to stop short. It suddenly seemed terribly ill mannered to be speaking of money in such an interested, knowing way, and Holland's strained expression had returned. 'But I should prefer the Navy, if I were a man and having to make my way in the world,' she continued, as if she had not noticed the *oh*. 'Or the artillery; which is also very heroic, I am sure.'

He smiled again. 'Well, maybe, but I don't know as you should count too much on heroism; the money's surer. But tell me, whatever happened to that other Tracey — the one in history. Afterwards, I mean.'

Mary thought for a moment. 'I never heard that anything happened to him,' she admitted. 'I do not think he was ever punished.'

'Ah, well, there's some justice in the world, then.'

'Justice? But he committed a terrible murder!'

'He was following the king's orders. The country would be in a hell of a state if soldiers were allowed to question their orders.'

'Yes, but . . . the king did not precisely *order* him — not like in a battle. He was at dinner, I believe, and he was annoyed with the archbishop, and he said, "Who will rid me of this turbulent priest?" And William Tracey and the others went straightaway to Canterbury and killed him.'

'That was an order,' nodded Holland, 'just not in plain words. The dodgy ones are always given that way. It was bad luck for Tracey and the others who heard it.'

'They could have refused to carry it out.'

'Oh, no, you couldn't have that. And for all we know the archbishop *was* turbulent, sticking his nose into things and causing trouble.'

'Yes, I believe he *was*,' Mary agreed, 'that is why the king was so angry. In fact, the archbishop had said—' She hesitated, remembering that her original foray into historical allusion had not been particularly successful, and allowed her sentence to trail off. 'But I still think that if Tracey and his friends had been better men, they might have done something. Warned the archbishop, perhaps, or waited until the king was in a better mood and . . . reasoned with him.'

Holland shook his head mournfully. '*Not* followed their orders . . . *warned* the king's enemy what was in store for him . . . I don't know, Miss Finch, it sounds like you're suggesting treason and dereliction of duty. Anyone would think you were a Jacobin – a revolutionary trying to corrupt me. And I shouldn't listen to you, being a loyal officer of His Majesty, but have you clapped in irons.'

'Oh,' Mary countered, laughing, 'but if I were a revolutionary I should never have suggested *reasoning* with the king. I should simply have said, "Cut off his head and have done with it."'

'Well, maybe you aren't quite so bad, then.'

Mary nodded, as if reluctantly mollified. 'Certainly not. And a truly loyal officer would not be affected even by treasonous talk,' she added, with the lift of the chin that Holland was already coming to recognise as characteristic. 'He would scorn it.'

Holland smiled. 'Agreed.'

It had been arranged that they would hire a carriage and driver to take them from Woodbridge to White Ladies and a horse for Holland's return journey. Consultation with the coachman revealed that the former were easily secured at the Crown, but a decent saddle horse was probably to be found at the Bull. Accordingly, when they arrived in Woodbridge, Holland asked Mary to remain at the Crown, while he made his way to the Bull.

Attended by their respective luggage, Mary sat in the parlour and thought neither about coaches nor horses, but about money. Holland had paid her fare from Ipswich, and his expression when she attempted to mention the subject convinced her that she would not be contributing to the price of the next stage of the journey either. He *was* an officer, of course, and used to taking charge of things – saying, go and they goeth, like the centurion in the Bible. Captain Holland was happy to make others *goeth*, but not to let them *payeth*. But surely he could not afford to throw money about, any more than she could; he certainly did not look very wealthy. In fact, he was probably *less* able than she, for there was no wealthy uncle waiting for him at the end of their journey. And he was helping her, after all; she ought to do what she could to help him. She considered how she might do this without causing a row. Perhaps if she made the enquiries about the carriage it would at least show that she was not wholly dependent upon wealthy relations and benevolent artillery officers.

It was in that frame of mind that Mary made her way to the snug: the small room at the rear of the Crown where she was told the landlord could be found. Her satisfaction grew with every step; Captain Holland might do the actual paying but she would prove herself an efficient administrator. She might even negotiate a better price for the hire, or resolve a detail that he would have forgotten. Yes, this was an excellent plan.

She stopped short at the sight of four men huddled around a table playing cards. Their coarse, unshaven appearance robbed her of some of her confidence, and she stood uncertain in the doorway. Before she could withdraw, however, one of the players looked up from his cards and muttered, 'Customer for ye, Joe.'

A man with his back to Mary turned in his chair and then stood up. 'What can I do for ye, miss?' He was a big, heavy man. His rolled up shirt sleeves and dirty white apron indicated that this was indeed the landlord of the Crown, although he was wearing red carpet slippers on his feet, which Mary found rather surprising.

'I beg your pardon,' she said, blushing, 'but can you tell me about hiring a carriage, please?'

'Oh, aye, miss,' said the landlord, 'right this way.' He gestured toward a large, overflowing desk against the far wall. 'Never mind that lot,' he urged, as she hesitated under the appraising glances of the other men, 'they don't mean no harm. Now, sit yerself down, and tell me where yer wantin' to go.' He settled himself on a stool and indicated a broad, deep-seated armchair for Mary.

'Thank you.' She perched on the edge of the chair and stated her requirements in what she hoped was a businesslike manner, but was actually a rather nervous pipe: a carriage and driver for Lindham, please.

'Makin' a visit, are ye?' asked the landlord. He squinted at her with one eye, as if he could not quite trust what he saw with both, and stroked his chin with the battered feather of his pen.

Mary cleared her throat; the air in the room had a stale, smoky smell, a consequence of the windows rarely being opened. 'Yes, I am.'

'Aye, well, it's a pretty place, Lindham, closer to the sea than we are. Young lady here makin' a visit to Lindham,' he announced to the card-players.

Two of the men turned round to observe Mary, while the third solemnly gathered up the cards. There was a general agreement on the charms of Lindham. 'Oh, aye, a fair old place is Lindham, miss.' 'You'll find the sea air grand for yer health out that way, miss.'

'Well, now,' said the landlord, 'the hire is eleven pence a mile, for a journey of—' He leaned past Mary and called to one of his colleagues. 'Six miles to Lindham, ain't that so, Tom?'

'Near enough,' replied the man so addressed. 'Have ye family thereabouts, miss?'

'Ye-es.' Mary had not considered that her travel arrangements would be a general topic of discussion. She shifted her chair to show that she was speaking exclusively to the landlord, but she was the only one who seemed to understand the significance of the gesture. Anything remotely interesting, such as her admission that she actually wished to travel further than Lindham, was immediately passed on, and soon the other men had left their table and stood gathered round her, leaning against the desk or propping up the wall. One of them tapped the leg of her chair with his foot, and it seemed to Mary as if the air was becoming close.

'Ever heard o' White Ladies, Tom?' demanded the landlord. 'Tom Scott, there, he's a Lindham man.'

Tom Scott acknowledged his authority with a slight nod of the head. Then he rubbed his chin meditatively. 'Funny old house, miss? Past Rooks' Hollow?'

Mary admitted that she did not know, and this widened the discussion. 'Ain't you thinkin' of old Mother Tipton's place?' asked the man called George Trotter, who had praised Lindham's sea air.

'No, I do not think so,' said Mary. 'I have never met anyone by that name.'

'Well, I guess you'd know if you'd met her,' agreed George, and he made a wry face, 'but there ain't no other big house in Lindham, not as I've heard of. Not till you get right close to the sea.'

Tom started to dispute this statement, or some part of

it, and the fourth man, speaking for the first time, advised George not to be so free with his opinions, for they weren't worth a brass farthing.

This advice was not taken up, however, and the questions continued. 'And it's your family you're visiting, miss?' 'What did you say the name was?' George Trotter and Tom Scott seemed to loom over Mary as they asked their questions, and she could feel herself growing hot. She wanted to reply tartly that she had not given *any* name, and that it was no business of theirs, but she could not nerve herself to do so, with them standing so close. Someone kicked her chair again, and she admitted that the name was Finch; her uncle was Mr Edward Finch.

Tom frowned and said he did not know it. Mary knew immediately that he was lying, and her courage swelled. 'Why do you say that White Ladies is a funny place?' she asked.

'No reason. Ain't never been there, ye say? Well, it's that old, and—'

'Old and mouldy, eh, Tom?' cajoled George.

'Just pipe down, George,' urged the fourth man. 'Young lady ain't interested in your nonsense.'

'Shall we say seven and six for the hire, then, miss?' asked the landlord, apparently remembering the original reason for the conversation, but Mary was still watching Tom Scott and only half heard the landlord's remark.

'Well, Miss Finch, all sorted?'

That voice, both familiar and unexpected, made her jump. There was Captain Holland standing in the doorway, his expression evenly divided between amusement and irritation. 'Ye-ss,' she nodded.

As Holland advanced Mary was aware of an exchange between him and the landlord, and of the other men seeming to melt away. The black-bearded man flourished the pack of cards and gestured toward the table on the other side of the room. 'It's yer deal, George,' he urged, 'if you've not forgotten. Let's get back to the game. Are ye in, Joe?'

'Oh, aye,' said the landlord, good-naturedly, 'keep yer shirt on. Thank-ee, sir,' he added to Holland, on receiving the fare. 'I've a very pretty curricle that'll see you and the young lady to Lindham in style.'

He escorted Mary and Holland to the parlour and then shuffled ahead to prepare the vehicle. As soon as they were alone, Mary turned to her companion. 'I apologise for not waiting, as you bade me,' she began, 'but I thought it would help if I hired the carriage.'

'That's all right.' Holland was not normally phlegmatic, but he was coming to think that Miss Finch was simply an odd sort of girl, and it was better to humour her.

'But you must have wondered where I was.'

'No, no. They told me the landlord liked playing Three Hand Brag of a morning, and I thought you'd asked to be dealt in for a couple of hands – to pass the time. Didn't lose much, did you?' he asked innocently.

'I did not,' Mary complained. 'I am sure I would never gamble with strangers – and besides, I do not know the rules of Brag. But now you have distracted me! I wanted to tell you – there is something wrong about those men. Did you see them gathered round? I am sure they were very strange.'

Holland considered saying that there was nothing strange about men gathering round a pretty girl, especially a pretty girl who went into places where she didn't belong and then turned as a red as her hair when anyone spoke to her. He shrugged instead and observed that they were probably just trying it on.

He was not surprised to see the lifted chin. 'They were

not trying it on,' she assured him, although she was not altogether certain what the expression meant. 'Those men were questioning me about Lindham, and White Ladies, and my uncle. They *know* something; I am sure of it!'

Holland was adjusting the straps on his bag, and he did not look at Mary. 'Well, what did they say?'

'One of them said that the house was an odd one and very old, but his manner was not quite right, if you understand me. He also said he did not recognise my uncle's name, but I could see that he did. The man called George Trotter said – well, I forget quite what he said, but he was very impolite; I did not like the way he looked. Another of them – the one with the dark beard – was very quiet, but from the glances that passed between him and Tom Scott – that was the other man, who lied about not knowing my uncle – it was clear that he did not want Tom or George to say anything more. They wanted to know what *I* knew.'

Holland seemed oblivious to the avalanche of words, but at last he stopped fussing with his bag. 'What happened then?'

'*You* arrived,' said Mary, with a dramatic sigh, 'so naturally they had to go back to their game, as if nothing extraordinary had happened.'

She looked at Holland, waiting for his reply. He was silent for a moment, considering, and then answered in the flat, eminently reasonable voice that Mary found particularly irritating. 'My uniform must have done it. There's a fair bit of smuggling hereabouts, and they wouldn't be taking chances.'

'Ah, I understand,' she nodded. At least he was not going to try and fob her off completely! 'Of course. You believe them to be *freetraders*.'

'Free— How do *you* know about that?'

Mary explained what Mr Treadgill had said about the freetraders and their wickedness, and she was taken aback when Holland did not immediately confirm that view. Instead he remarked that smuggling must be a damn sight easier than working a tuppenny ha'penny piece of land, after all, with nothing to show for it but a broken back and a poor harvest; and then there was the thrill of keeping one step ahead of the Revenue and the Navy. Some men would risk a lot for the excitement of the thing, and the chance of a big reward.

She frowned at him. 'But *you* do not approve of smuggling, surely? Especially not while we are at war?'

'It doesn't much matter what I approve of, though as it happens, I don't hold with smuggling. But don't *you* run away with the idea that those men are ... up to anything. If your uncle's house is very grand, it's probably well known – a sort of landmark, and they've seen it. They don't talk much to strangers because they don't want trouble – and nothing more. There's no point in creating a lot of mysteries and difficulties, you know.' He gestured vaguely, as if that was how such things came into the world, through some unconsidered motion of the air. 'You'll only upset yourself.'

'No, I see that,' Mary conceded. She did not see it at all, really, but she was coming to think that Captain Holland was simply a discouraging sort of man and it was better to humour him.

5

To begin with, the final stage of the journey to White Ladies was sufficiently interesting to prevent Mary from thinking too much about what might happen when they arrived. She had never seen a windmill before, and Woodbridge boasted two of these large machines, their long, rotating arms visible on the hill above the town. From the vantage point of that rise, it was also possible to view the considerable traffic in and out of the bay. Their own road took them across a river about a mile north of Woodbridge and then turned southeast. The river was the Deben, which reached the sea north of Felixstowe. Holland explained that Woodbridge had once been a great port, but the Deben had shifted its banks over the centuries so that now only smaller boats could come so far inland. He was less knowledgeable about whether these were the sorts of boats favoured by smugglers, as Mary suggested, and merely allowed that they *might* be.

As they left Woodbridge behind them, the road took them into an open, rolling landscape of gorse and bracken, with only the occasional tree to obscure the horizon. They encountered one other vehicle, a cart laden with

75

reeds already bundled for thatching, and two men, probably keepers, out with their dogs. Beyond the village of Shottisham they passed a man repairing a hedgerow. None of these sights particularly inspired conversation, and the overcast sky had become steadily darker, while the air grew heavy with the threat of rain.

Gradually this sombre atmosphere had its effect on Mary. Even under normal circumstances the journey to White Ladies would have been an anxious one, but now she began to imagine more particular difficulties. It was over forty miles from St Ives to Lindham; what would she find when she arrived at her destination? She had stopped thinking that the French were lurking in Suffolk, but what of the local inhabitants? Perhaps they would be unfriendly, or behave very differently from what she was used to. What of her uncle himself? He was much older than her father, that much she knew, but would he exhibit any familiar habits or expressions? Close relatives did that, sometimes, even if they had been parted for many years. They laughed in the same way, or had similar features. She did not know if she *wanted* to be reminded of her dear father by a stranger; it could make things so awkward, and as they had been brothers, there might be a very marked resemblance. And then there was this strange business of Mr Tracey, and the men at the Crown, and the watch – her uncle's watch. What did that mean? Did her uncle know Mr Tracey? Would he be distressed to hear of his death? She found that she wanted their vehicle to hurry, to speed her toward White Ladies and the resolution of all her questions, and yet she was starting to dread arriving.

'What's the trouble?' asked Holland, breaking in upon her thoughts.

'Trouble? What do you mean?'

'You've gone quiet, and just now you looked like a terrier that's seen a rat.'

She smiled, although, really, his image was far from flattering.

'That's better,' Holland nodded. 'I was starting to worry.'

She smiled again, could think of nothing witty to say in reply and blushed instead. Somehow she did not feel like explaining herself to Captain Holland at that moment, and instead gazed resolutely forward in an attempt to prevent the recurrence of disturbing thoughts. By this time, however, the landscape provided even less in the way of distraction. The rain began to fall in a heavy mist that almost obscured the bleak heath land. The driver stopped, and he and Holland manhandled the roof into position. They halted again when they reached the village of Lindham. The driver reckoned it another four miles to White Ladies, but he despaired of the condition of the coast road, given the recent bad weather.

'You see how it is, sir,' he complained. 'This here sand is terrible hard going, and the horses can't get no purchase. Another bad storm comin' on,' he added lugubriously.

'Looks like it,' agreed Holland, glancing skyward. 'But we're not stopping here, so the sooner we push on, the better. I'll ride the rest of the way; that will make the curricle easier to manage.'

The driver had much more to say on the inadequacies of the coast road, but the look on Holland's face stopped him from uttering any of it. Instead, he expressed his opinion by shrugging his shoulders, moodily flicking his whip and, while Holland adjusted his horse's girth and stirrups, voicing his grievances to his own animals. 'There you are, Ben, old feller; come on, Tally. Can't wait around all day; might miss the thunderstorm. *You* know

77

the coast road ain't fit for it, but I dursay there's some folks knows better.'

They resumed the journey, therefore, in no good humour. The driver, in fact, became increasingly disgruntled when the rain stopped and the road out of Lindham narrowed, but did not actually worsen. He would have preferred to suffer wind, rain, or quagmire if only to prove his point. At last, however, he got his wish. The road had divided, and they were progressing along what must be the drive leading to White Ladies. Indeed, the roof of a substantial building was visible beyond the trees. Where the drive began to curve toward the right, however, a large fallen tree blocked further progress, and the driver nodded with a sense of triumph. 'Most likely come down in the last storm,' he observed. 'Hit by lightning, mebee.'

Holland dismounted and studied the position of the tree, while the other two offered advice. The driver was adamant that his vehicle would founder if they attempted to leave the road, and Mary thought they must be able to walk the rest of the way; it was really no distance at all. 'All right, all right!' said Holland, frowning at both of them. 'You can leave us here— No, I'll take that, Miss Finch; it's too heavy for you. Just lead the way and leave the rest to me.'

The drive, a combination of sand, gravel, and fallen leaves, gave way to an expanse of large, frequently cracked, flagstones, apparently the remains of a courtyard. To the left of this stood a small stable and a length of old wall, part of which had fallen down. To the right stood the house itself.

To an impartial observer the description of White Ladies as both old and odd was certainly apt. The building was rectangular in shape, with a long, single-storey front

78

built of grey stone. A second storey, mostly of brick, was visible to the rear, and the difference in materials, as well as the different pitches of the roofs, created a very uneven effect. Moreover, several of the narrow windows to the front of the house had been sealed up and new sash windows inserted. While this transformation undoubtedly brought welcome light into the rooms affected, it also marred the older stonework and upset what had once been a balanced, if severe, facade.

Mary hardly noticed these details, all her mental energies being concentrated on the imminent meeting with her uncle. As they approached the stately porch, with its massive wooden door framed by a circular stone arch, she considered how she would introduce herself, according to whether a maid, footman or butler responded to her knock. When none of these individuals appeared, therefore, she was disconcerted. A second, more forceful application of the heavy iron knocker produced a similar result.

'Let's go round,' suggested Holland. 'Sometimes people turn their houses back to front, if you understand me. The other side of this one faces the sea, and maybe your uncle or your grandfather liked that view better.'

As they walked Mary took in a number of disturbing details: the absence of outdoor servants, drawn curtains at the upper windows and shutters at the lower, and no smoke from any of the chimneys. The modern stable to the rear of the house showed no recent evidence of either horse or carriage, and the cottage beside it was unoccupied. The house did boast a rather showy rear entrance, obviously built on to the older fabric by later hands. Even here, however, everything was closed, quiet, and apparently lifeless. Having ascended to the porch, Mary thumped vigorously at the door, numbing her hand on the hard wood, but she received no answer.

In all her attempts to imagine the welcome awaiting her at her uncle's house, Mary had so completely failed to imagine this situation that at first she could do little beyond framing unanswerable questions. 'What can have happened? Where are the servants? My uncle is not a young man – what can have caused him to close up his house and not employ even a caretaker? Where can he have gone?'

'We'll have to go back to Lindham,' said Holland, slowly, 'and try to find out what's afoot. You can ride my horse,' he added.

Mary agreed, wondering whether she ought to admit that she had never ridden a horse in her life. 'If only there were a way inside.'

'There is,' said Holland, joining her on the steps. 'We can break in.'

If he thought she would be shocked by the suggestion he was disappointed, for Mary responded as if this were an activity that she regularly pursued. 'And I am not certain that housebreaking would be the correct term,' she added, frowning at the unyielding door, 'as we would be acting without a felonious intention.'

He stared at her. He did not think he had ever heard anyone speak of felonious intentions, and certainly not a girl. 'Well, you're the lawyer, Miss Finch, so I'll leave all of that to you. But as we don't have a key, breaking a window is the only way I know, whatever you like to call it.'

'Yes, I suppose so,' said Mary, meditatively. She started to speak again, stopped, and then asked Holland whether he would mind *examining* the windows. 'You never know,' she observed, encouragingly, 'one might have a loose catch, or even have been left open.'

'I don't think—' he began, before amending it to 'oh,

80

all right,' and turning away. There was nothing to be gained by arguing with her, however odd her ideas.

He was conscientiously performing his task, albeit with little enthusiasm, when he discovered that her ideas were not so odd after all. She hurried over to hear his report.

'Here's your housebreaking,' he announced, rattling a loose casement. 'I may have to damage the frame a bit, but I can get in through there.'

'That is splendid,' cried Mary. 'You see, I *thought* there might be a way. Servants can be quite forgetful, especially if the usual routine is interrupted. That is what made me think about the key.'

'What key?'

'The key under the mat. It is quite common, you know, to leave a key under the door mat, or in a convenient flower pot, when you come out of your house – not if you intend to be away for long, of course, because then it is dangerous to leave a key lying about where any robber may find it.'

'And *have* you found a key, Miss Finch?'

'Yes. Under one of the loose flags at the bottom of the steps.'

'Does it fit the door?'

'I have not tried it. I found it just as you called.'

'Let's have a go, then,' said Holland, taking the proffered key. 'I would rather *not* break your uncle's window if I can help it.'

'Yes, certainly,' Mary agreed. 'Although really, if we *were* obliged to damage something very slightly, I do not imagine that he would wish either of us to be prosecuted.'

'No? Well, that's good news.'

The question of prosecution was, for the moment at least, avoided. The key fitted, the door opened, and they

81

entered the broad, surprisingly tall, rear hall. A cursory examination of the nearby rooms confirmed that the house was indeed closed. Dustsheets had reduced much of the furniture to anonymous mounds, and several carpets had been rolled up. Grates had been emptied of ash, and tables were bare of ornament. The negligible amount of dust and the lingering scent of polish suggested that the inhabitants had departed recently. More than that, however, was not immediately obvious. Certainly there was no indication of where Mr Finch had gone, and why.

Mary and Holland decided to separate in order to resolve these questions. He would discover what he could from Mr Finch's neighbours, while she examined the house more thoroughly. Before departing Holland insisted that they restore one of the parlours to something like its usual state of comfort and light a fire, and he urged Mary to remain there at her ease until he returned, if she preferred.

'Are you sure you don't mind staying on your own?'

'Oh, no,' she replied, as he had known she would, 'and I shall have a good look round. I may discover a letter, or a memorandum explaining my uncle's departure, or something of that kind. And I will try to find us something to eat.'

'All right; only bolt the door, and don't open it unless you're sure it's me.'

'You do not think—'

'No, I don't. But it doesn't hurt to be careful.'

Having made herself secure, Mary began a tour of the house. This, as had been apparent from the outside, was built on two unequal levels. The ground floor consisted of a central courtyard, or cloister, surrounded by rooms apparently given over to books, sport, conversation, and the working of the estate. At the south end stood the new entrance hall and what remained of the chapel, while the dining hall and kitchens occupied the north end. The first floor ran only along the eastern side of the house and could be gained by either of two staircases. Here Mary found a series of bedchambers suitable for family members, guests, and servants.

Everywhere, but particularly on the ground floor, the house proclaimed its age and its likely previous life as a monastic institution. Low-arched doorways, massive beamed doors, flag-stoned passages, and the large, curiously old-fashioned kitchen all suggested an age long past. In the chapel, a room sadly truncated by the new entrance hall, the physical evidence of Catholicism had been ruthlessly excised, but the cloister retained its tranquillity, and the large, undecorated dining hall could still properly be described as a refectory. Even upstairs, where the proportions of the rooms indicated a more recent creation, the absence of bedding and linens, and the relentless tidiness, echoed the austerity of the convent. Observing all these things, Mary congratulated herself on her guess that 'White Ladies' referred to the nuns who had made this place their home in former days.

In the kitchens and larder she also found much of interest. The kitchen was roughly octagonal in shape, with two enormous open fireplaces and a smaller, but still generous, oval oven. Open-faced cupboards contained a selection of pots, pans, moulds and bowls, while a number of more bizarre, and in some cases ferocious-looking, hooks, spits, cleavers and skewers adorned the walls. Food was evidently prepared for cooking at the two large wooden tables in the centre of the room.

Mary was not an accomplished cook, and during the past three years her culinary skills had been limited to making herb tea and toasting bread before the fire in her room. As she surveyed the large iron cauldrons neatly lined up in one fireplace and the complex piece of machinery that had been added to the other to turn the spits, she very much doubted whether she would prove capable of producing anything in the way of hot food. *And that is always assuming*, she mused, *that there is any food here to be cooked.*

A survey of the larder, which also contained the buttery, eventually produced ingredients for an eccentric meal. Quite obviously, the fresh food had been consumed or disposed of before the house had been closed. At first glance, Mary could find only such items as could withstand long storage: pots of preserves, nuts, spices, and several sacks of dried peas. A closer and more thoughtful inspection, however, revealed occasional lapses. Hanging in one of the kitchen chimneys was a quite respectable piece of bacon, and a box of earth gave up several potatoes that had only just started to sprout. In one of the cupboards she found a cloth bag of very hard, but apparently edible, biscuits. Some combination of these would at least keep them from starvation. Only in the area of drink were they well supplied, as Mary discovered a tea caddy, several bottles of wine, and a greater number of barrels, presumably containing beer or ale.

Leaving most of her treasures behind, Mary returned to the parlour with the not-quite-sprouting potatoes. These she placed among the embers of the fire, added more wood and resumed her survey. As she made her way from room to room, her lighted candle created glancing, flickering shadows on walls and ceilings, and she began to experience a vague, niggling sense of uneasiness. While unable to say quite why she was troubled, the very darkness and the stillness of the place made her feel

84

that an ill-defined *something* might happen. In the corridor a series of large, gloomy portraits scowled down at her, adding to her disquiet. To give herself heart she began humming 'O God Our Help In Ages Past' in a particularly confident manner.

The library proved a more tangible source of comfort. Apart from the dining hall, it was the largest room in White Ladies, and it was barely adequate to house Mr Finch's considerable collection. The bookcases were constructed so as to store volumes most efficiently according to size and subject matter. Thus, large, heavy books on astronomy were topped by smaller, and then tiny, works on natural philosophy. Literature of Greece, Rome, France, and England ran along the walls above theology and moral philosophy. Law and history gave way to physics and mathematics, and triumphed over atlases, dictionaries, and bound musical scores.

It was just the sort of room in which Mary could have spent a happy afternoon, browsing from book to book. She did, in fact, spend some considerable time doing precisely that. Eventually, however, she looked up from a ninth-century account of the life of Charlemagne and realised that she was both cold and hungry. She remembered the cosy parlour and the potatoes baking before the fire. And Captain Holland – surely he had been gone a long time? He would very likely return at any moment, and it would not do for him to find her absorbed in a pursuit so wholly unrelated to their goal.

Having carefully replaced Charlemagne, as well as the other volumes she had taken down, she left the library, closing the door firmly behind her. What was it about that sound that provoked a second, distinct wave of anxiety and even made the candle shake slightly in her hand? It was certainly possible, she knew, to frighten oneself – by telling ghost stories, or imagining that the tapping of an ivy tendril against one's bedroom window was someone outside, trying to force the latch, or . . . she shivered as she navigated the dark passage, and unconsciously hurried her steps. *This is perfectly ridiculous!* she told herself, and it was even worse to raise her candle so that it partially illuminated one of the portraits, and made it appear like a disembodied head, hovering in space above her. Yet having once thought about mysterious sounds and things moving in the darkness, it was extremely difficult to *stop* thinking of them, and what if her candle should go out?

Thankfully it did not, and she felt much better once she had returned to the bright, warm parlour. Having lighted all the candles, to guard against accidents, she chided herself for an over-active imagination and sat down to await Captain Holland's return. Of course, there was no need to mention anything to him. He did not have any imagination to speak of; he probably did not even believe such a thing existed. Well, she would not give him the chance to laugh at her. In fact— *Oh!* She jumped as Holland announced his presence by tapping on the window.

The rain was falling again, and his first act upon entering the parlour was to remove his wet greatcoat and hang it over the back of a chair. Then he drew another close to the fire and sat down. It was clear from his sober expression that something had happened, but he began by asking whether *she* had discovered anything in his absence. Only when she shook her head did he admit his own news: Mr Finch was dead.

Holland reported the event matter-of-factly. It seemed Mr Finch's health had not been strong for some time, and he had taken a chill, or something of that sort. It would not have troubled a stronger man, but in his case

86

it was a serious illness. He had died almost two months ago.

Mary was quiet for a moment. The news surprised her, and yet she thought that she had half expected it. The result was an odd, numb feeling. 'Dead. Yes, I *did* know something – he mentioned in his letter that he was not very well. It was delayed, you know; sent to the wrong address. That would explain the state of this house. How did you . . . learn of it?'

'There were some men on the beach.'

They sat for a while in silence, she with hands folded and eyes lowered, and he studying the changing patterns in the fire.

'I do not pretend to say that I grieve for my uncle,' she explained, slowly, 'for we had never met. But, it is . . . he was my only family, and now I shall never know him.' She was not conscious of any wish to confide in Captain Holland, but being in her uncle's house, sitting before the fire as he doubtless had done, inspired a sympathy for the dead man that she could not repress; and that too was troubling, and made her speak.

'I did not mention it before, but my father and my uncle quarrelled many years ago. That is why I never knew him.' She glanced at Holland, but his expression had not changed. 'The Finches were very wealthy. My uncle, being the elder, inherited everything, and my father trained for the bar. But before he could begin his career, he met and married my mother. As she had no fortune, it was necessary that he secure an immediate income. He appealed to his brother for help and was refused.' Mary paused. 'So, my father gave up his profession and became a schoolteacher, and he and his brother never spoke to each other again.'

Holland leaned forward and raked up the fire. When

87

he sat back again he turned to Mary. 'Do you know why he wouldn't lend your father the tin?'

Mary did not know; it had never been talked about at home, and she had only heard the story once, haltingly summarised, by her mother. She had often wondered about it, and having never known her uncle she had assigned to him various unpleasant motives. He was a miser, or wanted to bully his brother by wielding this power over him. Or perhaps he was jealous of his brother's happiness, or did not approve of his choice of wife. There were hundreds of reasons, if one thought hard enough.

'I have disliked him intensely for years,' Mary acknowledged. 'And I used to imagine what I would say to him if we should ever meet. Entire conversations, you know, and they always ended with my uncle crushed by mortification and guilt, and offering to share everything with my father as compensation for his past unkindness.'

She smiled ruefully, and Holland did likewise. 'Is that why you came?' he asked. 'To have it out with him?'

'In part, perhaps, and I know that makes me seem hardhearted.'

'You were defending your father; that's not so bad.'

'No, but as I never knew the actual cause of the quarrel I might have been badly wrong. And I am afraid my other reason for coming here was even worse. When I received my uncle's letter I believe I felt astonishment more than any other emotion. I had to read it twice before I was sure of what it said, for I never *really* believed that I would ever meet him, and certainly never that he would seek me out. And then I thought, well, this is my opportunity to . . . leave Mrs Bunbury's.' She flinched slightly as she spoke those words.

'What was wrong with that?' asked Holland, practically. 'A wealthy relation asks you to come and visit him. Only a fool would've turned him down flat and stayed at that damned school. You didn't like it there, did you?'

'No, but you see, I thought that perhaps—'

'That he would adopt you, or give you an allowance so that you wouldn't have to take up school-teaching again? Why not? It was worth a go, though you might have had to pipe down about what had happened with your father. Leave off your speeches, I mean.'

'Yes, I felt rather guilty about that,' Mary admitted, 'but I could not very well give my uncle a lecture and then ask him for a present! Oh, it does sound terribly weak and unprincipled of me, and I suppose it was. But it is not very pleasant, having to worry about money all of the time, and wondering what will happen when you grow old, or if you lose your situation. And we did worry about those sorts of things – all of us at the school – quite frequently.'

Holland started to intervene, but Mary shook her head. 'But now, sitting here in his study, I have started thinking about my uncle for a change, rather than myself. I think that, after all, the quarrel with my father must have troubled him, and he wanted to make it up at last. That must have been why he sent for me – he hinted as much in his letter.'

Without waiting for Holland's reply she knelt down and began rummaging through her grip. After a few moments she found what she was looking for and, leaning across the chair, handed him a piece of folded paper.

My dear Niece,
   I present my greetings and respectful compliments, and trust that you are not averse to receiving either from one

who is at present a stranger to you. Grieved as I am to learn of the decease of your parents, I am hopeful that some small good may come of it, in that you and I may become more closely acquainted with each other. As I am afraid that my own health is not robust, I am unable, at present, to come to you. Therefore, I would take it as a particular favour if you would honour me with your presence at my home. I hope to see you at the earliest opportunity. With all good wishes, I am, your respectful servant and uncle,

Edward Finch

Holland's expression did not change as he read, nor as he returned the paper, but he shrugged, 'Yes, I suppose so,' in answer to her questioning glance.

'And now it can *never* be made up.' She clasped her hands together and continued in a low voice. 'Perhaps he suffered in his last days in receiving no answer to his letter, and . . . even today I was thinking badly of him.'

'Don't blame yourself for that,' frowned Holland. 'You weren't to know. It was damned hard luck, that's all.'

The fire spat out a shower of sparks, and she moved out of reach of the glowing embers and returned to her chair. 'Yes, but . . . I am sorry for it; and sorry for him, whatever the rights and wrongs of the past.' She fell silent again, and after a few moments smiled dimly. 'Mrs Bunbury says, "the best cure for trouble is to be *doing*", and that must be good advice. Let me think . . . my uncle must have had a lawyer, or an agent, and I suppose we may discover from him whether— Oh,' she added, hurriedly, 'but all of this need not concern you. I mean to say, I mustn't impose upon you further—'

Holland shook his head. 'You're not imposing. I won't go till you're settled, so carry on with your ideas.'

'It is terribly good of you,' said Mary. 'I hate to – but if you *could* help me just a little bit longer, I would be very grateful.'

He watched as another slow blush rose to her cheeks, then he looked away. 'That's all right,' he muttered.

Conversation became more comfortable as they considered the immediate future, debating the merits of returning either to Lindham or Woodbridge, or of seeking out one of Mr Finch's more eligible neighbours. Neither could confidently remember much about the inn at Lindham, but its relative proximity made it preferable to Woodbridge. The nearest neighbour was also several miles away, and Mary did not like the idea of begging hospitality from utter strangers.

'Or we could always stay here,' Holland observed.

She stared at him for a moment. '*Stay here?*' she squeaked. '*At night?*'

'Mm,' he nodded, hiding a smile. So it *was* possible to surprise her after all. 'There's plenty of space, and we would keep out of the rain. Sort things out in the morning. It's the most practical solution.'

'Ye-ss,' she acknowledged, trying to disguise her dismay. Did he *really* think that she could spend the night with him – just the two of them? Surely he realised that such a thing would be highly improper – but she did not want to offend him. She launched into her next sentence with no clear idea of where it was going to end. 'I suppose . . . I mean we might . . .'

His laughter cut her short. 'No, no, I'm teasing. Of course we won't stay here.'

She laughed then too, and said she knew it was a joke. But should he like to have something to eat before they set out? Surely he must be very hungry, and the potatoes were probably baked by now.

'Better to eat when you have the chance,' he agreed, 'we might need it worse, later, and be without.'

Mary led the way to the kitchen, pointing out various medieval features until she perceived that Holland was not so interested in cornices and vaulted ceilings. 'And this is my grandfather,' she said, raising her candle to reveal a large portrait at the end of the passageway. The face was difficult to study in the flickering light, although Holland recognised the defiant lift of the chin. The artist had painted him sitting at a desk; before him lay a map, compass and the body of a limp animal. The latter, a beaver, probably indicated that Captain Finch had made his fortune in the North American fur trade. Holland thought he looked like a tough old bugger, but he kept this opinion to himself.

They dined contentedly on the food that Mary had discovered, helped along by a bottle of wine that Holland said would give them heart for the journey ahead. He proved particularly adept at grilling slices of bacon before the fire, transfixed on skewers retrieved from the kitchen. 'We often cooked our meals this way in India,' he explained, when she complimented his technique.

'Oh, were you in India?' asked Mary. 'How exciting. You were fighting . . . Haidar Ali, I suppose.'

'N-no,' frowned Holland, 'his son, Tipu Sultan. I probably shouldn't be surprised that you know about India along with everything else, but I am.'

Mary could not resist a smile. 'I am really quite ignorant on the subject, I assure you. Only Mr Treadgill told me a little about Haidar Ali – Mr Treadgill was in Madras in the year '80, and he had quite an adventure.'

'If he was there when they stormed the city he must've done.'

Holland had gone to India in 1785. With Britain at

peace, promotion in the armed forces had been slow, and in those regiments where commissions could not be purchased, it had been almost non-existent. The artillery regiment had simply stopped commissioning new subalterns. So, recently passed out of the military academy at Woolwich, Holland had jumped at the chance of immediate employment in the army of the East India Company. He had remained in India for the next seven years, only returning in 1792 when his commission in the Royal Artillery finally came through.

'So everything ended well,' said Mary, to whom the status of the East India Company and the relations between its officers and those of the regular British forces were a mystery. 'I am so glad. And you know – though I am sure there were a great many dangers and difficulties – it all sounds like such a marvellous thing to do, going out to India. A real adventure. I do not suppose that *I* could ever – but I believe that some ladies do go? English ladies, I mean.'

'Mm. It's not all fighting, not by a long chalk, and there's a lot to see. Palaces and temples, and the bazaars. But it's bloody – sorry, extremely hot, and during the monsoon you think the rain will never stop. And it isn't like England, of course.'

'That is what I should like about it,' nodded Mary. 'There would be no point in going all the way to India if it were quite like being at home, would there?'

'No, I guess not.'

He smiled, partly because he agreed with her, and partly because he liked her for saying it, and his friendly expression encouraged her to question him further about his time in India. Had he ever ridden on an elephant? Could they run very fast? Not faster than a horse, surely? What about tigers – were they really so very ferocious? Had he encountered any man-eating tigers?

Holland taxed his memory to recall incidents involving elephants. He had never ridden one (which Mary considered a great shame), but he had seen so many that it was hard to describe them with much of a sense of wonder. He was more informative when it came to tigers. 'There were plenty of stories about tigers carrying off goats and bullocks and just about every other sort of animal, and when you were encamped on the plains you laughed and said it was all bol— not true. But at night, in the jungle, you might hear 'em – they didn't ever growl or roar, but they could pant so hard that you heard 'em plain enough. And sometimes you saw their green eyes reflected for a moment in the campfire; then you believed it all and kept a pistol beside you until morning.'

'How could you manage to sleep on those nights?' breathed Mary, 'when you heard them or saw them prowling round your fire?'

'I don't think I did sleep much.'

Then it was time to depart. Mary made several trips back and forth to the kitchen, and on one of these she heard Holland moving about, presumably ferrying their baggage out to the stables. She mused on the illogical nature of men, in that they would not even consider replacing dustsheets, but would insist on carrying one's baggage. This led naturally to the perils of the imminent journey, for Holland had repeated his assertion that she would ride his horse. But perhaps it would not be so terrible. After all, Captain Holland would be on foot, so the horse would simply walk along beside him, and it must be very difficult to fall off a horse that was only walking.

Before she put on her cloak and hat, she determined to look into the library once more. Perhaps there was something that might identify her uncle's lawyer. It was not until she was actually standing at her uncle's desk that she began to get the anxious feeling for the third time. Hearing footsteps advancing along the passage, she rebuked herself sternly. It was only Captain Holland, come to fetch her and doubtless ask why she was taking so long.

She turned to face him, but it was not the captain.

6

He was just visible within the circle of light cast by Mary's candle; an outline that dissolved and reformed as the flame wavered. She saw a cloak, a flash of silver buttons on a sleeve, a hint of a white shirtfront. And he was tall, certainly a man and not a boy.

'Who— Who *are you*?' Mary demanded, surprise lending more strength to her voice than she felt. 'What do you want?'

'Quiet,' he ordered, and advanced into the room. A leather mask and dark kerchief disguised his features, but his confident stride, indifferent to the effect of heavy boots on the polished floor, suggested authority and decision. He gestured curtly, a soundless snap of the fingers. 'Come here, girl.'

This high-handed manner had an unexpected effect on Mary; her shock gave way to anger rather than fear. What did this man mean by telling her what to do, in her own uncle's house? She had no intention of complying with his demands, and she told him so. But with anger came prudence; she backed as he advanced, keeping the desk between them. 'Stay away from me,' she warned. Her hands scrabbled for something with which to defend herself. A paperweight – she threw it at him. 'Keep back.'

He sidestepped to avoid the missile, and in that instant of distraction she blew out the candle. Dropping to hands and knees, she pounded the floor to make it sound as if she were running, and instead crept under the desk. He cursed under his breath, and she heard him move swiftly to his left, to block the path to the corridor. *And now*, she thought to herself, *you do not know where I am*.

Mary's heart was pounding, but still she felt no fear, nor was she even conscious of having planned her strategy. She had a natural instinct to act rather than to remain passive. The stranger took a few more, aimless steps, and then he stopped and seemed to consider. 'Come here, girl, and stop wasting time,' he growled. 'I'll fish you out, never you fear, and the longer it takes, the worse it'll be for you.'

From within her stronghold under the desk, Mary's own brain now began to work. What should she do? Certainly she must not remain in that room. At any moment he would realise that he need only shut her in and then return with another light. Then she wondered whether he *was* so very likely to think of it, for he was speaking again, urging her to come out. He would not hurt her, he promised in a voice consciously softened; she had nothing to fear.

He is either a fool or he believes me to be one, thought Mary, and she listened not to his soothing words but to gauge whether he was moving in the darkness, perhaps creeping toward her. She must not give him the chance to catch her unawares, but if she moved now she would reveal herself. He would be listening for her step, and even if she crawled her dress must make a sound as it slid across the floor.

Again her course came to her without apparent reflection. There was a chair to her right; if she moved slightly she would be able to touch it with her foot. Using the desk leg for support she reached up and around to feel along the edge of the desktop. Her fingers came into contact with the candlestick just as she heard the man move again. With a gasp she threw the candlestick across the room and kicked the chair hard in the opposite direction. He sprang toward the chair and Mary scrambled out from under the desk and raced toward the corridor.

For a moment she was free in the darkness; then a light blazed suddenly, dazzling her. Someone shouted, and strong hands grabbed and held her fast. She kicked at her captor, furiously, and he grunted, calling her a hellcat, as the light crashed to the floor. Hands like bands of iron held both her arms, and then a third, gloved hand was thrust hard against her mouth. She struggled to free herself, gasping in pain as the grip on her arms tightened. Then she could not breathe; she could not move. 'Watch out fer them teeth of hers, mate,' urged a voice from close behind her. 'She'll bite you to the bone, I reckon.'

Pain, shock, and the sensation of being about to faint made her stop resisting. Would they now relax their hold? No. She began to struggle again, if only to draw a breath. They were smothering her! Then the light reappeared, raised deliberately by the man from the library. The man gagging her with his glove was also masked, and the third man remained behind her, out of sight.

'What happened?' he demanded. 'We heard a crash and—'

'Never mind,' ordered the other. The candlelight made his eyes gleam as he stared at Mary from behind his mask. 'She wouldn't come of her own, like she was told to, and she wouldn't keep quiet.' He nodded at his henchmen. 'Think you can make her keep quiet?'

The gloved man nodded eagerly. 'Nothin' easier, cap.' With his free hand he drew something from his belt and pressed it firmly against Mary's throat: the cold, hard blade of a knife. She could feel the sharp edge as she swallowed. 'No noise or we kill you,' he muttered. 'Got it?' The leader waited until she nodded, and then he murmured, 'Good. Bring her.'

The hand was removed from Mary's mouth, and she breathed in deeply, gratefully. Then the man pinioning her arms changed his hold, gripping both of her wrists in one hand, and pulling her back hard against him. His other hand covered her mouth, but not quite so tightly; she could breathe against his fingers. 'Don't you bite, now,' he warned, and then he propelled her forward, nearly lifting her off her feet.

They moved swiftly down the passageway, now barely illuminated by the light ahead of them. Mary struggled not to give way to fear, but her mind was racing with frightening possibilities. Were these men robbers? Did they mean to kidnap her? Why? Was it possible that there had been some mistake? 'Please, I do not—'

'*Shhh*, no talking,' snapped the man in charge, while Mary's captor added, 'Quiet,' pressing his masked face close to her ear. 'Hidin' from us, was ye? Thought we wouldn't catch hold of you? Well, we know a place that'll keep you quiet, and it's perfect for them that aren't scared of the dark.'

Then they were in the kitchen, then the larder, and one of the men was lifting a trap door. As the heavy stone scraped against its neighbours, Mary thought of the well in the kitchens at Mrs Bunbury's; suddenly she realised what they were going to do. 'No, no! Please!' she cried, and began to struggle again in a desperate terror. Her efforts were worse than useless, and she was borne easily towards the black opening, gasping as the bones of her wrists were ground against each other.

There was a damp, musty smell, and she closed her eyes, expecting any moment to feel the shock of cold water. But her captor's hold did not relax, and he forced her down some stairs. She opened her eyes again, but could see nothing except that they were descending into a room or space under the floor.

She sat down unexpectedly on the stairs, her captor close beside her. She could smell his rancid breath. Again he whispered menacingly, 'Don't stir, now. If you do, I'll hear you.' Slowly, he slid his hand from her mouth to her throat and closed his fingers. 'I'll come down here and snap your neck like . . . that,' and he illustrated his words with a deadening squeeze. She gasped, choked, the blood was pounding at her temples, and suddenly he released her. She barely heard the sound of his departing foot-steps or the bolting of the trap door. And then she was alone.

For several minutes Mary sat on the stairs, breathing in ragged gasps, too stunned to move or even to consider what had happened. She could only obey her orders – not to stir and not to speak. Gradually the power of inde-pendent thought did return, but the effect was even worse. Alone in that dark, silent room her fears grew like an unhealthy mould. Had she been abandoned? Left to starve? They were violent men, without mercy, and now they had entombed her in this room! *Entombed* . . . what an unlucky word, and yet, if they did not return and let her go, who would ever find her?

She swallowed, trying to ease the painful dryness of her throat. The darkness around her was heavy and impenetrable. She could feel the steps behind, leading up to the door in what was now the ceiling, and the cold, rough wall on her left side, but she dared not venture forward. For all that the prospect of a lonely death was before her, she began to imagine more terrifying perils. What if she were *not* alone? What if some other creature, who had doubtless gone mad with hunger, were down there too? Another person, or . . . The 'or' sent a prickle of fear down her spine, followed by a real, if unreasonable, belief that something might suddenly grab her, might even now be reaching up toward her. She could almost feel a touch against her foot, shrivelled fingers clutching her ankle.

And yet there were no clutching fingers. Slowly, slowly, her terror began to subside. The cold and damp were making her shiver, and as she did so, her other senses recovered their keenness. It was still impossible to see even her hand in front of her face, but she rebuked herself for cowering there on the steps. What was the good of frightening herself? She must do something . . . find a way out. Taking a deep breath she cautiously edged forward, lowering herself one stair at a time until her feet reached the floor. Then she stood up, slowly, with a steadying hand against the wall.

Suddenly she heard a sound — a scraping from somewhere in front of her. The word *rats* immediately formed in her mind, and she retreated up several stairs. The sound was not repeated, but she was unable to convince herself that she was quite alone. She strained her ears. Was that something . . . *breathing*? She experienced a greater panic when it seemed to move again. *It must be quite near . . . Oh God, what can it*— And then, having forgotten his existence until that moment, Mary whispered, 'Captain Holland?'

A tremendous surge of relief carried her down the last

few stairs and across the room. Feeling her way, she avoided treading on him and knelt down at his side. 'Captain Holland,' she repeated, shaking his shoulder. 'Is it you? Oh, please, *wake up*.'

He uttered a painful sigh and stirred again, raising himself to a sitting position. 'Bloody hell . . . what . . . Miss Finch?' he asked groggily.

'Oh,' breathed Mary, hugging his arm. 'Thank Heaven! Are you very badly hurt?'

He sighed again and then replied, 'No, I don't think so, but – where are we?'

'*Shhh*, they may hear us. We are underneath the larder.'

'In your uncle's house?'

'Yes.'

'What?'

'*Yes*, and, *please*, they are still up there.'

'Now, miss, if *I* can hardly hear you, your voice won't carry above ground. Tell me what happened. Are you all right?'

She assured him that she was quite well and quickly explained what had happened, passing lightly over some of her more colourful fears. The act of speaking helped to restore her confidence, and the possibility of ghosts faded almost completely from her mind. 'Are they robbers? Did you see them?'

'No, not really. I was in the stable – something startled the horse, and I turned round. There was someone, but, well, he must've hit me, and the next I knew I was here.'

'How could robbers know about this cellar? Do you think they come and go here as they please?'

'Well,' said Holland, slowly, 'the house has been empty for a few weeks; it wouldn't be hard to get a key, you know, like the one you found.'

'Oh, but I did not *really* find it there,' said Mary, and immediately wished that she had not spoken.

'What? Then how—'

'Mr Tracey had it on his watch chain,' she admitted, feeling a silent but intense wave of irritation emanating from her companion. She released his arm. 'I thought it might be important, and you see, it was. I . . . you were so angry about the watch that I did not like to tell you about the key.'

'I was not *angry*,' he insisted, 'but of all the – is there anything *else* you didn't like to tell me?'

'No.'

A tense, awkward silence ensued. Then Holland sighed and swore under his breath. 'Well, never mind. There's no sense arguing, as things stand. Sorry I barked at you.'

His words increased her sense of contrition. Her own conduct seemed ridiculous, even childish, although she had thought it very clever at the time. She asked him humbly what he thought the robbers meant to do with them.

'Doesn't look like they've quite decided. They could've killed us easy enough, and they didn't try to find out why we were here. Maybe there is something they don't want *us* to see, and they decided to put us in a safe place till it's over.'

'And then they will . . . let us go?' asked Mary, hopefully.

'Maybe.'

She heard him get to his feet. 'What are you doing?'

He did not answer immediately, but took a couple of deep breaths. 'Nothing yet, but I'm going to find a way out.'

'Oh, but surely there is only the trap door?' she cried, now fearful that they might hear him moving about. 'That is why they put us in this room.'

'That's what they think,' he corrected, 'but maybe they overlooked something. As you said yourself, you never know.'

'Yes,' she agreed, timidly. 'Can I . . . do anything to help?'

He was gratified by her remorse, but doubted it would last long. 'Well, what happened when they brought you down? Did you notice anything?'

'No, I could see nothing beyond the first few stairs,' she explained, dismally.

Even that information was helpful, however, and he questioned her more closely. Where were the stairs? In which direction were the outside walls of the house? Could she remember seeing a door or a window in the kitchen or the larder, apart from the doorway between them?

She answered as well as she could. 'Do you think they might come down here . . . to check on us?'

'No.' He was silent again. 'It doesn't look as if, when the house was built, supplies were brought inside from the kitchen or larder and then carried down here. And the old entrance to the house is at the other end of the passage. So unless the nuns – what did you call 'em? Sisters—'

'Cistercians.'

'Unless they heaved everything from one end of the building to the other, there must've been another way in. You're sure you didn't see anything up there like a blocked-up door?'

Mary thought hard, conjuring up the image of the two rooms. She could see the oven and the great hearth, cupboards and open shelves, but nothing unusual about the walls themselves. 'No. I mean, I do not remember a door. I am quite certain of it.'

'Then there was probably a way into this cellar from

outside. A tunnel, or a chute that was big enough for sacks and barrels.'

'And us?'

'That's right.'

'And we must try and find it.'

'Right again. It will be on one of the two outside walls – if there *is* one, of course.'

Because of the absence of light, the search was necessarily carried out by touch. Having cautiously located what they believed to be one of the outside walls, they felt along its surface from floor to ceiling, hoping to find some evidence of a door or grating. At first Mary imagined placing her hands in spiders' nests or touching something slimy. Neither occurred, but the rough, cold brickwork was unpleasantly numbing. Much worse was the nagging fear that Holland was unwell, that whatever injury he had suffered at the hands of their captors was more serious than he was letting on. What would happen if he were to collapse, and she were once again alone in that dark place? How would she look after him, and would she be able to carry on alone to find a means of escape? And what if—

All at once she realised that she had reached the end of the wall, and they had found no door.

The examination of the second outer wall proved more difficult, as wooden crates had been piled up against it. These had to be moved quietly, and in such a way that they did not create a new hazard. Slowly, and with great care, Holland and Mary found and removed each one, and then edged their way back to the wall, conscious that any significant noise must surely alert their captors.

After the crates they faced a second obstacle, a tall, shallow cupboard. Having ensured that every jar and bottle had been removed, Mary stepped aside so that Holland could drag the structure out of the way. Fortunately this manoeuvre was accomplished in comparative quiet. When there was sufficient space to admit Mary, she made the first survey of the newly revealed wall. 'Oh, it is here!' she whispered triumphantly. 'There *is* a door here – or something. It is not very large.'

She felt Holland leaning over her and heard the buttons of his coat scraping the wall. Reaching up, she guided his hand down to a rough, but obviously wooden surface. After further lifting and heaving of the cupboard, they knelt down together to study their find more closely.

'I can feel a small— perhaps a keyhole,' said Mary, 'but nothing more. How does it open?' She heard a scraping, grinding sound. 'What are you doing?'

'I'm . . . trying . . . to pry it . . . open.'

'Oh, have you managed it? Well done.'

'The wood is thick,' Holland explained, feeling along the outer edge of the door where part of the lock had been torn away, 'but mostly rotten.' He found her hand and pushed something hard and heavy into it. 'Hold that, will you?'

She flinched as she felt the sharp edge. 'What is it?'

'A knife, of course. I don't want to lose it in the dark – but don't cut yourself. And now . . . there.' The ancient hinges groaned as he forced the door open the rest of the way.

They were immediately aware of a dank, stale odour. 'It will be all right once the other end of the passage is opened,' Holland assured her. 'I'll do that now – back in a moment.'

'Yes, good luck,' said Mary. She returned his knife, and he laughed, asking whether she thought he was going to meet anyone coming the other way.

I wish you had not said that, thought Mary, as he crawled

into whatever lay on the other side of the opening, and she was alone again. It was all very well to joke, but what if something *did* happen to him in there? Or what if the robbers came back, now, while he was in the tunnel, or if he became trapped? What if there was no door at the other end?

Then she heard a series of actual heavy thumps. What was happening? How long could the tunnel possibly be? Was he stuck? There was a scraping sound, and then she felt Holland close beside her again. 'Is there another door?' she whispered. 'Can we get out?'

There was a door, and they could get out. She listened with trepidation as Holland explained what she must do to gain her freedom, but she answered confidently. Then he was gone again, and after a short while his voice, sounding strangely hollow, floated down to her. 'All right; the artillery's made a breach and the infantry may advance.'

Mary took a deep breath and backed carefully through the opening into a low, sloping tunnel. Lying on her back she began to inch forward, pushing with her feet as Holland had advised. It was quite easy to touch the surrounding walls, and when she was completely in the tunnel the sense of being trapped was almost overpowering. She stopped for a moment to recover her nerve, but the effect was precisely the opposite. Her heart was hammering away, and she could almost feel the walls closing around her, making it hard to breathe – and what if one of their captors suddenly entered the cellar, perceived that they were escaping, and dragged her back? She tried to draw up her legs at the thought and bumped them hard against the roof of the tunnel. This shocked her back to sensibility, and she told herself not to be such a coward – a ridiculous coward.

'Come on,' urged Holland's voice, now reassuringly

nearer. 'Almost there. Give me your hand.' Mary reached up, gasped when Holland's hand tightened first on her injured wrist, and then relaxed while he pulled her the last few feet. 'Well done, Miss Finch,' he added, helping her to stand. 'You're a brave girl.'

'Oh no—' She swallowed. 'I was very frightened.'

'Which is why you were brave to do it.'

'Well, perhaps; but I only did as I was told. It was you that got us out.'

They stood for a moment in the lee of the house. Night had fallen, and only a faint moonlight shone through the breaks in the clouds. To eyes used to the inky void of the cellar, however, this sort of darkness seemed light and almost comforting. Mary perceived that Holland was smiling at her, and her hands moved unconsciously to smooth her gown. 'Oh,' she murmured, suddenly shy, 'it is good to . . . breathe the fresh air again.'

'A damn sight too fresh,' he replied, stripping off his coat and handing it to her. As she struggled to put on the heavy, roomy garment he explained their situation. To reach the magistrate they must head north, a distance of six or seven miles, but westward lay Lindham Hall, where a lady named Mrs Tipton lived. It was closer, probably only a couple of miles if they went across country.

Holland thought Lindham Hall the better option, and Mary agreed. Anything sounded better than remaining where they were, within reach of their captors. Why, any moment one of them might come out of the house and—

'Right,' Holland nodded. 'We'll go into those trees, to avoid the courtyard, and cross the drive under cover. There may be some of 'em about, so be ready to stop if I say so, and be as quiet as you can.'

They set off, cautiously while they were still close to the house, but with increasing confidence as they left it behind them. Mary could see the road ahead, but Holland stopped her before they abandoned the comparative safety of the undergrowth. 'What is it?' she whispered.

'When it's safe to cross, I want you to walk twenty paces into those trees on the other side and wait for me.'

'*Wait for you?* But where are you going?'

'Back to the stables. We'll go much faster riding than on foot.'

'Oh no,' Mary cried, and then lowering her voice again she urged, 'but they will *see* you – there may be men anywhere about, you said so yourself. Or what if they go down into the cellar and see that we have escaped? Surely we can do without the horse. It is much too dangerous!'

He disagreed, but he also refused to let her come along. Instead, she was instructed to kneel right down in the bracken and not to stir, *whatever happened*.

Mary tried to argue with him. It was easy to imagine all sorts of terrible *whatevers*, and besides that, his argument made no sense. How could he claim that it was not dangerous to go back into the very lair of the robbers? Or, if it *was* safe, why must she remain behind. 'But—'

'*No.*' Holland glanced quickly up and down the road. 'Do as I say – I'll be back before you know it. Now go!'

The hand on her shoulder was somewhere between a pat and a shove. She darted across the road, and such was her nervous energy that she had to restrain herself from exceeding the allotted twenty paces. She did, however, kneel right down, and when her heart had stopped trying to leap out of her chest she told herself, not very successfully, to remain calm. He had been so sensible about finding the tunnel, he *must* know what he was doing now – but it seemed madness to risk capture by going back when they had only just escaped!

A heavy cloud drifted across the moon, and Mary suppressed a shiver that was only partly the result of anxiety. Her hands and feet were no longer merely cold; she could scarcely feel them, and she cautiously shifted her position amid the fallen leaves and damp clumps of bracken. A sudden light patter from somewhere behind her – no, in front of her – made her start, until she realised that it was only rain and not someone creeping toward her.

She sat up to ease the stiffness in her back and thrust her hands into the pockets of Captain Holland's greatcoat. Her fingers touched his knife, and she was immediately back in the robbers' clutches being bundled roughly toward the cellar prison. She could hear their voices threatening her, and she swallowed convulsively. If they caught her again, might they not . . . She drew her hand away from the knife in a futile attempt to cut short her imagination.

Nothing seemed to be happening. It was well known that minutes passed slowly when one was waiting for something, but surely Captain Holland was taking a very long time? She was reminding herself that he had to be extra vigilant, advancing into the enemy's lair, when she thought she heard footsteps. Her heart leaped in relief until she realised that the sound – and it was definitely footsteps this time – was coming from the wrong direction. Might the captain have circled round, or even made a wrong turning in the dark? It was possible, she told herself, but she crouched right down again.

The footsteps grew louder, and now Mary could make out the dim figure of a man advancing toward her. What was he doing on that lonely stretch of road on a dark, inclement night? It seemed impossible that he was an innocent traveller, however much she wished he might be. His tread was too cautious, almost furtive, and he was carrying something . . . it looked like an unlighted lantern. Surely an honest man would not *choose* to travel in the dark?

She held her breath as he drew near. Would he sense her presence? She dropped her gaze, so that he would not feel her watching him. He must be one of the robbers, but what was he doing? Had their escape been discovered? Was he searching for her? Or perhaps keeping a lookout for anyone else who stumbled upon the house that night? His footsteps seemed to slow, and then become louder as he crossed to her side of the road. Oh, God— Surely he would never see her, if she simply kept still and did nothing foolish . . . The steps halted, but she dared not look to see what he was doing, and then, cautiously, he moved on.

If time had passed slowly before, it seemed to move with great rapidity now. The footsteps faded, and suddenly she perceived a pale, ghostly figure looming up out of the darkness, almost in front of her.

'Hello?' it whispered, cautiously. 'Are you there, miss?'

Overwhelming relief at the sound of his voice. 'Here I am,' she whispered back, and staggering to her feet she hurried forward. Almost too late she perceived another darker, larger shape and narrowly avoided blundering into the horse's side.

'Careful,' Holland cautioned, his arm steadying her.

'Thank Heaven you – did you see him?'

'Who?'

'The man in the road. You must have seen him – he was just here!'

'No.'

Mary gazed anxiously up and down the road as Holland completed the adjustments to the saddle. The rain was pattering all around them, and the horse seemed to be making a terrible racket, stamping and tossing his head. 'You either passed him,' she insisted, 'or . . . but surely you could not have crept by unnoticed, not with the horse.'

Holland seemed not to be paying attention. 'Right,' he said, 'you'll have to sit sideways at first, but then you can shift round.'

'But I have never rid— Oh!' Her admission was interrupted by the sudden sensation of being lifted off her feet and placed onto a high, unstable seat. She grasped Holland's shoulders to maintain her balance.

'It's easier if you don't have time to think about it,' he said. 'Now if you—'

His words were interrupted by Mary's startled cry as a light flashed suddenly behind them. A lantern was held high, and a voice demanded, 'Oy! You there! Stop!'

'Bugger!' muttered Holland. A quick glance over his shoulder, and then he was swinging up behind her as the voice repeated, 'Stop!' The horse sidled awkwardly, and Mary gasped as she tipped backwards into nothingness. Holland pulled hard on the reins with one hand and clasped Mary with the other. She clung to him, eyes closed, as they shot forward.

The thundering beat of their horse's hooves and Mary's own terror drowned out any other sounds, but it was clear that they had been seen. Were they also being pursued? They seemed to be setting a tremendous pace, but no sooner had Mary begun to accustom herself to the strange, leaping motion beneath her than the horse checked his stride and sprang to the right. 'Go on, you bastard,' urged Holland. Mary gasped as the unexpected shift thrust her hard against Holland's restraining arm. Then they were galloping forward, then turning again, and this time she was tipped forward as well. The rain was falling harder now; she felt herself slipping sideways

112

but she had no way to stop it and was too frightened to try. She was bumping and slipping with each stride. *Oh God*, she prayed, *please let it be over.*

And suddenly it was. Or, at least, they slowed to a trot, and then to a walk. Mary let out her breath in a long, shuddering sigh, and Holland shifted her to a more comfortable position in front of him. When she opened her eyes all had become quiet; the only noise was the patter of the rain and the puffing of their horse, who was apparently little used to sudden gallops. They had left the road and were proceeding upon a narrow path of some sort; the leaves underfoot, and the stunted trees and bushes on either side seemed to absorb all other sounds.

'Are you all right?' asked Holland.

'Yes, I— Have we – are we free of them?'

'I think so. He was on foot, but I didn't want to hang about. They have horses in the stables and might come after us, but—'

'Oh, then we mustn't stop,' cried Mary, although she dreaded another wild flight.

'No, let's wait a bit. There's no sense running unless someone's after you – especially when you're not sure where you're going.'

'Are we lost?'

'No, no, but I may have turned us round when we left the road. Old Dobbin here can catch his breath, and then maybe the moon will give us a bit more light.'

They halted in a small copse, and their horse coughed and tossed his head, the final complaints against his unexpected treatment. 'Oh, my,' gasped Mary, as he lowered his shoulder and she felt herself slipping again.

Holland lifted her back into place. 'I don't suppose you can sit astride in that dress,' he remarked, 'but you'll feel

113

better – more comfortable – if you turn a bit so that you're facing forward.'

'Yes, but how will I . . . I have never ridden a horse before,' she admitted.

Holland would not have called her current activity 'riding', but he only said, 'No? Well, you're doing very well; you only have to turn round. That's right,' he continued, as she made a series of slow, tiny movements, bracing herself against his arms, 'now put your leg . . . sorry, there you go. Now lean back.' He placed his hand on her shoulder and drew her firmly against him to illustrate his suggestion.

'Oh— I beg your pardon,' said Mary, her face flaming. She could feel his arms close on either side now as he held the reins in both hands. She had been clutching him far more tightly only a little while ago, but then she had been too frightened to think about what she was doing. Now, however, fear dissolved into acute embarrassment. She was almost sitting on his lap – it was practically an embrace – and his hand on her knee . . . Oh, it was terrible – well, not exactly terrible, but thank goodness for the dark!

'Better?'

'Yes,' she answered in a small voice. 'But what if we have to . . . go fast again? What shall I . . . ?'

'Don't worry, I won't let you fall.'

She was sitting bolt upright against him, and after a moment he asked whether she was cold. 'Oh, no,' she lied, and then, feeling that she must make an effort to converse normally, asked what had happened when he went back to the house.

Holland explained that his actual task had been quite easy – nothing to worry about, as he had said. On his way to the stable, however, he had overheard a conversation

114

that had surprised him. Two men, smoking on the back steps of the house, had been discussing landing conditions and the state of the tide. They seemed to be waiting for a boat and wondering when it would land.

'A boat? So . . . perhaps they are not robbers at all, but smugglers?'

'Yes, that's what I thought,' said Holland, slowly. 'And it makes sense that they wouldn't want us to see what they were doing, only . . . it seemed as though they were talking about taking a cargo *off*, not *landing* one.'

'Would that be very unusual?'

'I think so, but maybe not. At least they weren't bothered about *us*.'

'But now that they know we have escaped – will they come after us again?'

He shrugged his shoulders. 'Maybe, but I doubt we're worth it.'

They were silent for a moment, and then, as if in consolation, the sky cleared and the pale moon shone down upon them. 'Ah,' said Holland, looking skyward, 'that's better. Now, let's see if we can find Lindham Hall.'

7

They rode for a time in silence and, almost in spite of herself, Mary began to relax. It was actually quite comfortable to lean back against Captain Holland, and as the minutes passed, pursuit seemed increasingly unlikely. She no longer dreaded falling, and their future course had become imponderable, unalterable, and impossible to worry about. Lacking money, belongings, or any notion of where they were going, it was proposed that they should beg shelter from someone about whom they had absolutely no knowledge other than that she was called Mrs Tipton. Only yesterday the very idea of doing such a thing would have been amazing, yet now it seemed almost sensible. And Captain Holland – he was really a stranger, when their acquaintance was measured by any normal standard, yet now she was associating with him in *very* familiar circumstances. It was almost as if . . . well, she was not quite sure she could complete the parallel.

With an effort she turned her thoughts to less disturbing matters, and remarked that their horse was really quite well-behaved, once one was used to him. But then, horses probably did not generally bite or trample one, except in extreme circumstances. The horse that drove the cart at Mrs Bunbury's, for example; it was hard to imagine *him* misbehaving, but then he was very old. Everyone called him Old Niggle, because of his frequent ailments, but his true name was Ajax.

Fortunately Mary could not see Holland's face during this report, and when he asked whether she had ever been driven by the mighty charger his tone gave nothing away.

'Once, when we went to Cambridge for a concert of ancient music, but generally the cart is only used for school business. Mrs Bunbury says we cannot risk his knees for mere pleasure, although why his knees should have been singled out, I do not know. He once had a particular cough, I remember, which was very loud. In the hot weather he sometimes wears a hat, and—'

'A *hat*?' demanded Holland, finally unable to contain his mirth.

'Yes, a straw hat, to keep off the sun. Mr Taft − *Mrs* Taft is the housekeeper and her husband does all sorts of jobs, including driving the cart − made a hat for Niggle. I suppose it is good for him, but really,' she added, now laughing along with Holland, 'he *does* look a sight, and I am convinced that he knows it, poor old fellow. Some animals are easily embarrassed, you know. Like dogs . . . and horses, I daresay.'

'I daresay,' Holland agreed.

Their pace slowed as they crossed a boggy stretch of open heath. Once or twice Holland looked behind him, but if he heard anything untoward, he did not acknowledge it, and maintained their steady, careful progress. For Mary it was like a dream, where nothing made sense, and one simply kept going − through tunnels, on foot, or on horseback. Even Niggle's hat seemed to belong to another

117

world. She considered mentioning this strange feeling of helplessness to Captain Holland, but decided that he would probably say that they were not helpless at all, and what was she thinking of? Instead she looked up at the stars, spangles of light emerging from behind the clouds. How far away they seemed. How far away everything that was normal and regular seemed. She wondered how Holland knew where they were going. Sailors navigated by the stars, and perhaps soldiers too, when they were marching by night – which she supposed they must do, sometimes. Would he be offended if she asked him again about their location?

The horse halted at Holland's brief command, and Mary wondered fleetingly whether she had voiced her last question out loud. Then a more alarming possibility struck her, and she sat up anxiously. 'What is it?' she whispered. 'Is someone coming?'

'No, just getting my bearings again. Not much farther now, I think.'

Gradually the going improved, as bog and tussock gave way to meadow, and then to a field of rough stubble. They followed a hedgerow and, at a gap, crossed it to join a path. This in turn brought them to a large, half-timbered house. Below all was in darkness, but lights showed at the upper windows.

'Is this Lindham Hall?' whispered Mary.

Holland dismounted. 'If not, it will do just as well.' He lifted her down, and she took a few tentative steps. In addition to her sore throat and wrists, she felt stiff and uncomfortable in places she did not care to mention.

His firm knock on the front door caused an immediate commotion within, consisting chiefly of the voices of several dogs, but also that of an elderly woman, who called, 'Cuff! Mr Cuff!' The dogs continued to bark, then quieted as another voice, masculine this time, called them to order. There was a pause, and then this same voice ordered, 'All right, hold 'er steady, Peggy,' and the door was unbolted and opened.

A pool of light revealed a stocky, grizzle-haired man wearing a nightshirt and overcoat, and pointing an old-fashioned but serviceable blunderbuss. Two dogs edged in front of him, growling and offering to bark, while on the stairs behind him stood a plump, middle-aged maid, also in her nightclothes, wide-eyed and brandishing the lighted lantern.

'What'll yer business be?' demanded the man.

'I'm sorry to wake the house,' said Holland. 'I am—'

Before Holland could finish, a querulous female voice from somewhere within demanded, 'Are they gypsies, Mr Cuff? Turn the dogs on them.'

Hearing themselves mentioned, the dogs growled more authoritatively. 'Hush,' said Cuff, and nodding to Holland said, 'go on.'

'I am Captain Holland, of His Majesty's Regiment of Artillery, and I must ask you to rouse your master or mistress.'

'What are you doing down there, Mr Cuff?' called the voice. 'Why are you talking to gypsies?'

'Aye, ye've done that a'ready,' said Cuff, jerking his head upwards. 'It's no gypsies, missus,' he bellowed.

'Nonsense, of course it is. Who is it?'

'Military chap. Captain Hol . . .'

'*Holland*. And this young lady,' he continued, raising his voice to a volume that would carry up the stairs, 'is Miss Finch, the niece of Mr Edward Finch! We've had an accident at White Ladies!'

'*Is* that Mr Finch's niece, Mr Cuff?' demanded the voice. 'What is she doing with the Army?'

'I cannot tell ye that, missus,' called Cuff, peering at the two visitors, 'but they surely did have an accident.'

'Peggy! Come up immediately.'

'Aye, Peggy,' agreed Cuff, 'you have a good look on 'em, and tell missus. Leave yon lantern.'

Peggy descended timidly, glanced quickly and rather suspiciously at Mary and Holland, and set down the lantern on a sideboard beside the door. Then she retreated up the stairs. While she was gone, Cuff maintained his forbidding stance, and one of the dogs pushed past him onto the porch. He sniffed enquiringly in the direction of the strangers. After a few minutes Peggy's slippered feet could be heard on the stairs, and she rejoined Cuff in the doorway. 'Mrs Tipton says you are to go into the second parlour, and she'll be down directly. Mr Cuff, you're to put that horse in the stable and see to him, but then you're to come back inside right quick with no dawdling.' (The last was Peggy's own injunction.) 'You're to bring Prince with you, not letting him on to the furniture.'

'Aye, aye, a thousand and one orders,' sighed Cuff, lowering his gun and standing aside. 'Lead the way, then, Peggy, and I'll be back in half a tick. And ye might give us a bit o' fire.'

'Half a chance, Mr Cuff, half a chance,' complained Peggy, busily lighting candles. 'Right this way, miss, if you please.'

As Mary stepped inside, her gaze quickly took in a panelled hallway, now bravely lit by several wall sconces. To the right stood the broad, highly polished staircase, with a thick but worn carpet running up the centre. There was a similar carpet on the floor, and to the left, above the sideboard, a mirror. Its glass was cloudy, but that could not disguise Mary's disordered appearance. Her

120

hair was wild; her face streaked with dirt, and the captain's coat was now sodden and disreputable. The mirror was not long enough to show her grimy skirt or her filthy hands, but it did reveal something of her shock and exhaustion. Instinctively she straightened her back and tried to look cheerful – or at least less like someone on the brink of tears.

Following Peggy into the parlour, and now painfully aware of the state of her clothes, Mary thought that she, like Prince, ought to be banned from sitting on the furniture. Fortunately, Holland had no such qualms, and he guided her into a chair by the hearth, where Peggy was lighting a fire. Mary sat down tentatively and turned to her companion. His white breeches were grimy and spattered with mud, but it was the sight of livid cuts on his forehead and right cheekbone, and smears of blood across his shirtfront that shocked her into speech.

'Captain Holland! You *have* been badly injured! I thought— Please,' she turned to Cuff, who had settled into a chair near the door with Prince, an enormous rough-coated dog at his feet, 'might he have a drink of water?'

Holland frowned and shook his head slightly, but she was paying no attention.

'Reckon he'll want sommut stronger 'n water, miss,' said Cuff, cheerfully. 'But best wait till missus comes down.'

In a little while the sound of slow, deliberate tapping on the stairs and hallway floor announced her coming. A peevish voice ordered those dogs that had been denied admittance to the second parlour to 'look out', 'stand aside', and 'get down, sir'. At the sound of that voice, Prince got up on his own authority and retreated to an out-of-the-way corner, gathering his tail carefully around him.

121

Mrs Tipton was a small, elderly woman, who navigated unsteadily by means of two stout canes. As she processed across the parlour, frail, tottering, and dwarfed by everyone else in the room, she seemed incapable of withstanding a harsh word or a moderate breeze. When she had settled herself in what was obviously her particular armchair, however, a transformation occurred. Her dark, sparkling eyes peered shrewdly at Mary and Holland from behind steel-rimmed spectacles, and her neat, sober appearance in a black silk gown and lace cap gave her a distinct moral advantage over the bedraggled visitors. With her canes crossed in front of her like a pair of ceremonial wands of office, she proceeded to the inquisition.

She had to be convinced, initially, that Mr Finch could have possessed a niece, since *she* had never heard of one. 'Hmm. Well, you do not favour him, but I suppose that is just as well. And what are you doing with this fellow?' She nodded in Holland's direction. 'What did you say your name was?'

'It's Holland, ma'am.'

'What? Not those frightful Whigs?'

'No, ma'am. I'm not related to Lord Holland.'

Mrs Tipton studied him for a moment. 'No, of course not,' she agreed, in a tone that made him redden. '*Hollands* . . . I trust your family is not engaged in the making of gin?'

Mary instantly recalled her first conversation with Captain Holland and her confident production of Mrs Oldworthy's bottle of cordial. He seemed to remember it too, as he glanced fleetingly in Mary's direction. His expression never changed, however, and he answered Mrs Tipton in his usual curt tone. 'No, ma'am, nothing like that.'

'Hmm. Well. And why are you traipsing about with this young person, knocking at my door in the middle of the night and putting my servants in fear of their lives? If this is the way that government proposes to save us from the French, I do not think very much of it.'

'If I could explain—'

'I hope that you can. You look as if you have been to the wars already. Let him speak,' she advised Mary, to whom the idea of intervening had not previously occurred. 'Men usually explain things better than women, and even if they do not, they think that they do, and one must humour them if one is to have any peace.'

Mrs Tipton's notion of letting Holland explain did not include letting him do so without prompting, comment, or further questions. Nevertheless, he managed to present a fairly clear account. 'So you escaped through an ancient serving passage,' she observed. 'I have never heard of such a thing. It was very enterprising of you, young man. But if we cannot expect enterprise from our officers, what hope have we? Mr Cuff, first thing in the morning, you will conduct a thorough examination of our cellars. If you find any similar disused passage, I want it closed up immediately.'

'Aye, missus, first thing.'

'And when you have done *that*, you must go straight-away to Woolthorpe Manor and inform Mr Somerville of this *criminal outrage*.'

'We are sorry to give you any trouble,' said Mary.

'It is no trouble *to me*,' Mrs Tipton replied, 'and Mr Cuff can use the exercise. But an armed band of brigands – robbers, I daresay, after your uncle's silver.'

'I think they may have been smugglers.'

'Smugglers, brigands, disreputable rogues,' said Mrs Tipton, contemptuously. 'What do you say to that, Mr Cuff? I imagine *you* have some inkling of what goes on at the dark of the moon.'

Cuff assumed an expression of appalled innocence that affected Mrs Tipton not in the least. 'Mr Cuff,' she explained, 'does his fair share of poaching, although I have warned him time and again, and if the law takes him up, he knows that I shan't intervene. And I have no doubt that some of his cronies turn their hand to other illegal activities when the opportunity arises.'

'Oh, missus,' protested Cuff, 'I swear they'd none of 'em treat a young lady rough,' nodding at Mary, 'nor knock a chap on the head like the poor captain, here.'

'It is all one,' said Mrs Tipton. 'They begin by knocking rabbits on the head, and soon they are doing the same thing to officers of artillery. Now, I suppose, they will betray us to the French, and the entire mob will set about robbing decent people and calling it a revolution.'

Holland frowned, but merely remarked that he would be glad of a word with the magistrate.

'I am not surprised,' agreed Mrs Tipton. 'Eager to be after them, I daresay. Fellow has no politics, but rushing about the countryside after brigands, that is a different matter. Well, what do you think of all this, Miss Finch? What do you mean to do? You must visit your uncle's grave before anything – pay the proper respects.'

Mary acknowledged that she would.

'Mr Hunnable must call, of a certain, and I daresay Mr Somerville can enlighten you on the legal side of things. Well, well,' Mrs Tipton continued, 'you seem a good girl – what did you say your Christian name was? *Mary?* Hmm. Rather old fashioned, but I suppose it cannot be helped. Now, both of you require some looking after. Peggy, you had better see what there is in the way of supper, and find Captain Holland something to drink. We have no gin, but perhaps he might make do with a rum punch, and some hot milk for Miss Finch. Do not wake

124

Pollock – that woman could sleep through the last trump, but if once she is made to leave her bed at an unseasonable hour we shall never hear the end of her grumbling – but see to it yourself. What is the state of the guest rooms?'

Peggy looked aghast. 'Oh, ma'am, I shut them rooms up proper, after Mr and Mrs Arthur's visit, as you said the dogs was always on the beds.'

'So I did and so they were, the rascals. Well, you must put things in order straightaway – Mr Cuff, you must help her. Fetch some hot water and towels, of course.'

Mrs Tipton fixed her gaze on Holland, as if about to give him an order, and he quickly offered to see to the proper stabling of his horse.

'Certainly. Mr Cuff will direct you to the stables. Peggy, there are nightclothes belonging to Mr and Mrs Arthur in the press. Lay them out for Miss Finch and Captain Holland. And Mr Cuff, you will do as Peggy directs you – no answering back or saying you did not understand her.'

'Yes, ma'am,' said Peggy, with a glance of triumph in Cuff's direction.

'No, missus,' he agreed, gloomily.

Having thus delivered her orders, Mrs Tipton announced that the hour was late for an old woman such as herself and she would leave them. She waved aside any attempts to thank her for her hospitality and said that she looked forward to whatever developments tomorrow might bring – it was better than a play. With a further command that Prince and Hero should remain downstairs to discourage any smugglers from playing their tricks *here*, she departed.

Her leaving had a liberating effect on those who remained. Mary and Holland exchanged smiles, and several dogs nosed their way through the incompletely closed parlour door and began visiting. 'Well, well, what a to-do,' said Cuff. 'Who'd a thought it, eh, Peggy?' 'Never in all my born days, Mr Cuff,' Peggy agreed.

Peggy had very decided ideas of what constituted a sufficient meal for gentlemen – particularly those who had suffered wounding and hardship – and in the absence of her employer these views were allowed full sway. Thus supper consisted of sausages and onions, a cheese omelette, bread and butter, and the generous remains of an apple tart. The unusual circumstances of the meal, and the fact that it was served in the kitchen instead of the dining room, encouraged Peggy and Cuff to join in, or at least to hover more openly than they would ordinarily have done. They both spoke freely with Captain Holland. With Mary they were rather more shy; Cuff because Mary was so much younger and prettier than the females with whom he regularly dealt, and Peggy because she wondered – just at first – whether the young lady was as good as she ought to be, out with a gentleman late at night, whatever the reason.

Mary took little notice of either admiring or critical regard. Instead she realised that she was famished and set to her meal with a will. With each mouthful, however, she found herself growing increasingly drowsy, until she wondered if it was possible to eat oneself to sleep. The comfortable domestic atmosphere contributed further to her lethargy. The warmth of the oven, whose fires had been banked for the night, and the pots of preserves and condiments, all neatly labelled with reassuring titles like 'sweet strawberry jam' and 'best long acre honey', made her feel that nothing else dreadful could possibly happen and she could relax at last. She was aware that a conversation

126

of sorts was occurring around her, but she lacked the inclination to join it.

At last she was allowed to leave the table and make her way upstairs to the chamber that had been provided for her. While not a particularly grand room and very old fashioned, its furnishings were finer than any Mary had ever seen, and ordinarily she would have taken in every detail. Tonight, however, she was unable to appreciate the velvet bed hangings, or the Dutch tiles of the fire surround, or the vast walnut cabinet, whose inlaid doors depicted bearded faces, to the willing mind. Instead she sat down wearily at the foot of the bed and gazed at her own reflection in the dressing-table mirror, while Peggy whisked about the room, plumping pillows and adding more wood to the fire. Mary's own face seemed strange to her, not merely tired, but somehow different. So many things had happened since she had left St Ives – had she changed too?

Peggy finished her labours and stood with hands on hips, watching Mary speculatively. She *had* endured a very nasty experience, after all, being fair choked to death by villains, and she *did* seem to be a proper young lady, for all that her gown had been darned more than once. 'Reckon you'll be comfortable, miss?'

'Yes, thank you,' Mary nodded, smothering back a yawn. 'I shall be . . . perfectly comfortable.'

'A good sleep, that's what you need,' Peggy affirmed, and her expression lost its prim severity. 'Well, good night, then, miss, and pleasant dreams.'

The door closed and Mary began unpinning her hair, but she lacked the energy to do much more. A few moments later her reverie was interrupted by a brief knock. She thought it would be Peggy with a final query or renewed offer of a hot drink, and was surprised to find Holland in the passageway. He smiled when he saw her and held a finger to his lips.

'I wanted to make sure you were all right,' he whispered.

'Yes, thank you – I mean . . . We *are* safe here, are we not? They would not—'

'No, no. They were probably glad to be rid of us.'

This did not quite make sense to Mary, but she nodded and said that she was not really worried. Nor was it a lie, for her predominant feeling at that moment was of being wide-awake. How could she have thought she wanted to sleep? A ridiculous notion. But he was not going, was he? She struggled for something that would prolong their conversation. 'Mrs Tipton seems . . . do you think she is rather an odd sort of person?'

'She's odd all right.'

His tone of voice, even when whispering, made Mary want to laugh, and she had to bite her lip to stifle a giggle. 'But it is terribly kind of her to take us in,' she reminded him, trying to be serious. 'How strange it must have seemed, our appearing as we did in the middle of the night.'

Holland shrugged. 'We're good entertainment. Like she said, "better than a play". I'm the fellow with no politics who's knocked on the head like a rabbit.'

This time she did giggle, adding, 'At least you are not one of those "frightful Whigs".'

'No, that's something,' he smiled. 'And you're the long-lost relation. Every play has one, hasn't it?'

'Yes, I think so. "*You do not favour him in looks, Miss Finch, but perhaps that is just as well*".'

Then they were both laughing and telling each other to be quiet at the same time. '*Shhh*,' she admonished, 'she will hear you,' while he added, 'and likely say I've been at the drink.'

128

Mary glanced at him shyly. 'Yes, I did not understand – what did she mean?'

'She meant that she's a silly old woman. There's a sort of gin the Dutchmen make that's different from English gin. It's generally called "Hollands", but nobody *called* Holland makes it.'

This set them laughing again, especially after Mary admitted that she had always thought that 'Holland' referred to a kind of linen – 'Holland cloth' – but she had not imagined Captain Holland to be a tailor or a draper, in consequence.

'Well, don't suggest it to her,' Holland pleaded, 'or she'll have me darning the napkins.'

As their hilarity subsided, however, the silence that followed began to feel awkward. Mary was conscious that she was blushing and looked at the floor, only to realise that she had taken off her boots before answering his knock, and that she had been talking to him in stockinged feet.

Her hair fell in tumbled curls against her shoulders, and the light from her candle produced highlights of copper and gold when she turned her head. Holland was aware of her curls, and her delicate feet and ankles, and the curve of her neck as she looked away from him. He was carrying his uniform coat over his arm, and he began rubbing a smear of dried mud. At last he murmured, 'Well, good night, then.'

'Good night.' She sounded relieved, and smiled up at him again. 'And Captain Holland?'

'Yes?'

'Thank you.'

He returned her smile. 'That's all right, Miss Finch.'

Mrs Tipton was an early riser and so, perforce, were the other permanent residents of Lindham Hall. She was so far from believing that her guests should adopt this practice, however, that she insisted upon all chores being completed in strict silence until after breakfast. The execution of these two mandates resulted in Peggy stealthily taking away Mary's dress to sponge and press it before first light and, having replaced it, failing to close the bedroom door tightly behind her. This, in turn, directly contributed to Mary awakening, several hours later, with the distinct sensation that she was being watched. She opened her eyes to find that five dogs, of varying sizes and breeds, had not only pushed open the door and entered her bedroom, but that the three smaller ones had joined her in, or rather on the bed. These animals were all asleep – one actually snoring – but their larger colleagues had waited for an invitation, or for sufficient space to be made for them, and now they stood staring at Mary, wagging their tails hopefully.

For a few moments she simply returned their gaze and reflected upon the changeable temperament of Mrs

Bunbury. Having repeatedly railed against dogs as noisy, dirty creatures, and never to be tolerated upon school premises, she had obviously relented and was now affording them access in great numbers. As the last remnants of sleep receded, however, Mary began to look about her more carefully. The snowy eiderdown, the stiff, embroidered curtains at the windows, the heavy furniture here and there ornamented by Mary's own meagre belongings . . . this was *not* Mrs Bunbury's school for young ladies but Lindham Hall — and the events of the previous day and night came flooding back.

She dressed hurriedly and went downstairs accompanied by the dogs, who had interpreted her motions as indicating a willingness to play with them. (They were disappointed, therefore, when she excluded them from the dining room, and they lay in the passage, whining, until Peggy chased them away.) Closing the door behind her, Mary encountered a large, oak table with places set for three, only one of which was occupied.

'Morning,' said Captain Holland, rising to his feet. 'I hope you're well?'

Mary replied with an anxious smile. 'Good morning. I am quite well, but I am afraid that I overslept. Have you been waiting long? Where is Mrs Tipton?'

'She's been to church, and now she's taking her morning constitutional, meaning Cuff is pushing her up and down the lane in an invalid chair.'

'Oh dear, I ought to have— Did *you* go? To church, I mean.'

'No, I think we were both excused duty. Better have some breakfast, instead.' The thought of sitting down to a hearty meal when she had already failed to display a proper piety caused Mary to hesitate, and he continued, 'Pollock, the cook, is in a passion at having missed the excitement

131

last night – she has been rattling the pots and pans about – and if she hears that you've turned up your nose at her cooking . . .' He shook his head. 'Very likely poison us to get her own back. How about some tea, at least?'

Mary smiled, in spite of herself, and sat down opposite him. 'Very well – I mean, yes please. Shall I pour out?'

Shaking out her napkin, she surveyed the scene: the snowy cloth with hints of lace, a jug of red and white campions, the delicate, porcelain breakfast service . . . really, Captain Holland was the only incongruous element. Of course, gentlemen must eat breakfast, but there was something inherently feminine about that meal, especially in such a dainty setting, that made them seem out of place. Would a man appreciate the pretty, bone-handled knives, or the plates adorned with scenes of water gardens, with long-legged birds preening beside arched bridges? She doubted whether most men would take any notice at all.

As Mary passed Holland his tea she smiled again, a secret smile. What could be more incongruous than that she herself should be in such a situation – that she should be a guest at Lindham Hall! This was certainly not the sort of breakfast she usually had at Mrs Bunbury's, where the bread was often stale and the contents of the teapot highly suspicious. There were never little rolls with jam, while bacon and eggs, which Mary could smell sizzling in a chafing dish on the sideboard, were strictly a Christmas treat. How strange to find herself in a place where these luxuries were an everyday occurrence. It might make sense if one were in a fairy-tale, enduring hardship and danger to win through to the enchanted castle. Mrs Tipton was certainly odd enough to act the part of the fairy godmother, but it was all rather difficult to accept in the course of one's ordinary life.

Yet what *was* ordinary life? After yesterday, it was difficult to know. Mary tried to explain her feelings to Holland, not quite sure whether he might be part of the strangeness, for how often did she breakfast with a captain of artillery, with whom she had been imprisoned in a cellar? 'It is as if . . . as if somewhere on the road from Mrs Bunbury's I left all of my true, *real* life behind me, and now none of that is real at all, but only this.' She glanced around her. 'And yesterday.'

'Mm,' said Holland. 'Battles are like that. Sometimes, if there's a lull in the fighting, you think about ordinary things and can't believe you ever did 'em. And then afterwards, the battle itself sort of fades in your memory. Especially the worst parts, which is a good thing, really.' He hesitated. 'You're not . . . it doesn't worry you now, does it? To think of what happened yesterday? No bad dreams, I mean?'

Mary shook her head but his words gave her pause, for late last night she *had* seen something – or thought she had, from her bedroom window: an odd shadow moving across the courtyard. It was Captain Holland's fault, really; his unexpected visit had awakened her too thoroughly, and afterward she had been unable to sleep. She could not explain why she had gone to the window, nor describe the shadow itself, for it had melted away – there one moment and then . . . not there. And so now she shook her head with a clear conscience. It was not the sort of thing that one admitted in the light of day, especially to someone like Captain Holland, who never believed anything and might think that she had insufficient faith in his assurances that all was well. Of course, all *was* well; but how strange that he should ask whether her dreams had been upset.

'Have you heard any news about the magistrate?' she

133

asked, consciously dismissing other uncomfortable thoughts.

'I have. Cuff left a message, asking him to come here as soon as he can. And in the meantime, there's the parson paying us a visit, so it looks like we won't have missed church after all.'

The Revd Hunnable did indeed pay a visit to Lindham Hall that afternoon. He was a mild, earnest little man, who could call upon few reserves in the way of physical, spiritual, or intellectual strength when striving with life's difficulties. He was dimly conscious of this; at least he knew that interviews with either Mrs Tipton or the late Mr Finch were rarely of a wholly easy, pleasant nature. Mr Finch had had the unfortunate tendency of fixing one with a speculative, or even a scornful eye, and of conveying the feeling that he was not quite *listening* as he ought. Mrs Tipton's manner, on the other hand, was quite the reverse. One *always* knew what she thought, although one did not always know how to respond to her opinions, having once – and frequently more than once – received them.

Mr Hunnable had not, therefore, looked forward to his interview at Lindham Hall nor, having been installed in the first parlour, did his mood lighten. That room, which was never used except to entertain visitors, was not generally comfortable without a substantial fire. On this occasion, however, the fire was only a few minutes old, and its modest size made it almost useless against the pervasive chill. Mr Hunnable could not quite see his breath, but he was convinced that it was colder in Mrs Tipton's parlour than it was outside. And then there were his inquisitors – for so he considered them – gathered around him. He could not be sure of Miss Finch, but Captain Holland was a rough, turbulent-looking man, probably violent, and he knew Mrs Tipton of old, of course.

Had he but realised it, in Mary Mr Hunnable had a sort of ally, at least as regards the first parlour. It was so much less cheerful than the second parlour, lacking chairs that countless Tipton posteriors had made sunken and comfortable, and possessing a chill that reminded her of all the rooms at Mrs Bunbury's. Over the fireplace hung a portrait of a gentleman in an old-fashioned wig and lace cravat, and he stared gloomily down the room at a woman in a grey silk dress who occupied a similar place on the opposite wall. A slight cast in her eye gave her a suspicious expression, as if she were wondering what these people were doing in *her* parlour, and doubting whether they were good enough for it. For her own part Mary thought the doubt very plausible, but that if people could not look more . . . charitable they really oughtn't to have their portraits painted.

Everyone sat in silence, gently shivering and drinking luke-warm tea. Mr Hunnable felt the oppression of the situation most keenly; he, after all, must eventually speak. He sighed, and wondered whether another slice of toast might ease his burden. Well, well. It was best to begin with Miss Finch who, after all, had first claim upon his attentions. He explained how sorry he had been to learn of Mr Finch's demise, though he could not assert a particular intimacy with the departed in this case. One did one's duty . . . and naturally one ought not to grieve in circumstances when death was a relief from present suffering. Suffering, of course, was the lot of mankind on this earth, and illness, particularly when it was prolonged, could be a severe burden. Mr Hunnable's own health was not the strongest, but one mustn't complain. And was it not a comfort, in any case, to reflect upon how our troubles in this present life were a preliminary to the greater joys of Heaven?

When this peroration came to an end, Mary nodded politely and said she was grateful for his sympathy. 'Do I understand it, sir, that you were not with my uncle when he died?'

Unfortunately, Mr Hunnable had not been present, but had learned the melancholy news from Mrs Collins, the housekeeper at White Ladies. He had been suffering from an illness himself at the time and had been keeping indoors.

Mary would have liked to meet Mrs Collins, and Mr Hunnable lamented that this was likely to prove impossible. 'A dour woman, I always thought, but very much affected by poor Mr Finch's death. She departed the neighbourhood shortly after the funeral. She was not a local, you know.' The housekeeper, it was revealed, was a native of distant Sudbury, and had only been with Mr Finch for ten or eleven years. It was hardly surprising, therefore, that she would wish to return to her own people when that flimsy tie was severed. Certainly she had always been regarded as a foreigner in Lindham, and so the object of grave suspicion.

'Suspicion of what?'

The question, and the forthright way in which Mary expressed it, took Mr Hunnable aback. 'Of foreign, outlandish conduct, I suppose. It is quite usual in places such as this, where the locals have little knowledge of the outside world.'

'Was that your own experience, sir, when you came to this parish? Or perhaps you are a Lindham man yourself?'

Mrs Tipton uttered a snort of surprising volume, given her size. 'No, no. You were born in Oxfordshire, were you not, Mr Hunnable?'

He admitted that fact and added that he was, of course, a clergyman.

Mary frowned. Were clergymen especially numerous in Oxfordshire? Or did ordination render one immune to local gossip? Neither interpretation seemed very likely, but rather than pursuing the matter she expressed her surprise that a house such as White Ladies should have had only the one servant. Mr Hunnable believed, and Mrs Tipton was certain, however, that this was the case. There had been a steward, of course, but White Ladies had never been notable for its gardens during Mr Finch's time nor, indeed, for its hospitality. 'You were not in the habit of calling upon Mr Finch, were you, Mr Hunnable?' demanded Mrs Tipton.

'No, not quite in the habit. Indeed,' he added, clearing his throat, 'I found it rather difficult to know what to do in the matter of the funeral. Of course, I am well versed in the clergyman's part in that solemn and important ritual, but where the deceased has not made his wishes known, one cannot be certain how to proceed with regard to those elements of a personal nature. One strives for delicacy, you know, even when the arrangements must, of necessity, be circumspect. The headstone was particularly vexing, but I trust that my decision – which I felt bound to take – will prove satisfactory.'

Mary was watching Holland throughout this speech. She doubted he was paying the least attention. It was really too bad of him, and Mr Hunnable was bound to notice. This condemnation distracted her, so that Mr Hunnable drew to a conclusion more quickly than she anticipated. Not entirely certain whether she ought to nod or frown, she murmured, 'How vexing for you. My uncle did not leave a will?'

'Ye-*ss*, I believe he did. Certainly Mr Todd thrust himself

137

forward most officiously, informing me that everything must be done with the least expense possible, which I imagine had been Mr Finch's instruction. He would not have dared to interfere otherwise, surely?'

She was paying attention now, but it was impossible to offer a comment until Mrs Tipton revealed that Todd was the name of the late Mr Finch's solicitor. 'I see,' Mary nodded, 'and very likely his executor, or at least privy to the terms of the will.'

'Privy he may have been,' complained Mr Hunnable, 'but *I* was left completely adrift. Moreover, Mr Todd has also seen fit to throw out hints of a devise – or is it bequest?'

'Bequest, sir, I believe.'

'A bequest, then, of a charitable nature, and this too has, apparently, been left in Mr Todd's hands. Well, I am not complaining. One does one's best, and if charitable bequests are left in the hands of lawyers – not that I am casting the least aspersion against Mr Todd, although he rarely attends divine services – but, well, there it is. And we all thought – we assumed – that poor Mr Finch had no relations. I am certain that was *quite* understood.' Mr Hunnable nodded and then, as if conscious that he might have given offence, added, 'But, of course, I am very happy to have been mistaken on that point.'

'Yes, sir, thank you.' Mary struggled to keep her voice steady, and Holland rolled his eyes and shifted impatiently in his chair. She did not dare to look at him, in case their glances should meet.

Just then there was a knock and Peggy presented herself in the doorway. 'Mr Somerville to see you, ma'am.'

The atmosphere was transformed by this announcement. 'Ah, at last,' cried Mrs Tipton, and Captain Holland rose to shake hands with not one but two new arrivals.

The first was the magistrate himself, large, florid, and rather boisterous. His clothes, a bottle-green frock coat with gold buttons, and a yellow striped waistcoat, were as loud as he was. The second was a tall, swarthy gentleman, both younger and more fashionably dressed. He had an exotic air about him, and this was confirmed when Mr Somerville introduced him as Mr Paul Déprez, lately of St Lucia in the West Indies and presently residing at Woolthorpe Manor, the Somerville estate.

'I hope I do not intrude upon you, ladies,' said Déprez, his glance taking in Mary and Mrs Tipton. 'I was fascinated by the story my friend Somerville told of what happened yesterday, and I took the liberty of including myself in your invitation to him.'

Mrs Tipton offered her reassurances and, having quickly looked him over, said that she understood the West Indies to be most notable for the production of sugar, and did he have property there? Mr Déprez admitted to having owned a sugar plantation – he would have owned it still, if it had not been destroyed by the present warfare. He did not wish to intrude upon his friend's official duties, however, and retreated to a chair beside Mr Hunnable, indicating with a gesture that he meant to take no further part in the conversation.

'Indeed,' nodded Mr Somerville, 'official duties.' He was standing before the hearth, effectively blocking the meagre heat produced therein, and now he frowned pugnaciously. 'If there is one thing that I cannot tolerate – well, two things – it is smuggling in wartime and Republicanism,' he announced. 'Look where this Republican nonsense has landed the French. And the other is just as bad, for it is helping those same damned Republicans.'

'Very troubling,' murmured Mr Hunnable.

'I have been playing hide-and-seek with smugglers for

the last ten years,' Mr Somerville continued, 'and now to hear that they have had the . . . the audacity to break into the house of a respectable gentleman, and him barely cold in the— Er, I beg your pardon, Miss Finch. I only meant . . . well, it is an outrage.'

'Yes, sir,' said Mary, blushing as all eyes turned to her. 'Were you . . . well acquainted with my uncle?'

'I would not venture so far as to claim a friendship,' Mr Somerville acknowledged. 'He was a close man – kept to himself. Am I correct, ma'am?' Mrs Tipton frowned and turned her head slightly, as if to fend off the booming query.

'Indeed, yes. The result of Mr Finch being such a great reader, for books were all he cared for, and very few people wish to make their society solely out of literary disputations. You would do well to remember that, Mary,' she added, as if referring to some previously expressed weakness on Mary's part.

'I had the honour of meeting Mr Finch shortly after I arrived in the neighbourhood,' Déprez remarked, and he inclined his head more courteously in Mary's direction. 'I found him a very witty, intelligent gentleman, in all ways pleasant, despite his poor state of health.'

'Oh yes, undoubtedly,' said Mr Somerville, 'sound as a nut was old, er, ahem. But if you will forgive me, ladies, I believe we ought to leave the . . . encomiums for another time. I propose to depart for White Ladies immediately, to investigate the . . . the scene. We can discuss the details of what happened as we go.'

'By all means,' Mrs Tipton agreed, thinking that conversation was not particularly Mr Somerville's strong suit. 'Undoubtedly an investigation is in order.'

Captain Holland and Mr Déprez were to accompany the magistrate, and two of the three were taken aback

140

when Mary shyly added her request. Mr Somerville gaped in surprise, but admitted that he could see no harm in it. Judging, moreover, that her presence would transform the exercise into something like a pleasure outing, he extended the invitation to include Mr Hunnable.

'Oh, I—'

'Good, capital,' cried Mr Somerville. He clapped Mr Hunnable companionably on the shoulder, upsetting that gentleman's plate and napkin in the process, and then he was in the passageway, asking Peggy for his hat and coat.

They all piled into the Somerville carriage, Mr Hunnable sitting between Mary and Déprez, with Holland and Mr Somerville opposite. Mary had seen splendid vehicles in Bath, but she had never ridden in one, and now the fairy-tale feeling was taking hold again. Mr Somerville was not quite her idea of a prince, but his coach boasted pale, leather-upholstered seats and backs of a quite luxurious softness, and outside a coachman and groom in blue and silver livery awaited the signal to depart. This was given smartly by a thump of Mr Somerville's walking stick, and as the wheels started to turn the magistrate began his interrogation. He wanted to understand more precisely how Mary and Holland had come to White Ladies in the first place, and what had actually happened on their arrival. Mary answered most of his questions, and everyone seemed so interested in her account that she began to relax, and even to feel at ease. The fairy-tale was not fading, but perhaps it was one in which she actually belonged.

It was quite pleasant, she found, to be the centre of attention, and as her contribution drew to a close, she experienced a pang of regret. When Mr Hunnable looked as if he were going to speak, therefore, she carried on, mentioning for no particular reason the dire warnings she and Holland had received about the condition of the coast road. Mr Somerville shook his head dismissively. 'This machine,' he affirmed, 'is much lighter than you would imagine, looking at it. Light, but sturdy. You are not concerned by the motion, Miss Finch? Some people find it awkward.'

'Oh, no.'

'And I daresay they can pull us out, if necessary.' The vehicle gave a sudden lurch and Mr Somerville shouted, 'Steady on, man!' while thumping the ceiling with his walking stick. Then he straightened his wig and continued, 'You know, Miss Finch, that fellow Tracey interests me. We might have learned a great deal, if only he had lived. I do not believe *you* ever spoke to him, did you, Captain Holland?'

'No, sir.' Something in Holland's tone, a hint of uneasiness, attracted Mary's attention, and she looked across at him.

'Perhaps they may tell us something about him in Ipswich.'

'He wasn't a local,' muttered Holland. 'That's what Bamford said – landlord at the Great White Horse.'

'What a pity. Still, I shall make enquiries among my fellow magistrates.' Mr Somerville peered out of the window at the dull, overcast sky. 'I hope we are not due for another shower. Worst Michaelmas I can remember for bad weather.' A long, undulating hedge was rolling past them on Holland's side of the carriage. He glanced at it fleetingly and then closed his eyes.

As Mary continued to watch him a half-remembered image from their previous journey appeared in her mind's eye. She smiled to herself as she perceived the secret, unspoken bond between them. When the carriage slowed as they came to a turning, she leaned forward and asked Holland if he would mind exchanging places. 'Thank you,' she nodded, as they slid past each other, her eyes betraying no hint of her knowledge. 'I *was* finding the motion a trifle . . . unsettling.'

'And you prefer to ride backward?' asked Mr Somerville. 'It is usually t'other way round. Of course, you must suit yourself.'

From her new position Mary could study Mr Déprez more closely — not stare at him, which would have been impolite, but . . . take him in. Her mother had said that one could learn a great deal about a gentleman from his hands. Whether he was a gentleman at all, for a start, or at least whether he engaged in a gentleman's pursuits. Soft, pudgy fingers never managed a horse's reins, while calluses and broken nails were not gained by turning pages. A gentleman, of course, should be equally at home in the field and the library. Too much jewellery suggested a dandy, and frayed cuffs were a sure sign that money was wanting. According to these criteria Mr Déprez was a gentleman through and through. Indeed, there was nothing frayed or foppish about him, and he exuded a quiet elegance that was in marked contrast with his neighbours. Mary wondered whether he might even have an appreciation of breakfast.

The exchange had left Mr Hunnable pressed more closely against Déprez, and the latter observed, 'I do not suppose you encounter many smugglers among your flock, sir?'

Mr Hunnable denied it most vigorously, but after a moment allowed that, 'Sometimes late at night . . . one may hear things, if one is a light sleeper, as I am. And I confess that in the past it has been my practice to keep away from the windows on such occasions and . . . But of course, all that has changed, now that we are engaged in this dreadful war.'

'Oh?'

Mr Hunnable explained that he had undertaken to ring the church bell in the event of a French landing, and Déprez nodded his approval. 'A highly creditable service.'

'It is not so very much,' admitted the clergyman, 'but when our community is under threat, the responsibility for safeguarding it falls as much to the men of faith as to those of the sword. Particularly when our foes are such godless creatures.'

'"Get thou behind me, Robespierre," eh?' chuckled Mr Somerville.

Mr Hunnable shuddered. 'I dread to think what will happen if we are so unfortunate as to suffer invasion.' He reflected upon it for a moment, nevertheless, and then added, nervously, 'You do not believe that there might have been *Frenchmen* at White Ladies, do you?'

The suggestion that she had been a prisoner of the enemy ought to have raised a fearful spectre in Mary's imagination, but the clergyman's train of thought actually inspired something quite different. She looked away to hide her smile and said she did not think she had encountered any Frenchmen, and Mr Somerville opined that if they *were* to land, Mr Hunnable would undoubtedly be the first to hear of it and sound the alarm.

'Yes. Well, I hope so. I would not like to be found asleep at my post.'

This reminded Mary of something else, and she turned back toward her companions. 'I believe Mr Tracey knew that something untoward was happening at White Ladies. He said the most curious things, and—'

'He was foxed with gin,' Holland completed.

'Ah, the famous cordial,' chortled Mr Somerville.

144

'Well, yes, perhaps,' Mary admitted, 'but after all, he had the *key* to . . .' her voice trailed off. Captain Holland had resumed a healthier colour, and she thought it prudent to avoid his eye.

'Yes indeed, the key which you so thoughtfully removed,' beamed Mr Somerville, as if he quite approved of pick-pocketing.

'Of course, I never imagined,' said Mary, still unable to look at Holland, 'and I know that it was very wrong of me to remove it, but when I saw the *watch*, I thought—'

'Yes, quite a bit of luck, your noticing that. I see how that would have "opened your eyes", as they say, what with it being so like your father's. Must have been rather a shock, seeing it on a stranger's waistcoat.'

'Yes, it was.' Mary supposed that the watches, along with the rest of their things, had now been stolen, and Mr Somerville declared that, from an official point of view, he hoped they had been. Stolen property was frequently sold, and the more unusual the items, the more easily they were traced. If recovered, they would provide valuable evidence against the villains, who might otherwise be hard to identify. Most smugglers were local men, but building a case against them, that was quite another matter.

'*Local men?*' queried Mary, blanching at the prospect of encountering one or other of her captors in some casual exchange in the Lindham high street, or on the front step of Lindham Hall. She might not recognise them by sight, but their voices . . . those would be difficult to forget, and the deadening grip of a large, callused hand against her throat. She swallowed nervously.

Some of her anxiety was communicated to Mr Somerville, and he strove to calm it. 'I do not mean to say that you are in any *danger*. This whole business will have given them a very bad fright, and I daresay they will have gone to ground.' He patted Mary's hand comfortingly. 'And perhaps some clue at White Ladies will enable us to dig them out.'

Having been warned of the fallen tree, Mr Somerville directed his coachman to take a different turning, so they were able to drive right into the White Ladies courtyard. They descended, not quite like a pack of hounds straining at their leads, but certainly keen to begin their investigation. Mary took charge, directing them to the rear entrance and pointing out the various details that had first raised their suspicions that the house was unoccupied. She was conscious of a tranquillity that surprised her. It was as if she were explaining something that had happened to someone else a long time ago – almost like a History lesson at Mrs Bunbury's. The idea was faintly amusing, and if Captain Holland had not been present she would have been tempted to make up a story about the house, or certainly to expand upon the incident of the key. As things stood, however, it was best to keep silent on that score.

The door was ajar, and they filed inside. While Holland and Déprez lit candles Mary made the first, sobering discovery. Her bag, cloak, and hat were still in the entrance hall awaiting collection, and in the pocket of her cloak she found both watches. The smugglers, it seemed, were clever men; they would leave no easy trail for Mr Somerville to follow. The magistrate expressed his frustration at this reverse in a series of muttered oaths, and he stomped along the passageway, prodding the rolled-up carpet with his walking stick. Mary's response was more restrained. She simply closed her worn, leather purse, replaced it in her cloak, and rose slowly to her feet. Yes, the smugglers had been very clever; they had left the watches and taken her money. No great sum in absolute terms, but it was very nearly all the money she possessed. She could not even pay her fare back to St Ives.

With that realisation her mood of cheerful self-confidence ebbed away. She was barely conscious of the flickering lights, or the pervasive chill, or the muted conversation around her. But instead of slipping further into helplessness, her thoughts swiftly turned to what she must do in the face of this calamity – write to Mrs Bunbury and beg an advance on her salary? She guessed that her employer would produce a modest loan, enough to return Mary to the school, but that would mean giving up everything here, and she could well imagine the lecture, the patronising looks, the . . . consuming sense of failure. If only she could contrive to remain in Suffolk. Her moral debt to Mrs Tipton was so large already; could she possibly add a financial one?

Mary did not consider mentioning her loss to any of the men. She was convinced that *their* money would flow freely and unencumbered by lectures, but to throw herself on their mercy was somehow unseemly – not a step that a young lady ought to take. She could not quite explain the difference between it and allowing Captain Holland to pay her fare from Ipswich, but she was certain that there was one. So she kept silent and instead joined Mr Déprez and Mr Hunnable, who were gathering up some papers that had been scattered across the floor. They belonged to Captain Holland, and he said they were only some notes and calculations, nothing important. He leafed through them, nevertheless, apparently putting them in order before stuffing them into a battered leather wallet. He coloured as Mary handed him the last few sheets, however, for these were compositions of a different sort, and took them from her without a word.

From the entrance hall they made their way to the library, and now Mary began to feel a different kind of uneasiness. Walking along the corridor she remembered that *they* had been here, and here. The library itself revealed the disorder from her attempt to elude capture – the overturned chair, the shattered paperweight, and the dented candlestick. When they reached the kitchen the picture became clearer still. In addition to the remnants of the meal made by Mary and Holland, there were several dirty glasses and two empty wine bottles. Obviously, the smugglers had taken some refreshment after disposing of their prisoners. This added a further callousness to the imprisonment, and when Mary turned her gaze elsewhere she could not help noticing the various spits and . . . skewering things on the walls. There seemed to be nothing domestic about them; on the contrary, they looked like gruesome instruments of violence.

When the trap door was located and opened, Holland and Déprez made the descent into the cellar, while the others remained above ground. Mary kept well away from the steps themselves and could not bear to look down them, although she did watch the lights of the lanterns bobbing about. Her heart seemed to be beating with a similar unsteadiness.

Déprez emerged first. 'Most unusual,' he said, dusting his hands, 'and not very pleasant.'

'No,' agreed Holland from below. As he ascended, his expression said to Mary, *you shouldn't have come*, as clearly as if he had spoken the words aloud, and she shrugged *I am not a coward* in reply.

'Why, when this is closed,' said Mr Somerville, examining the top of the trap door, 'one might walk upon it without the slightest notion that anything was below. I daresay I have done so, more than once, little guessing . . . Well,' he continued, after the door was heaved back into place and he had, indeed, walked upon it, 'I doubt we shall find out anything very useful here. Our friends have not left us much to work with.'

They shut the door to the house behind them, locking it with Mary's key. Mr Somerville proposed to have a man come to change the locks, but until then they could at least exclude the weather and any casual thieves.

'Gypsies,' said Mary, thinking of Mrs Tipton.

'Eh? Oh, ah,' nodded Mr Somerville.

Déprez wanted to see the other end of the tunnel, so they tramped around to that side of the house. Holland opened the low wooden door, and Mr Somerville poked his stick meditatively into the dark hole in the wall. 'It was fortunate that the door was not padlocked on the outside,' mused Déprez, 'but I suppose its very existence had long been forgotten, or the smugglers would have used it themselves.'

'Let us be thankful, then, for poor memories,' agreed Mr Somerville, 'and that you were not left to the mercies of those villains. Not,' he added quickly, in a more jovial tone, 'that you were probably in any real danger. Very unpleasant, however.'

He maintained his cheerful flow as they made their way back to the carriage. 'You know,' he observed, 'this is really a very charming old place. It suited Old Finch – I mean, Mr Finch – down to the ground. That covered walkway, the cloister, is a notable example of the early Gothic style, so they tell me. In fact, Mr Hunnable means to write a pamphlet on the subject – am I correct, sir?'

'Yes,' piped Mr Hunnable, 'such is my aspiration.'

Mary was walking beside Captain Holland, and now Mr Déprez came up on her other side. 'I hope that this affair has not spoiled the estate for you, Miss Finch. Caused you to dislike it, I mean.'

149

'Oh, no,' said Mary, trying to sound confident. She did not think that any of the men, with the possible exception of Mr Hunnable, would let a group of smugglers frighten them away, and she did not want to appear any less spirited. 'I would like to examine my uncle's library more closely, sometime,' she added, airily. 'Perhaps another day.'

'You are like your uncle, then, a great reader, as Mrs Tipton says?'

'I suppose I am, when I have the opportunity.'

'Well, you would find it hard to wade through all of your uncle's books, and I do not know that there is much to interest a young lady,' said Mr Somerville. 'He probably did not go in for novels or that sort of thing – I daresay you are very fond of novels?'

Mary wondered whether a fondness for novels was something she ought to acknowledge. Mr Somerville's smiling tone made her think that it was not. Captain Holland too had edged away slightly. Mr Déprez, however, seemed to regard the matter in a more positive light; she turned towards him. 'There is a very good lending library in Cambridge,' she explained, 'and when any of us at the school borrowed a book we would all tend to read it.'

Déprez nodded. 'Of course.'

'And one of my colleagues was particularly attached to novels.'

Mr Somerville's smiling acknowledgement forced her to assure him that she was also fond of poetry, and history, and books of all sorts.

'Well, I hope you stick to the ones with happy endings,' and now he was almost chuckling. 'Love and romance and happy endings. That is the sort of reading that suits young ladies best – would you agree, gentlemen?'

Mr Hunnable made a faint, bleating sound, but Déprez

150

frowned. 'I am afraid I would not. We like to think – we men – that ladies cannot understand the higher forms of art and are satisfied with the banal, or the sensational. But that is merely a tribute to our self-love, and bears little relation to reality.'

Mr Somerville shook his head indulgently. 'You are verging on the philosophical, sir. But I recall something in that line about the fairer form and the weaker vessel – and what about the Bible? Daughters of Eve, and so forth? What do you say, Mr Hunnable?'

'Well, I should hardly like to affirm—'

'Of course, I bow to Mr Hunnable with regard to the daughters of Eve,' said Déprez, gravely, 'but in my experience, a lady of taste and intelligence is as capable of appreciating literature, poetry, or philosophy as a man. And in Miss Finch, I believe, we have a lady of that description.'

Mary could feel a blush rising, but she found she did not mind it. It was even more gratifying to be told that her education had placed her above most men, particularly those of a purely mechanical or unreflective nature. She thought so too, but was surprised to encounter a man who shared her opinion. Why could not one of her colleagues at Mrs Bunbury's have had a brother like Mr Déprez?

'Come, come, sir!' protested Mr Somerville, 'you force me to enter the lists in defence of mankind. Captain Holland, will you assist me?'

'I don't think I can, sir,' Holland admitted. 'I expect I'm one of those dull, mechanical fellows Mr Déprez was talking about.'

'Not at all,' cried Déprez. 'You mistake me, sir; I meant no such insult. Indeed, I value science most profoundly, and yours is a scientific profession, is it not?'

'Yes, it is. I've heard it described as 'heroic', but I wouldn't go so far as that.'

Their journey back to Mrs Tipton's was undertaken in a different mood from that in which it had begun. The air of urgency was lacking, and more than one member of the party felt rather flat. It began to rain again, and the steady drum on the roof contributed to the heavy atmosphere. Nor did their conversation help matters. Drawing upon recent events and Mr Somerville's experience as a magistrate, they concluded that the smugglers had known White Ladies very well. Its location close to the sea, and with decent landing places nearby, made it a likely depot – where cargoes could be stored temporarily before being moved inland. Such depots were essential for an operation that could extend as far as London. When Mr Finch died the smugglers must have taken possession. As he had no family nearby, they would have guessed that the house would remain empty for some time.

'As for your own . . . mishap, that is where the smugglers' network came in,' suggested Mr Somerville. 'The gang learned of your presence and, thinking you might prove dangerous, they decided to put you under lock and key.'

'In what way could we have posed a danger to them?' asked Mary. 'They seem to have landed no cargo – there was nothing in the house for us to find. Why not simply let us come and go?'

'Ah, but smugglers are very suspicious fellows,' Mr Somerville replied. 'And having a military officer turn up – that would have given 'em a fright. But I do not mean to, ahem, blame Captain Holland for what happened. The two of you were outsiders, and that was enough.'

'Yes, I see,' Mary nodded, 'and our going to White

152

Ladies was no secret, especially at – oh, yes, I nearly forgot about the Crown.'

'What crown?' asked Déprez. 'Do you mean a coin?'

'No, the inn at Woodbridge.' Mary explained her encounter with the landlord and his cronies, and their furtive manner when the subject of White Ladies was raised. How much more suspicious it all seemed, in the light of what had happened! She, of course, had thought something was wrong straightaway, and now she was sure that the smugglers' network was operating at the Crown.

'Every man who keeps mum in front of strangers isn't a villain,' Holland observed.

'No, but villains generally know to keep their mouths shut,' said Déprez. 'At least, that has been my experience.'

'And mine,' Mr Somerville agreed.

'I am certain that they were up to something,' said Mary. 'A man named Tom Scott knew the most, and he is a Lindham man. I think you ought to— Oh, I beg your pardon, Mr Somerville. I mustn't tell you how to conduct your investigations.'

'Not at all, Miss Finch. You have been exceedingly helpful, and I am much obliged to you. Tom Scott, eh? I shall certainly speak with the fellow.'

'And you might mention Mr Tracey,' she added, hurriedly. 'If they knew each other – that would surely be important.' She directed her remarks particularly at Déprez, and felt gratified when he nodded thoughtfully.

Having first deposited Mr Hunnable at the parsonage, the rest of the party divided at Lindham Hall. Although invited to step inside, the gentlemen from Woolthorpe Manor preferred to go straight on and take their supper at home. 'One's own fireside is always best, is it not?' asked Mr Somerville, before drawing Mary aside for a

153

private word. She was glad of this, for there was something she wished to ask him, although she doubted whether anything the magistrate said could possibly remain private, as he habitually spoke in such a carrying voice.

'I was wondering,' she began, 'what you thought I ought to do now.'

'Do?' he frowned, 'well, I do not quite . . . you mustn't worry about any of the practical matters – locksmiths and so forth – and I shall have a word with your uncle's old steward. You will have to decide whether you want to re-engage him, of course, but there is no harm in asking him to have a look round the place.'

Mary reflected fleetingly that she could not possibly re-engage *anyone*, but merely nodded, 'Yes, of course,' and then asked her question openly. Ought she to remain in Lindham, at least for the time being?

The magistrate was blissfully unaware of the deeper problems hanging upon his answer. 'Certainly,' he replied brightly. 'Much more convenient for everyone, I should think. Unless you particularly wish to return to St Ives.'

'No, but . . .' Mary bit her lip, wondering how quickly she could obtain the necessary funds to prolong her stay. She might write to Miss Marchmont and Miss Trent, her particular friends among the teachers at Mrs Bunbury's, but they rarely had funds to spare. 'I really oughtn't to impose any longer on Mrs Tipton,' she finished, in the tone of someone who wished to be told that she might do precisely that.

Mr Somerville rose to the occasion. 'Impose?' he demanded, 'not a bit of it. I doubt if she would let you go – or if she did, she would be mortally offended.'

This, they agreed, ought to be avoided, and Mary breathed a secret sigh of relief. Here was one matter dealt with; the rest she would have to leave for the moment. She smiled shakily, and Mr Somerville patted her hand.

'That is settled, then. And it will make things easier when it comes to dealing with the legal side of things – of your uncle's death, I mean. Nothing can happen for good or ill without the law sticking its nose in – though I suppose I oughtn't to say such things, being an officer of the law myself.'

The solicitor, Mr Todd, had an office in Woodbridge, and Mr Somerville proposed to send someone with a message first thing in the morning. The prospect made him chuckle good-naturedly. 'Perhaps I shall go myself. I should like to see his face when he discovers that the very person he has been seeking has stolen a march on him!'

'Do you suppose he has been trying to find me?' asked Mary.

'Bound to have been. It is a big estate, you know, and I daresay your uncle had other investments. If you are his heiress – and I suppose you are – you stand to inherit quite a tidy fortune.'

9

'Well, Miss Finch, what do you think?' It was the following afternoon, and a brisk wind was blowing across the church-yard of St John the Divine, in Lindham. Mr Hunnable kept a tight grip on the brim of his hat, almost as if he were saluting, and Mary's cloak flapped and billowed around her. 'Of course, the stone will improve when it has weathered, and in the spring I believe you will find this a very peaceful spot . . .' He gazed up at Mary anxiously.

'Yes, I am sure you are right,' she agreed, suppressing a shiver. It was hard to think of spring at the moment, with the trees bare of all but a few dead leaves, and the brown, waterlogged grass lying in untidy hillocks where it had not been properly cut. 'Nothing is at its best at this time of year.' She studied the simple stone tablet.

EDWARD STRONGMAN FINCH
1738–1795
THE LORD IS MY SHEPHERD

'Was the twenty-third psalm a favourite of my uncle's?'
Mr Hunnable cleared his throat. 'Not precisely – that

is to say, I would not venture to affirm . . . but I cannot believe that he would have objected. Such a beautiful expression. I hope you agree?'

Mary was rewarded by a relieved smile from Mr Hunnable when she confirmed that it was precisely what she would have chosen. She was about to expand on the point when she noticed someone standing at the gate.

Mr Hunnable turned and stepped backwards into a puddle. 'Oh – botheration,' he exclaimed. 'Hello there,' he called, waving. 'Can I help you?'

The stranger acknowledged the greeting and approached them. He was soberly dressed in neat, but well-worn breeches and coat, and either time or outdoor work had given him an aged, weather-beaten appearance. When he removed his hat, the wind tousled his long, greying hair. 'Beg your pardon, Reverend. Hicks is the name, Jonathan Hicks. I am looking for Woolthorpe Manor, if you could direct me. Chap on the coach told me it was hereabouts.'

'Yes, it is,' affirmed Mr Hunnable, and he explained the directions more particularly. 'But I should tell you that Mr Somerville – the owner of Woolthorpe Manor – is away from home today. He has gone to Ipswich.'

Hicks started. 'Ipswich, you say? Now isn't that a shame. I have come up from London myself, you know, and passed through Ipswich. Daresay I passed him on the road.'

'What a pity,' Mr Hunnable agreed. He had a great sympathy with disappointed hopes. 'Have you business with Mr Somerville?'

'Indirectly, sir. I understand he has a visitor, a foreign gentleman, staying with him?'

'Mr Déprez, do you mean?'

'That's the one, sir.' Hicks glanced at Mary and then at the headstone. 'I am sorry to disturb you, miss, with my conversation.'

Far from being disturbed, Mary found it very interesting that Mr Déprez should have such a strange visitor, but she only smiled and said, 'Not at all.'

'Well, that's kind of you, but I had better be making a move. Good afternoon to you, sir, miss.' He replaced his hat and turned to leave.

Mr Hunnable called after him. 'I daresay someone will be driving out toward Woolthorpe who could give you a lift – you might enquire at the Sun.'

'Oh, no, sir, I wouldn't like to bother anyone.' Hicks opened the gate and picked up the worn leather case he had deposited there.

'Do you mean to *walk* to Woolthorpe?' persisted Mr Hunnable. 'It is above eight miles, and I fear the journey will not be a pleasant one in this weather.'

'Never you fear, sir. I'll take no harm from a bit of wet, and I'd like to stretch my legs after the coach. And then I am a stranger here myself, and walking, I find, is the best way to become acquainted with the neighbourhood.'

Mary watched him until he was out of sight and then turned to Mr Hunnable. 'What a curious person. What is his business with Mr Déprez, do you suppose?'

'Hm? Curious? I cannot imagine. Some sort of tradesman, I daresay.'

'Yes, perhaps, but would a tradesman come all the way from London? I thought he might be a clerk but it seemed to me that . . . his voice was not quite, or perhaps his tone . . .' Mary thought for a moment, frowning. 'I cannot explain what I mean, but listening to him, and paying no attention to his dress, I could not tell whether he was a clerk, or a labourer, or an educated man. His voice seemed a combination of all three.'

'Well, foreigners know all sorts of odd persons. Rather

odd themselves, if you ask me.' A particularly violent gust of wind made Mr Hunnable stagger. 'My goodness, I do hope the poor fellow is not blown down. He did not look altogether strong. Let us go inside, Miss Finch, and out of the gale. My housekeeper has promised us cake — or perhaps you would prefer crumpets?'

Mr Déprez dined that evening with Mrs Somerville — her husband having been delayed in Ipswich — but afterward he retired to his bedchamber for a private discussion with the lately arrived Hicks. It would have been wrong to describe the two men as friends; the differences between them were too great for that. Déprez was young and successful, whereas a good many years had passed since Hicks had landed on the island of St Lucia, defeated and seemingly broken. Yet each had a genuine respect for the other, and in private at least they spoke as equals and without reservation.

As soon as he opened the door and caught sight of Hicks drawn up in an uncomfortable-looking position in an armchair, Déprez knew the other's mood. He closed the door softly behind him and leaned back against it. 'You are going to say that our plans are in ruins,' he smiled.

'I wasn't,' muttered Hicks, 'but they are.'

'Things are not as I could have wished them, to be sure, or even as I would have predicted them only a few days ago,' Déprez acknowledged, 'but I would argue against any suggestion of hopelessness.'

Hicks shrugged. 'You always take an unreasonably optimistic view.'

'And you take an unreasonably pessimistic one,' replied Déprez, 'which means that we complement each other. Are you cold?' he asked, as Hicks stirred up the glowing coals and placed more fuel on the fire. 'I was going to suggest that we open a window.' Déprez unbuttoned his waistcoat and took his seat in a chair that Hicks obligingly pushed back from the fire. 'Mrs Somerville is a most considerate hostess, but the heavy meals that she orders must prove fatal to her guests. If my stay at Woolthorpe Manor is prolonged, apoplexy must inevitably result.'

Hicks smiled, but offered no opinion on his friend's diet or its likely consequences. 'I believe I may have a touch of the old fever, compounded by the English damp. I had forgotten how killing it can be.'

'You should never have walked from Lindham – it was madness!'

'I'll be all right,' shrugged Hicks, 'it always passes in a day or so, and the walk gave me the chance to have a nose around.'

'Indeed, and what is the result of your . . . nosing?'

'Well, the smuggling operation is shut up tighter than a drum, for one thing. There will be no cargoes of any sort for a good while. The affair at White Ladies put paid to that.'

'The smugglers always seemed to me the weak end of the chain, as soon as I learned of them. It cannot be helped now, however. You know what happened?'

'Yes, and Tracey's accident. What a bloody shambles.'

Déprez shrugged. 'A strange conjunction of circumstances . . . and individuals. Miss Mary Finch, for instance, the niece of the late owner of White Ladies. She—'

'Yes, I met her,' acknowledged Hicks. 'Only briefly. I can see why she would appeal to you, however.'

'You are a scoundrel,' Déprez laughed, 'but in fact she does appeal to me, for a variety of reasons, not least of which because I am thinking about the future of our enterprise. But we need not discuss that just at the moment. She is undoubtedly a charming young person, and the fortitude that she demonstrated in escaping from White Ladies must endear her to any right-thinking man. However, tell me about London – you met with an official of the City Police?'

Hicks nodded. 'A fellow called Hudson; he has an office in Bow Street.'

'And was the meeting satisfactory?'

'Not to begin with. I'm sure he thought I was up to some scheme or other.'

'Ah,' laughed Déprez, 'but that only shows him to be a man of intelligence, of discretion. Of course he must find a story such as ours incredible – I would myself! But you gave him the proofs?'

'Yes, and they whetted his interest, but he still wanted to know more, such as who you were, and why he should not raise the matter with anyone else if the danger was so great. Do not worry,' he added, as Déprez frowned and started to protest, 'I settled his mind on both points. I told him about your work last year on behalf of the Admiralty, and I reminded him that the best way to unmask a military spy was *not* to make a gift of our information either to Horse Guards or the Ordnance. Mr Hudson was not altogether happy when I left him, but he was satisfied.'

'We could not expect him to be happy,' Déprez agreed, gravely, 'the matter is too serious for that. And when you say that he was "satisfied", you mean that he will help us?'

'Yes, according to our instructions. I am to keep him informed of our progress.'

'Excellent. I expect the forces of the law to prove important, eventually, but we mustn't have Bow Street officers, however well-intentioned, blundering in prematurely. A case like this requires judicious handling.'

'Mm. I think I may have ruffled his feathers a bit when

161

I suggested as much – he's rather a prickly character, is Mr Hudson – but we have the promise of his support if and when we need it, and he promised that no one in the military would be alerted until we were more certain about who are the rotten apples.'

Déprez nodded. 'Good. And well done, Mr Hudson, for all your prickles.'

'Well, I am glad that *you* are satisfied, but Hudson is a detail,' Hicks growled. 'It is all well and good to speak of our progress, but what progress can we hope for now? And what the devil are we going to do?'

'Do? We wait upon events. I have some ideas, and I think it likely that we shall have to return to London, but let us see what happens. Patience is a virtue, they say. Is Rede still in Ipswich? Good, then tell him to come here – somewhere close by in case we need him, but out of sight. And you mustn't be downhearted. This is not the first difficulty we have encountered, after all.'

'No, but . . .' Hicks sighed. 'You would not consider narrowing our field of endeavour at all? Perhaps concentrating solely on *our* man?'

'And ignoring the wider military implications? No, not unless it proves absolutely necessary. I always believe in striking as many foes as possible with each blow. It is more efficient.'

And more glorious, and more likely to go wrong, thought Hicks. He contented himself with a shrug, but Déprez knew him well enough to smile at the unspoken rebuke. 'What is it that Virgil says?' he murmured, 'that "Fortune favours the brave"?'

'Yes,' complained Hicks, '*and* Terence before him. Virgil copied shamelessly, you know. And what do you say to the Book of Proverbs – that "pride goeth before destruction, and an haughty spirit before a fall"?'

162

'I say that I prefer Virgil, for all his copying,' laughed Déprez.

A note arrived at Lindham Hall that evening, as the inhabitants were retiring to the second parlour to drink tea after supper. Mr Horatio Todd, solicitor, presented his compliments to Miss Finch, and hoped to have the honour of an interview with her on a matter of great importance. Would it be convenient for Miss Finch to make the journey to Woodbridge tomorrow morning? Business kept Mr Todd in his office tomorrow, or else he would naturally come to Lindham and wait upon Miss Finch, and it was to be assumed that Miss Finch would not wish to delay a meeting. Mr Todd therefore proposed a time of eleven o'clock.

'It would certainly *not* be convenient,' pronounced Mrs Tipton, lowering her teacup. 'We have a far more pressing appointment with the dressmaker at that hour. Mr Todd will have to wait until we have completed our business, and he may keep his assumptions to himself.'

Mary and Holland exchanged covert glances, and Mary was obliged to bite her lip before answering. 'Yes, ma'am. I believe that Mr Todd's servant is waiting downstairs for my reply. What answer shall I give?'

Mrs Tipton uttered a distinct *humph* and toyed with one of her canes, her thin, pale fingers opening and closing nervously upon the polished wood. 'Decency and propriety demand that you have some suitable clothes before appearing in public – a mourning gown, at the very least. Not that Mr Todd is entitled to an explanation or any other mark of distinction, in my opinion. A flighty man – no bottom. Tell him . . .' she concluded, 'that your affairs require your presence in Woodbridge tomorrow, and that you will condescend to visit Mr Todd at two o'clock in the afternoon. "Mr Todd proposes" indeed!'

Mary sat down at the small, inlaid writing table in the corner of the room and hurriedly composed a more temperate reply. She was looking forward to meeting the solicitor, and even more, she privately acknowledged, to the appointment with the dressmaker. She had been pleasantly surprised when Mrs Tipton had mentioned it, although *mentioned* was perhaps not the right word – when Mrs Tipton had *decreed* that they would do Miss Cheadle the favour of bestowing their custom upon her. But however it had come about, the prospect of a new gown – silk, perhaps, and made to her measure – provoked a smile, and Mary supposed there might also be gloves, lace collars, even a pelisse.

This contemplation on luxurious adornments reminded Mary of her father's watch. Perhaps it could be repaired, at last, and set running again! That would doubtless prove an expensive proposition, for Mary would not trust the work to any but a very skilful watchmaker, but the possibility no longer seemed daunting. Everyone was assuming that she would inherit a considerable fortune from her uncle – even Mr Hunnable had spoken of it – and surely this letter from Mr Todd confirmed that assumption. *A fortune.* She smiled to herself. How fickle she was, ready to spend vast sums of money before she had so much as a penny to her name and only a few days ago weighed down by the fear of destitution! Still, the solicitor was unlikely to write with such urgency if he merely wished to report bad news.

That view of the matter comforted her as she sealed her reply and delivered it to the clerk, who was waiting in the kitchen. She was still smiling when she returned to the parlour to hear that Captain Holland also had plans for the morning; he would be taking his leave. The coach for Norwich departed Woodbridge at eight o'clock.

Mary's smile faded. She sank into a chair opposite Holland, but without looking at him.

'I believe it is an excellent service,' Mrs Tipton affirmed, in the voice of one who presumed that her good opinion would naturally affect the recipient's mode of travel.

'Yes,' agreed Mary, weakly, 'you . . . you mustn't waste any more of your leave of absence.'

'Ah, so you are on a . . . holiday of sorts,' cried Mrs Tipton. 'I understood your journey to have some official purpose.' She gazed shrewdly at Holland, as if information had purposely been withheld from her but she had discovered it nevertheless.

'No, ma'am,' Holland admitted. He disliked talking about his personal circumstances, particularly with someone like Mrs Tipton, and he attempted to curtail the discussion with a casual reply. He had relations in Norfolk and had been on his way to see them when he met Miss Finch.

It was a vain effort, and further questions produced the interesting fact that Holland's cousin was Sir William Armitage, now retired, but formerly of the Treasury and knighted for his services. The Norfolk address caused Mrs Tipton some irritation, as she had to cast her own net of acquaintances fairly broadly to determine whether she knew Sir William, and this task was made more difficult when Holland could not remember Lady Armitage's maiden name. Nevertheless, the family sounded very respectable, particularly when it was established that the Reverend Henry Armitage, whom Mrs Tipton had met through her late husband's sister, was also a relation. She gazed at Holland rather more benevolently than had been her habit thus far in their acquaintance.

Mary soon stopped paying attention to Mrs Tipton's interrogation. Going. Of course, she had known, with the rational, background part of her mind, that Captain Holland *would go*, but that was not the same thing as *going*. What with everything else there had been no time to think this through – to decide how she felt about it. And now, well, what did it matter what she felt, he was going. She would probably never see him again.

The names Susannah and Charlotte were mentioned, Sir William Armitage's daughters, and suddenly Mary remembered, 'My Dearest Susannah'. One of the scattered papers she had picked up in the hallway of White Ladies the other day had been a letter. She had realised that it was a letter and had tried not to notice anything further, but she had seen the salutation: 'My Dearest Susannah', and at the bottom, 'Yours ever, Bobs'. And Captain Holland had said they were nothing but calculations . . . what *sort* of calculations?

Mary pictured Susannah and Charlotte, extremely beautiful and accomplished, living in Norfolk and calling him Bobs. Yours ever, Bobs. He probably visited them whenever he had the chance. Whenever silly girls were not delaying him with mysteries and adventures that did not interest him in the slightest. She forgot about his threadbare coat and rough ways, and instead imagined him in a vast country property with servants, and carriages, and every luxury. Then she heard herself eagerly telling him about the murder of the archbishop of Canterbury and closed her eyes. No doubt *her* inheritance would be a mere trifle compared with the vast wealth of *Sir* William Armitage . . .

Suddenly she became aware that the conversation between Holland and Mrs Tipton had broken off, and both were gazing at her. 'Hm?' she asked. 'I beg your pardon?'

'You have been so quiet, I thought you might have fallen asleep,' observed Mrs Tipton. 'Captain Holland has informed me that Miss Armitage and Miss Charlotte Armitage were educated at home, and I asked whether you, as a schoolmistress, had an opinion on that practice.'

'Oh, no, I . . . have never thought about it,' said Mary, thinking that the appellation 'schoolmistress' had never sounded drearier. 'Dearest Susannah' had never been a schoolmistress – would not stoop to it. *Her* father was Sir William Armitage, lately of the Treasury, and she probably had a different gown for each day of the week.

Unconsciously she fingered the fabric of her own gown; it felt coarse and ugly. The conversation between Holland and Mrs Tipton resumed, but Mary made no effort to join it. How could an evening that had begun so well end so gloomily? She began even to doubt whether the interview with Mr Todd would prove satisfactory, for everyone knew that legal matters could be protracted *and* expensive, and if she turned out *not* to be an heiress, how was it all to be paid for?

Eventually Mrs Tipton retired for the night, but her departure left an uncomfortable void between the two who remained. Mary had been humbled by the imagined delights of Norfolk, while Holland's pointed interview on the subject had left him more withdrawn than usual. In the silence that followed, Mary began petting one of the dogs as a refuge from conversation. Holland had no such outlet, and after a few minutes he simply gave vent to the feeling that was uppermost in his mind. 'My God, that woman can talk.'

Mary sat back in her chair, but was obliged by an insistent canine head, thrust under her hand, to resume her ministrations. 'Yes, she is very . . . positive.'

Holland considered offering a different adjective, but

instead asked, 'Are you sure you aren't bothered? Staying on here with that old busybody?'

Her answer was the obligatory one – she was perfectly happy, but *he* must be anxious to resume his journey. He disputed the second point, but said that he really ought to go, if only to please Mrs Tipton, who was longing to see the back of him.

'Oh, no, I am sure you are wrong. She thinks very highly of you.'

'Ha,' he scoffed, 'you mean that now she thinks perhaps I wasn't born under a hedge after all?'

This forthright query broke through Mary's wall of politeness. Moreover, she was conscious that, before tonight, her own assumptions about his origins had been none too complimentary. 'I think it is just Mrs Tipton's way to say, or ask . . . whatever comes into her head,' she explained. 'I hope you were not offended.'

He shook his head, a gesture that was only partly a lie. 'No, I don't mind. What I really meant was, between her and Mr Somerville and Mr Hunnable, and now the lawyer, you're pretty well settled.'

'Yes.'

'So, I ought to go.'

'Yes.'

'They're expecting me . . . in Norfolk.'

'Yes.' Mary thought that their conversation would very soon disappear into nothingness, but she could not think of anything else to say. All she knew was that she did not want him to leave, and she could not possibly say *that*, not when he was clearly longing to go. If only she were witty – or at least one of those people who could easily think of things to say that were not actually foolish . . . She continued to stroke the dog and hope for inspiration.

Inspiration did not come, and the silence stretched on and on. 'I must go,' Holland repeated, at last, 'but . . . if anything *did* happen, I mean, if you thought . . .' He paused, glancing at her. She was not looking at him, but her face was flushed, and he knew that she was listening keenly. Abruptly he made a decision. 'I'll be at my cousin's place for about a fortnight – it's called Storey's Court, near Aylsham – and then back to Woolwich.'

Mary started at the implication that they might correspond – it was at once flattering, exciting, and highly improper. Did she dare? She fleetingly imagined writing the words, 'My dearest Bobs' and felt her face growing hot. But perhaps she had misunderstood. 'Do you mean . . . *write* to you? A letter?'

He grinned at her. 'Or a proclamation, I suppose – if the French land.'

'Oh, no,' she protested, laughing, 'I daresay Mr Hunnable has that well in hand. He has probably made arrangements with the printer.'

'That's right,' agreed Holland. '"MEN OF LINDHAM! TO ARMS!"'

'"THE HOST OF MIDIAN IS UPON YOU",' added Mary.

All at once conversation between them became easy again, and they talked about Woolwich, and India, and Mrs Bunbury's, and nothing in particular. Captain Holland was very droll, and it occurred to Mary that her own conversation was also particularly worth hearing. Why had she worried about having nothing to say? She felt as if she could carry on all night. Only after Peggy had come in for the third time, asking in a meaningful way whether they wanted anything, did Mary feel compelled to take her leave, although she was not the least bit sleepy. She wished Holland good night and a good journey, adding, 'And . . . thank you again, for all you have done for me. I am ever so grateful to you.'

Holland remained standing until she had left the room. Sitting down again, he said to the remaining dog, 'What do you think of all that, eh? Am I being clever, or a damned fool?'

10

Mary awoke very early the next morning and crept into the window seat in the corner of her bedchamber. Wrapped in the extra blanket, she had a fairly comfortable view of the courtyard below, and even in the faint dawn light she could observe anyone crossing between the house and the stables. No particular sound had alerted her, but rather a kind of sixth sense that something was going to happen, and now she waited attentively. Nor had her intuition played her false, for presently the door to the stables opened and a greatcoated figure emerged leading a horse. A second figure appeared from the direction of the house carrying a leather bag. He strapped this to the horse's saddle and took the reins while the first man put on his gloves and the horse swished its tail. It was a damp, frosty morning, and the breaths of all three of them floated in white clouds, as if they were smoking. Then the first man, taller than the other, took the reins and swung into the saddle; the shorter man stepped back a pace and thrust his hands into his pockets.

If he is thinking about me, thought Mary, *he will look up at this window – or at one of the windows, if he is not sure which is mine. But if he does not look up, then he is indifferent, and I shall be likewise. I shall resolve . . . not even think about him ever again.* An exchange of some sort occurred between Captain Holland and Mr Cuff; the latter seemed to be giving directions. *Well, that is all right,* she conceded, *very sensible, in fact; he needs to know where he is going.* Then the horse became impatient and danced sideways, and clearly the captain had to settle him down; he could not be gazing up at windows while his horse was behaving so wildly. Mary leaned forward, hugging her knees; her nose was growing cold, and she snuggled down into the folds of her blanket so that only her eyes were visible. She did not want him to see her, after all, only to *want* to see her. He had finished with Mr Cuff, it seemed, and brought his horse under control, and now . . . and now . . . and now he was riding away. He did not look back. Mary waited a few minutes longer, until it was quite clear that he was gone, and then she climbed back into bed.

A few hours later, when it was properly morning, Mary set off on a journey of her own, to Woodbridge, in the company of Mrs Tipton. It was, moreover, precisely the kind of activity to wake a person up. Mrs Tipton's carriage was not so grand as Mr Somerville's, and it did not seem capable of moving without emitting groans, squeaks and other mysterious noises. Also, the seats had removable cushions, and they proved just how removable whenever the vehicle rolled into a rut or turned a corner. If Mr Cuff achieved any degree of speed, the passengers were in serious danger of sliding onto the floor. Mrs Tipton had worked out a system of braces with her canes to avoid this calamity, and Mary held on to the edge of her seat with one hand and the frayed strap on the inside of the door with the other.

Fully alert, then, Mary was looking forward to the business of the day. It was surprising what a difference sunshine could make to how one felt about things; sunshine and exciting prospects. Their first appointment was with the dressmaker, Miss Cheadle, and this provoked both hope and anxiety. Mary's clothes were all homemade; plain, serviceable garments made up from ugly, hardwearing fabrics that were regularly mended and turned. Items were replaced when they had become unwearable, never because they were merely disliked. She longed to own a beautiful, stylish, *frivolous* gown – perhaps more than one – yet dreaded the means by which it must be obtained. She realised that Miss Cheadle's of Woodbridge could not rival the fashionable shops of Bath or even Cambridge, but she still worried about appearing ignorant in matters sartorial. Would she be expected to know whether sleeves were being worn long or short this year, and which were the most fashionable colours in London? What if she turned out to have poor taste? No sense of style? Was a confirmed frump?

In fact, she need not have worried, for the simple reason that Mrs Tipton had no intention of allowing her more than a nominal role. Mrs Tipton experienced some difficulty actually getting into Miss Cheadle's establishment, for the path outside was muddy and the shop itself was small, but once settled in a comfortable chair, she assumed full control over the process. This proved no bad thing, for while her notion of a young lady's wardrobe was rather old-fashioned, it was also sound, and like her opinions on everything else, those on gowns, chemises, petticoats, stockings, and handkerchiefs were delivered briskly and decisively. Poor Miss Cheadle was nearly worn to distraction by the repeated demands for bolts of fabric, samples of buttons and ribbons, and sketches from the several ladies' magazines depicting everything from necklines to

hemlines. The consequences, however, were worth the effort – a large, even magnificent, order with items to be despatched to Lindham Hall as quickly as Miss Cheadle and her assistants could produce them.

Mrs Tipton despised half measures, but in this case her conduct was also inspired by a desire to set the right tone on Mary's behalf with Woodbridge society. The unfortunate incident at White Ladies was already being talked about, and her career at Mrs Bunbury's was hardly a recommendation. Mary simply could not afford any further eccentricities, whereas a liberal shower of silk, lace, and satin would go a long way toward proving that she was the right sort of young person. 'Of course, a proper economy is highly desirable,' Mrs Tipton explained. 'You must never fall into debt, or let it be known that you cannot manage the household accounts. But economy must seem to come naturally; to *talk* about penny-pinching is so . . . *lowering*.' She waited for Mary's nod of acquiescence and then added, more brightly, 'Your hat will do, for the moment, but we must see about some shoes. Those boots of yours are a disgrace.'

The realisation that she was an object of interested speculation was a disturbing one for Mary, and coloured the short drive to the shoemaker's and thence to Mr Todd's office. Every passer-by appeared to be staring at them, and Mrs Tipton's slow descent from the carriage, assisted by Mr Cuff in a curious knitted hat with earflaps, seemed designed to draw further enquiring looks. It also prevented Mary from making a quick dash into the lawyer's office, as she would otherwise have done. In her anxiety she grasped Mrs Tipton by the other arm and tried to propel her more speedily toward Mr Todd's front door.

Fortunately, an attentive servant answered after only one furious knock. Once inside they were guided to a

comfortable parlour, and provided with tea and a selection of little cakes and sandwiches by Mr Todd's clerk. This gave Mary time to regain her composure and also went some way toward mollifying Mrs Tipton, who was annoyed by her rough handling, so that they were both in reasonably good spirits when their host appeared.

He conducted them to his office, a small, darkly-panelled room that smelled of paper and old leather, and directed Mary to the chair opposite his desk. Now highly conscious of her disgraceful boots, Mary drew up her feet onto the bottom rung of her chair, in an effort to conceal them. Mrs Tipton was obliged to assume the only other seat in the room, an armchair that had the advantage of being larger, more comfortable, and closer to the fire, but the distinct disadvantage of being somewhat out of the way, when it came to any exchanges between lawyer and client. Whether Mr Todd had been influenced primarily by the advantages or the disadvantages when arranging the seating was hard to tell.

He was certainly very deliberate in his manner. Softly spoken and gravely polite, he asked Mary a series of questions, carefully recording her answers in a notebook. He nodded as he completed each entry, slowly inclining his bald head, and then raised his eyes to continue his interrogation. He nodded again when he was shown the matching pocket watches, and after reading the letter that Mary had received from her uncle. Yes, he had seen the watch inscribed to *E.S.F.* before, and he certainly recognised the handwriting in the letter as Mr Finch's. Gradually the information began to flow in both directions. Mr Todd had not known of Mary's existence. He had been aware that Mr Finch had a brother, but the only address had been an Oxford one, sadly out of date. It was fortunate that Mr Finch had remembered Mr Richard Finch's residence in

Bath. There were indications of more remote relations but none near to hand: a family called Bagot in Hampshire, and a maternal cousin in Surrey.

Mr Todd paused then, and considered how best to proceed. 'Of course, some further enquiries will be necessary – necessary to persuade me in my fiduciary capacity as the late Mr Finch's legal representative – but I am hopeful that these can be completed with a minimum of time and inconvenience.' He cleared his throat. 'It would not be proper, in the light of those further enquiries, for me to disclose the *particulars* of Mr Finch's testamentary arrangements.'

'Indeed not,' snapped Mrs Tipton from deep in her armchair, her desire to hear said particulars adding to her vehemence. 'Quite *im*proper.'

'However, I think I may go so far as to explain the *nature* of those arrangements, in general terms, to Miss Finch.' He nodded again. 'Mr Finch – or I might venture to say, your uncle Mr Finch, was a close gentleman, little given to idle chatter and with few intimate friends or relations. He was also a very well-to-do gentleman, in respect of lands, goods, and chattels. This combination, I believe, inspired his choice of testamentary arrangements. A choice that might, at first blush, seem somewhat . . . eccentric, but was actually very sensible. Happily, I should add, this should not *materially* affect your position.'

'Did he leave a will?' asked Mary.

'Yes and no. He completed a testament of goods and chattels. This included several general and specific legacies, and named Mr Richard Finch as residuary legatee.'

Mary sat up sharply. 'My father – he named my father in his will!' she cried, and for a moment Mr Todd imagined that she was going to lean across his desk in an excess of emotion. That danger passed almost immediately, as she rocked back in her chair, but now she was smiling strangely at him. 'Oh, sir,' she breathed, 'this news has made me very happy.'

'Yes, indeed,' Mr Todd agreed, 'I should think so, for Richard Finch having *predeceased* the testator—'

'No, no, you do not understand. I am not thinking of myself, but of my father – and my uncle. There was an estrangement between them, you see, of many years, and they were never reconciled. And yet, in the end, they *were* reconciled, at least in my uncle's mind, for he wished my father to succeed him.' Mary's expression lightened again, and now she was fairly beaming. 'And that must be the reason why he wrote to me. I wondered, you know, for his letter was not quite clear. He must have wished to be reconciled *to me*. Of course, you will say that this makes my uncle's death the sadder, for we were not able to meet, and I see that. But at the same time, knowing for certain that he wished to make things right, it really does make *all* the difference.'

Mr Todd's countenance remained solemn, and Mary turned to Mrs Tipton. '*You* understand me, ma'am, I am sure?'

'Perfectly,' replied Mrs Tipton, glancing loftily at the solicitor. 'And it is an entirely fitting, ladylike sentiment.'

'Ahem, yes,' acknowledged Mr Todd. 'Family harmony is always to be wished.' He gathered the papers in front of him, tidied them unnecessarily, and then returned them to their previous arrangement, thus demonstrating his sympathy for Miss Finch's sentiments. Having done so, he continued in precisely the same tone in which he had been interrupted. 'Mr Richard Finch having predeceased the testator, the residuum lapses in favour either of the executor,' and here he bowed, 'or the next of kin where the testament indicates that no such claim on the part of the executor was intended by the testator.'

'I imagine that Mr Finch would never have intended such a claim,' Mrs Tipton remarked. 'He would never have been so foolish.'

'Indeed, ma'am, the will is explicit on that point; the executor has no claim. With respect to his landed property, which includes the estate of White Ladies and several other valuable farms and tenements, Mr Finch left no will. All of these, therefore, descend by law to his heir-at-law.'

'And can you identify the heir and the next of kin?'

'Yes, ma'am, I believe I can. Although different considerations apply to establish heirship and kinship, in this case they would produce the same result. Assuming that she can establish her identity as the only child, lawfully born to Mr Finch's only brother, Miss Finch is both heir and next of kin.'

'Ah.' Mrs Tipton nodded. 'Very satisfactory.'

Mr Todd agreed with her, particularly as the residuum of Mr Finch's personal estate and the whole of his landed property were *very considerable*. He paused as he uttered these words, and Mary was conscious of a strange giddiness, like nothing she had ever experienced before. She was rich – or rather, she *would* be rich! She would own White Ladies along with valuable farms and tenements! The very considerable residuum would be hers! She could have servants, and a carriage, and . . . anything she wanted! The news was not strange, nor even unexpected – but until this moment she had never really, wholly believed it. And now it was true – or rather, *would* be true. She could feel herself trembling and gazed fixedly into her lap, hardly daring to look or speak. Nothing must upset this perfect moment.

'What about debts?' Mrs Tipton demanded, as a lump of coal sizzled and collapsed in the grate.

'Negligible, ma'am. Now, Miss Finch, as you will have deduced, I am Mr Finch's executor, and in that capacity I must execute the terms of his will. While I am happy to assist you in whatever way I can, I strongly recommend that you take legal advice from another quarter, as your position is, in one respect, wholly unrelated to the will, and in the other, based upon an inadequacy in the will. Do you understand my point?'

She nodded. 'Yes, sir – your advising me might compromise your position with respect to my uncle.'

'Precisely. Mrs Tipton, I know, places her legal and business affairs in the hands of Mr Brownlowe of Bury St Edmunds—'

'Indeed I do.'

'—and I can also recommend him as an extremely knowledgeable, reliable individual. Mr Brownlowe, or someone of his competence, could both undertake to produce the requisite evidence of your status as next of kin, and also make application on your behalf for letters of administration.'

Mary tried to maintain a serious expression, but a smile kept threatening to emerge. She frowned to counteract any suggestion of levity and said that she would consult Mr Brownlowe straightaway.

'A wise decision. When I have received confirmation from Mr Brownlowe, we shall . . . put our heads together. These matters can never be as quickly resolved as one would like, but I think I can say that in this case I foresee no significant difficulties.'

'Thank you,' said Mary, gravely, and she shook her head. 'I am . . . I can hardly believe it.'

At last Mr Todd's demeanour underwent a faint softening.

'Well, well, I daresay it will become more familiar, with time. Now I wanted to say—' A discreet tapping from the passage cut him short. 'Ah,' he nodded, 'that will be Mr Sparrow, of Collier's bank. I asked him to step round.'

In contrast to Mr Todd's solemnity, Mr Sparrow looked like the sort of man for whom a humorous expression was rarely far away. He was short and heavyset, with a cheerful, jolly countenance. His wig was also slightly askew, and this contributed to the effect. While the clerk was producing another chair, Mr Todd endeavoured to alert his associate to the state of his wig by a series of looks and gestures, but these were sufficiently obscure to be misunderstood by the banker and almost caused Mary to laugh out loud. Mrs Tipton considered it further proof of that flightiness with which she had long associated Mr Todd. The sooner that Mary's affairs were safely in the hands of Mr Brownlowe of Bury, the better.

After the introductions had been completed Mr Sparrow sat down beside Mary and produced a sheaf of papers from a large leather wallet. These he handed to her with a flourish, smiling and twinkling at her from behind his gold-rimmed spectacles.

'Those should just about explain the situation, Miss Finch. As you will see, your uncle did not keep a very large balance with us; only enough for convenience. I would be happy to make enquiries for you with Coutts – his London bank – if that would be helpful. Or perhaps Mr Todd will act on your behalf?' He glanced at the gentleman in question and continued. 'Ah, yes. I must not get ahead of myself. Of course, until the forces of law are satisfied that you *are* Miss Mary Finch, and fully entitled to the late Mr Edward Finch's estate, neither Collier's nor any other reputable bank can release funds from any of his accounts.'

Mary froze as a sudden fear assailed her. Rich? How could she have thought she was rich? She hadn't a penny, and what had Mr Todd said about delays? Everyone knew that legal matters could take a great deal of time, and often they did not turn out as one expected. The enormous sum spent so frivolously at Miss Cheadle's appeared before her eyes. How would she manage to pay it? And then there were Mr Todd's fees . . . and very likely the tea and sandwiches. She had not merely plunged herself into debt, she was swimming in it! She would be fished out and put into prison, and what would people say?

'In the meantime, however, your credit with Collier's ought to be sufficient for any necessary expenses.'

'*My credit?*'

'Well, perhaps I ought to say Mr Somerville's and Mrs Tipton's credit.'

No drowning man ever felt greater relief. 'Oh, *Mrs Tipton*—' Mary began, but her thanks were cut short by that lady's queenly gesture, at once discouraging further speech and directing Mary's attention toward the banker. Mr Sparrow was a silly man, but he generally got things right eventually.

'As soon as your own affairs are put in order,' he continued, 'Collier's will be honoured to make an advance of credit up to a limit of . . . yes, just there, at the foot of the page.'

'Yes— Oh my,' said Mary, looking up at him in surprise. From heiress to pauper and back again. Everything was happening so quickly; it was difficult to take it all in.

His eyes twinkled. 'Now, as far as investments are concerned, the third paper – that is the one – sets down the bank's views on what may be expected in the longer term, should you care to commission us to act on your behalf. East India stock, in particular, is bound to rise as soon as there is some good news from the Continent, but the price of corn must remain high, with the appalling weather we have had, and agricultural rents . . .' He shrugged his shoulders.

'Thank you.' Mary nodded, still somewhat dazed, but trying to take account of the relevant papers. Rents and stocks . . . it was clear she would have to study them very carefully . . . the first responsibility of her newfound wealth. 'This is all . . . very helpful.'

'Excellent,' he beamed, closing up his wallet and rising to his feet. 'Then I think I shall take my leave. Time is money for us bankers, you know. I daresay it is for lawyers as well, but it seems to work for them in the opposite direction! Good afternoon, all. Read through those papers when you have time, Miss Finch, and if we may be of any assistance we should be delighted to see you at Collier's.' He shook hands with Mary a second time. 'A Sparrow could not very well turn away a Finch, now could he?' he chuckled.

While Mary was drinking her tea that evening, contemplating the purchase of an exquisite porcelain service, Captain Holland arrived at Storey's Court, a very pleasant country residence some sixty miles distant. Pleasant, if somewhat old-fashioned looking, with its gabled front and casement windows. Both these qualities, and the fact that he had grown up in it, endeared the house to its present owner, Sir William Armitage. As a young man he had looked upon Storey's Court as a refuge from his London life, and now, in retirement, he delighted in the familiar, comfortable rooms, the views of the lake and gardens, and the gardens themselves. He could afford a much grander house, and indeed Lady Armitage knew of several more desirable properties that would have suited them admirably, but Sir William would not be persuaded.

There was certainly a resolute streak in Sir William's character. Sometimes this equated to his sense of right and wrong, sometimes merely to his appreciation of what could or could not be achieved. His tenacity had proved valuable during his long career in government, although the results had not always been happy ones or ones with which he was thoroughly comfortable. Particularly in his later years he felt this. And yet, he often reflected, were not softness and sentimentality equally fatal? What had these qualities gained for Sophia, when all was said and done, but a broken heart and an early grave?

Sophia Armitage was Sir William's cousin, and she had married – neither wisely nor well – a man named David Holland. Both had died young, and Sir William had sent their son to the military academy at Woolwich because it had seemed a reasonable provision for an energetic boy with no other prospects. Sir William sometimes brooded on the wisdom of this decision. A career in the artillery – what sort of life was that? True, the gunners were the Army's professionals – the only officers actually trained for their jobs and barred from purchasing ranks in excess of their competence – but they also had far fewer opportunities for distinguishing themselves than the 'amateurs' in the infantry and cavalry. Who ever heard of a gunner taking charge of a battle or storming an enemy position? No, they might succeed in getting themselves killed, but they rarely performed the exploits that appealed to the public or, more importantly, the government.

And what was the result? Very few knighthoods, and even fewer peerages. How many gentlemen of the artillery – and not all of them *were* gentlemen – were even Members of Parliament? One needn't be a politician to appreciate that public honours enhanced a career, and a public situation rendered its holder so much more . . . eligible, in a variety of ways. One did what one could, of course, used one's influence. There was Robert's appointment on the regimental staff. Quite a good job for someone who knew a lot about gunnery and fortifications, and who did not mind the prospect of being blown to Kingdom Come if things went wrong. A fellow needed strong nerves for that sort of thing. Sir William meditated on nerve, its strength and longevity. It seemed to be something that declined as one grew older, for he had enjoyed a healthy dose of it himself in his younger days, whereas now . . .

Sir William took a sip of port and decided he oughtn't to sit alone like this after dinner. When there were guests it was a different matter, but when one was alone one tended to brood; it was bad for the digestion. That was what he was doing now, *brooding*, and he mustn't. Robert seemed happy enough, and the artillery was at least inexpensive. Only think what a commission in one of the fashionable regiments would have cost – and that would not have been the end of it, not by a long chalk! Dash, and swagger, and polish all cost a mint of money. Thankfully, Robert was not that sort of fellow . . . he was happy enough; content, at least. No, he never complained – not that he had any reason to! There were plenty of young fellows worse off than he. And yet, he *was* an Armitage on one side, though now, as things had turned out, one would scarcely credit it.

Sir William's thoughts were hovering uncomfortably around this point when Jeffries, the butler, appeared at his elbow. 'Eh?' murmured Sir William, blinking in the candlelight. 'Miss Charlotte feeling abandoned, is she? I shall be along directly.'

'I beg your pardon, sir,' said Jeffries, bowing gravely.

'Master Robert, that is to say, Captain Holland has arrived.'

'Has he, indeed?' cried Sir William, his gloomy expression vanishing. 'Send him in immediately. And bring in some more candles. I feel like I'm sitting in a dashed tomb!'

'Certainly, sir.' A deft hand beneath Sir William's elbow, only tolerated because Jeffries was a servant of such long standing, assisted him to his feet.

'There you are, Bobs,' Sir William exclaimed, as Holland strode into the room, looking more wholly at ease than he had done for the last several days. 'How are you? It is good to have you home again.'

'Thank you, sir. I'm always pleased to be here.'

Storey's Court was indeed Holland's home, in as much as he had one, although there was little to suggest any family tie between him and Sir William, apart from the warmth of their greeting. The Armitages tended to be small and fair-haired, whereas the Hollands, if Robert was any indication, were dark and built on a larger scale. Sir William had enjoyed a certain wiry strength as a young man, but now he might have been described as delicate, and he looked even more fragile in the company of his younger cousin.

Holland, however, said he thought Sir William seemed in good health. 'And I trust the rest of the family are well?'

'Oh, we are as usual. Anne and the girls blooming, and a bit of the *Anno Domini* with me. But you, my boy,' added Sir William after they had sat down, 'you look rather the worse for wear, I think.'

Holland said it was nothing, a bit of an adventure, and Sir William did not press for an explanation. He was interested, however, to hear of the Lindham detour. 'Whatever

185

were you doing there – or is my question indiscreet?' He sent Jeffries to investigate the leftovers, in case it was.

'No, sir,' replied Holland. 'I was just held up longer in Suffolk than I'd expected. Jeffries said something about Lady Armitage being away from home. Is she gone to Town?'

Sir William looked slightly uncomfortable as he explained that his wife and eldest daughter were visiting their neighbours, the Moltons. 'But you will remember old Tom Molton. Only a short visit, I expect— Ah, here we are,' he added with something of relief, as the butler swept into the room, bearing a large tray.

'It's just me, you know, Jeffries,' said Holland, as a selection of dishes was set down before him. 'There's enough here to feed a company.'

'Yes, sir,' replied Jeffries, lifting each cover with a flourish. 'And sir,' he continued to Sir William, 'Miss Charlotte respectfully wishes to—'

'It is an absolute *scandal*,' cried that young lady, pushing impetuously past Jeffries and throwing her arms around Holland before he could rise to greet her. 'Papa,' she scolded, 'how *could* you keep Bobs here, all to yourself, when you knew I was absolutely *dying* to see him.'

'Nonsense,' said Sir William, fondly, 'and do not strangle him in that hoydenish manner. It is bad for the chair, let alone your cousin's neck.'

'I am sorry, sir,' explained Jeffries. 'Miss Charlotte waylaid me.'

'Yes, yes, and wheedled the news out of you. My word, it is a good thing none of us depends on secrecy around here.'

'I do not know why Bobs coming home should be kept a secret from me,' Charlotte protested.

'It is not a secret, it is the principle,' said Sir William, none too clearly. 'Now do sit down and stop hanging over the chair in that absurd way. Do you want Robert to think you an Amazon, a hussy, ignorant of all proper behaviour?'

Charlotte sat down, looking rebellious. She was a pretty, rather than a beautiful, girl, who would probably become a pretty, rather than a beautiful, woman. Her sandy curls were a little too dark to be fashionable, and she had a liberal dusting of freckles across the bridge of her nose, against which her mother was endeavouring to do battle with lemon juice. She was also jolly, wilful, and terribly loyal to those she loved. Her expression resumed its usual sweetness when Holland gave her hand a comforting squeeze, and she kept hold of it, although this necessitated that he eat left-handed.

'What a lot of dinner you have, Bobs,' she observed. 'Are you going to eat it all?'

'Of course,' he replied. 'It's bad manners not to eat what you're given.'

'I think you will become very fat if you do. Like Mr Fortescue – the curate. He gasps when he eats,' she added.

'Am I in danger of gasping, you shrimp?' demanded Holland, grinning at her.

'Well, not yet, perhaps.'

Holland burst out laughing. '*Not yet!*'

'*Really,* Charlotte,' scolded Sir William. 'I wonder at you.'

She scrutinised Holland's lean profile. 'You are not like Mr Grantley Molton. He is younger than you are, and he has jowls already.'

'I suppose you think I ought to take some exercise, after all this dinner,' laughed Holland. 'Well, how about riding with me tomorrow morning?'

'Oh, *yes,*' cried Charlotte, her eyes shining. 'I have been practising ever so much on Clemmie and— Oh, you have not seen Clemmie! Papa bought him for my birthday, and he is simply lovely.'

Sir William shook his head. 'You see what I mean, Robert, an Amazon. She begged so for the beast, there was no living with her until it was bought. I needn't tell you that we do not suffer from such a clamouring for books, or music, or needlework, or anything that might be desirable in a young lady. I daresay next she will badger me to let her come out with the hunt.'

'Have you been out much yet, this season, sir?'

'Not really; what with this blasted rain, and Tom Molton so set on coursing rabbits until Christmas. Not that I mind the old ways, far from it. His nephew has one of these speed packs, and I daresay we shall all be expected to race about after it. That is the fashion now, to give over all the skill of the hunt to a mad desire for speed. God knows where it will end.'

'Oh, but surely, Papa, there is a great deal of skill in cross-country riding,' Charlotte urged. She performed an elegant rising trot in her chair and then stared over her hands as if contemplating an obstacle. 'And it must be so much more exciting to leap a fence than to stand about, waiting for the dogs to puzzle out the scent and one of the grooms to open the gate.'

'Miss Pert, you know nothing about it,' affirmed Sir William, glowering. 'Anyone who advocates flying leaps is a madman. Not only a risk to life and limb, but a confounded nuisance for the farmer, the hunt pelting across his fields and beating down his fences. But no one wants to take responsibility for things nowadays – for what things cost.'

The complaint was in no way directed at Holland, but he felt it nonetheless. 'I should've said, sir,' he explained, 'that I hope you don't mind if I take out one of the horses?'

'Of course not, my dear fellow,' said his cousin, quickly restored to good humour. 'Do not give it another thought. I daresay they could all do with some exercise.'

Charlotte wanted to know where Gunner Drake was, and she was disappointed to hear that he had been left behind in Woolwich. Drake held the post of officer's servant, and sometimes he accompanied Holland when he was travelling on regimental business. On his previous visit to Storey's Court, Drake had endeared himself to Charlotte by having a row with Jeffries over use of the boot brushes. Not only did he expose the tyranny of Jeffries' regime in colourful military language, but afterwards he performed a much admired impersonation of his defeated rival.

'And how did *you* come to hear of all this?' demanded Sir William. 'I wish you would curb this . . . unseemly interest in the servants and their affairs. You were in Mrs Tompkins' room again, I suppose.'

'No,' Charlotte protested, 'I was not downstairs at all. Jane and Elsie told me about it, and when I saw Drake, I asked him to show me, and he did. And it *was* very funny – he was *exactly* like Jeffries.'

'He's quite good at that sort of thing,' Holland admitted.

'Oh, very well,' frowned Sir William. 'But you mustn't gossip with Jane and Elsie— And for Heaven's sake do not tell your mother about it.'

When Holland had disposed of some, although not all, of the food placed before him, they retired to the drawing room. Here the absence of Lady Armitage was most evident, for the furniture had been allowed to reach a comfortable state of disorder that the lady of the house would not have tolerated. Armchairs were drawn up companionably before the large, marble fireplace, and Charlotte's paintbox was open and its contents strewn across an inlaid side table. Sir William, too, was partly responsible, for his newspaper was draped over the piano stool, and the two indoor dogs, Maisie and Budge, were reclining on a sofa without the slightest indication of guilt.

Jeffries set down the tea things among the detritus of Charlotte's artistic endeavours, and she poured out in a tolerably elegant manner. She waited until Jeffries departed before slipping off her shoes and curling up on the settle, on her cousin's other side. In that position she noticed his cuts and bruises for the first time.

'Have you been in a fight, Bobs?' she asked.

'No.' He smiled at her. They both knew that the less he answered, the more she would ask, and neither was averse to the game.

'Does it hurt?'

'No.'

'It looks as if it hurts.'

'It doesn't.'

'When are you going to go and fight the French?'

'I don't know.'

'Why not?'

'Because they haven't told me.'

'Well . . . why do you not ask?'

'Who?'

'I do not know – some general or other. And it is *whom*. *Whom* should I ask. I know because I got it wrong last week and Mama made me copy it out fifty times, which I do think was *very* hard.'

He gave in, laughingly. 'It was very good for you. And if I asked some general or other, he'd only say he had precious few troops *whom* he could send to fight anybody

190

– that's because we've evacuated Bremen. Do you know where Bremen is, shrimp?'

Charlotte thought hard. 'Ireland?'

'*Ireland?!* You ought to do a hundred lines, for such rotten geography.'

'Well, I hate lessons,' Charlotte pouted, 'and Geography is the worst.'

'It doesn't sound as if you do any of 'em enough to hate 'em,' laughed Holland, 'and you ought to learn Geography. It's much more useful than who and whom. Bremen is a free city, if you'd care to know, but it's next door to Hanover, which our king has charge of, when he's tired of England. But as you're an especially warlike shrimp I can tell you there's likely to be some action in the West Indies before long, but that's a dam— a confound-edly unhealthy place.'

'I am not warlike, and why are the West Indies unhealthy?'

'Because of all the fevers there, and it's fearfully hot. Some men die straightaway, and most can't stick it much beyond a season. So, you see, if you didn't know your Geography, you might go there for a holiday in wool stockings, and do you know what would happen if you did?'

He had assumed a stern expression, and she laughed delightedly. 'No.'

'There would be no more Lottie. You'd get heatstroke, or the sweating sickness, and that would be the end of you; just like that, dead as a doornail.' He snapped his fingers under her nose. 'It helps promotion, though, service in a place like that. If you're lucky, the fellows above you fall off the perch, and up you go, until you're—'

'Some general or other.'

'Exactly.'

191

Sir William found their banter difficult to follow, but the idea of promotion through the avoidance of disease was particularly distasteful and he intervened. 'You do not believe that the treaty with the Russians will have much of an effect on our military dispositions, then?'

'Not much, sir,' replied Holland, sobering. 'They aren't going to give us any troops, though they may furnish some ships. It's possible to serve on our bomb ships, sometimes, firing the mortars. I know a fellow on one.'

'It sounds terribly dangerous,' said Sir William. 'How does he find it?'

'Well, sir, in polite language, he says he's generally cramped, wet, and at odds with the sailors over discipline and authority.'

'You sound well out of it. And what about your own job, eh? That must be keeping you pretty busy?'

'Mm,' Holland nodded. 'And things will get more interesting if the war picks up again.'

'More interesting?'

'More lively.'

Sir William frowned impatiently. 'More *deadly*. War is not a game, you know, for all you young fellows like to joke about such things, and I believe this one will be even less . . . *merry* than usual. The French are not fighting for land, or power – though I daresay it will come to that in time – but a philosophy, and philosophies make men implacable, if history is anything to go by.'

The word 'history' made Holland's heart sink, and he thought, *that's what I get for coming over the schoolmaster with Lottie*. His slow nod was sufficient to convince Sir William, however, who continued, 'Consider our own experience with Republicanism in the last century. Men stopped at nothing to install their particular, hare-brained form of government and annihilate those of the opposite persuasion.

The Army in the hands of reforming firebrands and that tyrant Cromwell . . .'

While Sir William developed his theme, expounding on the Barebones Parliament and the Self-denying Ordinance – the last time Members of Parliament denied themselves anything, by God – the mention of Cromwell allowed Holland to feel himself on surer ground. Cromwell, of course, had been a very clever field officer, as evidenced by his victories at Marston Moor and Naseby. Or, at least, cleverer than his opponents, for the Royalist officers had been pretty thick-witted. *Cleverness and luck,* he reflected, as Sir William indulged in a lengthy aside on the Humble Petition & Advice, *those are the things that count – and knowing the sort of men you're up against.*

Charlotte sighed; she had very little interest in Republicans past or present. 'If only the war were over – then you could stay here with us, forever.'

'Oh, you wouldn't want me hanging about all the time,' Holland laughed, tugging her curls.

She gave him a playful shove. 'You will joke about it, but I am perfectly serious. I cried for days and days the last time you went away.'

'Did you, shrimp? That was nice of you, but I wouldn't make a habit of it.'

11

Captain Holland was used to rising early, but even military discipline could not equal Charlotte's enthusiasm for the promised morning ride. When he failed to present himself at what she deemed a reasonable hour, therefore, she proceeded to his bedchamber. Having detected a conversation between her cousin and Tibbs, the footman deputed to stand in for the absent Gunner Drake, she opened the door and entered without the least hesitancy. Tibbs looked away in prim disapproval, while Holland, who was shaving, addressed her reflection in the mirror.

'Morning, Lottie. I was just asking Tibbs what sort of day it was, but I'm sure you can tell me.'

'Good morning, Bobs. It is a perfectly glorious day for *riding*, if you have not forgotten. Good morning, Tibbs.'

'Good morning, miss.'

'No, I haven't,' said Holland, apparently concentrating upon his lather-covered chin, 'I've ordered the horses for half past, so don't think you can rag me for being late. And you shouldn't burst in on a fellow like that, you know,' he added, rinsing his razor in a bowl of water.

'Why not?'

'I might've cut myself, of course. Cut my throat, the devil of a mess to clean up, and *you* would have to do it. I doubt if Tibbs would lend a hand, would you, Tibbs?'

'I beg your pardon, sir?'

'Well, if you *will* take so long.' Charlotte sat down on the blanket box at the end of the bed and cast a critical eye about the room. It was smaller than her bedroom, and the wallpaper looked tired and faded. The rug would probably not suffer very badly if it *were* bloodstained, but that was not really a very great advantage. 'This is not a very nice room,' she announced.

'It isn't?'

'No, it is horrid. I wonder why Mama did not have it changed last year. Mine and Susannah's rooms were. I wanted navy blue hangings, but I was not allowed.'

'Well,' said Holland, 'I suppose she thought I wasn't here often enough to notice a change. Men don't care so much about such things, you know.' He rinsed his razor again. 'But I *have* noticed that you're looking very pretty.'

Charlotte was dressed in a dark green riding habit and a cocked hat of black beaver. 'It *is* lovely,' she agreed, smiling. She sat up and extended her arms to give him a better view. 'I have not worn it yet, apart from the tryings-on. The jacket is copied from the uniform of the Guards. You have seen them – do you think this is like?'

'Mm, apart from the colour.'

'Yes, but I could not very well have a red frock, you know. It would have been . . . *outré* – that is French for something extraordinary and not very nice. And you would not believe how difficult it was to arrange my hair properly under this hat. Do you think it looks all right?'

'First rate. I take it that this . . . outfit was a birthday present?'

'Yes, although Mama bought Susannah one as well,

which I do not think was really fair, as it was *my* birthday, after all, and Susannah hardly ever rides.' She caught her cousin's frown as he wiped his face with a towel and added, 'I hope you do not think me dog-in-the-mangerish. She *does* look very beautiful in it.'

He acknowledged that fair was fair, on one's birthday, and she pressed her advantage by mentioning that she was also wearing his present, a small silver brooch. She displaced him at the mirror in order to study it.

'Mm,' said Holland, as he tied his neck cloth. 'Yes, Tibbs, I know I've made a dog's breakfast of this damned thing – leave it. You don't think it's too small, that . . . pin?' He had dismissed it as paltry when he saw it in the shop, but he could not afford anything larger. The jeweller had assured him that it was in the Grecian style, and that size did not signify when the item was in the Grecian style, but Holland had his doubts.

'It is perfectly lovely,' Charlotte assured him, 'and I like it best of all my presents. Well, best after Clemmie. Are you ready at last? Older people take *such* a long time to do things.'

'Almost. Let me find my cane and then I'm with you.'

Holland shrugged into the less formal of his two civilian coats, while Tibbs hovered behind, uncertain whether to brush or straighten. Instead he offered a slightly battered hat, discovered among some other items rumoured to belong to Captain Holland because no one could remember Sir William wearing them.

Holland accepted the hat, and as he tucked it under his arm noticed a darn in his sleeve for the first time. God, he always felt like a damned scarecrow when he came to Storey's Court. 'Sure you don't mind coming out with me?' he asked Charlotte as they descended the stairs. 'I'm not quite up to your new rig.'

When he looked so hard and implacable he was difficult to tease, so she slipped her arm companionably through his. 'Oh, *Bobs*,' she chided, 'you know that does not matter. Now come and see Clemmie.'

Charlotte's gesture, and the fact that he did not generally dwell on things, soon lightened Holland's mood, and by the time they reached the stables he was thinking that, really, one could not find much wrong with Storey's Court. He did not profess to know much about hangings or furniture, but he understood light, and proportion, and sound construction. These were the necessary foundations for a comfortable property, and Storey's Court had them in abundance. When the good taste of someone like Lady Armitage was added, the house became elegant as well. Outside, the grounds and outbuildings were carefully, but unobtrusively, maintained. 'Maintained' was the right word, for nothing looked new and nothing needed repair. Exigencies of wind and weather, it seemed, made no difference to the quiet, good order, and everywhere one felt the mood of permanence and confidence. *And that's not surprising*, mused Holland, as Charlotte issued her orders to the head groom, *as the Armitages are a confident family. It would never occur to one of them to doubt his place in the world, or envy anyone else's.*

'Well, what do you think?' demanded Charlotte, as a sturdy, chestnut gelding was led out of his stall. 'Have you ever seen such a darling?'

'Not bad,' said Holland, thoughtfully, 'but let's see how he goes.' He turned to the groom and asked whether there was anything he ought to know.

'Ground's a bit heavy in the north meadow, sir, if you go that way, but otherwise, no. Miss has been out on Clemmie quite a bit lately – I think they know each other's ways.'

197

Clemmie tossed his head, as if stung that anyone should question his *bona fides*, but showed no further evidence of temper. Indeed, he proved a thoroughly good-natured animal, sufficiently lively to satisfy Charlotte's desire for excitement, but unwilling to be provoked by her tendency to jag her reins. And when a pair of rabbits scuttled unexpectedly across his path, he held his ground like a gentleman. From the greater eminence of one of Sir William's hunters, Holland expressed his approval of the new addition.

'I *do* enjoy riding,' Charlotte admitted, although her flushed, pleased expression rendered her words unnecessary. 'And I know that you love it too. Papa said that you were very cross not to have been allowed to transfer to the horse artillery, and I am sure it was unjust of them, but I did not understand what he meant. Surely you always use horses? How else could you move the guns about?'

'What? Oh, yes.' Holland had actually been thinking about the last time he had been riding with a girl, and how very different the circumstances had been. He could almost feel her clutching his arm as they galloped headlong into rainy darkness, or leaning against him, when she forgot her shyness. Her hair had been soft against his throat . . . With a sigh he explained the difference between transporting artillery generally, siting the heavy weaponry at the start of a battle, and moving the new, lighter guns perhaps several times over the course of the engagement. The third of these immediately gained Charlotte's approval. She had only the haziest notion of what a battle actually entailed, but she considered that advancing at great speed, and possibly firing as one did so, must be extremely desirable.

'You are so lucky, to be able to do such exciting things.

I mean, you *would* be, if they were not so unfair about your transfer.' She sighed then and toyed with her reins. 'It can be so very dull around here, you know.' Another sigh, and a glance in his direction. 'That is why I long to try jumping.'

'Jumping?' demanded Holland, vaguely, as if he had never heard of it.

She nodded excitedly. '*Yes*. Dear Bobs, will you teach me? I am certain Clemmie would be ever so good at it.'

'You are, are you? And what about your father? You heard him last night. He's dead set against it.'

'Yes, but I only meant *jumps*, not *leaps*,' Charlotte explained, 'and quite small ones. I am sure it is safer to ride if one is able to do small jumps.' When pressed she admitted that Lady Armitage was unlikely to be in favour of either jumps or leaps, but she rejected this as insignificant. The readiness with which she justified that view suggested that she had worked it all out beforehand. 'I have not asked her, so she has never actually forbidden me. And if we do it now, while she is away, no one can blame us for not asking permission first. And besides *that*,' Charlotte continued, aware from her cousin's expression that he was not wholly convinced, 'Mama does not know *anything* about horses. She and Susannah do not understand them at all. She would only be saying no because she always does whenever I ask about anything interesting, not because she knew it was wrong.'

'Somehow, I don't think—'

'And once I know how to jump, she cannot very well make me *forget*, can she?'

Holland uttered a curt laugh. '*You're* forgetting who will get the chop if something goes wrong.'

'But what could go wrong? And it would be such fun,' Charlotte urged.

'Jumping, or getting away with it?'

'Well,' said Charlotte, thoughtfully, and then she smiled. Holland smiled back. He didn't suppose there was much harm in putting Clemmie through his paces, if they were careful about it.

'Oh, Bobs, you *are* a darling.'

'Never mind that. Just remember that you're under my orders as far as what we do and what we say if anybody finds out.'

'I will remember,' Charlotte promised. She offered him her hand, and they performed the handshake that the Armitage sisters had devised to seal important undertakings, and to whose mysteries their cousin had long been admitted.

As they were returning to the house, Charlotte admitted that she had been quite gloomy when Susannah and Lady Armitage went away – there had been absolutely nothing to do – but now she scarcely cared *when* they returned. Could the jumping lessons begin that afternoon?

Holland nodded. 'Do they often visit the Moltons?'

'Oh yes. Ever since Mr Grantley Molton – he is Mr Molton's nephew – came to live at Fordham. His father was a Turkey merchant and became most prodigiously rich, but now he is dead, and his brother – *our* Mr Molton – has adopted Mr Grantley Molton as his heir. Wasn't that fine of him?'

'Tremendous. What's Mr Grantley Molton like, other than being prodigiously rich and the heir to Fordham?'

Charlotte considered this. 'He is a great sportsman and has been to the university, and Mama says he has quite civilised his uncle. You know how gruff and *bearish* Mr Molton has always been, and that horrible old coat he used to wear? Well, there was a great ball held at Fordham at midsummer, and everyone believes that this was Mr

Grantley Molton's doing. We did not attend, Papa and I, for Papa had toothache and Mama said I was too young. But she and Susannah went, and Susannah told me all about it. Mama wore her diamonds, and Susannah said that she was near to fainting on the journey there and back, for fear of highwaymen. *I* should have liked it better if there *were* highwaymen.'

'Me too. What did she say about Mr Grantley Molton?'

'I do not remember that she said anything, but Mama is *forever* talking about him. He is very eligible, you see. And Susannah must marry *someone*, after all. It would be dreadful to be an old maid.'

'Mm.'

'Now do let us go in to breakfast,' said Charlotte, blithely, grasping her cousin's hand and towing him along. 'I hope that Papa has not eaten all the sausages – Dr Chilcote says they are bad for him, and I am starving.'

Mary also rose very early that morning, when the air was still and dawn only a faint, grey glimmer. Anyone who saw her, creeping down the stairs in stocking feet and slipping on her outdoor things in the front passage, would have known that she had a definite, secret, object. But no one did see her, which was why she was able to leave Lindham Hall and set off alone for Woodbridge. She had important business there, and she was determined to pursue it without the assistance or even the knowledge of Mrs Tipton. Naturally, that meant that she must also do without Mrs Tipton's carriage, but it seemed to Mary that walking six miles – probably closer to four if one took the footpath across the fields – was a small price to pay for privacy. Mrs Tipton was a very dear old lady, and extremely generous beneath her fussy, crusty shell, but she did so like to take charge of things, and Mary felt as if *she* had been taken charge of quite ruthlessly in the course of the last few days. Today, however, would be very different. Her business in Woodbridge had nothing to do with Mrs Tipton, and her opinions on the subject were not required. Besides which, Mary hoped that she would complete her errand and return to Lindham before anyone knew that she had gone.

With that combination of incentives she strode purposely along the lane that would take her into Lindham village and thence onto the Woodbridge road. The way was muddy, and traces of a thin, chill vapour lurked beneath the trees and in dips in the road, but Mary scarcely noticed these inconveniences. She was used to walking in all weathers; she had frequently done so at Mrs Bunbury's, when her duties permitted. Moreover, as her walks had generally been solitary pursuits, she had developed the habit of reciting poetry to herself to pass the time if the views were dull. Now, such was her mood that she imagined herself sailing with Sir Patrick Spens, and when she passed a gnarled, leafless tree just before the road turned into Woodbridge she wondered whether it might not be the Eildon Tree, where true Thomas met the Queen of Elfland. '"*At every lock of her horse's mane / Hung fifty silver bells and nine.*" What a lot of jingling.'

Most of Woodbridge was still waking up when she stopped in front of a large, comfortable-looking, stone house, with a neat gravel drive and a spread of scarlet ivy along one wall. The house bore no further marks of identification, but Mary knew that this was the correct address. Squaring her shoulders, she climbed the three steps to the front door and rapped sharply with the brass knocker. Morning callers were clearly not so unusual at Ivy House, for Mary's knock was answered promptly by a soberly dressed maid, and Mary herself was shown inside.

Some time later the front door opened and closed again as Mary took her leave. She was frowning thoughtfully, stretching her fingers into her gloves, and she started at the sound of a familiar voice above the scrunching gravel.

'Is that Miss Finch?'

'Oh— Good morning, Mr Déprez.' His sudden appearance had disturbed a less pleasant train of thought, but now she smiled effortlessly. She liked Déprez, in so far as she knew him, and there was certainly nothing in his appearance or address to discourage a deeper acquaintance. Indeed, it occurred to her that he was very handsome. Of course, she had been aware of his features before, particularly the warm, brown eyes that did so much to soften the sharply chiselled planes of his face, but she had not consciously assigned a name to the result.

'A very pleasant morning, indeed, and a happy meeting.' He started to tip his hat but interrupted the gesture to ask cautiously, 'But is this not Dr Mallory's residence? I trust that everyone is in good health at Lindham Hall?'

'Oh yes, we are all perfectly well,' Mary assured him. 'I have been speaking to Dr Mallory about my uncle. He was my uncle's physician, you know.'

'Yes, of course, and I mustn't keep you talking in the open air or you may become a patient yourself. Where have you left Mrs Tipton? May I escort you?'

He offered her his arm and that gesture, or a slight embarrassment at having to explain herself, made her falter. 'No, I thank you, but it is quite unnecessary. I mean, she is not here. I came on my own.'

'Ah. But the carriage . . . where have you—' His look expressed surprise, but there was no doubting the laughter that sparkled suddenly in her eyes. 'Surely you have not *walked* from Lindham, Miss Finch, and *on your own*. Why have you done such a thing?'

'Why should I not?' Mary retorted, but her tone was mischievous, rather than affronted. Indeed, she was rather pleased at having shocked him. 'The distance is not so great, and I am perfectly capable. I frequently walked far greater distances when I was in St Ives.'

He found her banter, and the way she drew herself up to make her claim, strangely endearing. Without intending it his mood began to change from one of polite interest to something more akin to pleasure in her company. 'I do not doubt your capacity for walking, but . . . I hazard it is not the true explanation for this particular . . . adventure.'

'No?' she asked, and still her tone challenged him.

'No.' He considered for a moment, smiling. 'In fact, I wonder whether you were not escaping the vigilance of Mrs Tipton.'

Now it was her turn to register surprise. 'How did you know?'

'I merely consulted my own feelings. In your situation I should have chafed considerably under her supervision. However,' he added, as she opened her mouth to protest, 'I wonder whether on this occasion discretion might not have been the wiser course. Have you considered what you will say when she discovers your morning's perambulation? You think you will effect a secret entry? It may be possible. But you cannot hope to escape general notice during your return journey to Lindham, you know, unless you intend to creep among the hedgerows. Some passerby will undoubtedly recognise you and wonder . . . Perhaps someone already has.' He glanced surreptitiously at the windows of Ivy House. 'I am certain I saw one of the upstairs curtains twitch.'

'Oh, do you think so? Perhaps I had better remind Dr Mallory—'

'No, no,' urged Déprez, laughing, and his hand upon

her arm restrained her. 'Either he is an honourable fellow – in which case you insult him even by mentioning the subject – or he is not – in which case nothing you can say will prevent him from spreading such gossip as he chooses amongst his entire circle of acquaintances.'

'I should not like to be gossiped about,' frowned Mary, 'and doctors know such a lot of people.'

'Indeed they do.'

'Still, it would be very mean of him to give me away . . . If only I could be certain of Mrs Tipton! I see that I ought to have thought more carefully about how I would get back to Lindham Hall.'

'It is the first rule of good generalship,' Déprez agreed. 'Never set out until you know how you will return.'

'Yes, that is very well, but I *have* set out. What ought I to do now?'

'Adhere to the second rule,' said Déprez, bowing slightly. 'When in a difficult situation, call upon the cavalry.'

'But are not the *cavalry* . . .' Mary began, and then, smiling, shook her head.

'I am very grateful to you for this,' she said as Déprez handed her into Mr Somerville's carriage. 'And you are certain that your own business in Woodbridge is not urgent?'

'Very certain.' Déprez settled back onto the seat opposite and signalled the coachman to set off. 'I cannot promise that we shall reach Lindham Hall before your absence is noticed, of course.'

'No, but . . . I suppose it *was* silly of me, but I wanted very much to speak to Dr Mallory alone. No one seems to have known my uncle very well, but I thought that his doctor would at least be able to tell me something.'

'And was he? I beg your pardon. I do not mean to be inquisitive.'

Mary smiled at him. 'I prefer people who are inquisitive – not gossips, I mean, but people who are curious about curious things.'

'Such as?'

'Well, such as my uncle's last illness. He had not enjoyed good health for some time I think – perhaps he had never been robust – and I wanted to know whether his death was the result of that general . . . weakness, or something else.' She raised an eyebrow.

Déprez also looked his question, but Mary slumped back in her seat and continued in a flat, dissatisfied voice. 'Dr Mallory said that when he died my uncle had an inflammation of the lungs, which was a particular illness. However, it probably strained his heart, and his heart was probably already in a weakened condition.'

'I see.' Déprez would not, under ordinary circumstances, have found an elderly gentleman's last symptoms particularly interesting. For some reason, however, he was increasingly charmed by Mary's account. It might have been the raised eyebrow. 'Clearly the diagnosis did not content you, but did you expect something very different?'

'I do not know what I expected,' Mary admitted, 'but I cannot forget the fact that Mr Tracey had my uncle's watch *and* a key to White Ladies. My uncle was an invalid, and he was not especially friendly with any of his neighbours, nor with his doctor or his solicitor. And yet he gave a family heirloom and the key to his house to Mr Tracey. It seems so very curious to me, and yet no one else seems bothered by it in the slightest. *I* cannot help thinking that it has something to do with the smugglers at White Ladies. Perhaps Mr Tracey was part of the gang – or was trying to upset their plans. Perhaps *that* was his warning to me, but I could not understand it, because of the cordial.'

'Dr Mallory knew nothing of Tracey, I suppose?'

'No.' Mary smiled ruefully. 'And he hadn't the least interest in my uncle's condition – what might have affected it or how he might have contracted an inflammation of the lungs. The only *curious* point in the whole affair as far as he was concerned was my coming to question him!'

The carriage slowed at a turning, and then the horses had to be urged forward gently to prevent the vehicle being drawn into a deep, muddy rut. Déprez observed their progress from the window, and when they had set off again he released the curtain and turned to Mary. 'Well, perhaps the good doctor reflected that the truth is more often dull than the reverse, and that whether curious or not, the truth would not change the fact of your uncle's death. In that way, it could be of no comfort to you, and comfort, I imagine, is what he thought you were seeking.'

'Yes, but I cannot be comfortable about something if I do not understand it. Do you think that very odd?'

'No, but it is not precisely *usual* either, perhaps because it is so dangerous – by which I mean it is disruptive to the quiet life. I do not know whether Mrs Tipton would consider it a very desirable attribute, for example.' Mary's smile turned impish, and Déprez reflected that if ever she became aware of her beauty, she would be very formidable.

'Mrs Tipton has already warned me more than once about eccentricity,' she continued. 'I believe I should prefer to be an eccentric – then I might behave exactly as I liked.'

'No, you would not prefer it,' he urged, 'for eccentrics, after all, are only capable of eccentric utterances. Everything you said would be rejected or misunderstood.'

'Like Cassandra.'

207

'Precisely. And for someone of your temperament, I am convinced that such a role would be intolerable.'

'Yes, I suppose so. Perhaps Mr Tracey was another Cassandra.'

'Perhaps he was.'

Mary nodded. She felt better, although her questions about Mr Tracey and her uncle remained unanswered. Mr Déprez was a very sensible person; she was glad she had not challenged him on the true military value of the cavalry, which had very likely been underestimated in any case.

12

A fortuitous combination of a headache and loosened roof tiles meant that Mary's sojourn in Woodbridge was not discovered at Lindham Hall. The former had kept Mrs Tipton in bed until long after her usual time, and the latter had resulted in Mr Cuff being the first member of the household to perceive Mary's return. He had pursed his lips when he saw her alight from the Somerville carriage, but had offered no opinion on the matter. More importantly, he had not been tempted to enlighten his employer or his colleagues, and had even helped Mary win through to her room while avoiding the peril of the front door. Of course, climbing a ladder would not have been to everyone's liking, but Mary had not flinched at the suggestion, and so Cuff's decision to favour her above 'them old cats' was vindicated. Nevertheless, on sober reflection Mary appreciated that she had had a narrow escape, and that such activities ought to be avoided in future, if possible.

She spent most of the next day indoors. The rain had resumed, but more importantly, Mrs Tipton had decided that they should be 'at home' that afternoon to visitors.

It was a decision that had tried her conscience. Mary was, after all, in mourning for her uncle, and she could hardly carry out a full round of social engagements. On the other hand, a niece was not *such* a close relation, and it was possible to conform too rigidly to the rules of etiquette. A discreet invitation to ladies of a certain standing seemed to strike the proper balance. They would satisfy their curiosity, Mary would gain a valuable introduction into County society, and no one would feel that they were dancing on Mr Finch's grave.

Mary was less certain about the enterprise. She was in favour of County society, which she believed to consist of balls, assemblies, and elegant dinner parties, but she did not like being looked over by a panel of censorious ladies, some of whom reminded her of Miss Nichols, and enduring their stilted conversation. And their conversation *was* stilted, or concerned people whom Mary did not know. A stern critic, especially one who cared little for County society, might have called it tedious. Mrs Tipton, moreover, was continually interjecting some comment or other, or trying to influence Mary's own remarks through expressive frowns or winks, and this, on top of endless cups of tea, made the afternoon extremely wearing.

It was with particular pleasure, therefore, that she noted the arrival of Mr Déprez. He had come to collect Mrs Somerville, but as the only man among a gaggle of women, he was quickly pressed to remain. Mary watched as he made easy, polite conversation with each of them and also observed their responses – simpering, giggling, one actually grasping his arm when he attempted to move on. *How silly some women can be when there is a man about,* she thought, but her own heart fluttered uncomfortably as he crossed the room to join her by the tea things, where she had taken refuge on the pretext of being helpful.

He was conscious that she was wearing a far more attractive gown than he had presumed she would own, judging by the monstrosity she had worn the day they went to White Ladies. (He had made allowances for her appearance in Woodbridge, generously presuming that she had chosen it in anticipation of the muddy trek.) Today, however, she was dressed in a simple, but well-tailored affair in black wool crepe, upon which Miss Cheadle had laboured through the night to have ready. 'I hope I do not intrude, Miss Finch,' he smiled. 'Mr Somerville did not tell me that you would be . . . holding court to so many of our ladies of quality this afternoon,' and in a lower voice, more to himself than to her, added, '"*The Sprights of fiery Termagants in Flame . . .*"'

'"*In various talk th'instructive hours they past, / Who gave the Ball, or paid the visit last,*"' Mary agreed.

'Ah, I see you have read Mr Pope,' said Déprez, raising an eyebrow. 'Do you enjoy his poetry?'

'Yes, but we oughtn't to have said that, about the . . . termagants, I mean.' Mary had a sudden feeling of having been too clever for her own good. She shrugged and filled his cup.

'Never mind, it was I who said it, and I am duly chastened.' He took a sip and, gesturing toward himself, murmured, '"*The graver Prude sinks downward to a Gnome, / In search of Mischief still on Earth to roam.*" And speaking of mischief, I trust that there were no . . . unpleasant consequences yesterday?'

Mary shook her head and answered in a similarly confidential tone. 'She never discovered it at all. So long as none of the Woodbridge ladies informs against me . . . I daresay fretting about it has made me impolite.' She nodded gravely in the direction of a circle of cashmere shawls, in the centre of which the mayor's wife was holding forth.

'Ah, yes,' agreed Déprez. 'Well, I shall endeavour to shift the conversation if I perceive any of them to be on the brink of a revelation.' They parted then, and he made another leisurely circuit of the room, and Mary watched him, while telling herself that she ought not to. When he returned he begged for a slice of seed cake. 'I have been assured by that lady in the nightcap that it will be the best I have ever tasted.'

Mary had resolved to adopt a more reserved demeanour, but this was immediately defeated by his remark. '*Shh*,' she urged, stifling a giggle, 'that is not a nightcap!'

'No? It seems very like a nightcap, but I am glad you have warned me. I would not wish to cause offence by complimenting it.' He had a bite of cake. 'This is pleasant, but perhaps a trifle dry. What do you say to the ginger-bread?'

'Oh, I much prefer the gingerbread,' and she cut him a slice. 'Is *that* what they are all discussing – cakes?'

'Yes,' he smiled, 'cakes and lawyers. The particular cakes provided by Mr Todd, and the quality of his advice, and which are the most agreeable – of his cakes, I mean.'

'Mrs Tipton and I visited Mr Todd, you know,' Mary explained, lowering her voice again, 'about my uncle's will.'

Déprez nodded, and before he could assure her that she need not confide in him upon that subject, she began to do exactly that. She liked telling him things, and her uncle's will was a particularly fruitful source of information. For his part, Déprez found her enthusiasm attractive, and he really did not fancy yet another circuit among the . . . termagants. Soon, therefore, he and Mary were discussing such fascinating details as the practice of the ecclesiastical courts, which had jurisdiction over the disposition of Mr

Finch's property, and why Mr Finch had made a will of his personal estate but not of his real property. Déprez found the decision surprising, but Mary had questioned Mr Todd and so was able to explain it.

'It seems that where a man wishes his land to go to his heir, he is best advised *not* to do so by will, but to let it pass by inheritance, for the latter is the stronger title. In fact, if land *is* so devised, the will is useless and will be rejected, so that the heir takes by descent.'

'Indeed.'

'There is also the fact that if a man states in his will, "I bequeath all of my personal goods and chattels to . . . Mr Déprez," that statement will affect everything that he owns at the time of his death, but if he makes the same statement as regards his real estate, it will operate only upon such property as he owns when he makes his will. So, each time he purchases a new property, or even mortgages an old property, he is obliged to make a new will.'

Déprez smiled at her admiringly. 'You seem to have made quite a study of the laws of inheritance.'

'Well, it is very interesting,' she explained, shyly, 'and I . . . enjoy finding things out.'

'Of course; a perfectly sensible view. You would not be . . . *comfortable* in a state of mystification. And do you plan to continue your studies?'

'Oh, no,' smiled Mary, 'I am giving up the law – for the moment, at least. But I *have* engaged to assist Mr Todd in another way. His clerks are going to White Ladies tomorrow to make an inventory of the house, and I am going with them.'

Déprez did not attempt to mask his surprise. 'My word, Miss Finch, after all that happened there? I am— Of course, I honour your fortitude, but . . . or perhaps yesterday's adventure has inspired you to greater exploits?'

'No, indeed,' she protested, 'and I am not so brave as all that. I ought to have explained. Mr Mycroft, my uncle's steward, will be there as well, along with several of his men. They will make certain that the house is properly secure.'

'Ah, well, that is something, but what a dismal task! Counting chairs and cataloguing bits of crockery . . .'

'Perhaps it seems grasping,' Mary acknowledged, colouring slightly, 'but really, I do not think of White Ladies as in any way *mine* – only, it is all so interesting.'

'Yes, of course,' he agreed. 'I did not mean to imply any criticism. Why should you not take a hand in the proceedings if you choose?' He hesitated, frowning. 'However . . . would you allow me to make a suggestion?'

'Certainly.'

'I have an associate – he helps manage my plantation in St Lucia, but he has had to come away with me, because of the trouble there. He is a very capable clerk. Why not let him help with the inventory?'

Mary thought that she could not possibly agree to such a generous proposal, while Déprez thought that she could. His was the more logical argument, and he concluded it by smiling at her, which proved to be its strongest point. Somehow it was impossible to refuse him. 'Very well,' she agreed, 'if you think your associate would not mind. Thank you.'

'No, he will enjoy it, I am certain. His name is Hicks. I believe he met you when he arrived in Lindham. In the churchyard – he was asking about Woolthorpe Manor.'

'Oh, yes.' Mary frowned slightly. 'I thought—'

'That he seemed a slightly odd fellow? He often gives that impression to strangers, but you must not let that worry you. He has had some . . . hard knocks in his time, but he is completely reliable, and he has a great deal of experience.'

214

There was something in Déprez's tone of voice as he uttered these last words that drew her attention. Was he trying to tell her something? She glanced up at him, but his expression had changed, and now she was unable to read it. 'Do you think that it would be at all . . . *wrong* for me to go to White Ladies?'

'Oh, no, not wrong, but—'

'But it doesn't hurt to be careful?'

'Yes,' nodded Déprez. 'Why do you smile?'

'Nothing. That is what Captain Holland always said, whenever I was suspicious of something.'

'Did he? Well, it is a wise saying.'

When Mary arrived at White Ladies the following morning, she found it completely transformed. Dustsheets had been removed, carpets unrolled, and fires were burning in the principal rooms. The presence of several active, good-natured clerks and workmen also contributed to the changed atmosphere. Mary wandered through the house, frequently getting in the way, but marvelling at the difference between *this* White Ladies and the one she had experienced when she made her original tour. The house still did not quite feel lived in, but rather as if it had been woken up and taken in hand, and with light restored and his furniture put to rights, Mary could almost feel her uncle's presence. Would he have resented these strangers in his house with their lists and notebooks? It must have been a heavy burden living alone all those years. Not for the first time Mary thought how close she had come to lightening that burden, and to bringing a change from all this quiet.

In the course of her wanderings she met Hicks, Mr Déprez's associate, and to begin with Mary was rather shy of him. She found his manner unusual, sometimes rough and almost uncouth and at other times surprisingly urbane, and both completely natural. He was certainly very different from Mycroft, Mr Finch's taciturn agent, who seemed to know everything about coppicing and pasturage, but who recited the rent roll from memory better than he read it. Of course, a sugar plantation in St Lucia was very different from an estate in Suffolk; why should their managers not also be very different? But Hicks did not even *sound* like a West Indian – or, Mary corrected herself, he did not sound like Mr Déprez; at least, not all of the time.

They became friendly, however, over the White Ladies tableware. Mr Todd sent them to the pantry with the idea that Hicks should record the various items of porcelain, plate, glassware, and cutlery under Mary's direction. In fact, his knowledge in this area far exceeded hers. Once they ventured beyond the more mundane items Mary found herself unable to identify them. She soon realised, however, that Hicks not only knew what everything was called but also wished to avoid embarrassing her. Gradually a sort of game took shape between them, never actually acknowledged, in which they would trade hints and guesses. And as the one tended toward obscurity, the other became more outrageous.

'Now this spoon . . .' She frowned at the item, whose long, pointed handle was almost as strange as its round, pierced bowl. Why would anyone want a spoon with holes in it?

'"Why beholdest thou the *mote* that is in thy brother's eye?"' murmured Hicks, and he performed a discreet drinking motion.

'When thy own . . . *teacup* is full of them,' smiled Mary. 'Please to note a pair of silver tea – I mean, "mote spoons", Mr Hicks.'

'Very good, miss.'

'And this little shov—'

'Stilton scoop? Which some would wonder what on earth it was for? Yes, I'll note that, miss. I am very partial to Stilton cheese – after a meal, with a bit of fruit – and I daresay you are too.'

'Ye-*ss*, it is very nice. A Stilton scoop, then. These tongs, however, seem to me to have a most valuable purpose *after* the meal.' She brandished one thoughtfully. 'They are . . . for holding a gentleman's cigar, so that he may smoke in comfort to the very end, without the risk of burning his fingers.'

'Ah,' nodded Hicks, remarking that there were twelve of the ingenious devices. 'And during the meal, perhaps they might do double duty – picking up asparagus or the like.'

'Yes, what a good idea. I believe I shall serve asparagus at my first dinner at White Ladies for that very reason.'

Gradually they worked their way through casters, coasters, salvers, ewers, comports, and tasses, through glasses for water, for ale, for cordials, and for spirits, and through porcelain bowls and plates of every conceivable size and shape. Hicks revealed that Mr Finch's collection of silver, particularly, was a very fine one, and Mary began planning her first dinner party in greater earnest.

Mary also learned more about her colleague. Rather shyly Hicks admitted that he had been born to a life not so far removed from that of White Ladies. His father had been a gentleman of consequence, and Hicks ought to have succeeded to a comfortable, respectable life. Acknowledging that such an origin could not easily be reconciled with his present condition, he briefly described his fall. It was not an unusual story, but Mary knew little of moral degeneracy, and she listened attentively.

217

In fact, there was not very much of it actually divulged in Hicks' account, for he was sensitive to his audience and merely alluded to his misconduct. Nevertheless, Mary heard that whilst at university Hicks had taken up with a wild, rakish set of young men. Lacking other guidance, or spurning that which was offered, he had been reckless, selfish, and had generally 'lost his moral compass'. He had been obliged to leave Cambridge and had gone to London, where he had indulged himself further. For a time his life had been happy. At least it had been exciting and empty, which had counted as happiness for him in those days. Of course, the crash was bound to come, sooner or later, and a fraudulent investment scheme had done for him. He lost everything, and only avoided prison by fleeing the country.

Then had come the real hard times, when he had been ill, and friendless, and destitute. He had realised then what a mess he had made of things, but he was too badly lost to do anything but regret his fall. It was Mr Déprez who had given him his chance, or rather his second chance, plucking him out of the gutter and offering him a job on his plantation. For some reason Mr D had trusted him, and Hicks had resolved not to disappoint that trust. Gradually he had recovered himself, and had even become useful in a modest way. And now here he was, not quite what his father would have hoped for him, once upon a time, but having done his best.

Listening to Hicks' account, Mary experienced a series of emotions. Sympathy for the young man led astray by bad companions and his own weakness, sorrow for the parents who must have been cruelly disappointed, and admiration for the man who had taken the risk of helping another. How noble Mr Déprez had been, to have had faith in Hicks when most men would have left him to his fate! See what happened when one did the right thing – the noble thing? He saved another's life.

Some of these feelings were reflected on Mary's face, and Hicks urged her not to mention any of what he had said to Mr D. It was a private matter, really, and he wouldn't want to cause any embarrassment to his patron. 'Oh, no, of course not,' she agreed, and she clasped Hicks' gnarled hand.

Their exploration of the White Ladies' tableware eventually drew to a close in the early afternoon, and they were each sent to other duties – Hicks to the stillroom, and Mary to the library. Mr Todd explained that most of the books had been catalogued by their previous owner, but it was unclear whether the list was complete. One of the clerks would check it, for this involved climbing a ladder to reach the upper shelves, hardly a task for a young lady. There was also Mr Finch's desk, groaning under books, papers, and boxes of correspondence. Would Miss Finch be so good as to have a look at these?

The library. Mary experienced a slight tremor of uneasiness at the prospect of returning to that room, but the lighted passageway was reassuring, while in the library itself a clerk was studying a well-thumbed catalogue, and from the windows she could see Mr Mycroft giving instructions on the lawn. Everything looked so well-managed and orderly; it was highly unlikely that anything *dangerous* would occur.

The dullness of her task provided a further anchor. Her uncle, it seemed, had preserved a great many letters on not very interesting subjects: one half of a dialogue with Mycroft regarding diseased trees; copious descriptions of two lightweight fowling pieces to be purchased from Mr Nock of 10 Ludgate Street, London; receipts for a dozen gentleman's shirts and half a dozen plain cambric handkerchiefs. After wading through the smallest drawer she looked briefly into the others. All were stuffed with the detritus of everyday record-keeping; she would have to clear off the desktop to make sufficient space to examine them.

From across the room, Adams, Mr Todd's clerk, heard a slight, sharp sound. He was halfway up the ladder, and he glanced back over his shoulder. 'Everything all right, Miss Finch?' he enquired.

'Yes, yes,' she assured him, 'I . . . I have cut my finger on a bit of paper, that is all.'

'Oh, bad luck,' replied Adams. 'Paper cuts are such a nuisance. I cut myself once and bled on a set of instructions to counsel. Mr Todd was *not* best pleased.'

'What? Oh, yes— I mean, how unfortunate. This is not so very bad, however. No blood at all.' She spoke cheerfully, even holding up her hand to illustrate her point.

He uttered a faint grunt of acknowledgement and returned to his labours. Instantly Mary's expression changed, and she gazed in puzzled surprise at four sheets of paper. She had found them on her uncle's desk while moving a pile of books; they had been underneath. Inscribed on each was a series of letters in an apparently random order. On the first sheet these amounted to half a dozen lines, while the others were nearly full. It was . . . it *looked like* a codification of some kind.

She sat back in her chair and surveyed the strange collection. Why should her uncle have written in code, and why keep such documents hidden under a book? What could he have wanted to keep secret? He had no confidential business dealings – at least, she assumed not – and it was inconceivable that he was writing . . . *love letters*.

The heavy silence of the library, broken only by the

ticking clock, seemed to envelop her, and she began to feel anxious without quite knowing why. She wanted to do something – to speak, or open a window, or even walk about the room. Of course she could not do any such thing – what would Mr Adams think? And what was the matter with her? Why should sheets of paper make her uneasy?

She glanced across at Mr Adams, absorbed in his inventory. Perhaps she ought to show him what she had found – or Mr Todd. But what would she say to him? That she had found some secret papers? She doubted whether he would understand them any more than she did. Might they have something to do with the estate? But why write about estate matters in code? These papers must concern something that was meant to be kept secret. Then she remembered Mr Tracey . . . the watch, the key, his whispered warnings about White Ladies. And Tom Scott – he had known that something was wrong . . .

The smugglers. She felt a cold, shivery sensation, as if her blood was sinking into her toes. Secret messages to the smugglers! Of course! What could be more natural than that they would communicate in code to conceal their criminal dealings? But why would her uncle have their papers?

The library door opened, and Wallace, the junior clerk, poked his head into the room. 'Tea's just boiled if anyone is interested. My word, it's quiet as a tomb in here.'

'Of course it's quiet,' Adams retorted as he descended from his perch, 'we've been hard at work – not like some.' He dusted his hands.

'If you only knew,' Wallace complained. 'I've been in the stable block, while you have been inside with your lovely fire.' He glanced in Mary's direction. 'Uhh, correspondence,' he shuddered. 'Looks like you've drawn the

221

short straw this afternoon, Miss Finch. Would you care for a cup of tea?'

Mary had quickly hidden the papers, and she greeted Wallace with a nod and a smile, feeling terribly false as she did so. 'Oh, yes, that would be lovely.'

She followed the two men to the parlour, her mind in a whirl. They were still bickering about their respective workloads, but she hardly heard them, and she received her cup of tea from Hicks in a high state of distraction. It was only by the greatest effort that she heard Mr Todd's explanation of the excellent progress that they had made. He was very encouraged.

'Yes, how splendid,' she agreed, while privately she was asking herself whether it was conceivable that her uncle could have somehow been involved with smuggling. She remembered what Mr Treadgill had said about smugglers – their violence and criminality. Was it possible? After all, the smugglers had been very familiar with White Ladies; they had known about the cellar. She shuddered in recollection of her treatment at their hands – and they had come upon her *at the desk*! Perhaps they had known about the coded papers! They might even have come to White Ladies to find them! And had not Mr Tracey claimed—

'What? I beg your pardon,' she said aloud, as Mr Todd's voice interrupted her train of thought. 'Oh, no, I do not mind the work.' She settled back in her chair, as if making herself more comfortable. 'It is quite interesting.' Had Mr Tracey known about the papers? Perhaps been looking for them? But why? And why had her uncle kept such things on his desk? Buried, certainly, but not under lock and key. Had he only just received them? Perhaps been expecting to pass them on?

The coded papers, why her uncle had them and what they might mean, continued to play upon Mary's mind for the rest of the afternoon. She knew what she ought to do, but shrank from doing it. When the house was closed up for the day, and everyone said good evening, her contribution did not quite ring true, and she had forgotten all about asparagus tongs.

The return journey to Lindham Hall was a quiet one, and on arriving she went straight up to her room with hardly a word to Peggy or Mr Cuff. Closing the door behind her, she removed hat and cloak, and then drew the folded papers out of the pocket of her gown. It had cost her a great deal to remove them from White Ladies, deceiving Mr Todd and probably committing several crimes in the process. Doubtless she was tampering with evidence, but it was too late to worry about that now. She must find out what the papers actually said, in order to guess what they were evidence *of*, and that meant decoding them.

A secret code was all very well, but the message had to be coherent to sender and recipient; therefore it had to have a key. Suppose *she* had received these messages; how would she decipher them? The four papers seemed to have nothing in common – was that right? She looked at them again. Written in the top right hand corner of the first document were the numbers 1, 217, 12, while the second contained the numbers 1, 247, 16. The third and fourth bore similar series: 1, 299, 9; and 4, 412, 24. What could these mean? Were they part of the message? But why use numbers rather than letters? If the writer did not use the same key every time, he must have provided it with the message. She studied the sets of numbers; perhaps they were some sort of puzzle. Three times the series began with the number one and three times it ended with a multiple of four. Might that be significant? She tried adding the different series, and even adding the first, second, and third numbers in each series, but none of these provided illumination. She looked at the numbers again. If not a puzzle, what were they?

'Excuse me, miss. There's supper on the table, and missus asks, are you coming?'

Mary started. 'Oh, Peggy, I never heard you.' She felt her face flushing, and set about tidying the papers with an attempt at lightness. 'Yes, I am quite finished. Please tell Mrs Tipton that I shall be there directly.'

'Yes, miss,' said Peggy, wondering what there was about bits of paper that could be so interesting. She had knocked twice and received no answer, and had entered the room to find Miss Finch with them spread out in front of her on the bed, and staring out into nothing as if she were in a fit.

'Like she was in a fit,' Peggy repeated to Pollock, the cook, as she prepared to bring in the first course. 'And my own blood ran cold at the sight of her, I can tell you!'

'What happened then?' asked Pollock, her ladle poised.

'Well,' Peggy admitted, 'she roused herself, and neatened up all them scraps of paper, and come down.'

Pollock pursed her lips. She had expected a groan of remorse, or a faint, at the very least.

Conscious that her story had fallen rather flat, Peggy added, 'But she was that pale, and I never seen anyone walk so stiff like, and all over a tremble.'

'Humph,' sniffed Pollock. 'Just you see that you don't spill none of that soup, there, with your trembles.'

Mrs Tipton retired early to bed that evening, largely because Mary was so unresponsive. Mrs Tipton liked to feel that her words were having an effect on whoever heard them, and tonight Mary seemed hardly to be paying attention. One might as well save one's breath and go to bed. At Storey's Court, Sir William Armitage was also finding speech difficult, not because he lacked an audience, but because his subject was so awkward. He and Lady Armitage suspected that their elder daughter, Susannah, had become the object of Robert Holland's affections – affections that were no longer wholly fraternal. So long as Robert and Susannah remained apart, Sir William could regard this as a remote, almost abstract problem. The prospect of his wife and daughter's imminent return, however, necessitated a radical change of focus. He would be obliged to 'have words' with Robert, and that was unlikely to be a pleasant experience. For, of course, they could not marry. Robert was a fine fellow, but *every* consideration – birth, income, situation, even character – weighed against him. No, marriage to Susannah was impossible, out of the question. But how to say this in a way that did not wound?

The words 'dashed awkward' formed themselves in Sir William's mind whenever he imagined that conversation, and they were there now. He puffed his cigar thoughtfully. Charlotte had gone up to bed, and this was the perfect opportunity to speak with Robert – nothing complicated or overblown, just a simple statement of facts. 'Er, enjoy your smoke, my boy,' he advised, 'for there is an end to it after tonight. You may still smoke in the garden, of course, but I do not find that so comforting, not in this weather.'

'No, sir.'

They smoked for a while in silence while Sir William brooded on paternal responsibility and moral cowardice. Then Holland broke the silence with an observation that suggested an ability to read his cousin's mind.

'I'll be glad to see Susannah again.'

'Oh, ah,' was Sir William's somewhat startled reply.

'It's almost a year since I've seen her.'

'Yes, of course,' agreed Sir William, 'you have not been home since Christmas, have you?'

'No, sir.'

Paternal responsibility swelled in Sir William, and he drew himself up purposefully in his chair. It ebbed almost as quickly, however, so that he prodded the fire, quite unnecessarily, with a poker and complained, 'This blasted chimney will not draw properly. I must get Wainwright in to have a look at it.'

'Yes, sir. I thought Susannah and Lady Armitage were going to be in Town last spring, for the Season, but I never heard that they came.'

'No,' said Sir William, dusting his hands, 'Susannah was not particularly keen, and in the end Anne decided against it. Speaking of London, we . . . leased the house in Cavendish Square to Admiral Verney. A very sociable fellow, but his liver gives him a great deal of trouble. Do you know him?'

'No, sir.'

There was another silence, and when Holland started to speak Sir William interrupted with an affected lightness. 'You, er, you never told me of the adventure you had in Suffolk, on your way here.'

'No, sir – I'd forgotten.'

It had not taken three attempts for Holland to appreciate that Susannah was out of bounds, but now he abandoned the struggle, at least for the present. Instead he explained what had befallen him, and Sir William listened with a half-hearted, and then a genuine, interest. 'What an extraordinary situation,' he murmured, when he learned of the White Ladies' cellar. 'Charlotte will want to hear about your escape – and a very resourceful piece of work it was.' He brooded for a moment before adding, 'Perhaps you ought not to tell her, however. She is wild enough as it is, without tales of smugglers and secret passages. But to return to your story. You left Miss Finch under Mrs . . . Tipton's protection?'

Holland nodded, adding that he would return to Lindham if anything else happened – not that he considered that likely – but he had said that he would.

'She sounds a very remarkable young person, your Miss Finch.'

Holland supposed she *was* remarkable; the things she said, the way she argued with him, and laughed at him, and did not hang back even when she was afraid. He liked that about her, and the way she smiled. But it was mad to think about such things, and to his cousin he merely observed, 'A bit . . . fanciful, you know, the way girls are, but brave. She had nerve enough for anything.'

'Pretty?' As soon as he uttered the word Sir William wanted to recall it. Any discussion of feminine beauty must necessarily bring Susannah to mind. Before Holland could do more than nod, therefore, Sir William moved quickly onto another tack. 'Finch, hmm, the name sounds familiar to me. What did you say the uncle's name was?'

'Edward – he was a sort of recluse, on account of his health; and the grandfather was Thomas Finch, a sea captain on the North Atlantic run – the fur trade. Made a packet of money, and Edward Finch inherited it.'

Thomas Finch, that was the name Sir William knew. A cadet branch of an old Hampshire family, and the MP for East Salton when Sir William had joined the Treasury. Finch had never spoken much in the House, though he had generally voted with the government, and Sir William struggled for something to say about him. 'He must have made a packet, as you say; those Cornish boroughs are

227

dashed expensive. Still, he made his way, got on in the world. It shows what an enterprising man can achieve.'

'Mm.' Holland also fell silent, and then continued, 'Did you ever hear of a fellow who killed the archbishop of Canterbury on the king's orders, sir? In history, I mean.'

Sir William frowned in surprise. 'In his— Oh, yes, Henry II and Thomas Becket. "Who will rid me of this turbulent priest".'

'That's the one.'

'Yes, a very famous story, like King Alfred and the cakes. But what made you think of it? Not planning a spot of murder, are you?'

'No, sir,' Holland smiled, 'nothing like that.'

13

The ladies returned to Storey's Court on the following afternoon. Holland was in the timber yard, observing Charlotte's efforts to direct Clemmie over a very modest structure, when one of the stable lads announced that Lady Armitage's carriage was on the drive. The necessary precautions were instantly put in train: the structure dismantled, Clemmie taken away to his stall, and Charlotte ordered into the house to change her clothes and temper her mood of exultation. Holland undertook a hastier toilet as he passed through the kitchen garden, rinsing his hands at the well.

When he arrived at the front of the house, the carriage had already disgorged a great quantity of baggage and two passengers. Care of the former was given over to a pair of footmen under Jeffries' supervision. Sir William and Mrs Ramsay, the housekeeper, had taken charge of the latter, and Holland established a discreet position on their left flank. He caught Susannah's eye immediately, and she favoured him with a smile of delight. A few moments later Charlotte appeared beside him, looking demure in a gown of apricot muslin and actually carrying her needlework.

'Don't be daft, shrimp,' muttered Holland. 'She'll never

believe you've been pegging away at that damned thing and will guess you have something to hide.'

No sooner had he spoken than Lady Armitage called out that it was far too cold to stand about in such a light gown and Charlotte must go inside immediately. Apparently also noticing Holland for the first time, she advanced to greet him. Lady Armitage was a tall, fair woman, handsome, if a trifle severe. Although matronly, her attire bespoke a matron of wealth, fashion, and a certain dash. She had borne the six-mile journey from Fordham with the equanimity that comes from a well-sprung vehicle and a disciplined temper, and now she displayed neither a crease nor a tumbled curl.

'Ah, Robert,' she said, extending a gloved hand. 'How charming to see you.'

'Thank you, ma'am,' he replied. 'I hope you enjoyed your visit?'

'Yes, quite. We had not intended to stay away as long as we did, but Susannah is such a favourite with the Moltons that there was no getting away. I hope that you have been making yourself quite at home – when did you arrive?'

'Tuesday night.'

'Oh, what a pity we were not here. Still, you will be with us some time yet?'

'A few more days – then I'm due back in Woolwich.'

'Ah, yes, the call of duty. We mustn't chafe at duty, however much it interferes with our private pleasures, especially in wartime.' She beckoned her elder daughter. 'Susannah, here is your cousin.'

'Dear Bobs, how wonderful this is,' cried Susannah, hurrying toward him. 'We have all been longing to see you.' She was a softer, gentler version of her mother and very beautiful.

230

He smiled at her, taking her hand and saying something appropriate. Then Lady Armitage, having pronounced their greeting 'charming', cried that Sir William must not attempt to lift any of the baggage – she was quite worried about him. When Holland turned to see to this himself, Lady Armitage begged the favour of her daughter's arm and promptly led her into the house. By the time the men entered in their turn, the ladies had all disappeared upstairs to rest and prepare themselves for the evening.

The explanation of these manoeuvres would have been clear even to a dull-witted man, and Holland was not dull-witted. 'It won't surprise me,' he informed his reflection while doing battle with his neck cloth, 'if she's put an embargo on finery. Nothing but hair papers and shawls till I've gone and Mr Grantley bloody Molton turns up.'

The reappearance of the ladies in a splendid array of silk and lace put paid somewhat to this prediction, although Susannah's gown, with its high neck and broad white collar, had something of the puritan about it. Holland smiled to himself, moreover, when he saw the arrangement of the dining table, which placed him beside Lady Armitage at the foot and opposite Charlotte, while a considerable distance separated them from Sir William at the head. Susannah, on her father's left, had no opposite neighbour.

Whatever the initial constraints, the meal was a pleasant one. Everyone was happy to be at home and together. Such was Holland's relationship to the Armitages that they all considered his being at Storey's Court the natural condition and his long absences as exceptions. Sir William delighted in the presence of 'my favourite young people', none of whom was hesitant in conversation. Lady Armitage, too, when her maternal instincts did not interfere, was a gracious, thoughtful hostess. She held her tongue when her husband's remarks on saints' bones helped to shift a general discussion of ghosts toward one about executions and their associated superstitions. Sir William had seen several executions in his youth, and he reported on the great value that some people placed upon a piece of the noose or an article of the dead man's clothing. To have touched a condemned man or, better yet, shaken his hand, was considered the height of good luck.

'Why do they hang people?' asked Charlotte. 'Criminals, I mean.'

'Ah, well might you ask,' replied her father, nodding, but before he could begin an oration on penal reform, she made it clear that she was not interested in why criminals were executed, but why they were hanged in preference to some other method.

Thrown off his stride, Sir William had no ready explanation; he supposed that hanging had the advantage of being inexpensive.

Charlotte considered this. 'Which is worse, being shot or being hung – hanged?'

Something in her tone brought Mary Finch inexorably to Holland's mind. He could well imagine her asking such a question, and looking seriously around the table for an answer. But how could he be thinking of Mary Finch when his cousin Susannah was in the room? He told Charlotte that hanging was considered more dishonourable, and as he did so he reflected that Mary Finch would probably chime in with some fellow in history who was thrown off a cliff or boiled in oil, and what did he think about it? 'That reminds me of an odd story I heard at the Landguard fort,' he added. 'It's not about a criminal at all, but . . . a dead man's hand.' He smiled eerily.

'Oh, my goodness,' breathed Susannah, while Charlotte cried, 'Do tell us about it.'

'Well,' said Holland, in a low voice, 'the last lieutenant governor of the fort was named Thicknesse, Captain Thicknesse, and he was an odd . . . strange . . . fellow. Very learned and intelligent, but when no one was looking he wrote pamphlets, and he argued with people, especially his son, Lord Audley. When Thicknesse died they went through his papers, and what do you think they found? That he had left . . . his *right hand* to Lord Audley.'

'Oh, my,' Susannah murmured.

'The will said that when he was dead, they should cut off his right hand and send it to his son.'

'But what was the reason for this extraordinary conduct?' asked Sir William.

'He hoped the sight of that hand would remind Lord Audley of his duty to God, and that he would pay greater heed to *that* than he had to his duty to his father.'

'Extraordinary,' repeated Sir William.

'*Did* they cut off his hand?' Charlotte demanded.

'I don't know,' replied Holland in his usual voice. 'He died in France, so maybe they did. They're very fond of cutting off people's *heads*, so a hand, here or there, would make no odds with them.'

'Ohh,' cried Charlotte, 'I wonder what Lord Audley did when he received the hand. Do you suppose it came in the post, like a letter? Imagine receiving a hand when you thought it was a box of sweets!'

'But they would never deliver such a thing, surely,' Susannah protested. 'Bobs, are you certain this story is true?'

Holland wondered whether anyone else could be so perturbed and still so beautiful, and felt reassured. 'They swore to me at Landguard that he wanted it cut off and sent,' he shrugged. 'One of the officers had seen the will.'

233

'I declare these horrors will give you all bad dreams,' said Lady Armitage, rising at last. 'My dears, let us recover our spirits over tea, and leave the gentlemen to their wine.'

On Saturday evening Mr and Mrs Somerville held a small dinner party, to which Mary and Mrs Tipton were invited. On Mrs Tipton's scale of social engagements that could and could not be taken up during mourning, this fell comfortably on the right side. 'A private party of eight respectable persons,' she noted with satisfaction, 'is perfectly proper. You must wear your black silk, Mary – with the scalloped neck.'

Mary admired the gown in question and looked forward to wearing it; nevertheless, she would just as soon have declined the invitation. She was not in the mood for a social gathering, however respectable. In fact, its very respectability contributed to her uneasiness. Since finding the mysterious documents her mood had varied, sometimes wildly, but generally in a downward direction. Relief at finding no further coded papers had been followed by guilt at her own deceit in keeping quiet about those she *had* found. She had almost laughed aloud when she realised that the number series might refer to a book, with the first number indicating a chapter, the second a page, and the third a line or verse. But when neither the Old nor the New Testament yielded messages according to that scheme, and she could not even be sure that the Bible was the right book, she had relapsed into gloom.

The documents themselves were not Mary's only worry. If they *did* concern the smugglers, where did that leave her uncle? And indeed, Mary herself? Suppose Edward Finch was a scoundrel. If he had been engaged in smuggling, might not his wealth – and her inheritance – have a criminal foundation? What would be her 'rightful place' in County society under those circumstances? Mrs Tipton would withdraw her sponsorship – she might even think twice about allowing Mary to remain at Lindham Hall. And what of Mr Somerville? As a magistrate he would wash his hands of her completely. Everyone would feel as if they had been taken in – or they would feel sorry for her, the way one felt sorry for the ragged, shuffling people one passed in the street and did not look at. Yes, one felt sorry for them, but one did not invite them to dinner parties!

Mary was imagining her possible fall from grace during the journey to Woolthorpe Manor. She had reached the point at which Mr Hunnable gave a thundering sermon to the ladies from the tea party on the sins of the uncles when Mrs Tipton poked her with one of her sticks and demanded to know whether she was sickening with something.

'No, ma'am,' Mary assured her, straightening up and trying to look about her with greater vivacity. The carriage groaned, and she was obliged to speak up. 'I am quite well.'

'You are tired, then,' pronounced Mrs Tipton. 'All this work is exhausting you. When does it end?'

'Oh, I believe Mr Todd is nearly finished with the inventory.' Mary had no idea whether this was the case, but it seemed a safe reply.

'Mr Todd, indeed,' muttered Mrs Tipton. 'Still, you are quite right to keep an eye on him. If Mr Brownlowe were here, it would be a different matter, but with that man Todd . . . And he will not be the last person who attempts to impose upon you, of that you may be sure. As a lady of property – a *young* lady of property – you will attract

235

undesirables of all kinds. It is quite a responsibility, you know; and then there is the *personal* side. There you must be particularly on your guard.' She paused again. 'And of course there was that man.'

'*That man?*' Mary repeated in genuine surprise, and then she blushed rosily.

'Come, come,' scoffed Mrs Tipton. '*I* am not such an old woman that I have forgotten what effect a military coat may have. And if the officer concerned is dashing and performs heroic acts, the effect is doubled, or even trebled.'

Mary hardly knew what to say. She *had* thought about Captain Holland more than she ought to have done since his departure, given the terms of the ban, but to have him suddenly raised in conversation provoked a confusion of emotions. 'He seemed to me a very . . . worthy person,' she offered, tentatively.

Mrs Tipton expressed her opinion of Holland's worthiness with a scornful humph. 'I admit that he behaved creditably, and I trust you thanked him with a proper condescension. But any connection beyond *that* . . .' She shook her head. 'It is clear to the meanest intelligence that he has no fortune, and what do we know about his character, after all? His manner was certainly rough. His family *is* unexceptionable on one side – Sir William Armitage of Storey's Court in Norfolk, you know.'

'Yes.'

'But they are distant relations, whereas these *Hollands* – tradesmen, I daresay, and some bird-witted Armitage girl made a ghastly misalliance. I have no patience with such people, and *you* certainly mustn't become entangled with a . . . *brewer*, or a publican. It would be a disaster. Now Mr Déprez seems nearer the mark. A very good income, and his friendship with Mr Somerville also counts in his favour. He is well looking, too, with a dignified address. Not like that other fellow – *he* looked as if he had been in a fight.'

The reference to Paul Déprez only heightened Mary's discomfort, and she flailed about for a reply. Captain Holland *had* been in a fight, after all.

Mrs Tipton brushed it aside. 'Yes, well, he had the look of a brawler. And besides, you should not concern yourself with such things as whether a man is handsome. Appearances can be deceptive, and it is always the woman who pays for her lack of foresight.'

'Yes, ma'am.'

The carriage slowed, lurched, and Mary almost slid off her seat. 'Ah,' said Mrs Tipton, glancing out of the window, 'we have arrived.'

Woolthorpe Manor was much larger than Lindham Hall and, to Mary's inexperienced eye, almost excessively grand. Lindham Hall had a comfortable, slightly down-at-heel quality about it, as if generations of Tiptons had become so used to the loose banister rail and the door to the second parlour that would not close unless it was lifted slightly and pushed into place, that they had ceased to regard them as needing repair. Mr Somerville's estate, by contrast, exuded good, well-funded stewardship, from its carefully landscaped grounds to its succession of elegant, beautifully furnished rooms. While impressive, Mary found this elegance somewhat overpowering. Everything was very pretty, but was there not rather a lot of it? Much of the furniture looked too delicate to use, and with so many mirrors and gilded surfaces the very rooms seemed to sparkle. As she trailed after the liveried footman she was self-conscious in her new gown. Perhaps this was how it felt when one was presented at Court, and she imagined making such a low, respectful curtsy as to be unable to rise again. Was there an official who helped one up in such circumstances? It must happen all the time, to rheumatic ladies, and one could not expect the king to hoist them to their feet again.

That image of His Majesty stayed with Mary for the length of a very long corridor. At the far end a door was opened to reveal a parlour where everything inanimate seemed either to be painted, inlaid, or swathed in rose-coloured silk, and here they joined the rest of the party. The flesh and blood inhabitants were not quite so gorgeous, consisting of their host and hostess, Mr Hunnable and his aunt, Mr Déprez, and an elderly gentleman named Goudge, who was a neighbour of the Somervilles. He and Mrs Tipton fell straightaway into conversation, but Mary felt somewhat at a loss. She was not very good at making general small talk, and Miss Hunnable was distinctly hard of hearing, so that it seemed to Mary that she was shouting her pointless remarks to the entire group.

Mr Déprez took her in to dinner, however, which was a consolation, and gradually the combination of reasonably good food, better wine, and the pleasant attentions of Mr Déprez had its effect upon her. She began to enjoy herself, coping very well with the confusing range of glasses and cutlery and the unusual courses on offer, and even forgetting the burden of her uncle's possible treachery. If asked her opinion, Mrs Tipton would have affirmed that she had not seen Mary in such good looks since making her acquaintance. But had she not always said that Mary was a very lovely girl, if only she would make the most of herself? And this was a very pretty scene, to be sure. Cornelia Somerville set a good table, one had to admit (although she looked like a pig going to war in that pink satin). Mary simply needed something to maintain her glow when she was *not* in such a pleasing setting. Mr Déprez, now, he was certainly attentive; perhaps *he* might provide a useful tonic?

Mary and Déprez were speaking of poetry, while the other gentlemen pursued a rambling discussion of the weather and the likelihood of the ground hardening to allow any decent sport before Christmas. 'Not that I am likely to profit by any change,' complained Mr Goudge, 'if this wretched gout does not leave off. I have a touch of it every so often.'

'Indeed, sir, I hope that you do not suffer very severely,' said Mrs Somerville. She was a large, pleasantly dull woman. When first apprised of Mary's arrival in the neighbourhood, she had wondered whether *she* ought to take charge of the girl. Before the thought had been completely formed, however, Mrs Tipton had asserted overlordship, and this, in the opinion of both women, had rendered any alternative arrangements irrelevant.

'What was that?' asked Miss Hunnable, bending anxiously to catch Mr Goudge's remark. 'What is the matter with him?'

'The *gout*, Aunt,' replied her nephew. 'Mr Goudge has a touch of the gout.'

'Ah. He had better have it out straightaway,' she nodded. There was such a close physical resemblance between Mr and Miss Hunnable that it occurred to Mary that Mr Hunnable might easily impersonate his aunt, were he to feign deafness and alter his usual mode of dress. The thought made her smile, and she wished that Captain Holland were present to share the joke before she remembered that she should not be thinking about him at all.

She fleetingly considered mentioning it to Mr Déprez, but decided that she did not know him well enough to risk it.

'Fortitude, Mrs S, fortitude,' said Mr Goudge, smiling gamely. 'The Romans made it their by-word, you know, and we cannot do better than to emulate them.'

'You needn't feel sorry for him,' decreed Mrs Tipton, 'for it is entirely his own fault. Men will ruin themselves with anything they have a taste for, and frequently it is port wine. One would think that with advancing age would come the wisdom to avoid excess, but this is rarely the case.'

'One would certainly think it, madam,' nodded Déprez, 'but are we not told "when men grow virtuous in their old age" – if you will allow me, sir – "they only make a sacrifice to God of the devil's leavings"?'

'Ha! At my age you cannot help being reminded of it,' cried Mr Goudge, 'but what was that about sacrifices to the devil? Better ask the parson about that.'

'Is it a druidical reference?' asked Mr Hunnable, blinking attentively.

Mary looked down at her plate. 'It *sounds* like our friend Mr Swift,' she suggested, only raising her eyes when she could trust herself to keep an even countenance, 'but I do not recognise the quotation.'

'You are right,' said Déprez, with a smile that conveyed several types of amusement. 'It comes from his *Thoughts on Various Subjects*. What a pity he is so little in fashion nowadays.'

From Swift, they turned to Pope, Dryden, and Gray – 'Ah, his "Elegy" is the great English poem,' enthused Déprez.

'I understand it was a favourite of General Wolfe,' said Mary, 'a very heroic gentleman. He said that he would

240

rather have written Gray's "Elegy" than capture Quebec, which he did in the year '59.'

'In that wish I believe he had the sympathy of the other fellow, the French commander. What was his name? Montcalm? He would also have preferred his opponent to confine himself to literary endeavours,' laughed Déprez.

'Fancy reading poetry during a battle,' murmured Mrs Somerville. 'It hardly seems right, although they say that Frenchmen are very poetical.'

'No, no, my dear,' said Mr Somerville, 'you misunderstand. Wilson,' he motioned to his butler, 'the ladies' plates are empty. Help them to some more of the beef.'

As the sirloin made the rounds, followed closely by stewed venison, oyster loaves, fried celery, veal, and slices of turkey in prune sauce – and that was merely the first course – Déprez offered views on the dramatic productions he had attended during his recent stay in London. He confessed to having a great admiration for the stage, if an able company grappled with a work by one of the first class dramatists. When Mary admitted that she would like to see a London play, Déprez encouraged her. 'You will surely go to London, for the Season, and amuse yourself with concerts, and plays, and shopping. It is the principal ambition for young ladies of consequence, I believe, a Season in London.'

'You speak as one well acquainted with Town, sir. I take it that this is not your first visit to England?' asked Mr Goudge.

'No, sir. I spent some time in this country when I was a boy.'

'There was a Frenchman – two Frenchmen – living in Bury some few years ago,' said Mrs Tipton. 'Mr Brownlowe told me of them. Mr Brownlowe is my man of business,' she explained to Déprez, 'a very capable and respectable man,' this with a significant nod.

241

'And what account did Mr Brownlowe give of these two visitors?'

'Oh, I believe they were quite docile, biddable creatures,' she acknowledged, 'very interested in carrots.'

'I daresay the English practice of agriculture was superior to anything they had seen in France,' affirmed Mr Goudge, to murmurs of agreement from his neighbours.

'I remember them,' added Mr Somerville, 'the Count de la Rochefoucauld and his brother. And there was a third – a Pole, I think, or maybe a Russian. Capital fellows. Came to see some of our draught horses – punches, we call 'em, Miss Finch. Yes, and were mightily impressed. One of my tenants had a pair, absolutely unequalled for pulling power, and as sweet-tempered as any animals you could name. They put on a demonstration for those fellows and, well, they could hardly believe it.' He shook his head, remembering the occasion, and then his face clouded. 'I wonder where they are today. Dead, most likely, or turned Republican.'

The prospect of either of these fates having overtaken the two Frenchmen, and perhaps even the Pole or Russian, cast a pall over the conversation, and Mrs Somerville gestured frantically for the second course to be served. The swift arrival of tarts, a syllabub, jugged pigeons, a potato pudding, and anchovy toasts made a potent distraction, and Mrs Tipton's spirits, at least, were soon restored. She was aware, she said, that a great number of French noblemen and women, and even children, had been guillotined, but had many also professed sympathy with the new regime?

Mr Goudge thought they were bound to have done so to save their necks, although he considered it rather cowardly. 'They say that gentlemen have been afraid to appear properly dressed in the streets of Paris, for fear of being arrested and executed as aristocrats.'

'That is taking the tyranny of one's tailor too far, what?' chuckled Mr Somerville.

'Killing women and children in that horrible way,' shuddered his wife. 'I think they must be . . . What do *you* think, Mr Hunnable, from a theological point of view.'

Mr Goudge answered on his behalf. 'Oh, they threw aside religion when they did away with the monarchy and everything else that was decent and honourable. That was the whole point of their revolution. Out with the old and in with the new – and don't I hope they may like it!'

'That is the worst of your foreigners, you know,' affirmed Mr Somerville. 'They will set upon these wild schemes – there is no stopping them – and then, when they come a cropper – as was perfectly clear would happen from the start – they have no backbone for it. In fact, they quite lose their heads, ha ha!'

'And this war will be the same,' Mrs Tipton agreed.

'Oh, yes, ma'am,' said Mr Goudge. 'Without a doubt.'

'Amen,' intoned Mr Hunnable.

Mary had long since stopped eating, and as she pushed her food about on her plate it seemed as if her compatriots were engaged in a closely fought competition to see which of them could make the most tactless remarks. She was reminded very strongly of the raucous patrons at the Great White Horse. Turning to Déprez, who accepted everything with an easy tolerance, she asked, 'Do you find it at all awkward to be in England, Mr Déprez, now that we are at war with France?'

'Awkward? No, Miss Finch, not in the least. But why do you ask?'

'I beg your pardon,' said Mary, reddening, 'but I had imagined . . . is not Déprez a French name?'

He shrugged his shoulders. 'My grandfather came from Montreuil and my grandmother from Hampshire. You are surprised to see in me a countryman? But in truth I am a West Indian. Both my father and I were born in St Lucia, and when this war is over, and one can make a decent living there again without one's house being knocked about one's ears, then I shall return.'

'And in the meantime you will remain in England?' asked Mrs Tipton.

Déprez thought this very likely, for where could one go? 'The Continent of Europe is too dangerous for one such as myself, assuming it were permitted to undertake the journey. *I* am not a . . . man of the sword, and if one travels one is obliged to take up that occupation. I think it best that I stay here for some considerable time. Perhaps I shall visit my cousins in Hampshire. They live in a place called Minsted. Do you know it, Miss Finch?'

She did not, and they informed each other of the respective merits of Hampshire and Somerset, and of Bath, in particular, where Mary had grown up. Déprez knew nothing of her particular circumstances, other than that she had been a schoolmistress, and the calm, uncomplaining account she gave of her straightened childhood and the death of her parents strengthened his good opinion of her. He even experienced an unfamiliar pang of tenderness. 'We have felt very sorry for what you have suffered in coming to Suffolk, if you will excuse that liberty,' he murmured.

Mary's answering smile sent a warning to Mrs Tipton – even the most useful tonic could prove too potent – and she rapped her stick sharply against the floor. 'Yes, yes,' she demanded, 'but what of the campaign against the villains who attacked Miss Finch in her uncle's house? I trust the forces of the law are not resting upon their inconsiderable laurels? What is being done?'

'Not at all, ma'am,' began Mr Somerville, 'that is to say, I have learned something about that fellow Tracey, although perhaps the dinner table is not the best place to mention it.'

'Nonsense,' scoffed Mrs Tipton. 'Speak out, if you please. We shall not be shocked.' She gestured to indicate that she spoke for womankind, or at least for those representatives present at Woolthorpe Manor.

Mr Somerville cleared his throat and said that for several days before the accident, Tracey had visited the Great White Horse Hotel and seemed to be waiting for someone – a 'confederate'. He paused to give his listeners time to appreciate the significance of that word, and Mr Goudge promptly supplied the appropriate question. Why 'confederate'? Was this fellow Tracey – and here Mr Goudge amended his vocabulary in deference to womankind – not quite the thing?

Mr Somerville said that he used the term because the late William Tracey was well known to the Essex magistrates. He had been a thief, trickster, and all-round petty criminal, and he was bound to have confederates.

Mary was silent for a moment, toying with her fruit knife. 'Do you think that Mr Tracey might have had something to do with the smugglers at White Ladies? If they *were* smugglers, of course.'

Mr Somerville considered this. 'Might have done, I suppose, but a rascal like Tracey could have turned his hand to anything.'

'Yes, of course, only he must have . . . stolen my uncle's watch, and—'

'Ah yes, I was forgetting that, and the key. Good thinking! Perhaps he *was* part of the gang.'

Mary's heart sank. Part of the gang! A gang that might have included her uncle! Perhaps he *gave* William Tracey

245

the key to White Ladies, and the watch. Perhaps they had been good friends, dozing before the fire on winter evenings, talking about smuggling and composing coded messages for their *confederates*. Then she heard Déprez's voice, low and urgent, and felt the touch of his hand on her arm. 'Miss Finch, are you all right?'

'Yes, yes. I was just—'

'And I'll wager a guinea none of you can guess what Tracey had in his coat pocket,' continued Mr Somerville, beaming at the assembly.

Mrs Somerville frowned worriedly, but her husband raised his hand to reassure her. 'Never you fear, my dear,' he smiled, 'it was a section of Blackstone's *Commentaries*! Can you imagine?'

Mr Goudge appreciated the humour. 'Very good, sir, upon my word. What better reading matter for a confirmed scoundrel?'

'But sir,' urged Mrs Somerville, 'you mustn't be so hard on the poor man – surely this is proof of his good intentions. He must have wished to reform his character, if he carried a commentary with him.'

Mr Goudge gaped at her for a moment, and then smiled fondly. 'No, Mrs S, you mistake – though your generous feelings do you credit! We do not refer to a . . . *devotional* work, you know—'

'It is a book about the law, ma'am,' replied Mary, almost under her breath. '*The Commentaries on the Laws of England*.'

'What was that?' cried Miss Hunnable. 'I wish you would speak up, Miss Finch. What are you talking about?'

'The greatest law book in England, Miss Hunnable,' boomed Mr Somerville down the table. 'And I don't know whether my dear wife does not have the right of it, in a way, for that book is a godsend to those of

246

us who must administer the law. I will not call it the magistrate's Bible, at least not in Mr Hunnable's presence, but the phrase is apt, I believe. It has helped me out of a tricky situation more than once, at quarter sessions, when Henry Rushmore tried to play the lawyer with the rest of us. A line from Blackstone shut him up, I can tell you.'

'Lawyers of any degree are the greatest nuisance,' agreed Mrs Tipton.

'A book about the law,' murmured Mrs Somerville, thankful now that she had not ventured a comment on the 'Reverend' Blackstone. 'But how did *you* come to know of such a thing, Miss Finch?' One did not like to seem critical of a guest, but a knowledge of magisterial matters seemed, well, rather an odd accomplishment for a young woman in polite society.

Mary sensed something of her hostess's anxiety and therefore answered in as casual a manner as she could, while still endeavouring to speak loud enough to reach Miss Hunnable. 'My father owned several law books, ma'am, including Blackstone's *Commentaries*. He had studied for the bar, at one time, and reckoned that the *Commentaries* were a good general introduction to the subject.' She resisted the temptation to add that she had actually read some of the hallowed text.

'Well, well, perhaps that fellow Tracey was also meaning to change his career,' cried Mr Goudge, 'though they say that barristers are the worst kind of thieves, for they rob you *and* expect a fee!'

Mr Goudge and Mr Somerville erupted into laughter at this sally, and Mary had to raise her voice again to make herself heard. Did Mr Somerville recall which part of the *Commentaries* Mr Tracey possessed? 'For the work comprises a number of volumes, I believe?'

'Indeed it does – four hefty volumes,' Mr Somerville replied, still smiling. 'But Tracey only had a few pages – torn from another man's copy, I daresay. Part of the section on civil juries – I recognised it at once.' He chuckled again. 'Fellow ought to have read the chapters on the criminal process instead.'

'Yes, indeed!' laughed Mr Goudge.

Mary returned to her fruit knife, turning it over and over on the tablecloth, and seeming to study the gleam of reflected candlelight created by the motion. Again the confidential voice of Mr Déprez intruded into her thoughts. 'Forgive me, but you have grown very pale. Perhaps a glass of wine?' He moved to fill her glass.

'Thank you, no,' she murmured. 'I am really quite well. It is only—' She studied him for a moment, thinking hard. It was a risk, of course, to confide in him, but she needed help. 'When we . . . leave the table, might I have a private word?'

He nodded slightly, and even Mrs Tipton did not catch his whispered, 'Of course.'

'Well, it sounds like the passing of Tracey was all to the good, but I do not envy you your task of bringing the survivors to justice, Somerville,' said Mr Goudge. 'I imagine they have made themselves scarce, what with the attack at White Ladies having caused such a rumpus.'

'Indeed,' agreed Déprez in a louder voice. 'And I understand that a considerable naval vessel has been seen in Hollesley Bay. That must surely dissuade them from any further villainy.'

'Very likely,' Mr Somerville agreed. 'Well, I daresay there will be some other mischief soon enough – poaching or thievery. It is all grist for the magistrate's mill, and there is nothing new under the sun when it comes to crime.

The Garden of Eden and so forth. Am I correct, Mr Hunnable?'

'Yes, I am afraid so,' Mr Hunnable agreed. 'We live in a fallen world.'

14

'*Encoded documents?*' repeated Déprez in an incredulous whisper. 'How did—'

Mary glanced around. '*Shh,*' she warned. 'The others will notice and ask what we are talking about.'

'Ah, yes indeed,' muttered Déprez, and in quite a different voice asked, 'Dr Johnson, I believe, makes the very same point – in one of his *Rambler* essays, or perhaps *Rasselas?*'

'Yes, it was the second essay of *The Rambler.*' Mary was conscious that Mrs Tipton was watching her from across the way and so spoke somewhat at random. 'We had a copy of the bound essays at home.' The rest were talking amongst themselves – debating the possibility of a rubber of whist – but it was impossible wholly to escape Mrs Tipton's scrutiny. After rising from the dinner table the ladies had proceeded to a richly furnished sitting room, where Mrs Somerville produced cups of tea. Mary had waited in tense anticipation for the arrival of the gentlemen, and when Mr Déprez joined her on the settee she wasted no time in telling her story – at least in its essentials.

'And Blackstone's *Commentaries* contains the key – I am

certain of it,' she urged. 'The number sequences in the documents always begin with either a one or a four, and there are four volumes of *Commentaries*. The sequences *must* relate to something on particular pages in one or other of those volumes. When we examine those pages we will be able to understand what the encoded documents say.'

'But the documents themselves – where are they?'

'At Lindham Hall.'

'Somewhere safe, I trust?'

'Yes, of course. I know that I ought to inform Mr Somerville, but—'

'No, no,' agreed Déprez. 'This is not the time – it is better to be cautious. Afterward things can be explained to him.' He nodded thoughtfully. 'So . . . you believe that Mr Tracey had *two* keys in his pocket.'

'Yes. He must have been intending to write a coded message, or perhaps he had come to the Great White Horse to receive one. In either case he needed those pages from Blackstone.'

Déprez nodded again slowly, and appeared to examine the porcelain jar on the table in front of him. He started to speak when a servant appeared with a tray of sweets. Mary fumed in silent exasperation, but Déprez seemed pleased by the interruption. He offered advice on the various delicacies, and encouraged Mary to indulge in a selection of sugared fruits and Naples biscuits. He had a decided sweet tooth, he admitted, and quickly filled his own plate.

When they were alone again, however, he added in a lower voice, 'I must tell you, Miss Finch, that I am . . . very interested in these documents, more so than you might imagine. And you . . . think you can decode them?'

Something in his expression, suggesting both urgency and uncertainty, inspired her to answer with confidence. 'Yes – once I am able to examine the *Commentaries.*'

He hesitated. 'If I could *see* the documents—'

'But that cannot happen until tomorrow. Whereas, if I had a copy of the *Commentaries* – just volume one – I could begin working on the code tonight.'

'Yes, perhaps.'

Mary pressed her point. Very likely there was a copy there, at Woolthorpe Manor – Mr Somerville had acknowledged how important it was – if only they could lay their hands on it. And it could be done. She was not familiar with the Woolthorpe Manor library, and in any case she could not easily leave the sitting room. For Déprez, however, it was a different matter. He could . . . borrow the volume for her without the least difficulty.

Déprez bit into an almond tart and chewed meditatively. 'You know, even if you are right about the numbers being references to pages in this book, using it to decode the documents may still not be so simple.'

'No, but I would like to try.'

'Very well.'

They agreed upon a plan. Déprez would shortly excuse himself and go in search of the first volume of the *Commentaries*. If successful, he would hide it under the rear-facing seat in Mrs Tipton's carriage. The rest would be up to Mary.

'And I shall see you tomorrow?' she asked, her eyes shining with excitement. 'To report my progress?'

He smiled in reply. 'Oh, yes. That is certain.'

Some time later Déprez was able to escape the sitting room on the pretence of locating Miss Hunnable's shawl. A grim, sombrely dressed figure met him in the passageway and together they turned, not toward the gaudy parlour, where Miss Hunnable's shawl had fallen behind a chair, but toward the library.

'You are still determined to carry on?' asked Hicks.

'I am. We *must* encourage Captain Holland to return to us.'

'We should never have let him leave!'

'And how, precisely, ought we to have restrained him?'

Hicks frowned, and shrugged an apology for his outburst. 'But this . . . rigmarole to try to get him back – do you think it wise?'

Déprez raised his hands questioningly, but his tone was urgent. 'No, perhaps not, but I am more nearly convinced that it will succeed, and that is the important thing. I tell you, Hicks, she is a girl in a thousand – with such a quick understanding.'

'She found the documents, then?'

'Yes, of course she found them, but it is her performance tonight that gives me confidence. Old Somerville did nothing more than mention Tracey's having a scrap of the *Commentaries* in his pocket, and she grasped its significance in a flash. And she is so keen! I doubt she will fail us now.'

'No, I expect you're right,' said Hicks, gloomily. 'It is only . . . it seems so underhand. I wish we did not have to involve her.'

'Ah, I thought she would touch your old heart, for all your jibes at me! Naturally, I do not wish her ill – far from it – but in our present circumstances we are in need of an ally, and she is ideally qualified. Holland is not a fool, you know, and enough has happened to raise his suspicions. We must tempt him, therefore, but in a way that he is unlikely to suspect.'

'Yes, yes, I know. But I do not like it.'

'It *is* distasteful,' Déprez agreed, 'but our object is sufficiently important to risk a bit of indigestion.'

It was a cold, sombre drive from Woolthorpe Manor to Lindham Hall, with only a trace of moonlight filtering through the carriage window and Mrs Tipton dozing on the seat opposite, but Mary was intensely awake and eager. She could feel the promised volume under the cushion beside her, and a sense of excitement, curiosity, and determination grew each time she placed her hand on the all-important bulge. What information did the documents really contain? How was the code to be deciphered? Soon, hopefully, she would have the answer to both questions. Blackstone's *Commentaries*. Blackstone's *Commentaries*. The words repeated themselves in her head to the rhythm of the horse's hooves. Then the synchronisation was lost as Cuff chirruped his team, and Mary smiled approvingly. For her the journey could not be over fast enough.

Thank goodness the fashion is for oversized capes, thought Mary as she entered Lindham Hall clutching the volume under the considerable folds. There was a slight disturbance while Mrs Tipton was divested of hat, scarf, shawl, and pelisse by a yawning Peggy, and Mary took advantage of this to arrange her cloak – another of Miss Cheadle's creations – over her arm and hurry upstairs. In her bedchamber at last, she quickly cleared her dressing table of combs and hair ribbons, and instead set out a more useful array of pens, paper, ink, and the four encoded documents, with the pale leather-bound volume of the *Commentaries* in the centre. Trimming the wick of her candle to produce a more even light, she set to work.

The four encoded documents each included a sequence of three numbers: 1, 217, 12; 1, 247, 16; 1, 299, 9; and 4, 412, 24. If she had guessed correctly, volume one of the *Commentaries* should enable her to decode three of the four documents, with the crucial information contained on pages 217, 247, and 299.

She turned to the first of these. There did not seem

anything remarkable about the page itself. What was the twelfth word? *Treason!* She almost knocked over the bottle of ink in her eagerness to find the next clue – the sixteenth word on page 247 – and was immediately faced with a problem. The first word on that page was divided – should she count it or not? If she did, the sixteenth word was *formerly* and if she did not it was *shewn*. Neither was as thrilling as her first discovery, but she tried to be hopeful and turned to page 299. Unfortunately, the ninth word on that page was a wholly unsatisfactory *the*. She wrote the words *formerly the treason* and *the treason shewn* on a sheet of paper before running a line through them. How could a single word, even one so interesting as *treason*, decode an entire document? She had taken the wrong track entirely.

Turning back to page 217, she read the sentence that began on line 12.

A queen dowager is the widow of the king, and as fuch enjoys moft of the privileges belonging to her as queen confort.

On page 247 she found the following on line 16:

In refpect to civil fuits, all the foreign jurifts agree, that neither an embaffador, nor any of his train or comites, can be profecuted for any debt or contract in the courts of that kingdom wherein he is fent to refide.

And then turned to page 299, where line 9 contained:

The other antient levies were in the nature of a modern land tax; for we may trace up the original of that charge as high as to the introduction of our military tenures when every tenant of a knight's fee was bound, if called upon, to attend the king in his army for forty days in every year.

She read each of them again. Two of the sentences mentioned the king, but otherwise there did not seem to be anything significant in their substance. Certainly there was no common feature amongst all three. The importance, therefore, must lie elsewhere – in the letters themselves? She tried adding up the letters in each word in the first sentence. That produced a number sequence, but to what end? And besides, she reasoned, such a process would be too complicated; it would be too easy to make a mistake. She felt sure that the security of the code lay in the identity of the book, which would be very difficult to guess – certainly she had not been able to do so! Once the book was known, however, the code was probably very straightforward.

The code may be straightforward, she mused, *but if these sentences from the Commentaries provide the keys to the three documents, how do they work? The code uses letters, but not in their proper order. Therefore, each key sentence must provide that order. To do that, the sentence must contain all of the letters in the alphabet – or at least, it must contain all of the letters in the particular coded message with which it is associated.* She shook her head. *No, all of the letters, otherwise one would have to know what was in the message before one could apply the key and decode it.*

That meant there were two alphabets – the 'real' one, and the one that the code used. She looked again at the shortest of the Blackstone sentences – could it provide a code alphabet? She wrote out the sentence and crossed out all the repetitions. So that from:

A queen dowager is the widow of the king, and as fuch enjoys moft of the privileges belonging to her as queen confort

she produced:

A Q U E N D O W G R I S T H F K C J Y M P V L B

which left her two letters short. How could she plot the letters in that sentence against the real alphabet if the former only contained twenty-four letters? Which letters should she leave out? The last two? Z was not very often used, but Y? That did not seem very likely. Perhaps X and Z, the two letters actually omitted from the 'Queen dowager' sentence. Those were very uncommon letters unless one were writing about the ancient Greeks, and it did not seem likely that English smugglers would be writing about Zeno or Xenophon! It was certainly worth a try. So she matched the 'Queen dowager' alphabet to the real one,

A	Q	U	E	N	D	O	W	G	R	I	S	T	H	F	K	C	J	Y	M	P	V	L	B
A	B	C	D	E	F	G	H	I	J	K	L	M	N	O	P	Q	R	S	T	U	V	W	Y

and turned to the relevant coded document.

It took only a few tries to establish that her plan was not going to work. The coded passage began with the letters D U C N P F C N D D N D A C N, which produced a similarly incoherent F C Q E U O Q E F F E F A C D according to the alphabet in the 'Queen dowager' sentence.

She had clearly made a mistake, but she was also sure

that she was almost right. The 'Queen dowager' sentence had twenty-four different letters – was that significant? She looked at the other two sentences. By performing the same routine of copying them down and crossing off all of the repeated letters she came up with the same number, although the omitted letters were not the same. Might that mean that her first idea was correct? The omitted letters in the Blackstone sentences were simply not in the associated coded messages? No, probably not, as one of the omitted letters was L, which seemed far too common. Perhaps she was not so close to the solution as she had thought.

She took a deep breath and sat back in her chair. Staring at the letters had made her brain feel heavy, sluggish. A glance at her uncle's watch revealed the lateness of the hour; no wonder she felt tired. And cold; the embers of the fire were glowing faintly, their warmth long overwhelmed by the seeping night air.

Such had been her eagerness to tackle the decoding that she had begun immediately upon returning from Woolthorpe Manor, without even stopping to hang up her cloak or change out of her new clothes. Now, when she rose to stretch her cramped muscles, she felt not only sleepy, but also jaded and uncomfortable. She would just get ready for bed, she decided, and perhaps a new idea would occur to her.

There was a rule at Lindham Hall that fires should not be added to after ten o'clock, except under extraordinary circumstances. One ought to be in bed by ten o'clock, and with sufficient bedclothes one ought to be perfectly warm. An appendage carelessly left outside the bedclothes, of course, was subject to whatever glacial conditions might exist in the bedchamber generally. Thus far Mary had not challenged this rule; she was used to far more austere conditions at Mrs Bunbury's, where blankets were thinner and draughts more pervasive. Tonight, however, she built up the fire almost recklessly. If ever there were extraordinary circumstances, they were happening now.

As she tidied away her clothes and brushed her hair, Mary tried hard *not* to think of the documents waiting for her on the other side of the room. But it was a very difficult task. Everything seemed, sooner or later, to bring her round to them again – White Ladies, her inheritance, even Mrs Bunbury's school. For, of course, if she had not left Mrs Bunbury's, she would never have encountered Mr Tracey, never come to White Ladies, and never become mixed up in all of this.

Well, there was no point thinking about that now. Whatever it was, she was certainly mixed up in it. She gazed thoughtfully at herself in a hand mirror, and gradually her mind returned to the evening's dinner party. With the party came Mr Déprez. He was indeed very handsome – although apparently she ought not to concern herself with such things – but he was also intelligent, thoughtful, and they had several interests in common. Without meaning to she imagined a similar conversation with Captain Holland on the subject of poetry, and could not help smiling. If she had mentioned the works of Pope to *him*, he would probably have thought she meant the Pope of Rome! *He* would not have read *Rasselas*, or been able to discuss Addison's essay 'On the Pleasures of Imagination'. Mr Déprez, on the other hand, seemed to know about art, and music, and literature, and the theatre . . . Even as these thoughts formed, however, she experienced a pang of guilt. Surely it was not fair to compare Captain Holland and Mr Déprez, and besides, was not the Captain also very clever – in a different way? He probably knew all sorts of

259

military things, which were highly significant, only they did not tend to be discussed at dinner parties. And he had saved her at White Ladies – that was more important than poetry, after all!

This sudden turmoil of feelings made her toss the mirror on to the bed and walk purposefully up and down the room. She informed herself that she was a very silly girl to be worrying about two men whom she hardly knew and who, in a month or so, would have disappeared completely from her life. How could she be so foolish? And why *compare* them, for goodness' sake? Captain Holland was unlikely ever to return to Lindham, and Mr Déprez . . . well, it was all castles in the air.

She sat down at the dressing table once more and considered her fruitless jottings. Three keys – for the Blackstone sentences *must* provide the keys to the three coded documents, mustn't they? – but each sentence contained an alphabet of only twenty-four letters. How to make up the difference to twenty-six? Her gaze fell upon the volume of the *Commentaries*, which was opened at page 104, and she began reading at random about the islands subject to the crown of Great Britain that were comprised within a neighbouring county. One thing contained in another. Suddenly an idea occurred to her. Rather than omitting two letters from the real alphabet, why not add them to other letters?

The typeface of the *Commentaries* gave her the clue: the long S and the F looked very similar and *might* be considered a pair. Was there another? Her heart began to beat faster. 'Think, think, think!' she said, palms pressed together, tapping gently against her lips. 'Think.'

She sat back in her chair, smiling faintly. I and J could be interchanged – not in English, but in Latin. Was it likely that a smuggler's code would incorporate a peculiarity of the Latin language? Perhaps not, but neither was it impossible. Seizing a fresh sheet of paper she quickly constructed a new 'code' alphabet using the letters from the 'Queen dowager' sentence.

A	Q	U	E	N	D	O	W	G	R	I	S	T	H	F	K	C	J	Y	M	P	V	L	B
A	B	C	D	E	F/S	G	H	I/J	K	L	M	N	O	P	Q	R	T	U	V	W	X	Y	Z

And when she applied it to the first few letters of the particular coded document, D U C N P F C N D D N D A C N became F/S C R E W P R E F/S F/S E F/S A R E, and, after further consideration, SCREW PRESSES ARE.

She had done it. The code was broken.

Mary was not the only person kept awake that night by secret messages. In a quiet, respectable village north of London, a quiet, respectable man stood outside his house, accustoming his eyes to the dark. He carefully buttoned his greatcoat, adjusted his hat, and then locked the door behind him. After he had put on his gloves he checked the door again and patted his pocket. Hearing the reassuring chink of his keys, he set off. His journey had no particular object other than deliberation, for he thought better when he was walking. Now he walked steadily, silently past his neighbours' darkened windows. He carried his head with a characteristic twist that indicated he was thinking deeply.

His neighbours would certainly have been surprised by the tenor of his thoughts, which concerned a message he had received a few hours earlier. A single sheet of paper, folded and sealed to form its own envelope, and slid by an unknown hand into the gap between the sash windows in his study. He often received messages of this kind, tersely worded instructions or queries, easily translated so long as one had the correct alphabetical key and applied it carefully, but never a message like this one.

OPERATION TO CEASE. SERIOUS RISK OF COMPROMISE. HOLD FAST AND AWAIT FURTHER INSTRUCTIONS.

He asked himself unanswerable questions as he walked. What could have happened? How had he been compromised? He was certain *he* had done nothing wrong. Perhaps someone else had been careless, further up the chain . . . undisciplined men with slipshod habits – very likely drinkers. He had no patience with men who could not control themselves, and now he fumed at the injustice of it all. But what did it matter, if *he* was in danger as a result? And what was going to happen now? 'Further instructions', what did that mean? Would he have to leave his home? His comfortable life? A life so apparently placid and ordinary that no one would ever suspect he had any . . . untoward pursuits?

This led to a more frightening thought. He had heard stories of agents who had become . . . difficult, awkward in some way, or had been seen to pose a risk to their masters. It had been easier to get rid of them than to extricate them. Of course, these *were* only stories, but he had heard them, and his heart beat faster as he remembered them now. Then he frowned and consciously slowed his pace. Nonsense, he scolded himself. The warning had been sent to protect him. If *they* thought—

He stopped abruptly at the brief, scuffling sound somewhere behind him, and darted into a doorway. For a heavy man he was light on his feet. A fierce yowl and the sight of two low grey shapes streaking past made him breathe easier, and he stepped cautiously out of his hiding place. Damned fool to be afraid of a couple of tomcats. He altered his course, however, to avoid the tavern up ahead. It would doubtless be closed at this time of night, but there was no sense courting danger. There were such things as robbers, after all, and trouble-makers, even in respectable neighbourhoods.

What to do, that was the question. The message said 'Hold fast', but did that mean he should go to work on Monday morning as usual? If there was only a *risk* of compromise that must mean that nothing had actually been discovered, and if he diverged suddenly from his normal course that might confirm any suspicions. But who held these suspicions? Home Office spies? Agents connected with the military? Every government, whether Royalist or Republican, had its 'confidential departments' and 'offices of public security', whose job it was to root out enemies of the state. Working in the shadows and often scarcely acknowledged by the official organs of government, the men employed in such departments and offices tended to be extremely tenacious once they had picked up a trail. Perhaps even now they were closing in, or were waiting for him to turn up to . . . arrest him. A proper fool he should look if he walked blindly into a trap, and he prided himself on *not* being a fool.

He skirted the green and turned back toward his house. The cold was seeping into him despite his steady pace, and he thought about his cosy sitting room. A warm drink and half an hour in front of the fire, and then to bed. There was nothing like a good night's sleep to calm the senses. That was what he needed; he would think about the rest tomorrow.

The front of his house was visible from the top of the

lane. His hand fished into his pocket, searching for his latchkey. Coins, handkerchief, a stub of pencil. Why was it always the last— He stared at the light visible from an upstairs window; his bedroom. Surely he had not left a candle burning?

He crossed quickly to the other side of the lane, his gaze still fixed on his bedroom window. The curtains were drawn, but . . . A slight movement, a shadow, and then the light dimmed and returned, as if someone had passed between it and the window. Oh God! They had come for him!

For a moment he stood frozen with fear, then he crouched down and scuttled behind a low wall. He leaned back against it, suddenly breathless, as the sweat poured down his round, gleaming face. Gone were all thoughts of a good night's rest and a calm decision in the morning. He must get away – now – before someone saw him. A second fevered search of his pockets – yes, there was his wallet, thank God. But where to go? London? And how to get there at this hour?

Do not worry about that now, he told himself, *just go!* After a cautious glance first up the lane, and then down, he slipped quickly through the narrow gap between the houses opposite his own and disappeared into the dark.

15

Some people were not at their best first thing in the morning; they either looked or felt weary or bedraggled, and required several hours before they were fully sensible. Lady Armitage was not one of those. In a pale nightdress and robe, with an Indian shawl draped across her shoulders and a trim lace cap not quite concealing her golden curls, she presented an elegant image of dishabille. Her morning spirits were as refined as her dress, and as she sipped her chocolate and surveyed the garden from her dressing-room window they were in particularly fine trim. Ever since the children had left the nursery, she had taken the first meal of the day upstairs. She objected to their boisterous habits, which had resulted, at one time or another, in the introduction of dogs, snakes, and even freshly caught fish into the dining room. Not only did she prefer serenity, she also appreciated the opportunity to discuss important matters tête-à-tête with her husband before he was distracted by his own affairs.

'My dear,' she said, handing Sir William a plate of buttered toast, 'do you not think Susannah is in very fine looks since our return from Fordham?'

Sir William agreed, having a high opinion of his daughter's beauty on all occasions. Appreciating, however, that something more was required of him, he asked whether Lady Armitage could account for this particular degree of bloom. As he expected, she *was* able to account for it: Susannah and Lady Armitage had won the admiration of the Moltons, and their society had proved equally enjoyable.

'I did not know that *you* were such an admirer of Tom Molton's society, my dear.'

'Yes, well, I confess that I may have been rather harsh in the past, but you know he does encourage everyone to think him the merest countryman. He quite hides his light under a bushel. But I was pleased to find myself mistaken, and Jane Molton is a very sensible woman.'

'And young Mr Grantley Molton?' asked Sir William, smiling behind his napkin. 'I trust *he* was all that could be desired?'

'Well, my dear, I admit he is no phoenix – and do not think that I cannot see you smirking there – but he is a good creature, and so eminently suitable. And he fairly dotes upon Susannah.'

This last observation, while gratifying in itself, caused Sir William's smile to fade. He saw now where the conversation was tending, and he realised that his own failure would shortly be revealed. Despite his best intentions, he had not managed to 'have words' with Holland on the subject of Susannah, and this would undoubtedly displease his wife.

He was correct on every point, and yet her response was to pose questions to him as if she doubted his powers, and not merely those of execution. Had they not agreed that a marriage between Robert and Susannah was impossible? That unequal entanglements never succeeded? Surely, speaking privately to Robert was the kindest solution?

Could Sir William possibly have forgotten what happened to his cousin, Sophia? Did he wish to see Susannah entangled in a similar catastrophe? 'I know you think well of Robert – I do myself, in his own sphere. And you have done so much for him; you have been *more* than just. But we must consider Susannah first. She can do *much* better for herself.'

'Yes, yes,' he flailed, 'I daresay you are right. In fact—'

'*In fact*,' said Lady Armitage, with a steely glance, 'I am convinced that with only the slightest encouragement, her affection will be firmly settled upon Mr Grantley Molton. At one stage during our visit I was almost certain that they had come to an understanding – he was so very attentive – but I could not learn that anything actually happened. I am quite tranquil about her, however.'

'Well, that is a comfort,' grumbled Sir William. And he privately added that she could thank her stars that it was Susannah and not Charlotte whom they were endeavouring to manage. *Then* there would be an end to all tranquillity, if *she* wished to marry a penniless . . . But there must be no repetition of Sophia's tragedy, that was clear. Of course, Robert was not necessarily like his father, but one never knew. The apple did not fall far from the tree, after all. Sir William wondered who had come up with that expression in the first place. Newton, perhaps? He smiled at his little joke and even contemplated revealing it, but his thoughts trailed off as he perceived that his wife was still speaking.

'Yes, I think his coming *here* would be quite the thing,' she concluded.

'Hmm? Coming where?'

'Why to Storey's Court, of course. Did I not say?'

'No, you did not. Young Molton, do you mean? Coming

here? Good God, I thought we were only just rid of the fellow. He is like a dashed octopus.'

'Octopus? Whatever do you mean?'

Sir William gestured vaguely. He wished he had not made that last remark; it sounded distinctly odd. 'Clinging – you know . . . tentacles, or feelers, or whatever they are called.'

'Please, Sir William, do not excite yourself,' urged Lady Armitage, who looked as if she also thought it distinctly odd. 'Nothing is settled. It merely occurs to me that it would be quite a good idea not to leave things . . . up in the air. Susannah will feel more comfortable receiving a proposal here, in her own home, and if I were to write and suggest . . . merely a casual visit. He would be quite keen to accept, I have no doubt of that.'

'No, there is no stopping these young Romeos. It is dashed hard on poor Bobs, however, the other fellow being welcomed with open arms while he is at home. It must be . . . salt in the wound.'

'He shall survive it,' shrugged Lady Armitage, and she confirmed that she would write to Mr Grantley Molton straightaway. In the meantime, it was vital that Holland and Susannah not be placed too much in each other's company, and certainly not without supervision. Anything like a declaration at this stage would be extremely unfortunate. Lady Armitage was relying on her husband to take the necessary steps. She looked at him meaningfully before condescending to refill his cup.

'Yes, yes, very well,' Sir William frowned, eager to have done with the whole business.

While Sir William and Lady Armitage were shaping the destinies of the junior members of their family circle, Mary Finch and Mrs Tipton were apparently employed in less masterful pursuits. This was because they were among the congregation of St John the Divine waiting for Mr Hunnable to find the place in his notes and begin his sermon. Appearances, however, could be deceiving. In its long history, the Tipton family pew had been the scene of joy, grief, boredom, and even a certain degree of religious enthusiasm, but rarely had it witnessed such a level of contained and wholly secular excitement as on that particular Sunday morning. Having discovered the secret of the *Commentaries*' alphabets and translated the coded documents Mary had actually enjoyed a good night's sleep, but now she was eager to take the next step. Mr Hunnable's remarks on the Good Samaritan passed unheeded, and she had to resist a growing temptation to look behind her and see whether Mr Déprez had entered the church. When they rose to sing 'Awake Our Souls!' she *did* look, but could see nothing beyond the broad expanse of waistcoat belonging to the man immediately behind her. He took her glance as a criticism of his singing and, being of a truculent nature, increased the volume of his performance in consequence.

At last the service drew to a close, and Mr Hunnable offered the benediction. Mary turned swiftly in an attempt to see past the roaring man, and would have slid along the pew had not a firm grasp on her forearm dissuaded her. She turned back with a sheepish smile and helped Mrs Tipton rise. 'Have a care,' warned that lady, as Mary handed her the canes. 'If you lose your head you will surely lose everything else.'

'Yes, of course,' Mary acknowledged, striving to keep her tone demure even as she nodded meaningfully at Mr Déprez, whom she had picked out several rows behind. 'I beg your pardon.'

'He is very attentive, to be sure,' observed Mrs Tipton,

'and you might do worse than the richest man in St Lucia
– or so Mr Somerville tells me.'

'What? Oh.' Mary had almost forgotten that aspect of
the situation. She remembered it more keenly when
Déprez smiled at her and made a slight gesture toward
the rear of the church. The prospect of impressing him
gave an additional lustre to her information. 'Excuse me,
Mrs Tipton, but . . . I would not like to do anything *excep-
tional*, of course, but do you think it would be all right
if I were to . . . take a turn with Mr Déprez in the churchyard? Just a turn.'

Mrs Tipton pursed her lips. 'Very well,' she sighed, 'but
no giggling or fooling about. You mustn't carry on a flir-
tation in a churchyard, after all, and certainly not on a
Sunday! Peggy? Where is Peggy?' And when Peggy had
slipped forward to escort her mistress, Mrs Tipton continued
to Mary in an authoritative whisper, 'Now, do not make
a fool of yourself! You are not a milkmaid, after all. I shall
wait for you on the porch. Peggy, mind my shawl. I can
feel it slipping.'

Nodding in acknowledgement, Mary hurried toward
the south door. She blushed at the curious glances from
those she passed, but they did not make her stop. Déprez
met her in the vestibule, and there was a brief delay as
they thanked Mr Hunnable for his sermon and exchanged
a few words with Mrs Somerville. Then they walked
quickly outside and around to the churchyard. A cold
wind was blowing, but Mary found it exhilarating.

'Well?' asked Déprez, the moment they were alone. 'Do
you have them?'

'Yes,' Mary replied, smiling, 'the originals *and* the translations.'

'You have done it?' He stopped short and stared at her.
'Let me see.'

270

The breeze ruffled her cloak as she produced several folded sheets of paper from her muff and handed them to him. As his expression changed from scepticism to surprise, Mary crowded beside him, the story of how she had decoded the documents tumbling out. He held up his hand for a moment, trying to read each paper, but then he smiled and said, 'No, please, tell me.'

He listened attentively, growing more impressed with her intelligence and tenacity. It was precisely how he would have solved the problem, and *she* had no experience with this sort of thing. 'You did not by any chance teach cryptography at your inestimable school, did you?' he teased.

It was not really very funny, but he was smiling and so she laughed. She sensed that her efforts had surprised him, and she was basking in the warmth of his admiration. 'Oh, no,' she assured him, smiling, 'but once I realised that there were two *combinations*, rather than *omissions*, it was quite easy. Each document had a different key, on the three different pages, but they were all organised according to the same principle.'

'Yes, quite easy,' he affirmed, shaking his head. 'Miss Finch, I am amazed that – no, I commend you. It was very well done.' He glanced again at the coded originals, and then her translations. Then he lowered the final sheet and looked sharply at her. 'Do you know what these papers concern?'

SCREW PRESSES ARE GIVING TROUBLE AGAIN. NOT MERELY THE DANGER OF THE PROCESS BUT CONCERNS ABOUT CONSISTENCY OF THE CAKE PRODUCED. THERE IS TALK OF A MORE DELICATE THREADING DEVICE TO INCREASE AND EVEN OUT

TENSION WHICH MAY SOLVE THE SECOND PROBLEM BUT SAFETY FEARS REMAIN AND MAY BE INCREASED IF THE MECHANISM IS IMPROVED. A LIKELY NEXT TARGET FOR OFFICIAL RECONSIDERATION.

GLOOM STOVES ARE TO BE REPLACED BY NEW STEAM PIPE APPARATUS. NEW STOVES SAID TO DRY CORNED POWDER MORE QUICKLY AND EVENLY. PLAN OF STOVE TO FOLLOW IF POSSIBLE. NOTE THAT PRESSURE MAY PROVOKE FAULT. A SERIOUS RISK FEARED. REQUEST ORDERS TO CONFIRM OR REMOVE.

RUMOURS OF RENEWED COMMUNICATIONS WITH BISHOP WATSON FOLLOWING FURTHER TESTS ON IMPROVED CYLINDRICAL DISTILLATION. RESULTS SAID TO BE SURPRISINGLY GOOD. TINKLER, BRIDGES, PIGOU TO ATTEND DEMONSTRATIONS AT WALTHAM ABBEY. MOST PROMISING WORK NOW BEING DONE ON ALDER AND WILLOW. CHARCOAL PITS VERY LITTLE USED NOW IN ADVANCED MILLS. RECENT RESULTS

BATTLE	10	12	10
DOUBLE BATTLE	16	15	18
ORDNANCE LARGE GRAIN	13	12	12
ORDNANCE FINE GRAIN	23	20	24
EXCISE	21	20	20

STANDARD MORTAR

'Not really,' she admitted, glancing at them again, although she knew very well what they said. 'I thought that they might have something to do with weapons, but—'

Again her words surprised him. 'How can you tell that?' he demanded.

'The reference to ordnance. I remember that Captain Holland used that word when he was talking about the Woolwich arsenal. I do not understand what is meant by "cake", or why a bishop should be involved, but is not a mortar a type of gun, or perhaps a cannon?'

'Yes, indeed,' Déprez nodded. 'But how interesting that you should mention Captain Holland. Did he . . . say anything else about armaments?'

Mary frowned. 'I do not think so, but he might have done. He is a soldier, after all.'

'Yes, of course he is, and England is at war. Well. You are right; these documents *do* concern weapons, and so you must also know what that means.'

She certainly did, but she hesitated to acknowledge it. The smugglers were passing information to the French. A shiver ran down her spine as she spoke those words. Treason! And the two of them were discussing it now as if it were the most natural thing in the world! 'It is wrong, of course, to give away *anything* to the enemy, but do you think this information is very important?'

'I do not know, but espionage is a very dangerous game, and one that must be stopped.' Déprez paused, his expression grim. 'Now, I will speak plainly – you have earned it. I said last night that I was interested in these documents, and so I am. Some time ago I became aware of certain leaks of information within the military establishment – first in St Lucia, and then here, in England. I do not yet know the extent of the corruption

273

– the treason – but that is another matter. It was clear that the French were using English smugglers as go-betweens, and I managed to trace the flow of information to this area. That is why I am here.'

Mary gaped at him. 'Are you a kind of . . . *agent*?'

'That is a grand word,' Déprez cautioned. 'Let us rather say that I have a curiosity for such things, and sometimes it gets the better of me and draws me into matters that I might well have left alone.'

'But not if you can prevent this . . . treason,' Mary cried, grasping his arm. 'Surely you must act! It is very noble of you, and right!'

'Well, we shall see.'

'Does Mr Somerville know about your work?'

'Yes, to a certain extent. He is a very good fellow, of course, but my real partner is—'

'Hicks.'

'Yes, Hicks.'

'So that is why you sent him to White Ladies,' Mary concluded. The recollection that her uncle had hidden the documents gave her conscience an uncomfortable twist, but she merely frowned and asked, 'Did you . . . expect him to find something?'

'Ah, I have no secrets from you,' Déprez laughed. 'To tell you the truth, I was not certain about anything to do with White Ladies – it had already been the scene of one very surprising incident. But I wanted someone on the spot, and Hicks could join Mr Todd's men more easily than I could. I did not guess that you would prove a more attentive . . . agent than either of us.'

Mary flushed at the compliment, but Déprez's revelation about himself was even more interesting – it could change everything, and important questions quickly occurred to her. Had Mr Déprez known about Mr Tracey as well? *Had* Tracey been waiting for someone at the Great White Horse? Surely he must have been! Did Déprez know the man's identity?

Déprez answered cautiously. He had known something of Tracey, but not the identity of his associate, and while that information was crucial, they must proceed cautiously to obtain it. 'First we must translate the remaining document. It ought to be quite easy, now that you have shown us the way, and the message may give us a clue. But as for the next stage . . . I think the hunt may be on again. Things have become too awkward for the smugglers hereabouts, so if the French do not decide to go completely quiet, I expect they will shift their man to another location.'

'But where?' sighed Mary. 'Surely a boat may set out for France from a great many places on the English coast.'

'Yes, precisely, and we should have to guess. This time, we were lucky to trace our men – or some of them – to Lindham. I doubt we'd have the same good fortune a second time. So, I think we must work backward to the source of the leak, rather than forward to the point of departure.'

'I see,' Mary nodded, 'and can you do that?'

'It would be difficult, just at the moment,' Déprez acknowledged, 'but there may be a way to improve our chances.'

As she poured out her husband's tea the following morning, Lady Armitage announced that she had written to Mr Grantley Molton. She undoubtedly believed that the news would be of great interest to Sir William. In this she was mistaken, and in fact Sir William was absorbed in his letters and only dimly aware that she had said anything. Over the years he had cultivated the ability to

275

disguise his distraction, however, which was one of the reasons for their happy marriage.

'Have you, my dear?'

'Yes, and I expect an answer *very* soon.'

Sir William nodded vaguely. 'Hm, well, I daresay you do – I mean, I daresay it will all turn out for the best.'

'I *daresay*,' agreed Lady Armitage, more sharply, but her expression mellowed into thoughtfulness. She would have to consider very carefully how Mr Molton would occupy himself during the visit. If only it were spring, he and Susannah might go for walks. There was nothing more romantic . . . but in bad weather outings were positively dangerous, with every peril from deep mud to rain and high winds. A gentleman did not propose marriage after he had fallen into a bog, or to a red-faced young lady whose hair looked like straw. Indoor pursuits, then; wholesome family games . . . and Susannah could play something for him on the pianoforte. She played well enough, and she looked *very well* whilst playing. It would also be a good idea to serve some of Mr Molton's favourite dishes when he visited. Food generally put men in a good temper – sweets especially. She would have a word with Cook on the matter.

'I hope he is not overly fond of oysters, then,' remarked Sir William, breaking the seal on a small envelope with a black border. 'Ah, poor Willoughby has died at last. Well, well. I wondered how long he was going to hang on. He has suffered dreadfully from palsy, you know, these last two years. No, the last time she ate them Susannah came out in red spots.'

'Ah, yes, well remembered,' nodded Lady Armitage. 'No oysters.'

While devoid of spots, Susannah's face at that moment was decidedly pensive. She had risen early and was strolling listlessly along the leaf-strewn paths of the kitchen garden. The air was damp and blustery, and all about her there seemed to be nothing but bare earth and sparse, dead stalks. The scrunch of footsteps caught her attention, and she waved briefly at her cousin and sister. 'Going for a ride?' she called.

'Such a glorious morning!' waved Charlotte in reply. 'Come with us.'

'I am hardly dressed for it.'

'Go and change, then,' said Holland, practically. 'We'll wait for you.'

Susannah favoured them with a watery smile. 'No, no, you go ahead. It is too cold for riding.'

Charlotte recommended a good gallop as the best means of warming oneself, and repeated her invitation. Even this had no effect, however, and Charlotte quickly lost patience with her sister's lethargic mood. 'Oh, you are *such* a stick in the mud! Come on, Bobs, let us go.'

She plucked at her cousin's arm when he seemed to linger, but he did not heed her. 'What's the matter, Suz?' he asked.

'Nothing.'

'Let's *go*,' Charlotte repeated.

'No, you carry on,' he murmured. 'I'll catch you up.'

Charlotte frowned at Holland's back as he walked toward her sister. Then she huffed impatiently and flounced away. 'I shan't wait forever, you know.'

'No, I know,' Holland agreed, over his shoulder. 'But don't go out on your own. Take one of the grooms with you.' As Charlotte's petulant footsteps died away he repeated his question to Susannah. 'And don't tell me "nothing",' he added.

Susannah smiled apologetically at him but did not answer. Bending, she picked up a long, thin twig and rolled it slowly between her palms. He watched her speculatively, arms folded across his chest. 'Come on, out with it,' he urged.

'Oh, Bobs,' she sighed at last. 'Why can things not remain as they are? Why must they always change?'

Although odd, the questions did not surprise him. 'Well, things would be hellish dull if they didn't change.'

'Yes, I know, but . . .' She sighed again. 'It is different for you.'

Holland pulled the twig from between her hands and tossed it aside. Then, sliding his arm through hers, he began to walk. 'Of course it's different,' he agreed, 'but you don't have to hang about here, waiting to marry that fellow Molton, if you don't want to.'

She had allowed herself to be drawn forward with only a slight protest, but now her head snapped up in surprise. 'How do you know about that?'

'I'm not a complete fool, that's how. Are you going to do it?'

'I . . . suppose so.'

'What kind of answer is that, for God's sake?' he complained. 'You *suppose* so? Has he asked you?'

'Yes.' She hesitated, and then her explanation came quickly and not quite coherently. Mr Molton had made his affections known during the visit to Fordham, but he had not pressed her for an answer. He meant to give her time to think about it, only she had not *wanted* to think about it. But now she supposed she *must* do, for she had felt so deceitful, keeping it from Papa, and last night she had Revealed All. Of course, that was the right thing to do, but it had not made her feel any better, and she hoped that Bobs was not vexed with her.

He looked at her. 'Would it matter if I was?'

'Why, *of course* it would,' she replied, avoiding his gaze.

278

'I would never— But I did not know what to say. He is a very honourable, decent young man, you know, and I am persuaded—'

'Persuaded by Lady Armitage, you mean.'

'Well, yes, *and* Papa. He said that I must do as I liked, but that this was a very sensible match, and he would not withhold his consent. So you see . . .' She raised her free arm in a helpless shrug.

Holland did not know what he was supposed to *see*. It was quite simple, surely – either she wanted to marry the fellow or she didn't. Susannah, however, did not understand the situation in that way. So much of her comfort lay in knowing that everyone around her was pleased, or at least not displeased, that she could not easily be a source of discord. This particular decision was difficult because she sensed that, however she chose, she would upset someone.

Of course she would not agree to marry Mr Molton if he were a bad man, but this was not the case. Fordham was nearby, which was very convenient, and old Mr Molton had always been so kind. Everyone seemed to think that she ought . . . it was very difficult to disappoint people.

She gazed up at Holland hopefully as she made these points. 'Do you think I am wrong?'

'You don't want to hear what I think.'

'Of course I do,' Susannah protested, but she wanted even more to avoid hearing anything very severe.

'Well then, I think your mother knows you don't give a damn about this . . . Molton, and she is trying to hurry you into marriage with him as a way out.'

They had stopped walking, and she shrugged free of him. 'What do you mean?'

'She knew I was coming here, didn't she?' Holland demanded. 'She would do anything to keep me away from you.' He paused, observing the blush that spread across Susannah's cheek, and then he continued in a gentler tone. 'She thinks I'm not good enough for you.'

'Oh, no,' Susannah cried.

'It's what they *all* think, and they're right. But . . . she . . . must've thought there was a risk, or she wouldn't have tried so hard to save you from me.'

He waited again for her to speak, but she remained silent and only fidgeted nervously with the folds of her gown. After a moment he drew a deep breath. 'Look, Suz, I know I'm not . . . eligible the way Molton is, but suppose . . . suppose I had more money. Suppose I could get some.'

'But . . . *could* you?' She raised her eyes in wonder. Bobs was poor; everyone knew that. He was very dear, and she longed not to hurt him, but he had nothing beyond his pay, and they did not pay officers so well, nowadays.

He did not answer her question, and his suggestion of what they might do with this mysterious income was even more astonishing. '*Go out to India?*' she repeated, staring at him. '*Me?*'

'Why not? You could . . . go tiger hunting instead of managing the accounts. Ride elephants – visit the bazaars. You'd like that.'

'But I like managing the accounts. And Mama says—'

'Will you stop thinking about your mother?'

'You mustn't say that, Bobs,' she urged. 'And, of course Mama advises me – that is only right. But it does not mean—'

'Just tell me,' he interrupted, speaking slowly and resting his hands on her shoulders, 'would it make a difference if I had money?'

She glanced up at him fearfully, biting her lip, and did not answer even when he cajoled her. 'Well, but what if— Oh, Charlotte,' she murmured, and quickly stepped away from him. 'Who is that man?'

Holland turned round as Charlotte waved at them from the other side of the garden and called, 'Bobs! Bobs!' Beside her stood a rather rough, almost elderly-looking man, grey haired and travel-weary.

'What the— Yes?' Holland called. 'What is it?'

'There he is,' said Charlotte to her companion. 'This man is asking after you, Bobs!'

'All right, all right, you don't need to rouse the neighbourhood,' Holland complained, advancing toward them.

'Captain Holland, sir?' asked the stranger. 'A very good morning to you, if I may. Hicks is the name.' He tipped his hat respectfully.

Holland nodded. 'Do I know you?'

'No, sir, you don't, but I think you'll want to, if I may be so bold. I've come from Lindham, with a message of some importance from a young person of your acquaintance. Perhaps I might, ahem, speak with you about it?'

Holland started and then nodded again. 'Lottie, take Susannah inside. I think she could do with some breakfast. Go on,' he ordered, as Charlotte threatened to linger. He waited until the sisters had departed and then turned back to Hicks. 'You have a message from Mary Finch?'

'That's right, sir.'

'Did she send you?'

'In a manner of speaking she did. She and Mr Déprez.'

'Déprez? What the devil does—' Holland shook his head. 'All right, let's hear it.'

The morning that dawned clear and cold in Norfolk brought a damp chill to London, and Mr John Hudson was aware of the coldness rolling under the door, and through the ill-fitting window, and generally filling his office at Number 4 Bow Street. Hudson usually began work early on Monday mornings. Sunday might have been declared a day of rest, but Sunday nights were generally busy ones for the City Police, which meant that there was always a report to write. As he hated the exercise, he preferred to get it out of the way. So, on this particular Monday he sipped his tea, hot and sweetened with a generous helping of sugar, and turned with a sigh to his work.

Clerical work did not seem natural to him. His heavy build and broken nose gave him the look of a retired prize-fighter, and his irascible disposition might have completed the picture, but it did not. The experience of his police work had honed his powers of practical analysis to a considerable degree, making him a thoughtful, even meditative individual, at least within the sphere of criminal detection. Nevertheless, he hated these damned reports, and as he wrote his expression hardened. Rape, robbery, a street brawl that had ended in a knifing, petty theft; what a sordid list it made. And depressing. For all their work, crimes continued to be committed with the same dreary regularity.

A respectful tapping hardly pierced the gloom. 'Yes, come in.' Hudson continued to write, only looking up when his office door opened to admit one of the desk clerks. 'What is it?' he asked. 'I hope you've brought up the coal – it is colder than a witch's . . . nose in here.' He frowned as he made the wholly unsatisfying amendment, but the clerk was an elderly man, and Hudson was aware that he belonged to one of those sects that disapproved of alcohol and tithes, and so he felt obliged to control his language.

'Someone to see you, sir,' replied the clerk in a noncommittal voice. 'Says he's here on the St Lucia matter.'

282

St Lucia! Hudson had been so busy in the last few weeks that he had filed his conversation with Jonathan Hicks somewhere to the back of his mind, but the mention of St Lucia brought it all back – spies, and secret codes, and the loss of important military information. St Lucia was the signal that they had agreed upon, the signal that would precede a communication of some sort from Hicks and his associate. Hudson's damned report could wait! 'St Lucia!' he repeated, throwing down his pen. 'Send him up, man!'

'Yes, sir, here he is. And I'll see about that coal directly, sir.'

Hudson was already on his feet and moving round his desk, but he stopped abruptly as his gaze fell, not on Hicks, but on a small, thin-faced man. His dark clothes, greasy black hair, and bright eyes reminded Hudson of a rat, and the scar curving round his mouth like a whisker completed the picture. 'Who the devil are you?' he demanded.

The little man shot him a nervous, shifting glance. 'I'm Rede, gov. Mr Hicks sent me.'

The mention of Hicks' name was some reassurance, but Hudson wanted to be certain. The man before him did not precisely inspire confidence. 'To do with the St Lucia matter?' he repeated.

'That's the ticket, gov. St Lucia.'

'Where is Hicks?'

'He's in Suffolk, but I've got something, information like, as may be important to the case, and Mr Hicks said I should come show anything of that nature to you straightaway. So that's what I've done, and that's why I'm here.'

Hudson sat down again and motioned Rede to a chair opposite the desk. 'Very well, let's hear it.'

Rede slid onto the chair, not so much sitting as crouching upon it, as if ready to spring up again. 'That's right, gov, that's the ticket,' he repeated. 'Do you think you might . . . I been out all night, you see, and it's powerful cold.'

'Tell me what you know,' snapped Hudson, 'and I'll see what I can do.'

'That's right, I ain't holding out on you, gov,' Rede urged. 'Here it is.' He produced a bundle of papers from inside his coat and handed them across to Hudson. Each sheet had been folded several times and bore the mark of a seal – a plain seal – and each contained several lines of scrambled letters and a series of numbers. They looked very similar to the papers that Hicks had shown him a fortnight ago and which currently rested in one of the locked drawers of Hudson's desk.

'It's a code,' Rede explained.

'I know that,' frowned Hudson. 'Do you know how it works?'

Rede shook his head and then flinched nervously at a knock on the door. It was the constable with a scuttle full of coal. He switched it for the empty scuttle on the hearth and clumped out, although not before directing a sceptical glance at Rede.

When the door had closed Rede turned back to Hudson. 'Fellow put me off. What I meant to say is, they're to do with spies, them bits of paper.' He gestured vaguely.

'Perhaps they are. How did you come by them? From Hicks?'

'Naw, I got 'em off of a chap named Sault – from his house up in Waltham Abbey on Saturday night. He's been spyin' for the Frenchies, Mr Hicks says, and he told me to get hold of 'em.'

Hudson lifted a sardonic eyebrow. 'Relying on your experience as a housebreaker, no doubt? And where is Sault now?'

'I dunno, gov, and that's a fact. He weren't at home when I . . . came to call, so I just took them papers and scarpered. I hung about the neighbourhood, you know, till the morning, but he never come back. I reckon he must've got wind of it, somehow. He hadn't been gone long, though, when I turned up. Plenty of food in the house, and a fire in the grate. All very cosy.'

'Hm. Yes.' Hudson was silent for a moment. He was well acquainted with men of Rede's type, the petty criminal recruited to perform confidential and scarcely legal tasks for those who either did not wish to risk capture or who lacked certain important skills. 'How did you know where to find these papers?'

Rede smiled modestly and sat up straighter. 'Well, that's easily done if you've had a bit of . . . experience. Nine times out of ten whatever you're looking for's in a strongbox, all neat and tidy. And if it ain't there, it's likely to be under the bed, or in a desk drawer. With ladies it's the dressing table.' Sault had been slightly more discreet, although no one would call a box at the back of a wardrobe *original*.

'And I don't suppose that the lock on the front door presented any problem either.'

'Not much, gov.'

'Hm.' The letters had been tied up with a length of purple velvet ribbon. Hudson toyed with it before restoring the bundle. 'Looks like Mr Sault is a bit of a dandy. Unless this was your touch.'

'Not me,' grinned Rede.

Hudson sat back in his chair, and then he opened one of his desk drawers and fished out a bottle and a glass.

'Well, I don't know where this leaves things, Rede, but you've done a good job.' He poured out a measure of clear liquid. 'I think you've earned your drink – I presume you can make do with gin?'

'I can indeed, gov,' nodded Rede, his gaze fixed on the glass. 'I'm right partial to it, as it happens. Thank you very much.'

'I shall want a description of Sault,' Hudson warned, 'as much as you know of him. You give it to one of my clerks before you leave.' He waited until Rede nodded and then pushed the glass across the table.

Rede cradled it between his hands. 'And Mr Hicks says he's coming to see you himself as soon as he can. I expect him in Town in the next couple of days. He'll tell you more about Sault, I wager. A very honourable gent is Mr Hicks – more'n happy to do his duty.' He raised his glass. 'Well, cheers, gov. Your very good health.'

16

Charlotte was in the breakfast room, reaching for the marmalade, when she heard the sound of her cousin's boots on the stairs. Thrusting back her chair, she dropped her spoon with a clatter and hurried after him, deaf to her sister's call. Holland disappeared into his bedchamber as she reached the landing, but she ran after him and flung herself down on to his bed. 'What has happened?' she demanded, trying to catch her breath.

'What do you mean?' asked Holland. He was fishing for something inside the wardrobe. Turning to face her he continued, 'Why should anything have happened?'

'Susannah is in a dither, practically in tears, and now you look funny too. Who was that man? I did not like him.'

'No reason why you should. He brought me a message – and at least I'm not gasping.'

'But I ran all the way. An important message? What about? You— You are not *going*, are you? It is so unfair!'

'Yes, I'm afraid so.' He was unbuttoning his waistcoat and pulling his shirt out of his breeches. 'Cut along now, shrimp, I have to change.'

'No one ever tells me *anything*,' she fumed, sitting up

and hugging one of the pillows. 'Mama came downstairs and wanted to know why Susannah was carrying on, which only made Susannah cry the more, and now *Mama* is in a fearful wax as well.'

He smiled briefly. 'Serves her right. Where's your father?'

'I do not know. In the library, probably, waiting until it is over. That is what he generally does, when one or other of us is in a state.'

'Wise man.'

'*And* we have missed our ride.'

'Yes, sorry about that. Maybe next time.' He sat down beside Charlotte and gave her a hug. She suffered it, but not very graciously. 'That reminds me,' he continued, 'we have to think about your jumping, and how that's to be managed now that your mother is back.'

Charlotte did not answer, but a sulking shrug of the shoulders conveyed very eloquently her belief that the inevitable termination of her jumping career was simply the latest in a series of injustices that had blighted her life, and that Holland did not care in any case. Holland, indeed, was remarkably unaffected by her mood. He explained calmly that all illicit activities would hence-forth be transferred to the north meadow; it was a safe distance from the house and beyond Lady Armitage's regular sphere of influence. The meadow was not so well drained as the lumberyard, however, so Charlotte must expect that *sometimes* jumping would have to be curtailed. Chaplain, the head groom, would have the final say.

'And listen, shrimp, do you know the best way to keep this a secret?'

'No.'

'You make sure that no one suspects you of anything in the first place. Behave yourself and don't cause any trouble. If your mother thinks you're up to something, even if she doesn't know *what*, it will be there in the back of her mind. And sooner or later she'll get at you, or Chaplain, or one of the lads, and it will all come out.'

Charlotte received this advice sceptically, sensing that it was really an attempt to make her attend to her Geography lessons. She nodded more enthusiastically, however, when Holland said that of course she must continue her regular outings on Clemmie – a sudden and exclusive preference for lessons would be extremely suspicious. In fact, it would have precisely the opposite effect to the one they were trying to achieve. On the other hand, submission to *some* of the burdens of scholarship would probably be quite helpful.

'And about Susannah,' Holland continued, 'I'm sure you can trust her, but . . .'

'But she would give the game away if anyone asked her even *slightly*,' finished Charlotte, her faith in her cousin restored. 'Susannah is rotten at scheming – not like us.' She beamed happily at him.

'No, she's not so good at it. And shrimp, there's no need to say anything about the man who brought me the message. I doubt if Susannah paid much attention to him, and . . . you might as well forget about him too – *officially*, I mean.'

'I *knew* there was something odd about him,' cried Charlotte, and now she was smiling conspiratorially. 'Are you on a secret mission?'

'Sort of, and you're the only one who knows about it.' He gestured to cut off a threatened cheer of triumph. 'But remember, *nothing suspicious* – agreed?'

'Yes, agreed.'

'Good. Now I really must go. I'll try to come back again soon but, well, it may not be possible.'

★   ★   ★

The carriage, a particularly smart one despite the splashes of mud along its side, was waiting on the drive. It belonged to Mr Somerville, and had been entrusted to Hicks because the timing of the regular service did not suit. Hicks thought that with luck they ought to be back at Woolthorpe Manor by early evening.

Holland climbed aboard. 'Who thought to ask me about these papers?' he asked, as the driver eased his team into a slow turn that would take them past the front of Storey's Court before turning on to the road.

'I think it was Miss Finch and Mr Déprez together,' Hicks explained. 'Myself and Mr D, we've been on the trail of the smugglers for some time, but neither of us is what you might call a military man. So when Miss Finch decoded the messages we needed someone who could say for certain what they meant and where they might've come from. And naturally, they thought of you.'

'Mm.'

Hicks glanced back toward the house. 'Now that is what I call an elegant property, if you don't mind me saying so. Your flash new houses, with all their modern styles and what have you – I cannot see the attraction.'

'Can't you?'

'No, sir. I don't say that White Ladies was exactly to my taste – a grim old pile, to be sure – but these others, I have seen a fair few in my day, and most of them can't hold a candle to a place like this. A very fine spread, any way you look. I am sorry to be taking you away from it, Captain.'

Holland pushed his bag under the seat. 'Don't be. Storey's Court is nothing to do with me.'

'No? Well, it is something to dream about, I guess, and— There, sir,' cried Hicks, 'someone is waving to you.' He pointed and Holland turned quickly to catch a glimpse of a figure at one of the upper windows. It was Charlotte, and now the wind made the curtains billow out beside her as she hung on to the casement and waved her handkerchief.

Holland turned away with a crooked smile. 'If you ask me, dreams are nothing but a bloody waste of time.'

Mr Somerville and Paul Déprez were waiting in the vestibule of Woolthorpe Manor that evening when the owner's carriage drew to a stop, and Mr Somerville himself opened the door and peered inside. 'Ah, Captain Holland, excellent. Hicks, you have made good time. No trouble on the road, I see?'

'No, sir. We made good changes, and it was all very easy. I mentioned your name at Halesworth, like you said.'

'Capital, capital.' Mr Somerville clapped Holland on the shoulder as he descended from the coach. 'This is a damned business, what? But come into the library. You will want a drink, I daresay, and we can speak there in privacy.'

The library at Woolthorpe Manor was actually given over more to sporting than to literary pursuits. The four men who gathered there stood round a mahogany table littered with a confusion of equipment: a disassembled pistol, a box of fishing flies, leather dog collars, and part of a correspondence with Tattersalls. As Mr Somerville cleared space in the centre, he continued, 'I expect Hicks has apprised you generally of the situation, Captain Holland?'

'That's right, sir,' Holland nodded. High on the wall opposite, and directly in his line of sight, was an improbable portrait of his host, apparently seated among the ruins of a temple. The difference between that youthful traveller and the stout magistrate indicated that a fair number of years had passed since Mr Somerville made the Grand

Tour. The cheerful, boisterous, slightly naïve expression, however, was little changed.

'Good. Now, Déprez is the expert on all of this – I shall leave the rest of it to him.'

'Hardly the expert,' Déprez corrected, 'that is why Captain Holland has returned. And here,' he added, opening a large leather wallet and placing it on the desk, 'are the documents.'

Holland scanned the four translated messages while the other men leaned forward, eyes fixed on his face. Only the fire hissing in the grate broke the silence. He read them through a second time, more slowly, and then looked across at Déprez. 'Do you understand any of this?' he asked sternly.

'Well,' Déprez hesitated, 'under correction, I should say that they have something to do with gunpowder.'

'You're right. Gunpowder production and testing.'

'*Gunpowder*, by God,' echoed Mr Somerville. 'And is this information secret? Is it valuable?'

'Well, it shouldn't be given to the Frogs.' Holland asked to see the originals, and when these had been handed over he laid them and the translations side by side on the table.

Mr Somerville frowned over them. 'I am damned if I know how you are able to understand all of this. Even when it is written out in plain English, I cannot make sense of it.'

'Well, sir,' Holland acknowledged, his expression softening slightly, 'I know a fair bit about gunpowder, as it happens, so these references are all familiar to me.' He turned again to Déprez. 'You say Miss Finch figured out the code?'

'Yes, sir. Much to my surprise, I must admit. She is . . . an extremely perceptive young woman.'

292

Mr Somerville could not suppress a chuckle. 'She certainly is. Quite extraordinary. I have always known that women's brains worked differently from ours, but I cannot recall ever being grateful for it until now.'

'Yes, sir,' said Holland, 'she's damned clever.' He was still looking at Déprez, and he asked, in a low voice, 'Do you mind telling me how you fit into this?'

Déprez's initial reply, stressing the sympathy and confidence that existed between himself and Miss Finch, neither pleased nor satisfied Holland, whereupon Déprez acknowledged that his involvement did have a broader foundation. 'I was able to perform some services for the Admiralty when I was in St Lucia. That is why I had to leave when the island was overrun; I was not very popular with the French. When I came to England, I . . . took it upon myself to investigate certain information I had acquired having to do with espionage being committed inside the English military. You see the result – valuable information on its way to France. We have followed the trail to this area, but now it has gone cold.' He shrugged. 'I thought you might help us trace the leak in the other direction – backward to its source.'

'Mm.' Holland had been leaning forward, hands braced on the tabletop, but now he stepped back and folded his arms across his chest. 'Tracing the leak backward . . . that *could* mean the Warren. But the more I think about it, the less sure I am.'

'How so?' asked Déprez.

'Well, all of this information relates to gunpowder . . .'

Mr Somerville nodded. 'Yes, so you assure us.'

'But if it came from Woolwich I'd expect at least *some* of it to relate to weaponry. There's more to the arsenal than just powder. I wonder whether our spy isn't working at one of the powder mills instead.' This sounded like a breakthrough, and it produced expressions of approval, but Holland quickly explained that it would actually widen the search. In addition to the two owned by the government, several private mills also sold powder to the Ordnance on a more or less regular basis. Any of them might be the source of leaked information.

'Then what ought we to do?' asked Déprez.

Holland considered for a moment. 'It would be hard to investigate all the mills without the spy getting wind of it, and besides, *my* duty's clear. I should go straight to Woolwich and hand these papers over to my commanding officer.' He hesitated again and then indicated the fourth pair of papers. 'But then there's this.'

The original message of

CAVFGQUGBOGEAQAROTCVDDOCCCVF
FBIOEOYOLCQODOCCAIBEADAQTDOFF
CCGDAGWAILQOCAFFOBCOYOQUDFU
DSCLICGKVAIGOI

had been translated to read:

FAULT NOT YET MANAGED SUCCESSFULLY
REMOVE IF NECESSARY MACE AND CELLS
ST CATHARINES ALLEY SEVEN O'CLOCK
FIRST QUARTER.

Mr Somerville peered at it. 'You have lost me, I am afraid. What does it mean? More of your gunpowder jargon?'

Between the two of them Holland and Déprez explained that it might concern a meeting where the information was passed on. The Mace and Cells was probably a tavern, and the meeting took place there at seven o'clock. Mr Somerville frowned his scepticism. The whole thing sounded very far-fetched. 'Does either of you know of a tavern called the Mace & Cells?'

Déprez admitted that he did not, but Holland thought there might be an establishment of that name in London. He knew a neighbourhood called St Catharine's not far from the Tower. They agreed that a London venue was extremely likely and that 'the first quarter' probably referred to the position of the moon. This would provide a fixed day every month, which made sense if meetings were held regularly.

Still doubtful, Mr Somerville located a copy of the almanac, and after a couple of false starts declared that the moon would next reach its first quarter on the 21st of October, which was in two days' time. He admitted that this gave further weight to the idea that something involving the espionage network would shortly take place – he was the first to acknowledge that perhaps he had been wrong. Spies, after all, were not quite his line of country.

Holland and Déprez might have been expected to congratulate each other on their efforts, but they did not do so. Although polite, conversation between them lacked cordiality, and they both seemed ill at ease. Whether they or the situation had created this mood was difficult to say. A more perceptive man than Mr Somerville might have sensed the tension. Hicks certainly did, but his job was to keep silent. He had considerable faith in Déprez's methods, even when he did not fully understand them.

An uncomfortable silence was punctured by yet another query from the magistrate. 'But what about the "fault"?' he asked. 'Is that some sort of instruction? A warning of danger? I suppose it might mean a fault in the gunpowder, or in the plans of the conspirators.'

The question seemed to annoy Déprez. 'By God, what does it matter?' he frowned. 'We cannot expect to decipher every detail at this stage, but we must not lose this chance – we *must* find the Mace & Cells.'

'Oh, ah.'

'*We?*' demanded Holland, his expression hardening. He surveyed the others. 'This is my business, and not any of yours. I hope you don't take offence, Mr Somerville, but this isn't just to do with Lindham smugglers any more. And as for Mr Déprez, I know what you said about helping the Admiralty, but we're not in St Lucia either, and this is nothing at all to do with you, really.'

'No, of course not,' Déprez acknowledged, and now he was leaning forward, his fingers almost touching the nearest pair of documents, 'but neither am I a stranger to the affair, particularly in its wider context. I would not like to . . . give up the chase now. You will attempt to catch the spy at the place of rendezvous, surely?'

Mr Somerville glanced back and forth at the other two men. He frowned, trying hard to think of a suitable comment and even opened his lips to speak, but gave it up when Hicks touched him lightly on the elbow. 'Ahem,' he said, instead.

'I don't know,' said Holland, coldly. 'There's no sense charging in and making a hash of things. We don't even know if we're right about the mace and cells. And my duty's to report what I do know to my commanding officer.'

'But you must—'

'I *what*?'

Déprez recognised the dangerous quality in Holland's voice and consciously moderated his own. 'I beg your pardon, but might there not also be a risk in returning to Woolwich and revealing this discovery? We know that information is being given away, but neither the scope of the crime nor its authorisation. There may be only one man acting on his own, but there may be several – perhaps of considerable seniority.'

'Are you saying that the senior officers at Woolwich are spies and traitors?' snapped Holland. 'Because if you are—'

Again Déprez strove to avoid a confrontation. 'No, I am merely suggesting that it is a possibility, and if you return now, heedlessly, to Woolwich, you risk playing into their hands – surrendering the very evidence that would put their necks in the noose.'

Holland shook his head. 'I can't believe anything like that's going on. I'll go down to London tonight. That will still leave plenty of time to arrange something before the meeting – if it *is* a meeting.'

'I would like to come with you, if I may,' said Déprez.

Holland looked as if he were going to refuse, but instead acquiesced grudgingly. 'All right, but I want your promise not to try anything on your own.'

'You have it, sir. By all means. I place myself under your orders.'

Mr Somerville consulted his watch, relieved at last to make a valuable contribution. The London mail coach departed from Ipswich at nine o'clock, and he would have a pair of horses saddled. Captain Holland would undoubtedly want to take some refreshment before he set off, but fortunately there was time for this.

'Thank you, sir, but I'd better push on. I've . . . a few things to see to before I leave Lindham.'

Déprez frowned but said nothing. After a moment Mr Somerville observed, 'Well, I should never advise travelling on an empty stomach, but it is just as you like. Tell Coombes – or Mr Greenaway will very likely be in the stables — to saddle Trumpeter. He will get you to Woodbridge in good time — or Ipswich, for that matter, if you miss the connection.'

'Thank you, sir. It's very good of you.' Holland arranged to meet Déprez either in Woodbridge or at the Great White Horse, where they would join the London mail. Then he gathered up the papers, both originals and copies. 'I'll keep an eye on these.'

The two of them walked together down a long corridor toward the stables. A series of mirrors caught their reflections as they passed. Holland looked grave, and his shabby uniform made a sad contrast to the handsome attire of the man beside him. Déprez's expression was harder to read: thoughtful, calculating, but also apprehensive. Their steps were muffled by the thick carpet that ran along the middle of the floor, and Déprez's question was voiced in a low, mildly enquiring tone. 'Are you going to see Miss Finch?'

The change in topic did not render conversation any easier. Holland knew he was making things more difficult for himself by going to see Mary and, in any case, he had no intention of discussing her with Déprez. 'That's right,' he replied.

'I did not wish to exclude her from our discussions,' Déprez continued, 'and naturally, she was keen to be included, but any visit to Woolthorpe would have aroused Mrs Tipton's suspicions.'

Holland stopped in his tracks. 'Suspicions of what?'

'Of everything,' Déprez replied with a smile. He had stopped too, and then he motioned Holland forward. 'She is like a hen with one chick, you know. She has great plans for Miss Finch, and she . . . watches her very carefully.'

'Don't worry, I'll manage.'

298

'I am convinced that you will. Here we are – the stables are across the yard on your right.' Déprez opened the door and the candles around them flickered. 'Do not forget to be in Ipswich by nine o'clock.'

Holland nodded and disappeared into the gloom. Shutting the door after him, Déprez stood for a moment in silence, reflecting on what had just transpired. Had it been wise to reveal himself and his mission? If Holland bolted now, it might be difficult to recover anything like so promising a position, but if he did *not* bolt, the evident trust that Déprez had just displayed could prove even more valuable. It was a nicely balanced gamble, but Déprez was used to gambling, and he was very good at it.

'*Well?*' demanded a voice from close beside him, and Déprez flinched, despite his long training. 'My God,' he muttered, scowling at Hicks, 'must you creep about? And what do you mean by that . . . unhelpful observation? You saw what was decided.'

'I did. It was a damned fool decision. You could have prevented it.'

'Indeed. You seem to think that Captain Holland has no will of his own in these matters,' snapped Déprez. 'He is not mine to command, you know.'

Hicks shrugged. He was fully aware of his friend's anxiety, but for once he did not mean to humour it. 'Not now, certainly. You realise that we may have lost him?'

'He was not yet ours to lose.'

'*And* he has the documents – if he flies now we will be in a damnable position.'

'Further unhelpful observations,' replied Déprez. 'And let *me* observe that if he does not fly, then we have risked all to gain all.'

Despite himself Hicks smiled. One had to admire his friend's confidence, even if it led to the most outrageous difficulties. 'Would you enjoy this so much if there weren't the risk?'

'Ha! Do you suggest that I do this – any of it – for my own enjoyment?' Déprez seemed genuinely angry for an instant, and then he too smiled. 'Sometimes I think you are my *advocatus diaboli*, determined to make me see the worst in myself.'

'No, more like your good angel, if you will allow the parallel, warning you of danger.'

'Indeed, I will allow it,' laughed Déprez, 'even if I cannot always heed the warning. I do, you know, sometimes.'

Hicks did not answer, but Déprez was not offended by the silence. Instead he turned resolutely away from the door and gestured back along the passageway. 'Come, let us return to Mr Somerville.' As he walked he lifted his chin in a gesture of defiance not unlike Mary Finch's, although he did not appreciate the similarity. 'And as for Captain Holland, he will go to her, and then to Ipswich. I am certain of it.'

His confidence wavered, however, when his thoughts turned to another aspect of the matter. Miss Finch was not the first young woman that he had ever admired, but she had shown herself to be . . . unpredictable, and that added considerably to her charm. He did not want her to be hurt by anything that happened, and an injury was highly likely if she had much more to do with Holland. Despite all the help she had provided he almost wished that he had not involved her.

He did not mention this to Hicks, now padding faithfully beside him, his homily delivered. Rather, Déprez shrugged and told himself that he was growing soft, and softness made things dangerous. As for Miss Finch, she must take her chances like the rest of them.

Holland set off purposefully for Lindham. His horse, Trumpeter, was a good one and could cover the ground well. But he was also nervous. The atmosphere was strangely uneasy; the gusting wind blew in sharp, uneven bursts, and the patchwork of grey and black clouds rolled overhead. A storm was certainly brewing, and the horse was aware of it. He flattened his ears and began to twist and lunge, even as his speed increased. In the hands of a less determined rider, he might easily have come to grief.

His rider *was* determined, however, and the battle of wills did not last very long. Trumpeter was recalled to his duty by a series of well-executed checks, and made to understand that the surest way of avoiding the danger was not by out-running the storm, but by heeding his rider's commands. By the time Holland walked him into the yard at Lindham Hall, he was almost docile.

The stables were quiet, so Holland led him into an empty stall and loosened his girth. He had just slipped a blanket over the horse's back when the first drops of rain began to fall in a light patter, and the sound of footsteps could be heard crossing from the house. Holland retreated into the darkness, then stepped forward when he recognised the voice of the approaching figure, who was whistling through his teeth and talking to himself.

'*Mr Cuff*,' he whispered.

Cuff started and nearly dropped his bucket of hot mash. He was wearing his old overcoat, and now he peered into the darkness from behind his upturned collar and scarf. 'Holy Moses, sir, but you give me a fright. Thought you was a ghost at first.'

'I'm not a ghost, at least not yet, but you haven't seen me, all the same.'

'No, sir, I get you. More in the shadowy line, like. I reckon it's Miss Mary that you're wanting?'

'That's right. Can you let her know that I'm here?'

'Oh, aye,' said Cuff, smiling broadly, 'I'll tip her the wink. Reckon she's expecting it?'

'She might be, and I doubt the news will surprise her, in any case. But be careful.'

'Never you fear, sir. I weren't born yesterday, you know. Nor the day before.'

Cuff departed with those words, and after about ten minutes the stable door softly opened and Mary peered inside. Holland had taken the precaution of lighting a lantern, and she stepped tentatively toward the light. She was wearing a woollen shawl over her gown, and raindrops glistened on her hair and shoulders. After waiting to determine that she was alone, he emerged from an empty stall.

She felt a tremendous flood of relief at seeing him. Relief, excitement, shyness – all were making her heart pound and confusing her thoughts. She smiled up at him, nervously, and could think of nothing to say beyond a whispered, 'Hello.'

He was smiling too, although his first words were gruffly spoken, as if he were unsure of himself. 'Sorry about all of this, and in the rain, but— Are you cold?'

'Oh, no, I am quite warm,' she assured him, 'this shawl is very heavy.' She sat down on a bale of hay, and after a moment he joined her.

'Good. Well, I wanted to see you, to tell you . . .' He hesitated, unsure precisely *what* he wanted to tell her.

His diffidence was reassuring, and she stopped his halting effort with eager prompts. 'Have you seen the papers? Do you know what they mean?'

'Yes – I've just come from Woolthorpe.'

'And *is* there a spy?'

'Looks like there must be – either at Woolwich or one of the gunpowder mills. Or maybe both. I'm not sure.'

'Gunpowder mills,' Mary repeated uncertainly.

'Where it's made. We don't . . . dig it out of the ground you know.'

'No, of course not.' She remembered the references in the documents to stoves and cakes; could they have something to do with the making – or even *baking* – of gunpowder? It sounded very strange, but as she admitted to him, what did *she* know about it? She smiled when he said that he was glad to hear there was *something* she did not know, and asked whether the process was difficult.

'It's hard to get it right. Otherwise the powder doesn't work – or not very well, so we have to test it. One of the documents has the results of a test on different powder grades: large grain, fine grain.'

'Yes, I remember,' said Mary. 'And double battle. That must be the particularly powerful variety.'

'It's a sporting powder, actually. It's made in a place called Battle in Sussex.'

'Oh, I thought . . .' She smiled to herself. 'Like Hollands gin.'

'That's right.'

'But surely all of this information is kept secret – I mean, it *ought* to be kept secret. Who can have discovered it?'

'Yes, it is secret.' He paused for a moment. 'It's hard to say who would've been able to get hold of it, other than me.'

'Other than *you*?' Mary cried, and a sudden, horrible fear clutched her heart.

'Yes, you see I— Oh, damn it, Miss Finch, you don't think that *I'm* a spy, do you? Don't be daft.'

His indignant reply made her feel extremely foolish. 'No, of course not,' she agreed. 'It was only . . . everything is so . . . I hardly know what to think. I beg your pardon.'

'Well, never mind,' said Holland, frowning. 'What I meant is, gunpowder's one of my jobs. The Ordnance has a laboratory at Woolwich, and I work there.'

'On gunpowder?'

'Mm, and other things.'

It sounded terribly important – and terribly dangerous, especially when Holland acknowledged that even a small amount of powder could produce an explosion, and this could be triggered by a single spark. 'Perhaps the French intend to cause an explosion at one of our mills,' cried Mary, lowering her voice to an urgent whisper, as if the French might be listening.

'Maybe, but then they would only need to know how to get into the mills or the powder depots, and we know they're interested in our methods. But that's no surprise.'

'No?'

He shook his head. 'They've been having trouble with their powder, on account of the saltpetre. The best place for saltpetre, which you need for making gunpowder, is India. But some time ago – before the last war – we stopped the French from buying Indian petre, so they were bug— in a very sad way. They've been trying to find another good source themselves, and they're doubly keen to know what we're doing to make our powder more effective.'

'I see,' said Mary, 'and the information in the documents would be helpful to them.'

'So long as it reached France. That might be hard, with our Navy regularly sweeping up and down the coast, but smugglers – who already have French contacts and fast ships, and are used to dodging the Revenue men — they could do it. The same boats that land French contraband could easily take off secret English documents, or even spies.'

She nodded. Déprez had made the same point, as well as suggesting that the smugglers would now be too frightened to continue, so that the secret information would leave England by a different means. Unfortunately, that was where Déprez's knowledge ended. What route would the information travel, and who controlled it? Ignorance on those points had prompted him to call upon Captain Holland for his advice. 'But everything that has happened already — whatever has been given away . . . would you say it is *very* serious?'

'Damn right it is. Even if the actual information you found isn't so damaging, it would only be a matter of time before we lost something really important.'

Mary nodded. Again, Holland's view exactly mirrored that of Déprez. Nor was it surprising, really. One could not be lenient with spies merely because they had not managed to give away anything essential.

She looked at Holland; how stern he seemed, and remote. She had the feeling that his thoughts were taking him far away, and that he was barely listening to her. And yet, somehow, she felt that he might be easier to talk to than Mr Déprez. Mr Déprez did not seem to make mistakes — at least it was harder to imagine him doing so — and he probably would have less sympathy with someone who did. Captain Holland, on the other hand, made mistakes all the time, or did not know things. Imperfect people were much easier to confide in — as long as they were not *so* flawed as to be foolish or untrustworthy. 'And any Englishmen involved,' she said, as if there had been no pause, 'any who helped pass this information to the French . . . they would be traitors?'

Holland started to reply, but she quickly added, 'My uncle had those documents in his possession. He must have been involved somehow.'

For Mary that admission was like lifting a bandage from an infected wound; it was painful, but it meant that all of the uncertainties and secret fears that had been poisoning her thoughts for the last few days could be brought into the open. The words also had an effect on Holland, tugging him back more fully into the conversation. 'Your uncle? I hadn't thought about that. But maybe . . . maybe he didn't know what they meant. They were in code after all.'

Outside the rain fell steadily, and a cold wind blew open the half-closed stable door. Inside they could see their breath. 'But he must have suspected that there was something wrong. To be passing on coded messages while we are at war . . . he *must* have known.' Mary clenched her hands into fists and stared down into her lap. It was important that her admission be accepted in all its horribleness. She would not allow it to be explained away – she had tried to do that herself, and it would not work.

Holland said nothing, and after a long pause she continued, 'I have felt so angry, so mortified, and not only because of the wrongness, but because of . . . what people would think of *me*, once they knew what he had done.'

Holland frowned at her. 'What has that to do with you? And besides, you broke the code. If it hadn't been for you—'

'But he was *my* uncle. To have such a person – a traitor – as one's only relation . . . you can imagine what people will say. Anyone who is respectable . . .'

'And a goddamned busybody.'

'Well, if something is odd, or amusing, or . . . wicked, people *will* talk about it,' Mary reminded him. 'But it is

306

not only that. I have been thinking, wondering – please do not think me mercenary – but is it not true that a person who has committed treason suffers "corruption of blood", so that his property is seized by the Crown and no longer descends to his heirs?'

Holland blew out his breath. '*I* don't know.'

'When they first told me that I would inherit from my uncle, it was hard to believe that it was actually happening to me. It was more like something from a story than real life – a fairy-tale almost – for we had never been well off, and lately . . . But then it started becoming more and more real. My uncle wanting to be reconciled – he left everything to Father, you know – and Mrs Tipton talking about "County society" and buying new clothes. I started imagining living at White Ladies, and giving parties and having people to stay – as if these things would *really* happen. And I began taking notice of things, making comparisons, and thinking that I would have *that* sort of carriage, but not *that* sort of sideboard. Not what might happen in a make-believe world, but what I would really do, when I received my inheritance. It was very silly of me, I know, but—'

'No, it wasn't,' said Holland, shaking his head. 'Money makes a hell of a difference. You'd have been a fool not to think about it.' After a moment he added, '*I* do, all the time.'

'Well, after I discovered those documents, I wondered how much of my inheritance sprang from . . . criminal activities, and I felt terribly guilty that I should benefit from them. And that was right of me – that was the good side. But as well as that . . .' She bit her lip and began pulling loose pieces of straw from the bale beside her. He placed his hand gently on top of hers, stilling the motion. 'Go on,' he murmured.

'As well as that,' she repeated, slowly, 'I was afraid that someone would find out about it. I was thinking about my position . . . in society, you see, and I did not want everything to be spoiled before it had even begun. I think I must be the most selfish girl who ever lived – or at least *very* selfish.' She waited for him to remove his hand, but he did not do so, and she felt a slight stirring of encouragement that enabled her to carry on to the end. 'And now, if my uncle *did* commit treason, and we are right about the corruption of blood, perhaps I shan't have any inheritance at all.'

'No, maybe not.'

The matter-of-fact tone of Holland's voice and the confident pressure of his hand had a surprising effect on Mary. She stopped thinking about herself and instead thought about him – how awkward he must feel, listening to all of this, and burdened by the obligation to offer reassurance. It was suddenly important to reassure *him*. She smiled sturdily. 'Of course, I do not *really* mind it. I shall be no worse off than I was before – there is always Mrs Bunbury's, after all.'

He smiled back at her. She was brave; there was no doubt about that. 'Yes, there's always Mrs Bunbury's.'

'And then again, if I have no fortune, I shan't be of much interest to the grand persons of the County. They will just shake their heads and say something about the vanity of human wishes. It is hard to be the object of a moral lesson, but I do not suppose I shall hear very much of it.'

'They'll soon have something else to gossip about,' said Holland, 'you can depend on that. And I was wrong – about money making a difference. It might to those County people, but who gives a damn about them? It wouldn't matter to . . . to your friends.'

He was still holding her hand, and now it felt like the most comfortable thing in the world that he should do so. 'I hope you do not mind my telling you all of this,' she confided.

'No,' Holland assured her, 'I'm glad you did.'

'It was so difficult, not wanting anyone to know, but wanting to talk about it. I did not . . . I did not like to say anything to Mrs Tipton.'

'God, no.'

It did not seem right to giggle, and Mary struggled hard not to. Instead she asked about Holland's own plans.

'Report to my chief in Woolwich.' He consulted his watch and stood up. 'And I'd better get moving. I have to be in Ipswich to catch the London mail.'

Mary rose as well. 'I wish I might come too, but Mrs Tipton would never allow it.'

'You could always stow away on the coach,' said Holland, smiling down at her. 'No, I'm not suggesting that you do it,' he quickly added. 'I doubt you'd find Woolwich very interesting.'

He walked over to his horse's stall, and she followed. '*Is* that where you are going? To Woolwich?'

'Of course; why not?' He removed Trumpeter's blanket and began tightening his girth. 'Easy, now,' he urged, as the horse bumped against him, unhappy at the prospect of venturing out into the rain again.

'But how will you catch the traitors? And what about the mace and cells?'

Holland glanced at her sharply over the saddle. Then he eased out of the stall and returned to her side. 'What do you know about that?' he demanded.

Something in his tone – vexation? suspicion? – caused her to retreat a step. 'Mr Déprez thought that the mace and cells might refer to a rendezvous between the spy and the smugglers, or perhaps the spy and a French contact.' They had moved out of the circle of lamplight, and she could not quite read Holland's expression.

'It might,' he allowed, 'but it might not. Déprez doesn't know everything.'

'No.'

He paused, and then placed his hand upon her arm. When he spoke again his irritation seemed to have been forgotten, but she felt a different sensation in his touch. It was not quite so comfortable as before, and yet she found herself attracted to it. 'You're cold,' he murmured. 'Why didn't you tell me?'

'I am quite warm, really,' she protested.

'No you're not – you're shaking. You should go inside.'

His grasp was not firm enough to restrain her, but it had that effect nevertheless. She gazed up at him, or rather at his shoulder, and murmured, 'Yes, I will, but . . . I wanted to . . . I *do* hope that you catch the spy. And thank you for coming back.'

'That's all right,' smiled Holland, 'it didn't seem fair to leave you out of it. I meant to say before, it was damned clever of you, figuring out the code.'

'Well, I *did* have the book. I daresay anyone could have done it.'

She was blushing, and now she shifted nervously under his hand. He watched her for a moment longer, and then he leaned forward, bending his head toward hers.

'*Oy! Psst!*' came an insistent whisper from the doorway. Holland straightened, and Mary stepped back quickly.

'You have a hell of a sense of timing,' Holland complained.

'I know, sir, but—'

'What is it, Mr Cuff?'

'Ye'd best get back inside, Miss Mary,' he warned. 'Missus

310

is askin' fer ye. She'll be comin' out here herself in half a tick. And then we'll *all* cop it, and that's the truth!'

'Oh, my,' breathed Mary. 'Yes, of course.' She turned hurriedly to Holland, her face still flushed. 'I must go, but – please – be careful.'

'I will.' He smiled at her and touched her arm. 'You have a damned steady nerve, Miss Finch. Don't lose it.'

17

Paul Déprez looked up from the copy of the *Ipswich Journal* that he was not reading and nodded with relief when Captain Holland walked into the parlour of the Great White Horse. Déprez had been weighing up his options if Holland did not appear, and he was happy to abandon the exercise. 'You have cut it fine,' he remarked as Holland joined him by the fire. 'The coach is expected shortly.'

It was a quiet evening for the Great White Horse. The bad weather had kept many of the regular patrons at home, and the few travellers were dispersed in comfortable nooks, minding their luggage and keeping themselves to themselves. An attentive onlooker might have wondered at this rendezvous between two men who appeared to have little in common.

'Did you think I wouldn't turn up?' asked Holland. His greatcoat was sodden and mud-spattered. Stripping off his damp gloves he shoved them into his pocket and held out his hands toward the blaze.

Déprez was seated in an armchair, his legs crossed at the ankles. He was obliged to crane his neck to address

Holland's profile. 'No, but accidents can happen, especially if the weather is bad. There is still time for some food, if you are quick.'

Holland shook his head. 'I don't want anything.' Staring at his hands he added, bluntly, 'Riding in coaches makes me sick, sometimes. It's worse if I eat.'

'Oh, ah,' said Déprez, somewhat taken aback, 'how unfortunate. It is like, ah, seasickness, I suppose.' When Holland did not answer, he continued, 'You . . . managed to avoid Mrs Tipton, I trust? She is very protective as regards anything that affects Miss Finch.'

'So you said.'

Déprez was undaunted by Holland's brusque tone. 'Well, it is understandable. Miss Finch is a charming girl in many ways, but she lacks experience. And now she will be wealthy as well. She could easily become the object of unworthy, undesirable men, and—'

'*Undesirable*,' snapped Holland, his glance smouldering like the embers in the fire. 'What the hell do you mean by that? Are you warning me off?'

'Certainly not. Far be it from me to take such a liberty.'

Holland continued to frown, but when he spoke he seemed to have decided not to lose his temper. He explained what Mary had said about corruption of blood. Déprez was even more surprised at this turn in their conversation and, in a rare moment of frankness, both men acknowledged their ignorance of much of the law, and their dislike of that portion which they did know.

'Look,' said Holland, 'I have the papers now – it doesn't really matter where she found 'em. If her uncle was involved—'

'He might *not* have been, of course,' Déprez reminded him. 'I admit the case against him looks bad, but nothing has been proven.'

313

'Well, but even if he was, what difference does it make? He's dead now. Why not leave it at that? Whatever he did shouldn't hurt her.'

Déprez did not answer immediately, and then he offered a casual observation. 'I suppose – if he *was* involved – he received a handsome payment for his efforts.'

'That's what she's worried about,' Holland acknowledged, with a dismissive shake of the head. 'She doesn't want to benefit from his crimes. But that's daft.'

'You think that she *ought* to benefit?'

'No, I think she's daft to worry that she *would* be benefiting. Her uncle had plenty of tin before any of this started – he inherited and wouldn't share a penny of it with his brother, and that was years ago. I can't believe he was keeping White Ladies afloat by trading secrets to the Frogs.'

'Perhaps not.'

'So, we're agreed? We keep Mr Finch out of it?'

Déprez studied Holland thoughtfully. 'You would . . . deceive your superiors on this point? I am surprised, after what you said earlier about your duty.'

'This is nothing to do with my duty,' said Holland, curtly. 'It won't make any difference to what happens to the spy, and it will help Mary – Miss Finch. And you can square Somerville.'

'*Square* him?' Déprez frowned distastefully.

'You know what I mean – tell him to keep mum. He'll do whatever you say.'

Déprez's answer was interrupted by a call from Mr Bamford that the London mail had arrived, and would any passengers for the London mail get themselves outside straightaway, as they wouldn't wait for no stragglers.

Rising to his feet Déprez hurriedly shrugged into his greatcoat. 'Yes, very well,' he nodded, 'I agree. If possible,

Mr Finch will not be mentioned. Now come along, we had better try and get you a forward-facing seat, or you will have a miserable journey.'

Déprez had forgotten how cold it was: cold, wet, and unpleasant. He was reminded when they crossed the darkened yard. The light rain swirled round and round, as if trying to work its way into folds and pockets, and the churned up earth had begun to freeze, making the ruts and tracks awkward to navigate. They were the first to board the coach, so Holland did sit facing forward, while Déprez took the seat opposite. Two other men soon joined them: Mr Allenby, a rotund, middle-aged gentleman, and a banker named Jacobson. In the time that it took for the horses to be changed, introductions were made and baggage hastily stowed, and then the vehicle wheeled away into the night.

The conditions did not inspire conversation, and after a few non-committal remarks the four men gave up the effort. Instead they concentrated on keeping warm; hands were shoved into pockets, chins sank into upturned collars, and feet burrowed into the deep straw that lined the floor of the coach. Even before Stratford, where they made their first change, all was silent apart from Allenby's gentle snores.

Despite the silence, or perhaps because of it, Holland remained awake. It was easy to feel anonymous in the chilly darkness and safe from prying eyes, and as he relaxed his thoughts drifted. Corruption of blood . . . Mary Finch had spoken about a person's blood being corrupted, made worse. Holland supposed that *his* blood was already judged to be bad, which was why he couldn't have Susannah – that was if he wanted her, of course, and who said that he did?

Corruption of blood, he reflected, *but good blood is*

315

important . . . highly desirable. Bon sang – *that's what the French call it, though perhaps they don't care so much about it now. The French king had good blood, and look what happened to him. But then the Frogs . . . they're a strange lot.*

Charlotte was supposed to be learning the language, and Holland smiled as he remembered her heartfelt complaints on the subject. 'I am sure it is disloyal to be obliged to learn French while we are fighting them – and it is so *difficult*. I do not know how anyone manages to learn it unless they are French to begin with. People talk about *le mot juste* – that is a French saying, you know – but really, you have to get such a lot more right than the *mots*. There are accents and things . . . if you get only one letter wrong you have said something completely different from what you intended, and not like English at all!'

One letter wrong . . . corrupted . . . corrupted words, like who and whom, so not so very different from English. 'Oh, Bobs, you are a silly bugger' . . . *but surely Lottie had never said* 'bugger' . . . At last he too closed his eyes.

A change in the motion of carriage awakened him. The guard gave a short blast on his horn and knocked smartly on the roof. 'Chelmsford, gents.'

Mr Allenby awoke; this was his stop. As the coach came to a halt in the yard of the Black Boy, he groped about him for hat, gloves, and the bag at his feet. The horses, anxious for the stable, walked forward before they were unharnessed, and the consequent jolt thrust Mr Allenby on to the seat between Holland and Jacobson. The latter sat up with a start. 'Where are we?' he asked, drowsily. 'Have we arrived?'

'No,' replied Holland, helping Allenby back to his own seat. 'It's another four hours to London.'

Ingatstone. Brentwood. Rumford. Stratford. As the coach rolled through Mile End Mr Jacobson sat up and began to take an interest in his surroundings. He peered out of the window at the pre-dawn gloom. Now it was possible to measure their progress by the changing scenes outside their windows: the quiet of the London Hospital gave way to the din of the bell foundry at the other end of Whitechapel Road. There were upholstery warehouses and booksellers in Fenchurch Street, and the reek of butchered animals meant they were nearing Leadenhall market. When they passed St Dionis Backchurch, Déprez remarked how curious it was to find a church dedicated to a French saint in London. Holland shrugged, but Jacobson informed them that they were also not far from the famous synagogue of Bevis Marks. 'Which was built by a Quaker,' he added, as a further mark of interest.

The coach finally halted at the Post Office, where the yard was crowded with horses, post boys, and vehicles disgorging passengers and sacks of mail. Animals and people had a common appearance; all were jaded and travel worn, and while the former could muster enthusiasm only for their stalls, the latter were likewise trying to gather their wits sufficiently to carry on with their affairs. Jacobson seemed to be one of the more able. He climbed nimbly down, clasping his hat and bag. 'Goodbye, gentlemen, and a good morning to you both,' he cried, waved, and disappeared. Then their mailbags were handed down, and an inquisitive postal clerk peered in at the window. 'Spread Eagle, gents?' called the guard, thumping on the carriage roof. 'We're for the Spread Eagle.' Holland answered with a knock on the ceiling and a call to 'Carry on'. The carriage turned smoothly, and soon they were rattling back toward Gracechurch Street.

Holland did not often lodge in London, but when he did he usually stayed at the Spread Eagle. It was clean, moderately priced, and it ran a good service to Woolwich as well as the principal stages north and east. He jumped down now and walked quickly into the busy front parlour, with Déprez close behind him.

'Are you arranging your passage to Woolwich?' asked Déprez.

Holland answered over his shoulder. 'No, Waltham Abbey. One of our powder mills – a government mill – about twelve miles north of London.'

'But why—'

'Corruption of words, that's why. I think Miss Finch made a mistake in translating – the F and S.'

'*What?*'

'I think that one of the documents didn't mention removing a "fault", but removing "Sault", and I have to go to Waltham Abbey to be sure.' They had reached the desk and Holland turned to the landlord. 'What do you have for Waltham Cross this morning?'

'Well, sir,' said the landlord, considering the timesheets in front of him, 'the best I can do for you is the old Regulator. Steady as a clock, is that service. Leaves us at nine o'clock, and guaranteed to set you down at Waltham Cross at a quarter to eleven. Guar-an-teed, sir. And the mail can do no better.'

'But to have discovered an error,' hissed Déprez. 'Why did you not tell me?'

'I'm telling you now,' Holland replied, shaking off the other's restraining arm. 'Isn't there anything earlier?'

'Not from this here yard, sir,' admitted the landlord. 'And though it ain't for me to cry down the competition, I can't say as they'd answer in this case.'

'Why not?'

'Well, there's naught but the eight o'clock service over at the Savage, and consider: you must make your way up Ludgate Hill, which is near impossible, this time o' day, and likely as not you miss the coach, or find it full. And then it's a very slow service, and last week I hear they lost a wheel north of Hoxton. They don't maintain their machines proper at the Savage, and that's a fact.'

'Have you a seat on the Regulator?'

'Two seats,' Déprez corrected. 'You are not going without me,' he informed Holland, to which the other shrugged his shoulders. 'Suit yourself.'

'Two seats it is, sir,' beamed the landlord. 'Insides, of course. If you'd like to step through, you've time for a hot breakfast. Nothing like a good meal to set you up for a journey.'

Holland had no intention of setting himself up in this way, and he made his way to the waiting room. Déprez, however, was still not satisfied with his colleague's grudging explanation. 'When did you know that Miss Finch had made a mistake?' he persisted, manoeuvring Holland into a quiet corner. 'Did you discuss it with her?'

Holland shook his head. 'I don't know *now*, for certain. That's why I'm going to Waltham Abbey. To find out.'

'But why keep the matter to yourself? I have been quite open with you, and yet—'

'And yet I haven't? Well, maybe that's because I didn't think of it till last night, when you were asleep and dreaming of spies.'

Holland tried to push past, but Déprez quickly blocked the way. 'It takes two to make a quarrel,' he observed, his voice steely, 'so do not walk away if you wish to provoke one with *me*.'

They glared at each other, and then Holland looked away and shrugged in acknowledgement. 'You're right,' he admitted. 'Sorry. All of this . . . has me on edge.'

'I do not think either of us is quite awake,' said Déprez, relaxing in his turn. 'Come,' he urged, clapping Holland more companionably on the shoulder, 'I know that you are not one for breakfast while travelling, but let us get a pot of coffee, at least.'

Disconsolate would have been too strong a word to describe Mary's mood when she awoke that morning, but she was certainly feeling very flat. Captain Holland had gone, and what she privately called 'the adventure' was over, at least as far as she was concerned. It was as if she had been on an exciting journey – she had even been driving the coach for a stage – and now she had been set down at a particularly uninteresting stop while it carried on without her. She supposed someone would eventually come and tell her how it all ended – Mr Somerville, probably, or someone equally dull. And it was raining again. It seemed to rain every day, and she doubted whether anything thrilling would ever happen again. It was really very difficult having an adventure. Everything else seemed flat in comparison. After sitting for a good ten minutes in the window seat all she had managed to observe was a blackbird scuffling among some fallen leaves and the rainwater running down the stable wall where the guttering was broken. She dressed and wandered downstairs, wondering if she looked as gloomy as she felt.

Over breakfast Mrs Tipton provided the answer. 'You are rather down in the mouth today,' she observed, gazing at Mary over her spectacles. 'The result of too much mooning about after a certain gentleman, perhaps?'

Mary wished that her hostess would at least choose a different verb. 'Dreaming' might not be particularly wise, but 'mooning' sounded ridiculous. She was sure she had never done such a thing. 'Oh, no, ma'am,' she replied.

Pollock, the cook, had condescended that morning to produce the rich, buttery little rolls that were her specialty.

Ordinarily these were a firm favourite with Mary, and Mrs Tipton therefore passed the steaming basket along with her observation. On this occasion the rolls did not quite appeal, but Mary chose one – and then a second – to prove that she was not suffering in any way. It was well known that the lovelorn were never hungry.

Mrs Tipton, however, was not so easily convinced, and she proceeded to deliver a lecture on the circumspection required of a young woman exposed to masculine attentions. Mr Déprez featured prominently in her remarks. 'He seems a very gentlemanlike creature,' she allowed, 'and I am saying nothing against him but only *this*. A man, even a gentleman, may be light-hearted. Most of them are, and no one thinks the worse of them for it; but a woman, if she is a lady, *cannot* be so.'

'No, ma'am,' said Mary, thinking that the danger of light-heartedness was a remote one. 'Although I do not expect to see Mr Déprez again any time soon.'

'Indeed? Well, the principle is the same. Do not forget the principle, Mary. It will stand you in good stead when all the other young men hereabouts begin to pay you their attentions. For you may be sure that they will do so, when they learn that you are an heiress.'

'Yes, ma'am.'

After breakfast Mary wandered into the little room at the side of the house that Mrs Tipton dignified as the morning room, but which was really where all the odd bits of furniture that she did not particularly like but had not made up her mind to discard were accommodated. The fire was dying down, so Mary added an extra log, thinking that it would be a shame to bother Peggy. As she rose she was surprised to see a battered copy of her old friend Blackstone – or at least part of it. Volume One was propping up Hume's *History of Great Britain* in the bookcase that was itself leaning rather precariously against the mantel.

So, the *Commentaries* had been at Lindham Hall all along . . . she need not have bothered Mr Déprez. A series of images passed quickly through her brain – Déprez's look of approval when she produced the translations, and Captain Holland holding her hand in the barn – but then Mrs Tipton's word 'heiress' sent her thoughts in a far less interesting direction. There was still the disturbing question of corruption of blood, and Mary wondered gloomily whether she had not better read about that. Perhaps she would not be an heiress after all, and the light-hearted young men of the neighbourhood would direct their attentions elsewhere. She looked for the fourth volume of the *Commentaries*, where such criminal matters were probably discussed, but could not find it.

Volume One did not look as if it would provide much assistance, but she did not really want to read about treason. She flipped forward instead to page 217, where she would find the first of the code alphabets in the sentence beginning '*A queen dowager is the widow of the king*'. It was something to remember, after all . . . but the sentence was not there.

She looked again, up and down the page, but there was no discussion anywhere of queen dowagers. That was odd. She flipped backward – no, and then forward, and there she found it, '*A queen dowager is the widow of the king, and as fuch enjoys moft of the privileges belonging to her as queen confort*' on page 224. Frowning, she turned to page 247. The paragraph halfway down ought to begin, '*In refpect to civil fuits, all the foreign jurifts agree,*' but it did not. That sentence appeared at the bottom of page 254. And on page 309 she found the sentence about '*The other antient levies,*' which ought to have been near the

322

top of page 299. What was happening? She remembered the key numbers so vividly. How could she have got them all wrong?

She thought for a moment. Here was the book, proving quite plainly that she had been wrong, and yet she did not *feel* wrong. She was sure that the page numbers for the first volume were 217, 247, and 299, but following those references in Mrs Tipton's *Commentaries* did not produce the correct sentences. How then . . . She turned to the first page of the volume and read on the frontispiece:

WILLIAM BLACKSTONE, ESQ

THE FOURTH EDITION

OXFORD

PRINTED AT THE CLARENDON PRESS

M.DCC.LXX

And that explained it. The pagination changed between different editions, perhaps even between different printers. Mrs Tipton had bought the fourth edition, and Mr Somerville must have bought another. She shut the book and sat there with it on her lap. And her uncle had the same edition as Mr Somerville, because he had been able to read the code.

And yet . . .

Suddenly she experienced an odd, shuddery feeling, as if she had forgotten something important – no, not *forgotten*, never thought of. How did she know that her uncle could read the code? *What nonsense*, she scolded herself, *of course he could – he had the documents. He was the go-between; he passed the documents from the spy to the smugglers.*

And yet . . .

In her mind's eye she saw the coded sheets, each with their rows of neatly printed characters. There were different editions of the *Commentaries* and not all of them worked to translate the code . . . but which edition had her uncle owned?

She stood up so quickly that the book slid down her lap and on to the floor before she could catch it. Then she picked it up again and hurried to the kitchen, calling for Peggy.

The maid emerged from the scullery, wiping her hands. 'Yes, miss, what is it?'

'Have you seen Mr Cuff this morning? Do you know where he is?'

'I've not seen him since breakfast, miss,' Peggy replied. She called over her shoulder, 'You've not seen Mr Cuff, have you, Mrs Pollock?'

'Out in the stables, most like,' cried the cook. She was thumping mounds of dough into shape upon a floured table, her efforts sending up fine white clouds. Baking day always put her in a bad humour. 'Goes out there first thing, says he has sommut to fix on some bit of gear, and he's gone for *hours*. You'll find him, miss,' she added, addressing Mary's retreating back, 'smoking that old pipe of his and taking his ease, and you might just tell him that there's plenty of work wants doing *inside*.'

Mary ran across the courtyard, sliding on the icy patches and even breaking through to water in one of the deeper puddles. As Pollock had predicted, she found Cuff in the stables, apparently communing silently with Sally and Whiskers, Mrs Tipton's very docile carriage horses. Sally pricked her ears and uttered a warning snort when Mary appeared in the doorway.

Cuff looked up sharply at the intrusion, even whipping his pipe out of his mouth. Then he relaxed and afforded Mary a friendly wave. 'There ye are, Miss Mary,' he said. 'Just giving this old tack a good cleaning. What are ye in such a flurry about this morning?'

Mary instantly made her request – to borrow Mrs Tipton's carriage without her knowing. It sounded dubious, even to her, but there was no time to be lost in explanations, and this was too complicated to explain in any case. She must count on Mr Cuff's fondness for her and his general willingness to bend the rules when possible.

He rubbed his chin thoughtfully, a certain precursor to acquiescence. 'I reckon I might risk it, miss.'

'Oh, good. Thank you, Mr Cuff. Can we leave now?'

'Aye, if we're quick. Missus always has a bit of a rest this time o' day, and if Peggy don't blow the gaff, we might just slip away. Where we headed?'

'White Ladies.'

'*White Ladies?*' echoed Cuff, incredulously. 'Why ever do ye want to go there?'

'I have to – *do* something there, look at something,' said Mary. 'Oh, I cannot explain it, but it is *very* important, and it will not take me a minute.'

Cuff, however, had become cautious. He reminded her of the smugglers, and he was unconvinced by her airy assurance that they would never be so foolish as to return to White Ladies. 'Mebee,' he acknowledged, doubtfully, 'mebee. But some folk behave quite foolish, that's my experience. Sure you want to go there? Well, I'm going to bring along my old gun, just in case.'

'Very well – but hurry!'

The journey to White Ladies was an anxious one. Mary grasped Mrs Tipton's copy of Volume One like a talisman and told herself not to try to decide anything until she had seen her uncle's copy. Despite this sound advice, her imagination continually leapt ahead, posing questions and offering alternative hypotheses. What would happen if his edition of Blackstone did not work with the keys provided in the coded documents? What if he did not even *own* a copy of the *Commentaries*?

At last Cuff put an end to this wearing task. 'Here we are, miss,' he called from the box. To himself he muttered, 'And it fair gives me the shivers, it does.'

Mary leaned out of the window. Indeed, the grey stones looked very forbidding. 'It is much nicer inside,' she assured him. 'Drive around to the back of the house, will you? There will be less chance of anyone seeing – not that I think there is anyone *to* see us,' she quickly added.

They halted a second time in front of the rear porch. Mary jumped down, already fumbling in her pocket for the key. When she asked whether the horses could be left as they were, Cuff said yes, but that she must not hang about.

This advice brought her up sharply, the key in her hand. 'Are you not coming?'

'Reckon I'll stay here with the carriage,' said Cuff, doggedly, but not looking at her, 'in case of intruders.'

This was not at all what she had expected, and she did not welcome the proposed amendment. It was not that she actually believed there to be anyone lurking inside the house, but that was quite different from wanting to enter it alone. She reminded Cuff that Captain Holland had been outside when he was attacked.

'Aye, but they must've . . . come on him sudden – when he weren't expecting it.'

The realisation that Cuff was as frightened as she was stiffened her resolve. 'Very well, stay here then,' she announced. 'I will go on my own, and . . . and I will be back in a few moments.' *I am not afraid*, she told herself.

As she climbed the steps she heard his voice behind her. 'All right, miss, all right; don't hurry so, I'm coming.'

She beamed at him. 'Thank you, Mr Cuff. Oh, and you have brought a lantern. How clever of you.'

'Just ye hold it, now, while I load my gun.'

Cuff took up his stance beside Mary as she turned the key in the lock, ready to deal with any hostile forces that might be lying in ambush for them inside. The door opened and Mary stepped across the threshold, while Cuff turned round in case anyone had crept up behind them in the meantime. They paused in the entrance hall, and Mary lit the lantern.

After a moment she thought she heard him sniffing. At first she ignored it, not wanting to seem rude, but when he did it again she could not resist. 'Mr Cuff, what are you doing?'

'Having a good old smell,' he replied. 'You'd be surprised how places can take on a funny sort of smell, if they've been broken into, or had some sort of goings-on.' He glanced about him enquiringly, as if he were an elderly, and rather shaggy, bloodhound.

'And does everything . . . smell as it ought?'

'Aye . . . so far.'

Mary did not know whether to be reassured or not by this diagnosis. She could not help wondering whether she might gradually perceive some noxious fume . . . the odour of rotten things, perhaps, which might be even more frightening than a sight or sound. However, there was no help for it; she must go on if she was to resolve this mystery. 'I shall . . . lead the way, shall I?' Cuff made a brief, affirmative-sounding reply, and they set out.

As they left the entrance hall, Mary reminded herself that her last visit to White Ladies had not been so very dreadful, after all. Now the dustsheets had returned, so that the house looked as if it had gone back to sleep again. They looked ghostly, dimly visible at the edge of her lantern's light, but really, it was very silly to let that frighten her. 'You know, Mr Cuff,' she said, 'this is quite a beautiful house. I should say *very* beautiful. I shall probably come and live here, some day.'

'*No*, miss. You'd never want to stay in such a lonely old place as this?'

'It would not be lonely if it were being lived in,' she explained, talking to give herself courage. She described a particularly impressive fireplace, the panelling in one of the smaller sitting rooms, and then there were the cloisters. 'Why on a fine day— *Oh my!*' She stopped short as a large spider scuttled across the flagstones in front of her.

'What is it?' cried Cuff.

'O-only a spider,' she admitted, sheepishly. 'I am sorry, but it was enormous, and . . . I am afraid it startled me.' She hated spiders intensely but continued, 'They are very good luck, I believe.'

'Aye, miss,' he gloomily agreed. 'Good luck.'

'Well, here we are. This is the library,' and she hurried past the place where the spider had been. Then she opened the door and nerved herself to step inside. If Cuff had not been behind her, breathing heavily, she might not have been able to do it. 'If you would please draw back those curtains, that would be a very great help.'

While it certainly could not be called sunshine, the dim, late morning light did give the library a rather more cheerful appearance – less like a place where one might be attacked. Cuff sat down at the now empty desk, holding his shotgun across his lap, while Mary scanned the shelves that ran around the three internal walls of the room.

She found them, four volumes of neat calfskin, each with the word *Commentaries* clearly printed on its spine.

She removed Volume One from the shelf and opened the front cover, her eyes drawn immediately to the bottom of the title page: THE FOURTH EDITION. M.DCC.LXX. She shut the cover with shaking fingers and closed her eyes. Edward Finch had not been able to read or write the code.

'Find what ye were looking for?' asked Cuff.

'Yes, yes, just a moment,' said Mary, hurriedly, 'I am almost finished.' She whipped open the volume again, comparing it with Mrs Tipton's. She knew that the fourth edition did not work for the code, but she checked it nevertheless.

A final thought occurred to her – perhaps her uncle had had another copy. A faint possibility, but she wanted to make absolutely certain.

'Can I help ye, miss?' asked Cuff, as Mary began scanning the shelves again.

'Yes, I am looking for a book called Blackstone's *Commentaries*. Like this one,' she added, showing him the volume.

'Not them others you've piled up there?'

'No, not those, but quite like them.'

They duly searched the shelves, Cuff in a state of mystification, and Mary distracted by the speed and confusion of her thoughts. Edward Finch had never read the documents. He had not been a spy. He had not been responsible for any of it.

She felt a great surge of relief, and hard upon it, like a strong undertow, came a feeling of guilt. She ought never to have believed it of him. Her own uncle, and she had thought him a traitor! Of course, she was glad to be proven wrong – she had never wanted him to have been a spy, for Heaven's sake. But what had he been doing with those papers?

'I don't see nothing over here, miss,' announced Cuff from across the room.

'No, nor do I,' said Mary, 'but keep looking, please.' Might her uncle have passed them on without knowing what they meant? It was possible, but it did not seem very likely. She stopped, having reached the end of the last bookcase. Why had the papers been at White Ladies? It did not make sense.

'Well, miss?' asked Cuff, breaking in on her deliberations again.

'Hm? Yes, I am sorry, Mr Cuff, I am finished now.' She took a deep breath. 'We must go to Woolthorpe Manor as quickly as possible. Let us tidy everything up again, and then we can be off.'

'*Woolthorpe*, miss?'

'Yes. I must speak with Mr Somerville straightaway. Oh *do* hurry,' she urged, for, in his amazement, he was standing motionless in the middle of the room.

He helped to straighten a folded curtain and, picking up his gun, followed her back along the passageway. 'Well I never,' he murmured. 'And what are we going to tell missus?'

Mary set her jaw. *Not the truth, at any rate.* 'We shall . . . we shall have to think of something,' she declared, as she bolted the door behind them.

It was only twelve miles from London to Waltham Cross, and the Regulator was exact to its time. Holland and Déprez were deposited at the Four Swans, where the landlord knew Holland from his previous visits to the nearby mill. He was noticeably less friendly to Déprez, even implying that suitable mounts were few; a fellow couldn't expect to come in and hire a beast what he hadn't made no arrangements for. Prior arrangements, that is.

Holland would have argued with him, but Déprez adopted a more conciliatory approach, complimenting him on the furnishings of his establishment, its interesting sign, and particularly the notable piece of statuary not a stone's throw from the Four Swans. 'It is a great historical relic, I make no doubt?'

It was indeed, the landlord assured him, vastly historical; it was put up by King Edward in ancient times on account of his wife. There were statues like that – crosses, if you like – put up in all sorts of places, but this one here was the best. Many gentlemen had said so. 'You say you're for the mills, Captain?' he asked, thoughtfully. 'I guess you can take Jess, and there's Folly for your friend. They don't mind the bangs.'

'Hm, Folly,' remarked Déprez with a wry smile as they walked toward the stable. 'Tell me, Captain Holland, are there often *bangs* at the Waltham Abbey facility?'

'Not usually, but you can always wait outside if you're nervous.'

'No, I will go wherever I am permitted to go.'

Holland surveyed the other man's attire and warned that it would be necessary to change their clothes when they entered the facility. Any hard metal, even a button or a nail, could create a spark and was therefore risky. They would probably not enter any of the danger buildings, but—

'But it doesn't hurt to be careful?' finished Déprez.

'That's right.'

Jess and Folly were steady, reliable horses, and they made the journey in good time. Holland did not recognise the man on duty at the gate, but Holland's own name was certainly known, and he had no difficulty gaining admittance, either for himself or Déprez.

They left their mounts in the stables with the mill

horses, which were resting between their shifts spent driving the great crushing stones. After removing their coats and trading their boots for spark-proof magazine shoes, Holland and Déprez entered the central part of the facility, which included the charcoal mill and the carpenter's shop. A change in the breeze wafted the acrid smell of saltpetre in their direction, and this grew stronger as they approached the melting house. Holland recognised one of the workmen and waved a greeting before turning toward the main administrative building. There, by rights, they would find Mr John Marshall, the master worker and manager of the Waltham Abbey establishment.

One of the junior clerks, a pale young man with what sounded like the beginning of a cold, met them just inside the door. 'Oh, Captain Holland, sir,' he stuttered, 'we did not expect . . . I mean, this is not your usual time. Is it?'

'No. It's . . . Turner, isn't it? I want to see Mr Marshall.' Holland's voice had assumed the cold, uncompromising tone it usually did when he was dealing with professional matters or irritating civilians.

'Beg your pardon, sir, but he's not here.'

'What about Mr Sault?' Holland brushed past Turner and opened the office door bearing the nameplate 'Jos. Sault'. Inside was a small desk bearing ledgers, paper and pens, all neatly arranged, and behind it an empty chair.

'Mr Sault is not here either,' said Turner.

'I can see that. Where is he?'

'I don't know, sir. He hasn't come in today.'

'And Marshall?'

Turner blew his nose and nervously explained that Mr Marshall was not on the premises just at the moment, his presence having been required in the dusting house. 'He has been gone ever so long, sir. Should you like me to fetch him?'

Before Holland could answer, Turner opened a window and called, 'Wilson!' A very small boy appeared, whose dirty face and magazine shoes suggested that he spent his time in and out of the different buildings on the site. 'Run and tell Mr Marshall that Captain Holland is here and wanting to see him. I think he is in the dusting house. Hurry, now.'

Holland glanced around the main room. There was no place to sit, if they were not to perch on stools beside Turner, now sniffling heavily into his handkerchief. 'We'll wait in Marshall's office.'

'Oh, yes, sir, if you please,' came the somewhat muffled reply.

The Master Worker's office was graced by a massive oak desk – a fortunate barricade in the event of a nearby explosion – a couple of more-or-less comfortable chairs, and a glass-fronted wall cabinet. The latter contained ledgers recording various aspects of the site's regular production, as well as some of the more experimental work carried out at Waltham since its purchase by the government in 1787.

'I would not say much for the security arrangements in this office,' observed Déprez. He rattled the cabinet door, which looked as if it would break under more vigorous handling.

'No, but it's only because you're with me that you were let in at all.'

'Very true, and you are clearly above suspicion.' Déprez shut the door behind them. 'F and S. Remove fault – remove Sault. An easy mistake for Miss Finch to make, but thank God you realised it. Do you know him?'

'Not really. I've met him – he's Marshall's chief clerk. He keeps the results of test firings, and I guess pretty much everything passes through his hands. If the French wanted to know what was going on here, Sault would be able to tell 'em. Let's see what Marshall has to say about it.'

They sat down to wait, but the sound of raised voices in the corridor soon had them on their feet again. Holland opened the office door as Turner asked young Wilson whether he had delivered his message.

'I didn't dare, sir.'

'What's the matter?' demanded Holland. Turner was unable to reply without sneezing, and Holland turned impatiently to the boy. 'Tell me what's happened,' he ordered. 'Something gone wrong in the dusting house?'

Wilson shook his head; his face was pale beneath the grime. 'In the head mills, sir. Fred Buckland's caught his hand in one of the edge runners. It's mangled him some-thing cruel, and Mr Marshall don't like to move him.'

'Is there a doctor?' asked Déprez.

'Oh, yes, sir,' said Wilson. 'They've sent for him. It's all over blood in there,' he added, in a sudden fit of inspir-ation, 'and Fred Buckland's crying and begging for 'em not to touch his arm. He's afraid they'll cut it off.'

'All right,' said Holland, frowning. 'You run along now, and wait for the doctor at the gate. And don't let him bring in any instruments that are made of iron.'

The boy raced toward the front gate and Holland set off in the direction of the head mills. 'Oh, Captain Holland, where are you going?' cried Turner, standing in the doorway. 'Do be careful!' he added, his first query having failed to elicit a response beyond a dismissive wave.

Déprez pushed past him and hurried after Holland. He had just caught up when another voice called out, 'Captain, sir! Captain Holland!'

Holland did not answer, but then he stopped and smiled in recognition as a figure hobbled toward him. 'Tom!' he called, 'what's the news with Fred Buckland?'

'Captain, sir! Is it yourself?'

'Not likely to be anyone else. Steady there, the doctor's on his way. Is he bad?'

These questions were addressed to an elderly man, grey-haired and somewhat bent on one side. He would have been considered well past his useful working life but for the fact that he had a remarkable way with the mill horses. He generally accompanied them to and from their work in the head mills and, judging by his worried expression, he had been present when the accident occurred. Now he shook hands with Holland and observed him with a sharp, but friendly eye. 'Aye, sir, poor Fred's in a bad way.'

'Is he going to lose his arm?'

'I'd say so.'

'Poor bugger,' muttered Holland. 'How'd it happen?'

Tom shrugged his shoulders. 'Careless, I reckon, or in a hurry. And Fred was a great one fer talking on his shift. Talking's the devil when there's serious work to be done. But you yourself, sir, you're all right?'

'Of course – I've been in Walton's House.'

'Well thank the Lord for that,' said Tom, emphasising his words by clasping Holland's arm. 'I was that worried – not that I oughter have been, I know, but sometimes fellers can so *turn* a man, with all their questions—'

'What are you on about, Tom? Who's been asking questions?'

'He didn't say. I reckon he must've been from the Ordnance, or the regiment, or somewheres in government, though he looked more like a thief-taker to me, hanging about the main gates, and in the village. But if you've seen Mr Marshall—'

'Hold on,' said Holland, raising his hand. 'I haven't seen him. You'd better tell me what you mean.'

Tom glanced at Déprez, and Holland said, 'It's all right, Tom, fire away.'

'Just as you say, sir,' said Tom, and then he drew the two men into the lee of a supply shed. There he whispered that a stranger had been nosing round, asking all sorts of questions about the mill, and the men, and . . . Captain Holland.

'About *me*? What questions?'

'Oh, yes sir, he was full of 'em. He wanted to know how often you came to the mills, and for how long, and anything I could tell him.' Holland did not reply, so Tom continued. 'Don't you worry, though, sir. You can count on me – I didn't tell him nothing.' He nodded craftily.

'Damn it, man, what *could* you have told him?'

'No sir, no sir. I mean to say, I didn't tell him nothing *improper*.' He patted Holland's arm reassuringly. 'But, I mean, it *is* all right, sir, ain't it?'

'Of *course* it's—' Holland stopped and began again, more gently. 'Of course it's all right. You don't think I've been skiving, do you, Tom?'

Tom smiled now, but only an anxious grimace, a quick flash of gums. 'Oh no, sir.'

'You said that the man looked like a thief-taker,' said Déprez. 'Can you describe him more completely?'

'Well, he was a little feller, and everything about him sharp, if you take my meaning. And he had a scar right here.' Tom indicated the place on his own face. 'Not the sort of chap you'd take to straightaway. Looked like he knew what was in yer pockets.'

'All right,' Holland nodded, 'that's good. Now tell me, Tom, did this man ask about Mr Sault?'

'Mr Sault, sir?'

'Yes. You know, Marshall's clerk.'

The urgency in Holland's voice was making Tom fearful,

anxious to give the desired answer. Perhaps some of the questions *had* concerned Sault, but Tom could not be certain. *He* had been thinking of Captain Holland. Nor could he remember the last time he had seen Sault, although it might have been last week – or the week before. After thinking for a moment, and frowning deeply with the effort, he muttered that Sault might have gone to London.

Déprez looked up in surprise. 'Why do you say that?'

'Well, sir, I think I heard Mr Sault had family there, in a place called Marylebone. Yes, sir, that's it,' Tom continued, growing more confident. 'I think he went regular to see his mother – which is a good thing, too.'

'So it is,' Déprez agreed. 'A mother in Marylebone – what could be more convenient?'

Tom was watching Holland anxiously. 'I hope I did right, sir.'

'What? Oh, yes. And thanks for telling me.' Holland turned to Déprez. 'That other man – the one asking questions – he must be a friend of Sault's. They probably wanted to know whether Sault was suspected.'

Déprez's glance was sceptical, but he nodded, and said, 'Very likely. They felt us on their trail.'

'But what's it all mean?' asked Tom. 'What *is* the trouble?'

'I can't explain it now, I'm afraid. In fact,' Holland continued, 'I don't think I'll wait to see Marshall after all. He's busy, and . . . What we've just been talking about, Tom, it might be best if you didn't tell anyone else about it.'

Tom nodded again, slowly but firmly. 'Aye, Captain, you can count on me.'

'Thanks for that,' said Holland, pressing his hand. 'Carry on with what you were doing, now, and . . . look after Fred Buckland.'

'Aye, sir, and you look after yourself. And I hope we'll see you again soon, in the *usual* way.' Tom shook his head as Holland and Déprez hurried away. 'These young fellers, always in a hurry. That's the best way for accidents and no mistake.'

18

About a mile from White Ladies the narrow, winding track joined the main road that led to Woolthorpe Manor. As the Tipton carriage negotiated the turn, Mary sat back in her seat, relieved that they would at last be able to achieve something faster than a walking pace, whatever the perils of speed in that vehicle. She rehearsed what she would tell Mr Somerville, but after a few moments she leaned forward again. Why were they slowing? As the carriage swayed and creaked, as if it too were complaining, she opened the window and was surprised to see what looked very much like Mr Somerville's carriage approaching from the opposite direction.

She waved eagerly and called up to Cuff to stop. When the other vehicle drew level it proved to be Mr Somerville's, but he was not on board. Instead, Mary greeted an equally surprised Hicks. Noting the absence of Mrs Tipton, he asked Mary where she was going.

'Woolthorpe Manor! There is a— I was going to speak with Mr Somerville, but perhaps I had better tell you.'

'Well,' he temporised, 'I am in a bit of a hurry.'

Mary leaned out of the window and spoke in a loud

whisper. 'Yes, but this is very important. There is something wrong with the code.'

Hicks fumbled with the watch in his hands and almost dropped it. '*What* did you say?' But before she could speak he had climbed down and flung open her door. 'Wait a moment, wait a moment,' he muttered, and extended his hand. 'Please.' Then he bundled her into his carriage and continued, rather breathlessly, 'Much safer this way – privacy. Now – tell me what has happened.'

'I made a mistake,' she blurted, 'not about the text, but the source.' Briefly she recounted her discovery of the discrepancies between the first and fourth editions of the *Commentaries*. 'So, you see, this upsets everything that we thought was happening. My uncle, and . . . *everything*.'

Hicks sat silently, arms crossed and chin pillowed on his fisted hand, and then he spoke in a brusque, tense voice. 'I am on my way to London, as it happens, and I mustn't linger. But what you've said . . . Would you carry on with me – just until Woodbridge? I would like to hear about all of this in greater detail.'

'Yes, of course,' Mary agreed. She was vastly relieved by his attitude. There had been a slight doubt, when she had set off from White Ladies, that Mr Somerville would not quite understand her point, or would not take it seriously. With Hicks, however, she felt more secure. They understood each other, and in passing her information on to him she felt as if a great burden had been lifted. She smiled at him, and it was a smile of relief.

'Good girl.' Hicks patted her hand and then jumped down again. He returned in a moment, and then the carriages parted: one south toward Woodbridge, and the other north to the next turning place, and then back on the coast road to Lindham.

'Now, about the code,' said Hicks as they clattered along. 'You say that your discovery upsets everything, but I'm not sure that it does. Your uncle had the fourth edition of the *Commentaries*, but that doesn't mean he didn't have the first edition as well – only that you didn't find it.'

Mary admitted that there *might* have been another copy somewhere in White Ladies, and she was obliged to acknowledge that her uncle *might* also have passed on documents that he could not read. A person *might* have so little curiosity, even if Mary could not imagine it herself. Hicks reminded her that the information was secret, and there would have been no point in using a code if everyone who handled the documents knew what was in them. 'No,' he concluded, 'I am sure they were all hired and paid handsomely to do what they were told *without* knowing.'

The words 'hired' and 'paid handsomely' caused Mary's heart to beat uncomfortably, and she had to clear her throat before she could reply. 'Mm. I suppose so.'

'And, you know, sometimes people choose not to think too much,' Hicks continued. The excitement caused by Mary's unexpected appearance had worn off, and now he spoke more composedly. 'Once they've made up their minds to do something, they don't want to be talked out of it. Sometimes they won't listen to things for fear of losing their nerve.'

'Yes.' Mary paused. Only a short while ago her discovery had seemed catastrophic, and now, perhaps, it meant nothing. Her uncle was still a traitor, and everything was as it had been. The code *did* work, after all, and Captain Holland had been satisfied that the information contained in the documents was genuine.

Even as she privately acknowledged these facts, however, she felt that she was giving up too easily. If things did not

341

make sense, there was no point in saying that they did, merely to be polite or to pretend that you thought all was well. The facts did not satisfy her, and so she continued to pose questions to Hicks. What if an enemy of her uncle's had left the documents at White Ladies as an act of revenge? William Tracey was known to have been a villain, and he had had a key to the house. Mightn't he have secreted them, perhaps on some previous visit? Surely that would undermine the documents themselves? And what of the message regarding the first quarter? Mary had looked in Mrs Tipton's almanac and was aware of the date when the moon would next be in its first quarter – did a meeting tomorrow evening not seem strangely convenient?

Neither the questions nor their order was entirely logical, for Mary asked them as they occurred to her, and the female mind, as Mr Somerville had said, worked differently from the male. Nevertheless, Hicks answered as well as he could. He doubted whether an enemy would have waited until after Mr Finch was dead to seek his revenge – and revenge for what? If Mr Finch had not been involved in the smuggling of the documents, why would anyone have wanted to lay such a crime at his door? If Tracey had suffered some injury at Mr Finch's hands, it was surprising that no one in Lindham had ever heard of him, and why would Mr Finch have associated with such a low fellow in the first place? As for the meeting at the Mace & Cells being convenient, Hicks would only say that, for his part, he would have preferred more than a space of two days in which to arrange an ambush for the spies. The whole thing was extremely awkward, and he did not know how it would all work out.

Mary acknowledged all that he said. Her anxiety was not quite sensible, but it was real. 'I cannot quite— It is all so . . . strange,' she murmured.

'It *is* strange,' Hicks agreed, and then he fell silent.

It was not necessary to brace oneself in Mr Somerville's carriage, and Mary stared out of the window. She was aware of the countryside rolling past her, but none of the details of colour, sound or texture registered in her brain; it was merely a cold, flat landscape, with which she felt no sympathy. This sense of isolation did not enable her to resolve her own thoughts, however, and the silence between herself and Hicks was not helping. After a time she began to feel as if she ought to speak, but what could she say other than to repeat her sense of unease? She opened her mouth, and before she could begin Hicks said, '*Wait*,' and then, more gently, 'wait. I believe that I must take you more fully into my confidence in this matter.'

Mary was so taken aback by this remark that she made no answer. After a further silence he continued, and now he seemed to have left his rough, unmannered style far behind. 'As you know, Miss Finch, although we only recently tracked him to Suffolk, Mr Déprez and I have been on the trail of the spy for some considerable time. I do not say we have solved every detail, but a few things have gradually become clear to us. And I must tell you that we are not satisfied with Captain Holland's part in all of this.'

'Not *satisfied*?' cried Mary, even more amazed. 'What can you mean?'

'I mean that, while you believe him to be a very gallant fellow who came to your aid, rescued you from White Ladies, explained the translated documents, and carried them off to safety, his actions can be read quite differently.'

'You cannot think that Captain Holland is somehow mixed up in this . . . plotting,' said Mary, scornfully. 'It is too— I do not believe it.'

'Well, consider,' said Hicks, his calm tone providing an effective counterpoint to Mary's raised, anxious one. 'You met him *by chance* in Ipswich, and he *immediately* agreed to accompany you to White Ladies – though it was out of his way. Both of these facts strike me as rather remarkable. But perhaps they are not if we remember that William Tracey, who was part of the smuggling and spying network, was also in Ipswich at that time. Why was he there? Why was he waiting in the Great White Horse day after day? To meet his associate – the man further up the chain, or perhaps the spy himself.'

'But not Captain Holland!' Mary persisted. 'He was quite opposed to the notion that Mr Tracey knew my uncle or was involved in anything untoward.'

'Well, he was hardly likely to say differently, if he was himself involved in something untoward. Far better to dissuade you from any ideas of the kind. But Tracey's death had upset the usual routine. Captain Holland was obliged to come here and meet directly with the smugglers. And do not forget what happened when you arrived at White Ladies. He left you alone while he went off *in search of information about your uncle* – or so he said. It would be interesting to know what else he was doing.'

'But . . . Captain Holland was imprisoned in the cellar with me. You do not mean to say that all that was . . . a charade? What purpose could it serve?'

Hicks temporised, shrugging his shoulders. 'We have not reached the bottom of the scheme, and I would not like to say anything for certain. It may have been a trick, but I suspect it was a case of mistaken identity. Very likely the Lindham smugglers did not know Holland, because he always communicated through Tracey. Your enquiries put them on their guard; they followed you to White Ladies and clapped the two of you in the cellar, not realising that they were mistreating one of their own comrades.'

Mary frowned at this interpretation; it was possible, but not very likely. 'But if that were so, why did he not . . . attempt to explain things to the men? Why take the risk of escaping?'

'Men like that take a great deal of convincing,' Hicks reminded her, 'better a blow than a word with them. And of course your presence was a further complication. How could Holland explain himself to the smugglers without compromising his position with you? But by engineering a daring escape, complete with a knock on the head and a bloody nose, he became both innocent victim and gallant rescuer. There could have been no better means of establishing his *bona fides* with all of us.'

'But it was not like that,' Mary argued. 'You do not understand.' Even as she spoke these words, however, she began to experience a nagging doubt. Hicks' interpretation did not square with her own recollection, but could she *really* say that her memory was correct? It had been such a strange, frightening experience – perhaps she had not really understood what was happening.

'And perhaps he *did* manage to explain things to them,' suggested Hicks, 'when he went back, alone, for his horse. That business was rather surprising, I must say. Why endanger your escape by returning for the horse?'

'Ye-es,' Mary acknowledged, 'I . . . I thought so at the time.' She hesitated for a moment, biting her lip. She *had* thought so. And the man on the road . . . the man who passed close by her on the White Ladies drive, but who did *not* pass Captain Holland only a few moments later. Or at least Captain Holland said he had not passed anyone. 'But we did escape,' she persisted, forcing down her doubts. 'A man tried to stop us—'

345

'By calling out? The fellow gave up rather easily, by all accounts. No shots were fired, after all, and no one gave chase. And then Holland left you at Mrs Tipton's, but having established himself as a very heroic fellow in all our eyes – a very heroic *military* fellow.'

In her mind's eye, Mary could see Holland smiling at her on their last evening together at Lindham Hall – when he suggested a correspondence. The memory of his words, and how she had thrilled to hear them, provoked a vivid blush. Had she been a fool to believe in him? 'He could not have known that I would find those documents,' she protested.

'No, but he probably thought it highly likely that suspicious papers of some kind would turn up somewhere. And how convenient that the ones you found concerned matters particularly within *his* professional competence. He is probably the man best qualified in England to explain what they mean.'

'Yes,' Mary admitted in a low voice, 'he told me as much.'

'Ah, he did, did he? Did he say anything else?'

Mary nodded, and she almost whispered the next words. 'He said he was not a spy.'

'He said *that*?' demanded Hicks. Then he spread his hands as if all had been made clear. 'Well. He must have known that his position was suspect and tried to bluff you.'

'Yes, but . . . I do not know.' She shook her head, remembering her own sudden suspicions of the night before, but resolving in that moment not to reveal them to Hicks. 'These papers – why would he want them?'

'My dear Miss Finch, to put them out of harm's way – by which I mean out of the way of myself, Mr Déprez, and indeed, you. For you have had your doubts from the start. It only took you time to put all of the pieces together.'

346

'Yes, but I never— not *this*.' She sat up and squared her shoulders against the back of the seat. 'What does Mr Déprez think?'

'Mr Déprez has not been altogether happy with Captain Holland for some time. Holland is not a wealthy man, you know, and the information he acquired put him in the way of making a great deal of money. It would have been a severe temptation.'

Mary nodded, and as she did she could hear Holland's voice telling her that she would have been a fool not to think about her uncle's money – that *he* thought about money all the time. So sharp was the recollection that she missed the start of Hicks' next sentence. She turned to him suddenly as she caught a reference to 'the young lady in the case'. 'What young lady?' she demanded.

'I believe she is his cousin, or a relation of some sort,' shrugged Hicks. 'I understand she is very well off, and comes from a good family. They would never let her marry a penniless fellow like Holland, and he must have known it. That would have made his need to shore up his finances even more pressing.'

Dearest Susannah!

'And then there was his manner when he returned to Woolthorpe,' Hicks continued. 'Holland admitted that the information was secret, but when it came to taking steps to unmask the villains, he thwarted us at every point. This was *his* affair, he said, and *he* would decide what was to be done and what was to be left alone. Mr Somerville and Mr Déprez could sit and twiddle their thumbs. So, when Holland suddenly decided to rush away to London – taking *all* of the incriminating documents with him – Déprez did likewise. It is a very big place, you know, London, and it would not do for the captain simply to *disappear*.'

Hicks had grown more agitated during his speech, but now he sighed as he realised the effect of his remarks upon Mary. She was pale, and now she closed her eyes. 'I am sorry, Miss Finch. You would rather not believe this, and I do not blame you,' he said, gently. 'You thought he helped you, and—'

'He *did* help me.' She opened her eyes and smiled thinly at Hicks. 'I am trying to be sensible,' she pleaded, 'but I do not . . . There is much that I do not understand, and much that — forgive me — does not quite make sense.'

Hicks agreed. 'It is a highly complicated business, but Déprez will know best how to proceed.'

Mary nodded thoughtfully. Yes, Mr Déprez; he would make sense of this . . . mystery. It seemed as if all their hopes must rest on him.

The carriage slowed, and Hicks ducked his head to look out of the window. 'Ah, here is Woodbridge. We must change the team and carry on to Ipswich, but I will just see about a chaise to take you to Lindham Hall.'

Conflicting images continued to tumble through her brain, but she held on to the one fact that was clear — the code did not work, or at least, not completely. What did she owe Captain Holland, after all? *If he has done something wrong, why should I worry about him when there are other, more important considerations? Treason and spying . . .* And then the carriage lurched as the horses were unhitched, and Mr Somerville's coachman barked instructions about 'that goddamned snaffle bit'.

Mary turned impulsively to her companion. 'Mr Hicks, would you take me with you?'

'Take you . . . to Ipswich?'

'No — to London.'

He had started to rise, but her words made him sink

down again, and he stared at her in disbelief. 'You want to go to *London*?' he repeated.

'Yes. I allow your point about . . . my uncle, but I think there are much more important matters to consider. We have all relied on the code completely – Captain Holland and Mr Déprez—'

'But—'

'Yes, I know you do not trust the captain, and perhaps you are right.' She spoke those last words quickly and with a growing fervour. 'I am not certain. But regardless of that, Mr Déprez has taken decisions that he might not have done if he had known that the code was not quite right. He must be told the truth immediately. He may need to think again, or . . . he may be in great danger if he simply carries on!'

'I see that,' Hicks agreed, 'but . . . but I will tell him of your discovery. Of course I will, the moment I see him. How will the information be improved if *you* tell him?'

She smiled candidly. 'I do not suppose it will be. I know it sounds terribly selfish of me, but after everything that has happened – it is so hard to stand aside and not participate, especially when we have not worked it all out yet. I think I *must* see it through to the end. And I do know an awful lot about the code.'

'Yes, but . . .' Hicks frowned discouragingly. He liked Mary, but the thought, *ridiculous women, impossible to reason with*, was difficult to hold back. He managed, however, and after a moment even used the idea to his advantage. 'What about Mrs Tipton? How do you propose to explain all of this to *her*?'

The thought of her hostess was a sobering one. Mary knew that it would be impossible to explain anything to Mrs Tipton, certainly not in such a way that gained her approval. But simply to leave, to rush away without a word, was very bad – rude and ungrateful – and an absence in London could not be concealed. 'I will tell her that I am obliged – unexpectedly obliged – to go to London in great haste but in perfect safety on a matter of extreme importance and . . . propriety. I can write a note now, and someone from the inn can deliver it.'

'And you believe *that* will content her?'

Mary could feel herself blushing. 'No, but . . . at least she will not worry straightaway, and it is the best I can do without actually lying. So,' she added, after a slight pause, 'will you take me to London or . . . must I go on my own?'

'*On your own?*' cried Hicks, evidently scandalised.

'Yes,' said Mary, and her voice gained confidence as she spoke. 'They will advance me the fare at Collier's bank. I am an heiress, you know. I can afford to hire a vehicle – even *buy* one, if need be.' Then she smiled. 'But I would much rather go with you.'

Hicks sighed discontentedly, but the look of determination on Mary's face convinced him that further argument would only waste time. *Women!* Whatever their merits, they were no end of trouble. 'Very well,' he agreed, curtly. 'I suppose I must.'

Holland and Déprez returned to the Four Swans by way of the village of Waltham Abbey, not because either of them thought that they would really find Joseph Sault at home, but because they wanted to know whether his neighbours could be of any help in locating him. It proved to be an unsuccessful detour. No one had seen Sault leave, nor could they provide any credible information about where he might have gone. He was a quiet, respectable man who did not give any trouble. That is what everyone knew, and it was too difficult to imagine him as anything else.

Their hints and queries either rebuffed or misunderstood, Holland and Déprez had no alternative but to return to London. They were not alone on the coach from Waltham Cross, so it was impossible to discuss the question that concerned them most. As soon as they descended at the Spread Eagle, however, Déprez turned eagerly to his companion to resume their conversation.

'What now?' he demanded. 'What is our course?'

'There *is* no course,' said Holland, curtly. 'We'll never trace Sault now.'

'We could go to Marylebone.'

Holland shook his head. 'If they didn't know him in Waltham Abbey, they aren't going to know him there. And we don't even know where to ask.'

'But the old fellow . . . Tom said that he had family there.'

'Do *you* think he's off visiting his mother?'

'He might have done. A man in trouble, wanting a safe refuge . . . why not? A devoted mother is the best accomplice a criminal may have.' Déprez spoke urgently, but he received nothing more than a half-hearted shrug in reply. 'What is the matter? You seem very tired.'

'Maybe I am,' Holland agreed. 'Too tired to waste any more time.' He sighed and rubbed his eyes.

'What of the Mace & Cells? You said that it was near the Tower of London, in a place called St Catharine's.'

'St Catharine's is near the Tower, and I said there *might* be a tavern there called the Mace & Cells,' Holland corrected.

'Well, surely that is worth finding out? If the message did refer to a meeting tomorrow, perhaps Sault will attend. The message mentioned him, after all.'

Holland regarded Déprez curiously. 'You're very determined.'

351

'But you are not?'

The question prompted a change in Holland's demeanour. Whatever interest he seemed to have had in his associate faded, and his expression became guarded and cool. 'Yes, all right. We'll take a look, but that's the end of it.'

'Agreed. Shall we walk?'

They headed south toward the river, but on Holland's advice they turned on to Eastcheap, thus avoiding both the crowds at the Monument and the confusion of Billingsgate market. Even so, their way was repeatedly blocked by traffic as men and vehicles also tried to gain an advantage by using the narrower road. At this time of day most were heading away from the river; either fish-mongers who had shut up their stalls, or hauliers bearing goods from the docks. It would be even worse, Holland confided, on Thames Street.

'Ah yes, the customhouse traffic must be very great,' nodded Déprez. 'I have had some small experience of it, when I accompanied a cargo of my sugar some years ago. A very interesting voyage, which made the paperwork at the conclusion all the more tedious. Paperwork is the worst part of being in business – and losses, of course. Do you know, I had to pay a great deal of money to have my cargo landed promptly. I was informed that the usual practice was to store uncustomed goods on lighters, and one must pay a premium for anything else.'

'I think you were wise to pay,' said Holland. 'Thievery on the Thames is a big business. If the cargo had been left on board, or shifted onto lighters, you would have lost a fair lot of it.'

'Yes, so I understood. And the gangs have the most outlandish names: "Mudlarks" or "Scuffle Hunters". What can be their linguistic origin? And that,' he added after

Holland expressed no opinion, 'must be the Tower of London ahead of us.'

Déprez was looking up at the grim edifice as he walked. '"*With many a foul and midnight murther fed*,"' he observed, and Holland caught his arm to prevent him stepping into the path of an oncoming cart. 'Oh— I am obliged to you,' he said, sheepishly. They darted across the busy street, and Déprez continued, by way of an explanation, 'London is a favourite topic among literary men. Poets have frequently written about it – although not always in a complimentary manner.'

'Oh?' asked Holland, in a bland, perfunctory voice, and then, more naturally, advised Déprez not to cross to the other side of the street as they were going straight on. When they had eased past a crowd gathered round a wagon whose axle had collapsed he admitted, 'I don't know much about that sort of thing, I'm afraid. Poetry, I mean, and . . . history.'

Déprez glanced at the man walking beside him. Here was another of those unexpected turns that marked Holland's conversation. Were they planned? Intended somehow to disarm Déprez and gain his sympathy? Déprez did not think so, but they certainly made the job more difficult. He needed to understand Holland, and to predict his likely actions, yet – albeit unconsciously – Holland was keeping him off balance.

Déprez responded cagily. 'Indeed? You surprise me. I speak under correction, of course, but I understood that the gentlemen of the artillery attended an academy before they were commissioned.'

'They do. I went when I was twelve. When we were little we were supposed to learn . . . artistic sorts of things, but the fellow teaching us was drunk most of the time, and when he was sober he beat us. As we got older we were taught Fortifications, Mathematics, and Surveying by men who could hold their drink.'

'Of course, those would be the important subjects,' Déprez agreed, 'but—'

'I know, the other makes you more polished,' added Holland, 'and people think you're "eligible" if you can talk about Shakespeare.'

'Indeed, I am sure they do, although I was thinking more about the enjoyment of the thing. The beauty and power of great literature.' Déprez waited for a reply, but he did not receive one.

The Tower precinct was encumbered by a different sort of traffic. There were sightseers gazing up at the masses of medieval stonework or waiting in the queue to see the wild animals, and loitering off-duty soldiers. Wandering among both were street-sellers hawking gingerbread and hot chestnuts, while bands of shabby children preyed upon the charitable and the inattentive. 'You'd better mind your purse,' Holland advised as they shouldered through the crowd. 'They'll have it off you if you aren't careful.'

Déprez had already been aware of more than one attempt to pick his pocket and, confident of his ability to thwart any likely crime, he chose simply to do so rather than to publicise the affront. Instead he asked which was the Traitors' Gate.

'Round the other side. They brought important prisoners to the Tower by water.'

'Yes, I see,' said Déprez, looking about him. 'Much safer, I daresay.'

As they left the Tower behind them, their way became less inviting. In part, this was because the afternoon was drawing on, and the sky had darkened to a gloomy grey. More than that, however, the streets were narrow, with tall, ramshackle buildings that blocked out the light. Many of these were derelict, or partly so, with nothing but a rag hanging from an upper window, or a clothesline stretching high above the street, to indicate a continued habitation. At street level most of the shops had long disappeared, while those still trading consisted mostly of pawnshops and gin houses, while the presence of pale, slatternly dressed women and girls huddled in doorways suggested another occupation.

'My God, what a place,' muttered Déprez. They had stopped while Holland spoke briefly with a peddler of old clothes. 'I would not keep a dog in such a hovel, and now . . . God, the smell.'

'It's not very nice,' Holland agreed, as the peddler shouldered his load and set off in the direction they had come. 'Come on, it's this way.'

As he spoke the breeze shifted, bringing not just the acrid odours of filth and cheap coal but swirling smoke from ill-constructed chimneys, and the combination made Déprez cough and his eyes water. He glanced up at the gloomy, anonymous windows. Most were dark, but in some a candle flickered or a shadow passed, and he had the unpleasant sensation of being watched by unfriendly eyes. 'If one of us were to fall down in a fit,' he mused, 'I suppose he might only be robbed and not killed, but I would not like to put it to the test.'

'Neither would I. And it's best not to seem too curious, or as if you might be lost.'

At the bottom of a dark, narrow passage, whose broken cobbles were deep in mud, they found the Mace & Cells. Its name was said to mark a famous foreign adventure of the fifth King Henry. The village where the English camped before the battle of Agincourt was called Maisoncelles, and in his old age a veteran of that campaign had opened a public house near the river Thames, from whence he might still observe the comings and goings of soldiers and sailors. He had called his establishment the Maisoncelles as a tribute to the great victory, and only the rough learning of later generations had reduced the name to the more prosaic form.

That, at any rate, was the story, and it might even have been true. Certainly the Mace & Cells was very old, and its plastered front and small, dark windows made it look not so much impoverished as surrounded by a more recent, overwhelming poverty. It formed part of a collection of structures that had been built haphazardly over and against each other, so that it was difficult to see how they remained standing, except through mutual support.

'There it is,' remarked Holland from the shadow of a doorway part-way down the alley. 'Don't go any closer,' he cautioned, when Déprez would have kept walking.

'You do not mean to go inside?'

Holland shook his head. 'Two strangers turning up would put everyone on their guard. Especially the way you're dressed.'

'Have you not already done as much?' charged Déprez, 'alarmed the locals by asking for directions?'

'But I didn't ask about the Mace,' Holland explained, smiling, 'I asked about the house over there with the red door. There's a couple of girls at the top of the stairs — so I'm told — who cater to . . . all tastes.'

'I see,' said Déprez, smiling in turn; he could not help it. 'And might I enquire whether you asked for me or for yourself?'

'For you,' Holland admitted. 'I said you were too shy to ask.'

'Damn you,' Déprez laughed. 'But tell me, how did you know it was here?'

'I didn't. I told him the sort of thing I was after – *you* were after – and said I'd heard about a house near St Catharine's alley. It was a lucky hit.'

'Very lucky indeed.' Déprez glanced thoughtfully at Holland. 'Well, unless you propose to discover whether the young ladies' reputation is deserved, I suppose that means our work here is done.'

'Yours is.' Holland's voice had resumed its usual curtness.

'But you cannot let things go – not with what we have discovered.'

'I'm *not* letting them go. I'm going down to Woolwich, but that doesn't concern you.' Holland hesitated. 'Remember what we agreed, about not trying anything on your own.'

'I have not forgotten,' said Déprez. 'You . . . mistrust me, don't you?'

'No – but I don't like civilians shoving their noses into service business. I'm going to cross the bridge, but I can see you back to the Tower, if you like.'

Déprez shook his head. 'No, you needn't bother. I am very well on my own.'

'Well, goodbye, then.' They shook hands.

Holland had not taken more than a few steps when he was enveloped by an explosion of white light. He staggered, and for an instant was aware of a shattering pain. Then he fell to the ground.

Déprez bent over him and felt for a pulse, and then turned Holland over on to his back. One side of his face was muddy, and a trickle of blood ran from a cut on his forehead. 'You are rather too keen to get away from me, my friend,' Déprez murmured, 'and I am afraid that will not do.'

★   ★   ★

On arriving in London, Joseph Sault had not gone immediately to the safe house. His flight from Waltham Abbey had been too precipitous, and the threat of capture was still too real for him simply to go where he was known, even to a place that had always sheltered him in the past. So he went into hiding; first in an anonymous tavern where he hoped to remain unseen and unheard, and then, when the four dreary walls became too much for him, on the city streets. He walked up and down Oxford Street, scarcely looking at the shops, and into Hyde Park, where the soldiers drilled. He observed them critically; up and down, up and down, apparently oblivious to their surroundings. They excited little interest in him, and certainly no sympathy. In war there were bound to be casualties, and it was fatal to grant the enemy the benefit of human thoughts and feelings. The enemy was, simply, the enemy; an abstraction, or, if composed of individuals, then individuals marching about in that mindless way, whose elimination would be no real cause for concern. Cattle were slaughtered every day, after all, and no one shed tears over them. On the contrary, those who killed them skilfully were paid well for their work.

His feet began to grow cold, and with perfect assurance he strolled among the market gardens along the Edgeware Road, and then turned right, back into Marylebone and toward the house on Orchard Street.

His knock was answered by the same bland, unremarkable woman who had always answered, and he stepped inside. The house was well furnished; a retired gentleman of independent means was supposed to live there, and when Sault walked into the parlour he noticed that a small pianoforte had been purchased since his last visit.

To Sault it seemed as if he had entered a world

completely apart from the noise, dirt, and squalor of the streets; his feet sank into deep carpets, while a pleasant aroma of beeswax and lavender filled the air. There was a bowl of fresh flowers on the table, and interesting-looking books were piled casually on the sideboard. Above all, there was quiet – he could hear the well-modulated ticking of the longcase clock in the hallway. One of the servants escorted him to his room, the one he often used, and brought him a cup of tea. The very regularity of the place, everything calm and efficient, was soothing, and he began to recover something of his usual serenity.

After about half an hour he had an interview with one of the young men who generally saw to the 'business' end of things. Sault knew him and was glad that he did not have to explain himself to a stranger. He told his story carefully, omitting no details. 'And so, I had to come away,' he concluded. 'I know I had been told to hold fast, but—'

'No, you were exactly right,' pronounced the young man, as he recorded Sault's words in a notebook. 'There was nothing else you could have done.'

'I have always followed my orders,' said Sault. He did not want to blame anyone, but he felt that he could afford a little self-satisfaction.

'Of course you have. Paris has always been pleased with your efforts. I suppose no one would be able to trace your journey from Waltham Abbey?'

'No, I was very careful about that.'

'And your things? Those are not your hat and coat, I presume.'

Sault glanced at the greasy frock coat and battered tricorne he had been wearing since coming to London. He had bought them in a shop in Clerkenwell. His waistcoat, a garishly striped item, had come from a similar establishment, and he was mildly distressed that the young man imagined it to be part of his usual attire. 'No, I left all of my things at the Bolt-in-Tun, in Drury Lane — but I have not been staying there. Too obvious, I thought.'

'Yes, although sometimes it is easier to hide oneself in a crowd.'

'Well, in any event, do you think you could have them sent round? I am afraid I have no money left . . . coming away so quickly.'

The young man smiled reassuringly and told him not to worry — *he* would make all the arrangements. More than that, he praised Sault for having come through a very trying situation. 'I expect some instructions will be sent down in a few days, perhaps with regard to a new assignment. But for now, you should relax.'

He gathered together his writing materials, and when he stood up Sault did likewise. 'Are things . . . very bad at Waltham Abbey?' he asked. 'At the mill, I mean? My leaving so suddenly will cause problems for our operation, I know.'

'I am not certain of the exact position,' shrugged the young man. 'My understanding is that the real difficulty lies elsewhere, and the warning to you was merely a consequence. Now, is there anything else you need?'

'No, I am perfectly content, thank you. Perhaps I will have a rest — I am a bit tired.'

He *was* tired, and when he lay down he fell into such a deep sleep that he did not hear the servants come in to remove the unappealing clothes and replace them with his own, neatly pressed, and later, to deposit towels and a selection of men's toiletries. He noticed them when he awoke a few hours later, however, and felt a surge of happiness. How foolish he had been to doubt them. They were so careful, so discreet. They would not let anything happen to him. Everything was going to be all right.

He smiled at his reflection in the mirror as he washed his face and hands. How good it was to feel clean again; he hated a bristly chin. Then he retied his neck cloth, checked his watch, and put on his coat. His nap had refreshed him, and there was just time for a stroll before it became dark.

It was such a gloomy afternoon that he doubted there would be many people in the park at that hour, so he turned toward Oxford Street. There was no point inviting trouble, after all. He started thinking about the future. Very likely he would be given a new assignment, perhaps a more important one. Relocation would undoubtedly cost money, but he was a valuable agent, after all. Extricating himself as he had done — saving himself — had proven that, if proof were necessary, and it meant he was worth taking trouble over.

He was just another window-shopper, gazing bemusedly at a shelf of silver cigar cases, when he felt himself bumped and then jostled on one side. He reached automatically inside his coat to protect his wallet, forgetting that it was empty, and a hand gripped him firmly by the elbow and propelled him sideways. A small, thin-faced man with a scar like a cat's whisker was glaring up at him, and Sault flinched, just as Mary had done when she encountered the same man on the Stowmarket road.

'Oy!' grunted Sault, stumbling, and before he knew what was happening he was being pushed round the corner and into an alley. What was the meaning of this — sordid behaviour — wretched little vagabond. He tried vainly to shake off his attacker, and they slipped and jostled on the rough, rutted ground. Somehow it did not occur to Sault to cry out. Surely he need not fear this stunted fellow. 'Let me go – I have no money,' he warned.

'I know that,' sneered Rede. He had a wiry strength that belied his size, and he flung Sault hard against a wall, holding him there with his arm and shoulder. 'Left home in a bit of a hurry, didn't you?'

Sault froze. 'Oh my God— Who are you? What do you want?'

'What's owing to me, which I can't collect till I've sorted you out,' said Rede. He was fumbling for something in his pocket while still braced against Sault. 'You've caused me a lot of bother, traipsing about all over town like you have. I'm fair knackered.'

'Please,' begged Sault. 'Let me go. I have never— My information has always been reliable! I have always followed my instructions.'

'Have you? Well, that's nothing to me.'

Rede fished out a small pistol, hardly visible in the palm of his hand, but Sault caught a glimpse of it. 'No!' he cried, and gave a mighty shove that lifted Rede off his feet and flung him away.

The little man fell heavily, and the pistol slid out of his hand and across the cobbles, but he was quickly on his feet again. Sault stumbled, righted himself, and raced down the alley, even as Rede snatched up his weapon and sprang after him.

Sault was gasping, crying as he ran. Rede was faster, but lighter, and his flying tackle could not bring Sault down. They struggled together, Rede clinging fiercely as Sault tried to wrench himself free a second time. He staggered across the alley, heaving his assailant against a pile of crates just as Rede entangled their legs. They fell together, still fighting.

'Please, let me go!' Sault begged.

Rede smacked him hard across the face and Sault could feel his strength failing as Rede clambered on top of him. Then the metal was pressing against his side. He writhed hopelessly. 'No – wait! I have an idea!'

'I've got a better one,' Rede whispered, and pulled the trigger.

19

In a dark, draughty room that was bare of furniture apart from a crudely fashioned wooden table and a straight-backed chair, Paul Déprez sat motionless, deep in thought. Not so deep, however, that he was oblivious to his surroundings – the locked door in front of him, the pale shaft of moonlight that entered through the small casement window and crossed the floor, illuminating dusty footprints and bits of rubbish, and the darker shadow in the far corner of the room that moved, or seemed to move, from time to time with a restless shudder. The air was cold, and Déprez had not removed his greatcoat. On the table beside him were a candlestick and a double-barrelled pistol, and he grasped the latter and rose to his feet when he heard the sound of a faint tapping at the door.

He stepped quickly and noiselessly across the room, avoiding the moonlight, and slid the bolt. The door opened slowly, and a smaller figure crept inside, pushing the door closed behind him.

'Well?' whispered Déprez. There was anxiety in the single, curt syllable.

'All's well with me, gov,' replied Rede, 'and very quiet

outside – as quiet as you could wish for. Have you . . . done the necessary?'

'Hm. I have indeed *done* it, but it was a damned sight too much. Light that candle and take a look.'

Rede did as he was bid, and soon a faint, flickering light illuminated the table and Rede's thin, pale face behind it. Déprez lit a second candle and held it aloft, its light sending enormous, dancing shadows further into the room. 'Over there,' he nodded.

'Ah,' breathed Rede, as the shadowy corner was shown to contain a low pallet, or pile of sacking, on which lay a man covered with a dark coat. Rede knelt beside him and directed the candle light over him. His eyes were closed, but he did not seem to be asleep, for his breathing was ragged, and his hair lay wet against his face, despite the chill air. 'Captain Holland,' Rede murmured. 'Pleased to make yer acquaintance, at long last.' After a moment he lifted the coat, and his lips formed a silent whistle as he perceived a dark, wet stain on the man's white shirt. 'Put up a fight, did he, gov?'

Déprez bent over Rede's shoulder and frowned down at Holland. 'Yes, he certainly did, damn him, though really it was my own fault. I thought he was unconscious, but I must only have stunned him, and when I brought him in here he went for me like . . . like a man who was not unconscious. I was not expecting it and, as well as being on my own . . .' Déprez blew out his breath and shrugged diffidently. 'At the risk of stating the obvious, this is not how I had planned things.'

'Well, you've got him – in a manner o' speakin'. That's something, any road.'

'Yes, I have him, and it would be very much my luck if he were to die. What do you suppose are the chances of getting a doctor here tonight?'

Rede shook his head. 'Not a proper doctor — a respectable one. Never come near a place like this, day or night. I could try and find somebody — a butcher, say, or a horse knacker.'

'Damn you, man, I do not want him cut into pieces,' Déprez complained. 'I have patched him up as well as I could, but I could not remove the bullet — it looks to have mangled his ribs a bit. He needs skilled treatment, and sooner rather than later.' He was silent for a moment. 'Well, you will have to find someone — do the best you can, but bring him back quickly.'

'What'll I say about him being shot?'

'Say nothing — and do not bring a man who will ask. Now, help me carry him upstairs. I will take his shoulders. Can you manage his legs and the light?'

'Mm,' said Rede, and nodding at the injured man's bound wrists and ankles added, 'I . . . don't suppose he still needs to be trussed up?'

'Perhaps not — but you would not say that if you had seen him earlier. And it makes him easier to carry. Ready?'

They bore the limp body slowly upstairs, the light from Rede's candle wavering and flickering up the narrow passage and reflecting first on Déprez, backing up cautiously, then on Holland's pale face lolling against Déprez's shoulder, and then on Rede's left hand and arm as he held the candle aloft. He grasped Holland's legs firmly under his right arm and leaned against the wall to steady himself as he climbed. Bits of rough, flaking plaster were ground into Rede's coat or fell on to the steps in a gritty shower.

'Careful,' Rede urged, glancing upward. 'One more step and yer there.'

In the small room at the top of the stairs they found a dilapidated bed, chairs, and a washstand. After they had laid Holland down, Rede lit a fire in the grate, and then went back downstairs for a bucket of water. When he returned Déprez had Holland's shirt open and was examining his bandages.

Rede ran his fingers over the place where the bandage was padded. 'I think you're right about his ribs. What are you goin' to do with him?'

Déprez plunged his hands into the bucket and, finding nothing better, dried them on the grubby counterpane. 'That depends on what the doctor says, but I would be happier if this bleeding would stop. No word from Hicks, I suppose?'

'No, sir, not yet. I been over to the King's Arms, but there's no sign of him. But it's still early, if you figure he was comin' from t'other side of Woodbridge.'

'Well, we cannot worry about him now. He knows what to do, and in the meantime I need your help here. And first of all, find me a doctor.'

'I'll do that, gov. You can count on me.'

'Where are we going?' asked Mary, hurrying to keep pace with Hicks as he made his way through the crowded parlour of the King's Arms. It was a difficult task, for two coach loads of passengers had only just arrived and were streaming into the hostelry, eager for their breakfast, while Mary and her companion were trying to reach the courtyard.

'The office of the City Police,' Hicks replied, over his shoulder. He nodded at Mary as she won her way through the press and appeared at his side. 'Well, done, Miss Finch. Carefully, now.' Taking her arm he guided her across the yard and into Leadenhall Street.

The noise, the smells, the crush of people; it was London on a busy morning, but Mary had never experienced anything like it. She had thought she knew about towns. Bath was certainly busy, but London seemed to be busy on an entirely different scale. She hung back, aghast at the pandemonium of over-laden carts, carriages and horsemen, bawling street vendors and barking dogs, clerks, shop girls, and ragged children. Every face seemed strained, many were haggard, and no one seemed capable of moving quietly or even, she felt, courteously.

The chaos was even more formidable because she was only half awake. They had arrived in the capital at half past three, and their rooms at the King's Arms had been cold and comfortless. Not liking the look of the blankets and counterpane, Mary had laid down in her clothes with her cloak over her, only to be roused again after a few hours of troubled sleep. She had then drafted a second note to Mrs Tipton, but as this could state little more than the fact of her safe arrival she had not found the exercise very pleasant. All in all, it was not the best preparation for her first foray into London, and Mary was grateful when Hicks waved down a passing cab and handed her into it. 'Bow Street,' he informed the driver, and climbed in after her.

While the noise of the traffic outside continued to surround them, inside the journey was completed in silence. Hicks was eager and alert; he had cast aside any tiredness and appeared almost youthful. There was a closed tension about him, however, which also set him apart. Mary did not feel she could speak to him, either to point out interesting sights or to ask further questions. Instead she kept her own counsel and wondered what would happen next. What might the City Police add to the strange, confusing story of smugglers and spies? And where were Captain Holland and Mr Déprez?

The Bow Street office was also crowded with early

morning traffic, as constables returned from their nightly patrols. Several were accompanied by victims, witnesses or malefactors, and sometimes it was difficult to guess into which category they fell. That stunned-looking man with the black eye – had he been robbed or fallen down drunk? And those two quarrelling women – they did not seem at all surprised to find themselves in a police station. Mary stared as a man was led past her, his hands tied before him with a knotted rope. His face was bruised and bloody, and his grimy coat hung loosely off one shoulder. He tried to catch her eye, but she avoided him and moved unconsciously toward the safety of the front desk and the uniformed man behind it.

Hicks, it seemed, was known to the police authorities, for when he gave his name and mentioned that he had to do with St Lucia, the clerk's expression of jaded disinterest changed immediately. 'Of course, sir,' he nodded. 'Mr Hudson's just come in, but I'm sure he'll want you to go straight up.'

No one seemed to care what Mary did, so she followed Hicks up the stairs to the first floor. There she was introduced to a stern, implacable-looking man, who was drinking his morning tea. 'Miss Finch,' Hicks explained, 'has been much involved in our work, sir.'

'Indeed?' said Hudson. He was plainly surprised, but in neither tone nor expression did he indicate whether he intended to ask Mary to sit down or have her clapped in irons.

'Innocently involved, I ought to have said,' Hicks continued. 'Through no fault of her own – or no fault beyond being a very intelligent young lady.'

Mary added, hurriedly, 'I do not mean to intrude upon your work, sir, only, I . . .' It suddenly seemed ridiculous to explain that she had come all the way to London because she wanted to understand what was happening, that she had not wanted to be left behind, and her sentence trailed off.

'Of course, not at all,' said Hudson, with more politeness than clarity, and then he motioned her toward an armchair beside his desk. It bore a pile of papers and was partly overhung by a coat stand. 'Do, er, make yourself comfortable, and I hope you don't mind if Hicks and I discuss certain matters.'

'No, sir, indeed,' she replied, and as she removed the papers and shifted Mr Hudson's overcoat she reflected that he probably regarded her as only marginally more important to the present case. Still, it was comfortable to be slightly out of the way; to observe and not feel herself under observation. She would listen and learn what she could – but she would not have objected to a cup of tea, and her stomach rumbled at the thought.

'Right,' said Hudson. 'Now, Hicks, I trust my side of things is shorter than yours, so I'll begin. That fellow Rede came to see me two days ago with more of those coded papers.'

Hicks glanced up in surprise. '*More* papers, sir?'

'Yes. Said they belonged to someone named Sault, who has been spying for the French.'

'Ah, yes, sir, exactly right. But what of Sault himself?'

'Missing. He was not at home when Rede paid him a visit – not that a locked front door seems to have caused Rede any difficulties.'

'No, sir, it wouldn't have done.' Hicks watched as the other man opened the drawer of his desk and produced a file. From it he selected two bundles of documents and placed them on the desk. 'Here are the first ones you gave me, and here are the others. Different hands, but similar in essentials.'

Hicks nodded, pressing his lips tightly together, but Hudson's glance was sceptical. 'It is still just so much gibberish, of course, unless you are able to translate the damned things.'

'Indeed, sir, indeed I am,' Hicks assured him, 'that is to say, if you will permit me to defer to the expert in these matters. It was Miss Finch, you see, who broke the code in the first place.'

Mary smiled, but she found Hicks' deferential gesture off-putting. The sight of further coded documents certainly whetted her interest, and she was not a little proud of her achievement, especially in front of Hudson. But Hicks' manner made her feel like a child who was being placated, or a conjuror who had been asked to perform an interesting sleight of hand. And now Hudson was staring at her; she almost felt as if she ought to bow.

Hudson, however, was highly impressed by Hicks' commendation. 'By God, Miss Finch,' he cried. 'Please, if you can do so, tell us at once – let us know where we stand!' He snatched up the first bundle of papers and hastily untied the length of official red tape with which he had secured them. 'These are the ones you found, Hicks, so I daresay they're the earliest.'

Mary felt herself redden, and moved her chair so that Mr Hudson's greatcoat was no longer brushing her shoulder. The papers indeed looked very similar to those she had translated. 'Well, sir, if you can provide me with a copy of Blackstone's *Commentaries*, I can tell you what the documents say,' she affirmed, 'but they may not answer all your questions.'

'Blackstone's *Commentaries*?' repeated Hudson. 'Yes, certainly.'

'And it must be the first edition,' she added, glancing at Hicks.

It took some time for the requisite volumes to be found, and while they waited Hicks began his part of the story. Joseph Sault, he explained, held a confidential post at the Waltham Abbey gunpowder mills – one of the establishments owned by the government, as he was sure Mr Hudson was aware. At Waltham Abbey Sault learned a good deal about the tests and improvements carried out by the Ordnance. 'We had our suspicions about Sault for some time,' Hicks continued. 'Had him under our eye, as it were. But we were not certain until some documents were found in Suffolk – and decoded – by Miss Finch. They revealed Sault's part in the business.'

Hudson knew nothing about Waltham Abbey or any other aspect of munitions production, but he nodded sternly. Mary was less discreet. 'What do you mean?' she interrupted. 'I do not remember seeing anything about a man named Sault.'

Hicks shrugged and smiled reluctantly. 'Ah, well,' he admitted, 'there was only the slightest mistake in your translation – the F and the S. No one could blame you for it, for the man's name is a strange one, and if you did not know it, you would naturally translate FAULT rather than SAULT. If you look at these sheets,' he continued, turning to Hudson, 'copies of the Suffolk papers Miss Finch translated, you will see what I mean.'

Hudson scanned the proffered documents. 'But *Sault*,' Mary persisted. '*Joseph Sault* – you . . . knew about him already? You *knew* I had chosen the wrong letters?'

'We guessed that you had,' said Hicks, and then continued in a low voice. 'But we had to keep quiet about that, Mr D and myself, because, well, we were going to show those papers to . . . *another*, if you catch my meaning, and we did not want to give our hand away.'

'Captain Holland,' Mary whispered.

'Quite so. It will be . . . interesting to know whether anyone tried to make contact with Sault, to warn him, after Captain Holland had sight of the documents.' Hicks was silent for a moment. 'Rede went to Waltham Abbey on Saturday night, so Sault must have been warned sometime before that. Hmm. Very interesting, that is.'

'So, Joseph Sault is our man,' said Hudson, looking up from the White Ladies documents. 'That much is clear, even without translating the rest. But we also know he cut and ran before Rede could nab him, and now . . . Well, God knows where he's gone.'

'He is *one* of our men,' Hicks corrected. 'He was not acting alone.'

'Of course, there were the smugglers who transported the documents out of the country.'

'Yes, sir, and they were traced to a place called Lindham, on the Suffolk coast.' Hicks glanced at Mary. 'We cannot be certain exactly who else was involved at that end.'

'No, I daresay,' Hudson agreed. 'Smugglers are – I was going to say "thick as thieves", but that rather overstates the case. What I meant was, I don't imagine they would be easy to trace. But they're small fish, when it comes to that. Damned small fish, and not worth worrying about.'

'Yes, sir, indeed; I agree with you. But I did not mean the smugglers. When I said Sault was not acting alone, I meant that there is at least one other man in the same line of work. Not only passing the information on to the French, but *collecting it for them*.'

'And do you know the identity of this second man?' Hudson demanded.

Hicks glanced again at Mary. 'Well, sir—'

'We do not know for certain,' she urged.

'No, not for certain,' Hicks admitted, 'but the evidence points to an artillery officer named Holland – Captain

Robert Holland.' He cleared his throat and leaned forward in his chair. 'If I might explain the situation, sir.'

'Yes, yes, carry on,' Hudson frowned. He wished Hicks and this young woman would get to the point; he could not stand these wry looks and qualified suggestions.

'Captain Holland is, ahem, no ordinary captain of artillery. For the past year he has held a rather important post in the Ordnance laboratory at Woolwich – he is practically Colonel Congreve's right-hand man, in fact.'

'Who the devil is Colonel Congreve?'

'I beg your pardon – he is in charge of the laboratory, which is quite a little treasure house, in the military line. It is where they carry out their secret research, and Captain Holland is in the thick of it. What a prize he would be for the French – to gain his services! And as we know, he reports on the tests conducted at the government's gunpowder mills, and he makes regular visits to the Waltham Abbey establishment, *where Joseph Sault is also employed*. They must surely know each other.'

Hudson took out a sheet of paper and wrote down a few notes. 'Yes, I see that Captain Holland had the oppor-tunity to pass on information,' he said, slowly. 'What evidence do you have that he actually did so?'

It was not precisely evidence, Hicks admitted, but taken all in all, the facts amounted to a very strong case. He prefaced his account with a request that it receive a candid hearing – that was all he asked – but Mary soon stopped listening. She did not want to hear Hicks' suspicions, suspicions that she had been rehearsing to herself since the previous afternoon, nor did she wish to see their effect upon Mr Hudson. She had told herself more than once that the truth was the most important object, and that learning the truth was all that mattered. But she had not reckoned on the painfulness of the lesson. It was all so awful, so sordid, and everyone seemingly deceitful, while each revelation seemed to make matters more complicated and not less.

As a distraction, she returned to the coded papers that Hudson had given her. Like those from White Ladies, each document bore a numbered sequence in one corner. She glanced at Hudson, but he was listening to Hicks, so she opened the fourth volume of the *Commentaries* to page 412, where the sentence beginning on the twenty-fourth line would give her the alphabetic key to the first document.

Mary worked quickly. She was familiar with the task, and several of the documents were quite short. What they revealed, however, did not make for pleasant reading. They seemed to consist largely of instructions, or confirmations of information that had been received. Some of the references she understood, or at least recognised, such as Bishop Watson's experiments with charcoal distillation and a meeting of the mill owners to discuss production quotas. A mention of William Tracey in one of the documents did not surprise her, nor an instruction that certain test results were to be left for Tracey in the 'usual place'. Other messages were less clear. Two of them referred particularly to Woolwich and mentioned names that she did not recognise – the names of officers. Who were these men? Were they also passing on information? It certainly looked as if the circle of conspirators was very large indeed.

As she completed each paper, she laid it aside and turned to the next in the pile. The last, she noticed, used the same key as another she had already translated: 4, 266, 20. Well, that would certainly make things easier, and she retrieved the alphabet so that she could use it again.

The words appeared quickly under her pen: QUERY WHETHER RECENT WARREN INFORMATION

COMPLETE REQUEST CONFIRMATION FROM, and then more slowly, HOL. She stopped. Then, drawing her lip between her teeth she forced herself to write, LA. She checked each letter twice, but there was no help for it. ND. Her heart was pounding as she looked at the word. Then the sound of her own name pierced her concentration, and she looked up.

'. . . when Miss Mary Finch provided the most important help to our cause,' finished Hicks.

'Miss Finch,' echoed Hudson. 'Yes.' He made another notation and glanced at her, his pen poised.

She turned to him with a white face, her expression frozen. She had no idea what they had been talking about or what contribution she was expected to make. 'I think . . . you ought to see this,' she murmured. It was her duty to expose treachery, but she felt like a traitor. 'And . . . there are other names mentioned.'

Hudson read the documents quickly. On being assured that the translations were correct, he slid them across the desk.

Hicks snatched them up; his eyes narrowed as he scanned the messages. 'I think this proves what I have been saying,' he cried. 'Holland *must* be our man, and it definitely establishes at least one high-ranking link *within* the regiment. And these other names – MacLeod and Shrapnel – these look to be other senior officers. My God, what a find!'

'Steady on, steady on,' warned Hudson. 'Perhaps this does establish a link, though any knave can write an honest man's name upon a bit of paper.'

Hicks opened his mouth to speak, but closed it instead and ran a rough hand across his chin. 'That is so,' he admitted, in a low voice. He handed back the documents.

'On the other hand,' Hudson continued, 'an honest

man's name doesn't turn up among a traitor's papers for no reason. We must find Joseph Sault, but until we do— *Yes?*' he finished, irritably, as he was interrupted by a knock at the door.

'Sorry, sir,' muttered the clerk, 'but the lads have come in from the night rounds, and, well, I thought you'd want to see this.'

He handed over a file, and Hudson read it with a frown. 'Damn, damn, damn,' he muttered, and when he looked up, his face was grim. 'I think we shall have to do without Joseph Sault,' he informed them. 'From what this report says, it appears that he was killed last night. Shot down in an alley in Marylebone.'

Hicks sat back in his chair, looking wretched. 'Dead! Are you sure?'

'Looks like it. No witnesses, of course.'

'I doubt you need any,' Hicks complained. 'I'll wager this is Rede's work. Of all the damned blockheads! I should've known never to trust him with anything important.'

'Rede?' demanded Hudson. 'Did you send him after Sault?'

'No, not exactly, but something I said, when I told him to go to Waltham Abbey . . . he might have misunderstood. I let him know how important Sault was, and then when he missed Sault the first time – you saw for yourself the sort of man he is.'

'Yes, I certainly did.'

'He must have taken it upon himself to find Sault, and naturally, he does not tend to think much beyond a knife or a pistol. If Sault resisted, things could easily have gone wrong. But to have lost him!' All of the enthusiasm seemed to seep out of Hicks; he looked old and tired. 'You do not know . . . this is only one case to you, sir, but Mr D and I have been on the trail of Sault and his friends for months. Never letting up, always keeping an eye open for a new clue. And now . . .'

Hudson had some experience of professional disappointment, and he paid Hicks the compliment of regarding his in the same light. 'It's rotten luck,' he agreed, wearily. 'We shall make doubly sure when they bring in the body. I imagine you can say for certain if it *is* Sault. But in the meantime, we mustn't throw in the towel. What are we going to do about Captain Holland? You said that your friend Déprez left Suffolk in company with him, and that they were coming to London.'

'Sir, did you say "Déprez?"' asked the clerk, who was still hovering in the doorway. 'There is a man by that name downstairs.'

Everyone cried out at once, but Hudson's voice was the loudest. 'Good God, man!' he bellowed, 'Why didn't you say so? Bring him here! Send him up immediately!'

The steps on the stairs sounded eager, but the figure that opened the door looked very different from the Paul Déprez that either Mary or Hicks had last seen. His coat was mud-stained, while his shirtfront and cuffs bore spatters of blood. More than that, he looked grim and tired. He had shaved none too recently, and his face was cut and bruised.

'Déprez!' cried Hicks, springing forward. 'My dear fellow! You are hurt! What has happened!'

'No, no, never mind that; I will explain in a moment,' Déprez protested. 'But first, gentlemen – we have him.'

'Captain Holland?' asked more than one voice. 'How? What happened? Where is he?'

Déprez started to answer when suddenly he noticed Mary and stared at her in amazement. 'Miss Finch! How on earth . . . What are *you* doing here?'

He strode forward before she could answer, his expression changing rapidly between pleasure and surprise, and something like annoyance. 'How on earth,' he murmured again, edging round the desk.

'I came last night, with Hicks,' Mary explained, as he clasped her hands between his. She felt such a thrill of relief at seeing him that she could not continue for a moment, and then blurted, 'There was something wrong with the code, but it does not matter now. What has happened? Are you all right?'

'Yes, yes, do not distress yourself,' he urged, and now his glance fell upon the open volume of the *Commentaries* and the piles of documents. 'Something . . . wrong with the code did you say? What are these?'

And then everyone was talking at once. 'Those are Rede's papers,' said Hudson, 'but we haven't had a chance to go through them yet.' 'Not the code, I meant the book,' explained Mary, 'I mean, the *edition*.' 'Sault is dead, so we fear,' announced Hicks, 'of all the damned luck, but look at this – Holland is mentioned by name!'

Déprez continued to frown down at Mary's jotted notes, nodding at what was being said, when the reference to Captain Holland reminded him of his true purpose. 'Come,' he called, 'all of this can wait. I tell you, we have Captain Holland in our power – or we shall have him, if we move *now*.'

With that imperative, the heretofore random remarks gained focus. Where had Déprez left Holland? A house in St Catharine's rookery? Yes, Hudson knew the area. Holland himself was well secured? Yes, he was bound and under guard. The men turned then to logistical details – transport, a patrol of constables, and a surgeon to treat Captain Holland, who had been injured scuffling with Déprez. Mary was forgotten in the sudden shift from speech to action, and even she sensed that she had become irrelevant; a piece of furniture. Whatever was going to happen would do so without her.

In a very few moments the men were gone; Déprez lingering only a moment in the doorway, as if he wanted to say something to Mary before he plunged down the stairs after the others. She ran to the large, dusty window and watched as Déprez spoke to Hudson on the street below. He gestured and pointed, seemingly giving directions while Hicks looked on, nodding anxiously and clenching his hands. Then they were joined by several other men – members of the police force, judging by the way that Hudson addressed them. One of them hailed a pair of hackney cabs, and everyone climbed inside. It was all over very quickly. They departed with a clatter of hooves on the cobbles and the piercing shriek of a whistle, warning everyone to clear the way.

Mary stepped back from the window and sat down. All the life had departed the room, and it was suddenly cold. There was only Mr Hudson's cold cup of tea, the fire smouldering weakly in the grate, and a glove dropped by someone – Hicks, most likely – in his eagerness to depart. *She* was still there, of course, but she no longer mattered.

Hicks and Déprez were in the second cab along with two police constables. Déprez warned them to be on their guard when dealing with Captain Holland. Although he had been injured, he was still dangerous.

The constables nodded. 'We'll be careful, sir, you can count on that.' 'He won't play us no tricks.'

'No, of course not.' After a moment Déprez continued to Hicks, 'I wish that Miss Finch were not here.'

'Yes, I did not mean to bring her, but—'

'It is not right that she should be exposed to such things,' Déprez brooded. 'A young girl, tender-hearted – how could she not be hurt and distressed by what has happened?' He shook his head. 'Some of it could not be helped, but now to experience it again at close quarters . . .'

The constables understood this to mean that the young lady at the station had somehow been a victim of the traitor, her trusting nature taken advantage of, and their hostility grew. This Holland bastard could expect no mercy from *them*. Amid their growls Hicks muttered, 'It was the merest chance, you know. I met her on the road – she had been to White Ladies and was on her way to Woolthorpe Manor, to explain something that she had discovered about the edition of Blackstone! God knows what put it into her head to worry about such a thing, but it upset her. I showed her that it made no difference, but she was . . . upset, talking wild. She even said . . . and when I explained about Holland—'

'Ah, you told her of our suspicions?'

'Yes, I thought I had better.' Déprez did not answer, and Hicks added, 'She wanted to come – to make sense of it all. She would have come on her own!'

'To London? My God, she has some steel in her,' mused Déprez.

'Yes, well . . . I thought we owed it to her.'

'Perhaps. Perhaps we did.' Déprez was looking out of the window. The Tower of London loomed up beside them; even against the clear morning sky it looked cheerless and imposing. The conversation he had shared with Holland returned to him . . . *Traitors' Gate; they brought important prisoners to the Tower by water.* Then he lowered the window. The presence of four, unwashed men rendered the atmosphere close, and beneath that the cab had a sharp, unpleasant odour, as if someone even less salubrious had been a recent passenger.

'And then, it helped having her here,' Hicks continued. 'Hudson – Mr Hudson – was not easily convinced, but once she translated the documents that I had given him at the start and found Holland's name mentioned, he began to see things more reasonably.'

'Mm, yes,' agreed Déprez. 'That was well done.'

As he spoke the cab slowed and began to turn into a narrow alley. Déprez glanced out of the window and nodded. 'There it is, gentlemen, the Mace & Cells. Quite an appropriate name for Captain Holland's abode, I think.' He opened the door as the vehicle rolled to a halt. 'Come along. Our friends have already arrived.'

The police constables piled out, and for a moment the other two were alone. 'Ah, that damned whistle,' grumbled Déprez, as a piercing shriek echoed through the quiet alley, and then another. 'Can they do nothing quietly? We had better go and see.'

Several constables huddled around the door of the Mace & Cells. Déprez climbed out of the cab and started to ask what had happened when the sight of Hudson, pushing his way out of the crowd, made him hasten forward more quickly. 'What is it?' he called.

Hudson ran toward him. 'Holland's escaped!'

They met for an instant. 'What?' demanded Déprez, 'what do you—' And then he was running past Hudson, slipping over the muddy cobbles in his haste. He raced through the open door and up the stairs. In the little room at the top he found a scene of desolation: chairs overturned, the washbasin smashed, and no sign of Rede. The mattress lay partly on the bedstead and partly on the floor, and the blankets and counterpane had been tumbled into a heap. Captain Holland's coat was there, along with frayed pieces of the rope that had bound him. But he was not.

Hudson quickly ordered his men to make a thorough search of the building and the immediate neighbourhood. Holland did not have much of a head start on them, for God's sake – and the man was injured! He could not have gone far.

At least, Hudson hoped not. He gazed upward; even this alley was a goddamned warren. There were a thousand places where a fugitive might hide. 'Sergeant Harris! Make sure you go up into the attics.'

A commotion from one of the other buildings drew Hudson's attention. Shrieks, thumps, then a door flung open and a large, raw-boned woman with tousled red hair and dressed, more or less, in a ragged gown burst into the street. She was swearing furiously and two constables struggled to control her. 'There's a whorehouse, sir, top of the stairs,' cried one. 'We thought maybe he was hiding up there and—'

'You got no right!' screamed the outraged madam, and she began to flay one of the constables with what looked like a knotted petticoat. 'We ain't done nothing!' she cried, as her blows fell upon his head and shoulders. 'You leave us be!'

'Oh my God,' muttered Hudson. 'All right, all right. Calm down!'

As Hudson went to calm the situation, Déprez gestured faintly to Hicks and drew him aside. Then he whispered faintly that everything had gone to plan, and Holland was in fact safely under lock and key. Hicks visibly relaxed with the news, but he groaned in dismay when he learned that Holland's wound was in fact quite serious. 'Damn! A bullet wound may turn nasty if not treated properly – it may do regardless. What shall we do now?'

'Hudson is not going to hang about here much longer,' Déprez predicted. 'He will return to Bow Street, if only to organise a wider search. I will go with him. I trust there will be no problem with our friend Sault? Nothing to distract Hudson?'

'No, and the case against Sault is clear enough.' Then Hicks remembered something, and he frowned in exasperation. 'It would be as well to recover his papers, though.'

'Papers? What do you mean?' Déprez had been half observing the interplay between the constables and the madam, but now his smile faded.

'Sault's papers,' Hicks repeated. 'That bloody fool Rede collected all of the messages Sault had received and turned them over to Hudson by mistake. God knows what he thought he was doing. I don't suppose there's anything to—'

'*Turned them over?*' Déprez demanded. 'He turned over Sault's papers to the police before you had checked them?'

Hicks nodded, and his expression started to reflect the furious anxiety in the other man's voice. 'But—'

'My God, man! Have you taken leave of your senses? You left those papers with the police? *Sault's messages?* Think of what they might contain!'

'But no one else could read them – they had not been translated.'

'They had not been translated *yet*. Damn it, man, have you forgotten Miss Finch?'

384

20

Gone. Escaped. Missing. Mary was stunned by what she heard, and by the sight of Holland's bloodstained coat – all that was left of him. She had come outside when told that one of the cabs had returned, and there she heard Hudson's terse explanation. For a moment she stood on the steps, in the way, as police constables streamed past her; then a hand on her arm and a solicitous voice pierced her reverie. She was awake again, and even smiled faintly as Déprez asked anxiously whether she was all right. 'Yes, yes,' she nodded. 'It is only—'

'Of course,' he agreed, with his usual understanding and grave sympathy. He *did* feel sorry for her, and this rendered his task more complicated. He had to know – was she already dangerous, or must he only prevent her from becoming so? Gazing down at her, his forehead creased in a thoughtful frown, he decided upon the latter. 'It has been a cruel blow to us all, and so much worse for you, waiting for news. But now you ought to take some rest.' He turned to Hudson. 'Is there some quiet place nearby where Miss Finch may be comfortable?'

'Hm?' gaped Hudson.

'No, please,' urged Mary, placing her hand upon Deprez's, 'you must not concern yourself with me; I am really very well. What will happen when . . . you find Captain Holland?'

'*If* we find him,' muttered Hudson, while Déprez frowned. Her hand felt warm and confiding; he must be patient.

Mary stared at the two men, trying to interpret their glum expressions. 'Is there no hope at all?' she asked, in a low voice.

She was a lady, after all, and they consciously attempted to restrain their gloom, but they admitted that they were not very hopeful. Hudson was sending men to search the docks and to stop any likely boats, but he admitted the chances of finding Holland by these means were slim. There were many places where he might hide, and the police could not search them all. Once he obtained passage down river, it would not be difficult to hire a fishing boat that would carry him to France. Hudson shrugged. 'But then again, if he's too ill to travel, he might go to ground somewhere in Town – a safe house.'

'Safe house?' Mary repeated.

'Some snug retreat where he can be hidden, with friends to look after him until he can move without attracting our attention. I daresay they have one – this gang doesn't seem content with half measures – and that would be just as bad for us. Scouring London for a safe house would be like looking for a goddamned needle in a haystack, and I can't tie up my men on this one case forever, waiting for something to happen.'

'No, indeed,' agreed Déprez with perfect truthfulness, nor was the tone of his next remark wholly assumed, for nothing would be achieved by dawdling there on the doorstep with Mary Finch in tow. 'Hudson, if we are to discover Captain Holland we must decide upon our plan of action straightaway. Perhaps if we . . .'

Mary perceived his slight, upward gesture and turned to Hudson. 'What do you mean to do?'

Déprez grimaced as Hudson explained that they meant to translate the remaining coded messages, in the hope that these would provide some further clue about the gang. This was a dangerous line of conversation; Déprez could see nothing good coming from it, and very real danger. Mary's next question was even more unsettling.

'Would you allow me to help?'

'Miss Finch, I honestly believe—' began Déprez, shaking his head, but Mary cut him off and spoke eagerly to Hudson. 'Please,' she urged, 'I translated the others, remember. Let me finish the job. I would so like to do something useful.'

'—that you ought not to tire yourself.' Déprez completed his sentence in a murmur. The words came automatically and with little faith in their effect. He was already weighing up what Mary had said and gauging the risk of her proposal. Very considerable, he concluded, and he let out his breath slowly in a conscious effort to calm himself. *Sault, you fool, why did you not destroy those papers?* It was maddening to be so close to safety, and then to be forced to run a very narrow gauntlet. For he doubted that Hudson, for all his brusque ways, would resist Mary's plea.

'I am not in the least tired!' Mary assured them. 'Three heads are better than two, surely, and I daresay I could translate the papers faster than either of you.'

'Yes, I daresay you could,' Hudson growled. 'Well, come along then.'

They were soon ensconced in Hudson's office. Mary

387

had resumed her chair, now unencumbered by Hudson's greatcoat, while Déprez occupied a position at the opposite end of the desk, near the fire. Each had an open volume of the *Commentaries* in front of them; the remaining volumes, a lighted candle, and the small heap of encoded documents occupied the remainder of the desk. Hudson had taken up his pen, but he was prevented either by lack of space or ability from joining in the task of translating. Instead he merely observed the labours of the other two, whilst wrapping the violet ribbon round his fingers.

He had certainly done well to grant Miss Finch's request, he decided. While Déprez's efforts were so slow at times as to be almost non-existent, Mary's hand moved swiftly and steadily over the sheets, reducing the coded gibberish to recognisable words. More than once Déprez ceased his own work entirely to watch Mary, and as soon as she finished a document, he would reach for it and scan its contents, even before Hudson himself. 'Steady on,' complained Hudson, when the other man almost upset the candle in his haste.

If Mary thought Déprez's conduct in any way odd she did not say so. Indeed her voice was surprisingly cool when she lifted her eyes from her work to ask, 'Mr Hudson, can you tell me where Orchard Street is to be found? Is there such a street in London?'

'What?' demanded the two men.

She repeated her request and slid the paper she was working on across the desk into Déprez's outstretched hand.

'I don't know,' began Hudson, slowly, and then he paused. 'Have you found something? There may be . . . Yes, I believe there is an Orchard Street in Marylebone, near the Edgeware Road. What have you found?'

'Mention of a house in Orchard Street,' Mary replied, still in the same calm tone. 'Did you not say that Mr Sault was killed in Marylebone?'

Hudson snatched up the paper, not noticing that Déprez had become slightly flushed. 'Let me see that.'

'Do you think it is worth investigating?' she asked, glancing at each man in turn. 'It is not a very sure connection, but—'

'Yes, of course it is worth investigating,' said Hudson, his irritation giving way to an equal degree of enthusiasm. 'At this stage I would be willing to arrest my old grandmother if she were mentioned in these damned papers!'

'Perhaps Mr Déprez has heard of Orchard Street,' continued Mary. 'In his earlier investigations, I mean.'

Despite his considerable experiences of tight places Déprez's heart was pounding, but when he stared across the table, her expression reassured him. There was no accusation, he was certain of it. Her question made good sense, and she was an intelligent girl; there was nothing more to it than that. He shook his head, as if he were casting his mind back. 'No, I do not remember hearing it mentioned.'

Hudson was in no way set down by this news. 'No? Well, still, this is something,' he cried. 'A connection with Marylebone may be significant. Carry on, Miss Finch. You give us hope!'

'Yes,' echoed Déprez. 'Hope indeed.' *Orchard Street and nothing more,* he reminded himself sternly, *that is not so very bad. What does it matter if Sault is linked to Orchard Street? We will win through after all, if that is the only indiscretion, and there are but two papers remaining.*

Mary resumed her work and duly produced the last two translations. They were brief messages – one having to do with payment and the other querying the date of a meeting, whether involving the conspirators or their prey was impossible to discern. Neither document was particularly interesting or informative. She laid down her pen and observed the two men, noting their varying expressions of interest, concern, frustration, and . . . relief?

Déprez rose before she could be certain and went to stand before the fire. When he turned, his face was in shadow and she could no longer read any expression, either feigned or genuine. She sighed and stretched, thinking that this had not been a very profitable exercise. But what had she expected? And what would happen now? She was conscious of having set something in motion that she might not be able to control, but what choice did she have? Before she had quite resolved that point, she voiced her more obvious concerns to the others. 'These papers of Mr Sault bring us no nearer to Captain Holland.'

'No,' admitted Hudson. The lack of progress after Orchard Street had discouraged him somewhat, and now he was thinking about the distribution of police forces across the capital, and how he might go about organising a thorough search. A thorough, and very likely unsuccessful search.

'But worth the effort, this work of translation,' said Déprez. 'In a matter such as this, we must examine every clue and leave nothing to chance.' His tone was smooth and supportive, as it had ever been, but now it grated in her ears. *No*, she told herself, *you would leave nothing to chance.* She glanced at Hudson, but he seemed to hear nothing amiss. Nor would he, she realised, without help, and there did not seem to be any help at hand but herself. If only she could be certain . . .

'Do you suppose that the safe house you mentioned might be in Orchard Street? Ought you to look for Captain Holland there?' She directed her questions at Hudson, but watched to see their effect upon Déprez. He started – there was only the slightest flinch – but she had seen it, and it gave her confidence. She hardly heard Hudson's remark or Deprez's cautious affirmation. She must speak, and now was the moment.

'But before any decision is made,' she continued, producing a folded sheet from the pocket of her gown, 'you ought to see these papers.' Somehow, neither her hand nor her voice shook. Rather, all of her senses seemed to slow and fix upon this single task, and she spoke with a deadly coldness. 'This one says, "Expect instructions relating to the St Lucia matter in the next fortnight". Or this one, "St Lucia men arriving shortly. All operations to cease pending their instructions".'

She raised her eyes to Déprez and regarded him steadily. '*You* are from St Lucia; what do you suppose they mean?'

'Why you little—' He took a step toward her, and she retreated quickly, upsetting her chair. Immediately her wits were keen again, and she experienced both a flood of emotions and a consciousness that the struggle was not yet over. 'Keep away from me,' she warned, snatching up a volume as if she would throw it at him. Déprez halted; Hudson wrenched open the drawer of his desk and pulled out a pistol. 'Stay where you are, sir,' he barked. 'Everyone calm down. Miss Finch, what the devil are you talking about? Where did you get those papers?'

'Mr Sault – they were among those in the bundle you received. I translated all of the messages while you were away, but I put these aside because they prove that Mr Sault knew about the men from St Lucia! He was taking his orders from them – from Mr Déprez. They were working together from the start!'

'Miss Finch!' complained Déprez. With a supreme effort he managed to convey only annoyance, as if he had been played a nasty, if harmless trick, while new calculations whirled swiftly through his mind to the accompaniment of the words *Damn you, damn you!*

'Sault and Déprez working together?' growled Hudson. 'Impossible.'

'No, it is not,' Mary cried, backing further away from Déprez. Her heart was beating freely again, and she responded strongly to this challenge. 'Tell me, Mr Hudson, which of you suggested returning to Bow Street and looking at Sault's papers? It was Mr Déprez, was it not? I am sure it was.'

'He thought there might be a clue—'

'He was *afraid* there might be a clue,' Mary corrected, 'and he was right. There are two – Orchard Street *and* St Lucia. But if he had found them before I had, he would not have revealed them to you.'

Hudson scowled, but he turned to Déprez. 'Well, sir? Sault was to take orders from the St Lucia men, was he? Would you care to explain that?'

'I am hardly responsible for what some . . . anonymous document may contain,' replied Déprez. He spoke to Hudson, but he kept his eyes fixed on Mary. His look was hard, shrewd. He was sizing her up as an opponent. If he could make her back down now, all might still be well. 'So, Miss Finch, you believe that *both* Captain Holland and I are guilty.'

'Yes,' she nodded firmly, but she was not as skilled as Déprez in conflicts of this sort, and she hesitated. 'I . . . I am not certain about Captain Holland.'

'Oh, but he must be,' Déprez continued, and now his

392

tone became slightly coaxing. He had recovered his confidence, and he stood with his arms casually folded across his chest. 'After all, he also appears in these papers. By your reckoning, he is as guilty as I am – more so, for he is mentioned by name.'

'Perhaps. But he is not mentioned in Mr Sault's papers,' Mary countered, 'only the ones Hicks gave to Mr Hudson. Where did you get them? How do we know they are genuine?'

Déprez favoured her with a frown of curiosity. 'How do we know that *any* of them are genuine? And you forget, Miss Finch, that I have been hunting the traitors for these last several months.' Fleetingly he considered condescension, but rejected it as a poor strategy. He doubted she would ever submit to being patronised, and certainly not in her present mood. Instead he continued, reasonably, 'Why on earth should I go to all that trouble if I could simply produce coded documents with men's names in them? And what could I possibly gain from such an exercise?'

'I do not know,' she admitted, and indeed, that problem had taxed her while she sat alone in Hudson's office. But she sensed that Déprez was trying to confuse her, or distract her from the important point, and she shook her head. 'Why should Sault have mentioned the St Lucia men? And why did you want to see his papers? Because you *knew* they were real, and you were afraid they would give you away!'

Then they were both speaking at once, and Hudson called them again to order. 'Let me see if I understand,' he frowned. 'Miss Finch, you are saying that the papers from Sault are authentic, and that they accuse Déprez.'

'Yes.'

'But the others – those you found at White Ladies and those Hicks gave me – are not.'

'Yes . . . perhaps.'

'Though the code is the same throughout—'

'Yes, I know,' Mary acknowledged, 'and Captain Holland said that the information in the White Ladies papers was genuine.'

'Well, there are too many of these damned papers, that's for certain,' complained Hudson, 'but the fact remains that Captain Holland is the man we're after, and it sounds to me as if there is a good chance that he is in Marylebone. So that's where we must go.'

'Yes, of course,' urged Mary, 'but . . . what about Mr Déprez?' Could it be that Hudson did not realise the danger? He could not be so slow, surely – but perhaps he did not believe her?

'Mr Déprez will oblige me by remaining here.' Hudson raised his hand to silence the other man. 'I've heard enough of your explanations for the moment, sir. I think we must wait until Captain Holland can give us his. Miss Finch, be so good as to run downstairs and ask Constable Burt to step up, and I advise you, sir, not to make things any more difficult.'

'You do not say that you believe this nonsense?' cried Déprez. 'Remember, I have been trying to help you, man! Who caught Holland, when he would have disappeared? I did. And Miss Finch has had a bad shock, you said so yourself. She does not know what she is saying.'

'Oh yes I do.'

'Quiet!' ordered Hudson. 'We've relied on her for the rest of these damned papers, so we'll rely on her for these.'

'You mean to . . . take me into custody, while you go after Holland?'

'I mean to do exactly that.'

'Because you think I am *what*, precisely? A spy?'

'Because I don't know what you are, and I mean to find out.'

'You are making a mistake,' Déprez warned. 'I presume you have heard of false imprisonment.'

'I have, and I'll take the risk.' Hudson nodded in the direction of the door. 'Go ahead, Miss Finch.'

'Oh, for the love of— Let us not descend to amateur dramatics.' Déprez gestured irritably. He was silent for a moment, and then continued in a steely tone. 'Putting me under lock and key will achieve nothing. By all means go to Orchard Street if it pleases you, but you will discover precisely nothing and may do great harm.'

'Why is that?' demanded Hudson, and he frowned slightly at Mary, halting her progress.

Déprez pulled a chair toward himself and sat down. Hudson also resumed his seat, but he leaned forward, elbows on his desk and his pistol beside him. 'Because,' Déprez continued, 'your . . . visit would be extremely dangerous for Captain Holland.'

'Ah, then he *is* there,' Mary cried.

Déprez paused again before replying. 'Let us suppose that he is, for the sake of argument. In that case, it will not be so easy to get him out . . . alive. You know the street, but you do not know the house where he is being kept.'

'And you do, I suppose,' snapped Hudson. 'Damn it, man, he's been at Orchard Street from the start, hasn't he? All that rigmarole at the Mace & Cells was nothing but a blind.'

'Indeed it was not. I give you my word that Captain Holland was captured, by me, at the Mace & Cells. But that is an irrelevancy – he is not there now, as you discovered for yourself. Let us return to your Marylebone hypothesis. If he is in Orchard Street, he will be heavily

395

guarded, and those guards will be difficult to surprise. I observed your men's methods in St Catharine's alley – they are the reverse of subtle, and in Marylebone their employment could result in calamity. While your men were rushing up and down the street, banging on doors and blowing their infernal whistles, there would be plenty of time for Captain Holland to be . . . spirited away to another location or killed.'

'Why would they want to kill him?' Hudson demanded.

'Because your appearance would render him an encumbrance. You know the expression, I am sure, "there is no honour among thieves"; it must also apply to spies. Holland is injured, after all, and it would be easier to kill him rather than let him fall into your hands.' Déprez paused, watching as Mary grew pale and hardening himself against the sight. This was no time for compassion, and he pressed his point more strongly. 'Do not forget that Rede – the man who killed Sault – is probably there. He is not the sort of man to baulk at murder if his own safety is in danger.'

'No, I don't think he is.' Hudson spoke slowly, but he was almost pleased by the turn things had taken. All those codes and strange references had disturbed him; he had not known quite how to deal with them. The situation was still very dangerous, but it had clarified, and he thought he understood it. 'Very well,' he nodded curtly, 'how do we get Holland out?'

'*You* cannot get him out, but *I* could. I can employ certain tactics that will be effective on the men holding him.'

'*Certain tactics*,' Hudson scoffed. 'They take their orders from you, you mean.'

'As usual, sir, you exaggerate the situation,' Déprez replied.

Mary lost patience with both of them. What was the point of skirting round the question? 'But if you *can* get him away from Orchard Street, will you do it?' she demanded.

'I will,' Déprez replied, 'if Mr Hudson will agree to give up any . . . accusations against me in return. That is my offer – my freedom for that of Captain Holland.'

'That's a damned bad exchange, as I see it,' Hudson growled.

'On the contrary, it is an extraordinarily good one.'

'You've as good as admitted—'

'I have admitted nothing. It is not yet a crime to affirm that a man is in Marylebone. All the rest is . . . intelligent supposition. Without Holland, you can prove nothing against me, and you will never recover him alive without my help.' Hudson did not reply, and Déprez continued, 'Until five minutes ago you had no thought other than to arrest him. You ought still to want this. He may be guilty – a dangerous spy.'

'Not more than you are, I warrant.'

Déprez knew he could not risk a smile; his vanity was not so great as that, and Hudson was not quite a fool. He contented himself with a shrug. 'But then again, he may be an innocent man, and in either case he is worth having. Either he is guilty – and you may execute him – or he is innocent, and you have saved him.'

Hudson remained silent, and Mary had to bite her lip to keep from speaking. How could he hesitate? They *must* try to free Captain Holland, and if that meant trusting Mr Déprez, well, that was what they must do. She started to speak, but Hudson's stony expression stopped her. Advice, even very good advice, might not be kindly received at that moment.

The moment lengthened. Déprez knew what Mary

397

was thinking as plainly as if she had spoken the words, but he was not so sure about Hudson. The man understood the position, surely, and he could weigh up the chances of loss and gain, yet some scruple might stand in his way – some sense of duty – and that might upset everything.

'I don't make bargains with villains,' warned Hudson at last, 'but . . . very well. I suppose you have a plan?'

Déprez breathed a genuine, but wholly internal, sigh of relief. 'Yes, I do, as it happens. It is very simple. Some of your men can accompany me for most of the way – until their presence would constitute a danger. I will bring Holland to Hyde Park, where you will be waiting. He passes into your care, and I take my leave.'

Both men knew that this proposal would be rejected, and they began negotiating. Mary observed the cautious exchanges with little confidence in the outcome. Déprez was like a wild animal, superficially calm and aware of his proximity to the trap, but still extremely dangerous, while Hudson was the huntsman, uncertain whether a prod would make his quarry whimper or snap. Finally, however, they agreed that one of Hudson's men would accompany Déprez into Orchard Street, remain out of sight and not interfere, and then escort Déprez and Holland to Hyde Park.

'And it must be at night,' Déprez warned. 'Tonight, if you wish, but my actions must not seem . . . strange. It would be too dangerous to move him in broad daylight, and his captors would become suspicious if I suggested it.'

'But you control them,' Hudson asserted, bluntly. 'You can make them do as they're told.'

Déprez shrugged in self-deprecation. 'I believe I can achieve the desired result if I am not hampered by unreasonable conditions.'

When Hudson nodded in reluctant agreement, Déprez glanced first at him, and then at Mary. 'And I require one thing further. Miss Finch must be present.'

'What? Are you mad?' stormed Hudson. 'Absolutely not! It is far too dangerous. I won't hear of it.'

The men started arguing again, but now Mary thought she detected a change in tone. Déprez seemed to be taunting Hudson, implying that he was not to be trusted without a reliable witness such as herself, and she wondered whether this was part of some new scheme. She could not imagine how it would suit Déprez to give up his bargain with Hudson, but she did not trust him enough to find out. He was looking too comfortable, while Hudson was almost beside himself with exasperation.

'And then there is the practical point,' purred Déprez.

'Which is?'

Mary stepped into the breech. 'I can identify Captain Holland,' she said, in a tone that both supported Déprez and challenged him. She was willing to help – more than willing – but not out of any sympathy with Déprez.

'Precisely,' he agreed. 'I presume that you would not wish to . . . find yourself with the wrong man, would you?'

Hudson erupted with indignation, but Mary cut him off. 'Please,' she urged, 'I am sure you would keep your word, but I will come, if that will help the . . . plan.'

'Oh, all right, very well,' complained Hudson, and he leaned back in his chair in exasperation. Then another thought occurred to him. 'And how do I know *you* won't kill Holland, sir?'

Déprez shrugged again. 'You do not know.'

Once the decision had been made, the necessary arrangements swiftly fell into place. Mary had very little part in these, but nevertheless the intervening hours passed for her with a strange, dreamlike fluidity, and incidents of normalcy arose in the most unusual circumstances. In the early evening, Hudson awoke to the fact that Mary had eaten nothing since a slice of toast at the King's Arms. He told her she must remedy this situation immediately, and thus she found herself in a busy chop house in King Street, dining on a gristly steak, potatoes, boiled cabbage, and a jam pudding, chaperoned by a middle-aged constable whose astonishment at his chief's generosity had deprived him of all power of speech.

Mary surveyed the scene around her, the tables crowded with clerks and apprentices, and heard the talk of stocks and provisions bought and sold. It was a different world from any she had known, and she marvelled that she should find herself a part of it, even for a short time. Yet, what could she do but adapt as best she could, and soon she would be taking part in something far more challenging than a tough piece of meat. A rescue from criminals – or an exchange of one malefactor for another? She was reminded of her escape from White Ladies – had it been only eleven days ago when she had first felt caught up in remarkable events and carried far beyond her everyday experiences?

She tried not to think about Captain Holland. She wanted to believe him innocent, but wanting something would not make it so. When she considered the facts as objectively as she could, it was hard to conclude that he had no part in the plot. What would happen when the police recovered him? Would there be a trial? What if he were convicted? But she was getting ahead of herself, as who could even say whether the rescue would succeed? Mr Déprez seemed confident, but what comfort could one take from that? Mr Déprez was . . . a *villain* – that is what Mr Hudson had called him, and it must be true. But it was so extraordinary . . . and horrible. It was frightening to think that anyone could present such a false picture of himself, lead a life so utterly different from that which he presented to the world and *to her*. And she seemed to have uncovered not merely one person with that power of deception, but two.

They set off from Bow Street shortly before eight o'clock in a pair of dark, nondescript carriages. Two constables travelled in the first, and Hudson, Déprez, and Mary followed in the second. All three were extremely tense, although Déprez strove to project an air of calm. He gazed interestedly out of the window and offered remarks on passing sights. Neither of the others could be drawn into conversation, however, and Mary found his conduct extremely wearing. How could he expect her to speak to him as if nothing had happened? As if what they were doing was perfectly ordinary? Her irritation had another source. While she could not have explained it, she felt as if, somehow, her powers of concentration kept the forces of chaos at bay. If once she stopped thinking about what lay before them, something unexpected would happen and the rescue would fail.

The carriages turned a corner and slowed to a walk. 'Bloody traffic,' muttered Hudson. He shifted irritably and frowned out of the window at the people milling around them. 'What's the time?'

Mary wore her uncle's watch on a chain at her waist, and its face shone in the dim light when she opened the case. 'It is almost twenty minutes past the hour.'

'Ah, the famous watch,' smiled Déprez. 'Might I have a look?' He deftly unfastened the watch from the chain and turned it over in his hand. 'Very striking. That is how it all started, I believe, when you noticed this and wondered how it had found its way into William Tracey's pocket. What a fool he was to take it.'

Mary nodded, absently, and then started, her hand upon Déprez's arm. 'He never . . . he did not . . . *hurt* my uncle, did he?'

Her touch, and the urgency of her voice, moved him. 'No,' he replied, softly.

'And *you* never . . .'

'No.'

She was silent for a moment and then released his arm. Murmuring something under her breath, she turned away. Déprez studied her dispassionately. The pale light illuminated her profile like a cameo against the dark walls of the carriage. He noted the delicacy of her features, and the tilt of her chin that made her look like a stubborn child. She was very young, after all; clever, of course, but her intellect was essentially childish. Even as those thoughts occurred to him, however, he qualified them. He was as careful an observer of himself as he was of others, and he recognised that he could not dismiss his own feelings so cavalierly. It would be an insult to both of them to do so. 'I would have liked to explain everything to you,' he said, leaning toward her. 'You would have appreciated it, which is a rare quality. But now, I fear, I shall not have sufficient time.'

'She doesn't want to hear any explanations from you,' snapped Hudson, and Déprez raised his hands helplessly. He had no wish to impose his attentions where they were not welcome.

The carriages stopped part-way up Oxford Street. There Déprez was to change places with one of the constables and continue to Orchard Street, while Hudson's vehicle drove to the rendezvous in Hyde Park.

Déprez stood for a moment on the street, glancing casually about him. Then he leaned forward and spoke to Hudson through the carriage window. 'All right, I will leave you now. No more constables for the rest of the way – apart from my minder. And the coachman, of course,' he added with a smile.

Hudson shrugged irritably. 'I could hardly rely on a civilian.'

'Of course not. Well, I trust he has orders to remain on his perch.'

'He'll do that – unless he's needed.'

'Neither of them had better move, whatever happens,' Déprez warned, 'or I will not answer for the consequences. Well, Miss Finch, this is goodbye, I think. "*My bonds in thee are all determinate.*"'

He held out his hand and she took it. With the touch of his fingers she was suddenly conscious of a connection between them, that it had been real and that it was ending. 'Please tell me – *are* all the papers genuine?' she begged. 'The one that names Captain Holland?'

'Ah, I am afraid he will have to explain that himself,' replied Déprez, 'if he can. Goodbye.'

'All right, that's enough,' ordered Hudson. 'Get going.'

'Goodbye,' she murmured, and Déprez slipped away.

'What did he mean by that crack about bonds?' asked Hudson, suspiciously. 'I hope to God he isn't up to something.'

'It was probably a poem,' said Mary, shaking her head. 'I do not recognise it.'

'Poetry,' scoffed Hudson, 'that's all we need,' and then he thumped the ceiling. 'All right, Taylor! Let's go.'

Déprez's carriage stopped at the turning into Orchard Street and he climbed down. 'Wait for me here,' he ordered.

'Do nothing until I return.' Then glancing up at the driver he added, 'And try not to look like a damned police constable.'

'But Mr Hudson said—'

'Do as I tell you, man, or you risk more than his reprimand!'

Déprez glanced carefully along the street. At first it appeared empty, but as his eyes grew accustomed to the gloom he perceived one – no, two shapes, which gradually resolved themselves into the figures of men. Hudson was clearly taking no chances. Déprez smiled wryly and crossed the street.

Lights were burning in several of the houses, and from one of these the faint sound of a piano could also be heard. Déprez approached it and let the knocker fall once, and then twice quickly. After a moment the door opened and a golden light flowed out into the street, illuminating the visitor to anyone who happened to be watching. Déprez exchanged a few words with the servant, all the while conscious of the sound of approaching footsteps somewhere in the street behind him. The heavy, deliberate tread came closer, closer, and then moved further away, as whoever it was continued his journey. The servant stood aside and Déprez entered, the door shutting firmly behind him.

Orchard Street was quiet, especially after the bustle of Oxford Street. The piano was clearly audible, as a passage was played, repeated, and then a third time, as if the player were practising or receiving a lesson. No other sound, not even a cold shiver of air, disturbed the silence. After a few minutes the music was given up in favour of scales, and outside the driver shifted uncomfortably on his perch. Then the door opened and closed. There was no light this time, but two figures crept down the front steps and away from the house. The handle of the carriage door turned, first to the left and then to the right. The door opened, and the first man entered, awkwardly, the vehicle dipping beneath his weight.

Déprez stood on the step and whispered up to the driver, his face pale and tense in the lamplight. 'Now, slowly. You know where to go, but you mustn't lose your head, for God's sake.' And then he too climbed aboard.

Hudson's tension did not allow him to remain still for long. Shortly after arriving at the agreed location, he climbed out of his carriage and began to walk up and down. They had driven deep into the park and drawn up under the trees, and his footfalls made no sound on the damp, leaf-strewn grass. After a few minutes, the others joined him. Mary was afraid that something might happen if she were not present, and the constables could not very well sit in comfort while their chief did not. In fact, the carriage was not actually very comfortable, but the principle was the same, they felt.

Waiting, however, seemed even harder in the open air; feeling the cold rising inexorably through one's shoes and descending like a damp cloud, and all the while straining for every sound that might herald an approaching carriage. As she rubbed her arms under her cloak Mary thought about her hurried departure from Lindham Hall, and the hat and gloves she had left behind. Thank goodness she had been wearing her old boots when she had set off for White Ladies – they might be disreputable, but they were at least warm.

'I wish they'd hurry up,' complained one of the constables, stamping his feet.

'Quiet,' barked Hudson. 'What is the time?'

'It's a quarter to nine, sir, almost,' replied the constable, even as Mary cried, 'He has my watch!'

'What?'

'Mr Déprez – he was looking at my uncle's watch and has taken it away with him!'

'Aye, well, he's a slippery customer,' Hudson agreed, 'but don't you worry, Miss Finch, we'll get your watch back all right.' He sighed, trying to feel more confident. He hoped Déprez knew what he was about and could be trusted. The plan seemed straightforward, for Hudson did not doubt that Déprez was the guiding force among the spies and could do what he liked. But even the best plans could go wrong. Proper fools they would look if they lost both Holland *and* Déprez. 'Damn this cold,' he muttered. He took another turn and stopped himself from asking the time yet again.

As the minutes passed Mary tried to imagine what must be transpiring in Orchard Street. How long could it take? Had something gone wrong? What if they – whoever *they* were – suspected something and Mr Déprez could not get away from them? Or if Captain Holland was too ill to be moved?

A low exchange between the two constables inter-rupted her thoughts. Hudson stopped and listened intently. 'All right, this may be them,' he said. 'Get ready, you two, and Miss Finch, go back to the carriage and keep out of the way.'

Mary heard it now, horses' hooves and wheels on the road. Her heart began to pound and she forgot about the cold. She also forgot her instructions, but she retreated a few steps. As she did so she became aware of a greater activity around her. Men were moving in the shadows; she heard several clicking noises, as if pistols were being cocked, and muffled voices, and then the flash of a shaded lantern. All the while the sound of the approaching carriage grew louder.

Then it appeared on the road and stopped, almost in front of them. Hudson and the two constables sprang forward. One wrenched open the door while another thrust a lantern inside. The commotion frightened the horses and they sidled nervously, so that the vehicle rolled backwards. Someone stumbled and cursed, and the driver checked his team.

Mary tried to get closer, but the men in front were too tall. Then Hudson demanded, 'Is it him, Miss Finch? Is that Holland?'

'Yes, yes,' she cried. Standing on tiptoe and steadying herself against a constable's arm, she could only just see him in the flailing light. He was slumped in the corner of the carriage, pale and unshaven, and Déprez was beside him. A third man, a constable, was looming over them, and he held a pistol in his hand.

Hudson was also armed. 'Quickly now, let's have him out,' he ordered, and Mary's view was blocked. She stepped back, wondering what she could do to assist, as Holland was slowly helped out of the carriage. He could walk, it seemed, but he was bent over, and he was hugging his right side with his left arm.

Hudson had hold of his other arm, but suddenly he thrust Holland aside and pushed forward into the coach, colliding with the constable who came crashing onto him. 'Oy! Déprez!' Holland stumbled and almost fell. Hudson pushed past the constable and clambered through the carriage. It was empty! He leaped down on the far side. 'Déprez!' he bellowed, and blew a sharp blast on his whistle. 'Déprez! God damn it!'

He raced back to where the others were standing as more constables sprang out of the darkness, several bearing lanterns. 'Quick! After him,' he shouted, 'he's not far away. 'Sergeant Clark, have your men fan out to the left, and the rest of you come with me. We'll have that bastard. A guinea to the man who takes him – dead or alive!'

'But you said—' cried Mary.

'I said I don't make deals with villains,' Hudson snapped. 'Sergeant Riley!'

'Here, sir!'

'You stay with Holland. And if he moves – shoot him.'

Hudson disappeared into the darkness, together with the rest of the constables, and Mary, Holland, and Sergeant Riley were left alone. A few remaining lanterns provided dim pools of light. For a moment everyone simply remained where they were, and the park relapsed into silence. Then Holland sank slowly to the ground. 'Don't worry, sergeant,' he said in a low voice. 'I've no intention of moving.'

'Well, see that ye don't,' replied Riley, and when Mary brushed past him, warned, 'be careful, now, miss. Don't get too close.'

Mary ignored this advice and when she knelt beside Holland, he noticed her for the first time. 'Mary— Miss Finch,' he breathed. 'What are you doing here?'

'Are you badly hurt?' she asked, helping him to a more comfortable position. Whatever he had done, she had no shyness of him. Seeing him had excised every thought from her mind other than that he was there, and he looked so terribly unwell. 'Do you want to lie down?'

'No, I'm . . . let me lean against something.' He was tired, almost dazed, and the wound in his side was throbbing.

With Riley's help she propped him against a tree and opened his shirt. Riley laid his pistol on the ground, out of Holland's reach, and raised his lantern. The light revealed a wide bandage wound around Holland's middle. It was thickly padded on the right side, and in the centre of this there was a dark stain.

'You are bleeding!' cried Mary. 'Oh, what must we do? Should we open the bandages?'

'Best leave him be,' advised Riley.

'It's not so bad,' Holland agreed. 'They just . . . mucked about getting the bullet out. It's the . . . moving that's made it bleed again.'

'*Bullet!* I never— He said you had been hurt, but not—' She turned to Riley. 'We must not stay here any longer. He must have a doctor – surely you can see that!'

Riley frowned doggedly. 'I got me orders, miss, to wait here until Mr Hudson comes back.'

'But that is ridiculous – I mean, he may be gone for hours! We cannot remain here all that time. The ground is wet, and it is so cold . . .' Mary glanced up. One of the carriages had been driven away, but the other remained, without a driver. 'Could you drive that?'

'Maybe,' Riley allowed, 'but what about him? I can't leave him alone inside, with naught but you to guard him, miss. He might be dangerous, or he might break out, like that other feller did. And I got me orders.'

Mary started to argue, but Holland stopped her. 'Better stay put . . . for a while. They will probably be back soon. I doubt they will catch Déprez.'

Riley bristled at the lack of confidence in his chief. That was no common thief-taker as was in charge of the pursuit, but Mr Hudson of the City Police! And he generally knew what he was about when it came to catching criminals.

Despite this testimonial, Holland remained unconvinced. Paul Déprez, he felt, knew what he was about when it came to not being caught. But he did not want to argue the point. Turning instead to Mary, he repeated his earlier question. How had she come to be there?

She gave a brief and moderately coherent report – the

mistake in the editions, the additional coded papers, the murder of Sault. Holland could not follow all of it, but he appreciated the last point. 'Déprez must've killed him . . . or had it done.' Then he remembered what Riley had said and looked sharply at him. 'You don't think *I* did it, do you? Is that what you think you're doing? Keeping an eye on a desperate killer?'

'I dunno what you've been up to,' Riley admitted. 'All I know is there's been a lot of talk about spies and secret papers, and you're in it up to your neck. So I'd be careful about what I said, if I was you, unless you're wanting to make your confession. It's all evidence, you know.'

'Don't be a bloody fool,' sighed Holland. 'Spies and secret papers be damned. Déprez – he's the spy, him and his friends.' He turned to Mary; her expression was tense, and he frowned. '*You* don't think I'm part of it, do you?'

'Is that why he shot you?' she demanded. 'Because you had caught him?'

'No, that was a mistake. He was trying . . . to catch *me*.'

'But you said—'

'To hand me over to the French. That was the plan from the start.'

'Yes, and now it seems to have come undone,' said a voice, and Jonathan Hicks stepped out of the darkness. He was holding a double-barrelled pistol, and now he cocked it. From where he stood he could fire at any of them.

'Hicks!' gasped Mary. Until that instant she had forgotten all about him, and now he looked wild and dishevelled – completely different from her friend at White Ladies. She clasped Holland's arm in a gesture that was partly fearful and partly protective.

410

In his surprise Sergeant Riley had leapt to his feet, and now he stood uncertain, measuring the distance to his own weapon and wondering whether the other man had noticed it. 'I'm a police constable,' he warned, 'and I order you to put down that weapon.'

Hicks frowned irritably. 'I advise you to keep quiet, Mr Police Constable. I am not in a humour to hear the voice of authority just at the moment.'

'Wh-what do you want?' Mary whispered. Her voice was shaking, but she kept her eyes on the pistol.

'When things come undone, there are generally some loose ends that need to be tidied up,' Hicks explained, 'and Captain Holland is one of 'em. As are you, I am afraid. I do not mean you any harm, miss, but it is a damned shame you had to come to London. I told you not to, you know.'

Mary shook her head. 'You are not thinking clearly,' she urged, and indeed Hicks' expression did not seem normal. She forced herself to speak slowly. 'Captain Holland is innocent — we all know that. Mr Hudson, everyone. Hurting any of us now will do you no good. Please, put down your pistol.'

'No, you see, killing him will do us a great deal of good. We needn't have done it, but Déprez — I *told* him not to go back to Bow Street, but he would not listen. He is so damned ambitious — and stubborn — and this is the result. But then, so are you, miss — stubborn. But that is not my fault. So just move away from Holland, there's a good girl.'

Holland did not trust Hicks' growing unsteadiness; he was like a bomb waiting to go off. 'Mary — do as he says,' he ordered. 'Get out of the way.' He tried to shrug away from her, but it was hard to move.

'You do not understand! Mr Déprez has run away,'

411

she urged. 'His plan is finished, and there is nothing more for you to do – please.'

'He's saved his skin and left you to take the blame,' Holland added.

Hicks snarled angrily at the taunt. 'We will see about who is going to take the blame. Now move away from him,' he repeated, frowning, 'or you will be hurt.' He gestured with his pistol, but Mary refused.

'If you do this,' she warned, 'think of what will happen. The police – Mr Hudson – they will surely catch you. His men are all about here – all through the park; you will never get away. And you *cannot* shoot someone . . . an injured man . . . in cold blood.'

'Do not try me, miss, or I-I will not answer for . . . I will fire, and it will be your own fault, and none of mine!'

'Mary – go!' Holland commanded.

No one moved, and Hicks' pistol wavered slightly in his grasp. He was sweating now, but he nerved himself to carry out his threat. At the same time Riley was gauging the distance between them. Taking a deep breath, he prepared to spring.

'Hold your horses, cockie,' warned another voice, and a small, thin-faced man appeared at his side and placed a pistol against his chest. He casually kicked the sergeant's pistol into the undergrowth and pushed him back down onto the ground. 'Cockie here was goin' to try some heroics,' he informed Hicks.

'Oh, no, we mustn't have any of that,' Hicks agreed. He swallowed convulsively. 'You had better . . . sort things out, Rede.'

'Just as you like.' Rede moved quickly behind Holland, and Mary cowered as he reached toward her. She recognised him – the man who had frightened her when she was with Mr Tracey! 'Silly bitch,' he sneered, and shifting his pistol to his other hand, he grasped her arm and dragged her away.

'If you kill him it'll be murder,' warned Riley. 'You'll swing for it.'

'I'll be long gone before the bugger's cold,' Rede countered. 'Seein' as there's transport handy and all. You may not like driving it, cockie, but I don't mind.'

Hicks wiped his face on his sleeve. 'Now, on your feet, Holland,' he said, motioning with his pistol. 'On your feet, I say.'

Holland shook his head. 'You've got me. Go ahead and shoot if you want to, you stupid bastard. Shoot me and take the blame for Déprez.'

'Hicks! Please!' cried Mary.

'Go on, get up,' Hicks insisted.

'I know what'll make him move,' said Rede, and turning, he delivered a swift kick to Holland's side.

Mary screamed as Holland gasped and fell over; bright red spread quickly across his bandages. 'Ha! That'll do him,' laughed Rede. 'Don't hardly need another bullet. Kick him again, maybe,' and his boot connected a second time.

He chuckled as he leaned forward to grasp Holland's arm and pull him upright again. 'Come on, now, Captain, old son. I'll help you up. Can't say as I'm not kind—'

'Rede!' shouted Hicks.

'—hearted.' Rede's sentence ended in a gurgling cry as Holland lunged upward. Rede stepped back, clutching his stomach, and Holland rolled away from him, a long, thin knife in his hand. Mary scrambled to her feet as Rede staggered toward her. Then he fell, twitching, and she screamed again and retreated a step. At the same moment Riley sprang at Hicks, bringing him down. Hicks' pistol flew into the air and went off as it hit the ground. There was a momentary silence, and then Hicks began to sob.

'Quiet,' ordered Riley. He was sitting atop Hicks, and he remained there, catching his breath. Then he called over his shoulder, 'You all right, Miss Finch?'

She nodded, shakily, and then answered, 'Yes.'

'That's grand. Is the other feller dead? Don't go too near, now, but has he stopped moving at all?'

'Yes.'

'What about Captain Holland?'

Holland lay where he had fallen, crumpled on his uninjured side and still clutching the gory knife. He was breathing in short, painful gasps. 'I'm . . . still here.'

'Glad to hear it. Where'd you get the sticker, sir?'

'Took it . . . doctor . . . patched me up.'

'Ah, that was good luck for us, but if I'd known you had it, I'd have been more careful with me manners. Well, then, Miss Finch, there are three pistols lying about, and if you could find 'em for me and bring 'em here, I'd be much obliged. I think I can see one of 'em, and mine's over there in the long grass. Then I can get off this feller, and we can all be a bit more comfortable.'

'Yes, of course.' It seemed to Mary that she had no control over her legs, but somehow they moved of their own accord in the desired direction. She felt numb, but she retrieved the pistols and handed them to Sergeant Riley, carrying each by the butt, one at a time, as he instructed her.

'That's grand,' said Riley, when she had given him the last – Rede's single-barrel with the pearl handle. 'Now isn't that a pretty thing? Don't look quite real, does it? T'would have done the business, though, that's for certain. And now maybe you'd better have a wee look at the captain, Miss Finch, if you don't mind a bit of blood.'

414

'No, I–I do not mind.'

'Good lass,' smiled Riley. 'We don't want anything more happening to him, do we now?'

And that is where the police found them, recalled by the sounds of the struggle; Sergeant Riley keeping watch over Hicks, and Holland lying on the ground, his head pillowed in Mary's lap.

21

They did not apprehend Déprez. The park was searched thoroughly that night, as were the docks and other likely haunts over the course of the next few days, but to no avail. Whether he was still in London or had made his way to France by one of the routes mentioned in connection with Captain Holland when *he* had been under suspicion, no one could say. Certainly he had disappeared very efficiently, leaving no trail behind him.

At first Mr Hudson was furious that such an important spy had escaped, but gradually he recovered his spirits. Against the loss of Déprez there was the capture of Hicks and the recovery of Captain Holland, which did not make the score so very imbalanced, and if one added in the fact that Rede was dead and the Orchard Street safe house exposed, the sheet was almost even. Indeed, perhaps it was in credit. Hudson explained this to Mary when he called on her to enquire after her health, it being generally recognised that ladies suffered more acutely from shocks and violence than did men.

'Speaking unofficially and strictly between ourselves,' he informed her with an arch expression that sat uneasily on his battered countenance, 'it seems that some of those papers you translated were even more deadly than we supposed.'

'Indeed?' frowned Mary. 'But Captain Holland said they did not contain any *very* important secrets.'

'And I daresay he was right – but remember that he didn't have sight of 'em all, only those that you found at White Ladies. When I showed those that Hicks had first given me to the chap from the artillery regiment, he went white as a sheet.'

'Captain Holland was mentioned in Hicks' papers.'

Hudson nodded. 'Yes, as were some other officers – and very important fellows, apparently. Innocent, like the captain, but things would've been plenty hot for all of 'em if we hadn't confounded that devil Déprez and all his works. We've been questioning Hicks, you know, and he has admitted that their scheme was not limited to Captain Holland. He was the main prize, to be sure, but not the only one.'

'I remember Hicks said something about that, in the park,' said Mary, and she frowned in recollection. 'That . . . Mr Déprez was too ambitious.'

'Perhaps he was. But I must say this for him, he was damned clever and he almost succeeded. Only suppose what would have happened if Captain Holland had been "found out" as a traitor who'd decamped to France. Suppose then that we had had papers – which looked genuine – naming other officers along with Holland. What would have been the result?'

'It would have been assumed that the other officers were also guilty.'

'Exactly, and they would have had the devil of a time proving that they weren't.'

'The burden of proof reversed,' breathed Mary.

Hudson gaped at her, and then smiled. 'I don't need to explain much to you, I see, Miss Finch. Not in the legal line.'

'No,' she murmured.

'Then there would have been the scandal, and everyone blaming his neighbour for what had gone wrong – for that would have come next. There is nothing like a cock-up for bringing out the worst instincts in men – backstabbing and accusations – anything to place the fault somewhere else. A very nasty state of affairs, and not what we can afford with the war as it is.'

'And we prevented all of that,' said Mary. 'I had not quite appreciated . . .' Her chin lifted, and she smiled. 'It was rather heroic of us, when you consider it.'

'Indeed it was,' Hudson agreed, smiling in his turn. 'And I'm glad the thought gives you comfort, Miss Finch, for I daresay it is all we shall ever see in the way of a reward, or even notice of what we did – what *you* did, mostly.'

'I never expected a reward,' Mary admitted, flushing, and even as it was being dismissed as unlikely, the vision of a vast ceremonial, in which the king bestowed some unspecified accolade upon her while trumpets sounded, flashed through her brain. 'Did you?'

'No, no, but then I am philosophical. Don't have high expectations, and you won't be let down – that's what I say. And if you aren't philosophical in a job like mine,' he explained, 'you'll only break your heart.'

Mary did not know to which philosophy he was referring, but she agreed that it was a valuable guard against disappointment. Philosophers, she felt, did not so much *do* things as think about them, so when a person had finished whatever he was doing, he might

418

as well think philosophically about it. And she noticed that Mr Hudson had not been much of a philosopher so long as the capture of Mr Déprez had been a practical possibility. She did not mention any of this to him, however.

Nor was she free to indulge in much philosophising herself during the next few days. Her time was taken up in meetings and interviews with gentlemen from the Home Office, the Foreign Office, the Ordnance, and various other agencies whose purpose in government was not always made clear. They each had some particular interest in what had happened, what must be done in consequence, and what should be said about it. Miss Finch, they were relieved to discover, proved to be both extremely helpful on the first point and extremely sensible as to the third. She fully appreciated that, in so far as was possible, the St Lucia affair must remain confidential, and she agreed to adopt an explanation that obscured or omitted any sinister details. The Attorney General, with whom she spent a long afternoon, described it as a wholly innocent, but completely laudable, deception.

One person not wholly deceived was Sir William Armitage. As soon as he was informed of his cousin's injury, he posted down to London. Once there, his former status in the Treasury gained him access to certain confidential information. He knew, for example, that Holland had been in danger, that he had behaved with courage, and that Mary Finch had helped ensure that he emerged safely and creditably from the episode. Perhaps for that reason an immediate sympathy grew between Sir William and Mary. He also remembered what Holland himself had said about her – that she was brave, clever and pretty – and both what he heard and what he observed confirmed

419

these assertions. Thus he insisted that she take up residence at Dorant's Hotel, a highly respectable establishment close to his club. He also arranged that she had something approaching a sufficient wardrobe, for she had come away from Suffolk with nothing more than the clothes she stood up in.

Hudson's words came back to Mary when the various interviews were completed and the men from the several departments returned to their offices to produce their reports. Now was the time for her to think – not so much about what had happened – but about what might happen next. She had been almost a fortnight in London, and Sir William thought it was high time that both of them returned to their homes. Mary agreed, but she wondered whether she might be allowed to see Captain Holland before she left the metropolis. He had, she knew, required further medical treatment and been moved to Woolwich. But Woolwich was not so very far from London (she had checked this in an atlas supplied by the Home Office), and there was a regular coach service (whose details she had obtained from a helpful Ordnance clerk).

That she wished to see Holland was not in dispute, but she felt that she ought to examine her feelings more carefully. This was a difficult matter, however, for how *did* she feel about him? She liked him, certainly, but she had also liked Mr Déprez. She had even compared them, and not always to the captain's advantage. She and Mr Déprez had shared common interests and pursuits, while she had nothing in common with Captain Holland other than having shared and survived an adventure.

She drew out a piece of paper from the pocket of her gown. It contained the poem that Déprez had quoted to her in the carriage, which she had discovered through conversation with a particularly poetical gentleman from the Foreign Office; she read it thoughtfully.

> *Farewell! Thou art too dear for my possessing,*
> *And like enough thou know'st thy estimate:*
> *The charter of thy worth gives thee releasing;*
> *My bonds in thee are all determinate.*
> *For how do I hold thee but by thy granting?*
> *And for that riches where is my deserving?*
> *The cause of this fair gift in me is wanting,*
> *And so my patent back again is swerving.*
> *Thyself thou gav'st, thy own worth then not knowing,*
> *Or me, to whom thou gav'st it, else mistaking;*
> *So thy great gift, upon misprision growing,*
> *Comes home again on better judgment making.*
> *Thus have I had thee, as a dream doth flatter,*
> *In sleep a king, but waking, no such matter.*

Captain Holland could not have quoted such a beautiful poem – or any poem, for that matter. And yet . . . she felt comfortable with him despite their differences; with Mr Déprez it had been more a question of wanting to impress him. How lowering to admit that she had wanted to impress a French spy! And he had not written the poem, after all. *No*, she mused, ruefully, *he only appreciated fine poetry and fine watches*, and she bristled at the thought that her uncle's elegant silver repeater was probably being used to tell the time in Paris.

After a moment she crumpled the paper and tossed it on the fire. There – she was done with one, but the other remained. Did she . . . *love* Captain Holland? (a question which, even when posed silently, caused her to blush).

421

It was ridiculous to speak of love at first sight, for she had not even liked him at their first meeting, but perhaps her opinion had developed to something that might come close to that mysterious emotion? She remembered their last moments together, how he had lain quietly in her lap, in considerable pain but more comfortable because she had held his hand.

Yet the image of that night also recalled her common sense – or what she called her common sense. Captain Holland might have forgotten the affair – he *had* been very ill at the time. And as for everything else, she had probably imagined a great deal of it. Gentlemen were light-hearted, as Mrs Tipton had said. And what good did it do to resolve her own feelings, when she did not know his? Philosophy was really very silly, and she resolved not to think about any of it again.

Like many other resolutions of a dubious nature, this one was soon tested. Without the least prior warning, Sir William proposed that they go down to Woolwich on what was to be their last afternoon in town. 'I could not leave without seeing Robert,' he explained, 'and I have only just been given official approval. I thought I might take him to Storey's Court, but it seems that is not possible. It will only be a brief visit, I am afraid. The poor fellow is not quite well, yet, and we mustn't tire him.'

Sir William made his proposal casually, for he did not know how Mary would regard it. She had not said anything about wanting to visit Robert, and this had surprised him. Could it be an instance of feminine indecision? In his experience women had no hesitation whatsoever in making their wishes clear, and he peered at Mary as a rather unusual specimen.

Mary's heart soared with the suggestion, but she tried

422

to answer calmly. 'No, of course, we mustn't,' she agreed, 'and a long journey would not be good for him, I daresay.'

She was not so very adept at disguising her feelings, however, and Sir William felt reassured. 'No, indeed,' he chuckled. 'He hates riding in carriages at the best of times, poor chap. It has been the same thing, you know, ever since he was a boy.'

Sir William was still in good spirits when he went to collect Mary at Dorant's Hotel on the following day. He likened himself to one of those benevolent characters from literature who interceded to smooth the way for the young couple. Unfortunately, the only literary characters who came to mind in that context were the nurse and the friar in *Romeo and Juliet*. Not only was the first image rather unflattering for a retired Treasury official and knight, but that play was perhaps not the best model to invoke in any case. Still, the principle was laudable and he took quiet comfort in it.

He repeated his warning about the brevity of their visit when they arrived at the Warren, but Mary was in such a state of nervous excitement that she paid little attention, merely nodding mechanically. They were met at the main gate by a pinched, grey-haired soldier named Drake, whom Mary understood to be a kind of servant, or assistant, to Captain Holland. Drake seemed to know Sir William and greeted him almost casually, but he was considerably taken aback when he saw Mary descending from the carriage.

'I presume that there is no regimental objection to, ahem, ladies visiting officers in this establishment?' asked Sir William in his most pompous voice.

'Er, no, sir,' gaped Drake, 'it's only we didn't, I mean to say, Captain Haitch didn't say nothing about no ladies.'

'Ah. Perhaps I was not quite clear in my message,' Sir William admitted in his more usual tone.

'Do you think – perhaps I had better wait here,' said Mary, turning first to Sir William and then to Drake, and hoping that one of them would reject her suggestion.

Both men did so strongly. 'Nothing of the kind,' said Sir William, and Drake assured her, 'The captain'll want to see you, miss, no doubt o' that. It was only the surprise, is all. Caught me on the 'op. You come right along.'

Drake led them across the courtyard to the building where some of the officers had their quarters. Captain Holland's rooms were at the top of the stairs, and Drake urged them to go right on into the parlour – to make theirselves comfortable while he had a word with Captain Haitch.

'Is he well enough to have visitors?' asked Sir William.

'Oh, yes, sir, 'e's lookin' forward to it. It's only . . . you sit yourself down, now, miss, and I'll . . . see if 'e's awake.'

The 'parlour', as Drake designated it, was a small, cheerless room. Its walls and floor were bare, and the furnishings consisted of two battered leather armchairs, a small bookcase half filled with shabby looking books, a sideboard, and a square table with a single, straight-backed chair. There was a fire burning in the grate, but otherwise the room exuded an almost ruthless, barren tidiness. The armchairs stood at severe right angles to the hearth, with the bookcase against one wall and the table and chair against the other. An unmatched collection of plates, glasses, and cutlery was arranged in exact stacks and rows on the sideboard. Mary took in these details at a glance, and she experienced a fleeting, anxious empathy for the man who lived there.

It was only fleeting, however, for she was soon

distracted by the sound of voices arguing. Masculine voices, and none too quiet. While not every word was audible, there was clearly a dispute about the degree of undress in which a young lady might be received. At the words 'extra comforter' and 'won't even know you're in bed, 'ardly,' Mary walked over to the window on the far side of the room, but even at this distance it was difficult to ignore the forthright reply, 'I don't want an extra comforter, damn you, I want my goddamned breeches.'

'Ahem,' murmured Sir William, and in a louder voice he continued, 'perhaps there is something to read while we . . .' His eye caught the title of one of the volumes, *The Arms and Machines Used in War*, ' . . . wait. Hm. Perhaps not.'

'I had no idea that the Warren was so large,' said Mary, from her vantage at the window.

'Yes,' Sir William agreed, 'a very prodigious establishment.'

They exchanged a few more pleasantries on the subject of the arsenal, while occasional remarks such as 'you ain't 'avin' no waistcoat, sir, and that's final,' informed them of progress in the other room. At last the sound of a door opening made them turn. 'Ah, Robert,' cried Sir William. 'Here you are again. Excellent.'

'Thank you, sir, sorry to have kept you waiting.' The two men shook hands, and Robert looked past his cousin at Mary. 'Good afternoon, Miss Finch. I'm . . . sorry to have kept you waiting.'

Mary was determined to answer evenly, to avoid committing herself until she knew . . . until she knew more. 'Oh no, not at all,' she replied. 'We have been watching everyone coming and going down there – what a busy place this is – but I hope we have not put you to any trouble.' She addressed her remarks to a point near Holland's shoulder, vaguely aware that he was not wearing a waistcoat and pleased by the serenity of her opening effort. But then their eyes met, and all of her confidence melted away.

'It's no trouble,' he assured her, 'and besides that, I mean, won't you sit down?'

'I think we had better,' agreed Sir William.

Holland motioned his guests toward the dubious armchairs, while he lowered himself carefully onto the other. He was quite all right, he explained, only he was not allowed any unnecessary bending or twisting. 'And if I don't sit up straight as a board I'll have Drake in here, complaining about "doctor's orders", and making a fuss.'

'Well, I daresay he knows what is best,' said Sir William.

'He thinks he does. Once he gets a hold of anything official he's like a dog with a bone. Knows every regulation in the book – and some that he thinks ought to be there.'

Sir William interrogated his cousin for a few minutes on the state of his health, and Drake appeared with tea and a plate of muffins. He set these down on the sideboard with a significant glance in Mary's direction. She was all too pleased to have something to do, and she poured out while Drake handed round the cups and plates. 'Don't let 'im have none o' them cakes,' he warned, before retiring. 'Doctor says 'e ain't allowed nothin' fancy yet.'

'No, certainly not,' Mary agreed.

She was smiling as she returned to her place, but the tail-end of Sir William's sentence made her expression change. '—terrible uproar when she was not allowed to come with me. I believe she thought you were at death's

426

door, and considered it rank tyranny that she should be kept from your bedside.'

'That was good of her,' smiled Holland, 'but I'm sorry she got out of hand.'

Sir William humphed, and turned to Mary, 'You remember my mentioning Charlotte, my younger daughter? I have two daughters, the elder – well, ahem – but the younger flies from one scrape into another, and I believe Robert encourages her. He is her hero, of course – not that I mean to say that he oughtn't to be, but you see the predicament.'

'Yes, sir,' said Mary, cautiously. She watched Holland from behind her teacup. Had he been hoping for some message from 'Dearest Susannah'? He did not seem disappointed by Sir William's curtailed reference to her, and now he was rising and drawing something out of his breeches pocket. Could it be a letter for her?

'Perhaps this will put you back in Lottie's good books, sir,' he grinned. 'Spent pistol ball.'

'Good heavens!' cried Sir William, gingerly extending his hand to receive the flattened piece of lead. 'This is not—'

'No, it isn't, but she won't know the difference and she'll like to have it.'

'I daresay she will,' Sir William agreed, dubiously, 'and that is what worries me.' He wrapped the ball carefully in his handkerchief and dropped it in his coat pocket. He sat in silence for a moment, wondering fleetingly if he ought to mention Susannah's engagement, and then abruptly announced that he was going downstairs. He had never been to the arsenal before and was very interested in it. He would take a turn around the walkway, or parade ground, or whatever it was called. There was doubtless a great deal to be seen, and one was never too old to learn.

Holland offered Drake's services as a guide, but Sir William did not think that was necessary; he believed he could amuse himself. 'And then we really ought to go, my dear,' he added to Mary.

Mary could feel herself blushing furiously, and she was highly aware that both men were watching her. Without raising her head she nodded vaguely, but her thoughts were in a tumult. Sir William was a dear to leave them alone, but to be left alone *like that*! There was a bit of stuffing protruding from the arm of her chair, and she folded her hands resolutely in her lap to stop herself from plucking at it. What would she say to Captain Holland? What would *he* say to her?

The door closed firmly behind Sir William, and for a few moments neither Holland nor Mary said anything, and then he remarked in a low voice, 'It was good of you to come today.'

'Oh, I-I wanted to,' she replied, nervously, her hand wandering toward the bit of stuffing. 'We had heard – Sir William and I – that you were better, but, of course, we wanted to see you – Sir William and I.'

'And now you've seen Woolwich as well, or some of it. What do you think?'

She bit her lip; this was his place, and she tried to think of something to praise. 'It is quite . . . noisy,' she admitted, 'but so is London, and here – in the Warren – the noise is more orderly and I daresay more important. You have a very good view from your window of all the work carrying on below. It must be – it *is* very interesting.'

The tone of her reply, if not the words themselves, made him smile. 'Sir William says you're going back to Suffolk. There won't be any trouble, will there, about the . . . inheritance and everything?'

This at least was an easier question, and Mary smiled back at him. It had been officially decided that Mr Finch had not been involved with either the smuggling or spying, and that White Ladies had only been made use of for those purposes after his death. Therefore, no further inquiry on the subject was anticipated. As she spoke, Mary felt her confidence returning; it was almost a physical sensation. 'Of course, I am certain that my uncle was *not* involved – it was very wrong of me ever to have imagined otherwise. And now we have only to satisfy Mrs Tipton about *my* conduct! She knows that I am safe and well, of course, but Sir William has also written to her, and he is coming back with me to explain things – as much as we are *allowed* to explain them. The men from the government were very strict about that.'

'Mm,' said Holland. 'They were the same with me – not that I needed warning. I'm not likely to make a noise about it to anyone else. Knocked on the head – *again* – and then trussed up and handed back and forth like a blasted Christmas parcel . . .'

'No, it certainly does not sound very heroic,' Mary agreed, innocently.

He liked it when she teased him, and he warned, laughingly, 'No, but then I'm really a coward. I wouldn't fancy a grilling from Mrs Tipton, for a start. She didn't think much of me before, and now she'd be sure to think I was up to something. But she'll like Sir William.'

'Yes, I am sure she will. And then there will be White Ladies to see to – I expect she will want to advise me.'

'I doubt you could stop her! But you'll like that – not her telling you what to do, I mean – but . . . sorting out White Ladies.' He gestured vaguely. 'Making it a grand place, like you imagined.'

'Not grand,' she corrected, 'more *comfortable*. But, having been *un*comfortable myself for such a long time, I admit that I *might* be extravagant if given the chance.' Her eyes danced at the prospect. 'But I expect I shall find it all rather dull and quiet soon enough. I mean, it will not be nearly so interesting as what *you* will be doing.'

'No?'

'Of course not. You will have your work again, and Sir William says that he expects you will be given a regular command – is that the right term? I am certain you deserve one.'

'Well, maybe,' agreed Holland. It was his version of crossing his fingers.

'And nothing that has happened will affect that?' asked Mary, worriedly. 'Prejudice them against you? It *ought* to be counted in your favour, of course, but sometimes innocent people can be . . . tainted by association.'

Holland smiled. Her concern was even better than her teasing. 'It wasn't nearly so hard convincing 'em that *I* was innocent as it was that Déprez was guilty. One silly bugger from the Admiralty even wanted to provide him with a testimonial, because of what he'd done in the West Indies.'

'But *did* he help our forces there?'

'Maybe he did, but I bet if you looked closer you'd find that he helped us a bit and the French a damned sight more. Sometimes spies have to do that, you know, give away something to the enemy to gain his trust.'

'Like the actual spying that was going on at Waltham Abbey.'

'That's right. Most likely the French had already decided to close down the operation there, so they didn't suffer any real harm by giving it away, and it provided Déprez with real information, a real spy, and a real code. And he used it all damn well.' Holland became thoughtful. 'As it was . . . you wondered, didn't you, when you saw my name in that paper that Hicks dreamed up?'

This was a difficult moment. She had intended to acknowledge her doubts, but it was not so easy to have him ask her directly. She hesitated, which made matters worse, for he cursed himself for having put her in an awkward situation. His attempt to reassure, however, was even less successful, as she condemned herself for having misjudged his character in the first place.

The consequence of these gaffes was a painful silence, but fortunately Holland's candid admission had the opposite effect. '*I* used to think *you* were a bit mad, with all your plots and suspicions.'

'*Mad?*'

'Only at first, of course,' he laughed.

'I think it was rather longer than that!' she countered. 'But would you mind if I asked you another question?'

'Only one?'

'Well . . . I would like to understand it all, and some of it still seems so muddled.'

'Go on, then, fire away.'

'I understand that Mr Tracey was waiting for you at the Great White Horse and meant to bring you to White Ladies so that the smugglers could carry you off to France, but why should you have gone with Mr Tracey in the first place. Did he mean to force you?'

'I expect he was going to tell me something of the spies and the code, with the idea that I'd think it was my duty to investigate. And I probably would have done.'

431

'But if he was *waiting* . . . How did he know you would come to Ipswich?'

Holland shrugged. 'That wasn't so hard. They'd been watching me for some time, and my routine is fairly regular. Sault would've known whenever I was expected at Waltham Abbey. But then my job at the Landguard Fort took longer than usual, and in the meantime, Tracey had his crash. That put a spoke in their wheel, but the plan almost worked regardless, because I came to White Ladies with you.'

'Where you were knocked on the head for the first time.'

'Yes, thanks for reminding me. So, it almost worked, but not quite, and they had to think of something else – or someone else. They couldn't try anything a second time at White Ladies, and then I went to Norfolk. That must've been a test of Déprez's nerve, letting me out of his sight like that. They thought if they could get me to London they could . . . get a hold of me, so they decided to use genuine documents as bait, and they presented them to me through you, because they knew I'd swallow – I mean, *believe* whatever you said.'

'Indeed! *That* was very rash of them, for you never believed *anything* I said. I have never met such a . . . sceptical person.'

'Not sceptical, just careful,' Holland protested.

'And do you really know so many . . . secret things that such a lot of trouble should be taken to kidnap you? Twice? You mustn't think that I doubt it, of course.'

'Oh, no, of course not,' he agreed, but he did not answer her question.

'And if they *had* managed to take you to France, how would they have discovered these secrets? You would not have told them, I know.'

432

'I suppose they'd have tried to persuade me.'

Despite his jesting tone, or perhaps because of it, Mary paled, and he quickly reminded her not to worry about something that had not happened.

'No, but . . . they were ruthless,' she murmured, 'you were in very great danger. They killed Sault, after all – and he was one of them. I know Hicks *said* it was a mistake, but . . .'

'Did he?'

'Oh yes. When Mr Hudson received the news, Hicks behaved as if he were dreadfully sorry about it. He blamed that horrible man, Rede, and said that Rede had misunderstood his instructions.'

Holland grinned at her. 'He said that? Damn it! I'm surprised you didn't smell a rat straightaway!'

'Why? What do you mean?'

'It's the old archbishop of Canterbury again, of course. "Who will rid me of this goddamned priest?"'

She laughed as she realised his meaning. 'Oh, yes, how foolish of me. I really ought to have known. But it also proves that I was right to mention it to you in the first place, though I am sure you thought it was very strange at the time. And it was "turbulent" priest. That is what Henry II said.'

'It's what he *might've* said,' acknowledged Holland, 'but don't bet on it.'

'Yes, well, I suppose we shan't ever know for certain.' From Mary's expression it was clear she meant to continue, but before she could do so there was a rhythmic tapping on the door behind them. 'Oh,' she cried, turning at the sound, 'what is that?'

Holland got carefully to his feet and, without quite knowing why, Mary followed suit. 'Sir William's coming,' he explained. 'That was Drake letting me know. He has better timing than Mr Cuff.'

'What? Oh,' said Mary, blushing in recollection and flustered by this sudden crisis. Sir William back already? What should she do? Everything was happening so quickly! Nothing had been decided, and now there would be no time—

'He'll be here in a moment,' Holland confirmed, 'and then you're leaving. We had better say good-bye now.'

'Yes,' she nodded. They *ought* to say good-bye; only her heart was beating so strangely that it was suddenly hard to speak, or even to think. But she mustn't lose this last chance. 'I meant to say . . . I meant to tell you . . .' but her voice trailed off before she could tell him anything.

He uttered a hard cough and swore under his breath.

'Oh!' she cried. 'Your wound – it pains you!'

'No, I'm all right,' he said, 'just a bit sore, still.'

'You must be careful,' Mary urged. He looked flushed, uncomfortable. Was he going to be ill? She moved toward him. 'Perhaps you ought to sit down.'

'No, it's nothing,' he insisted, but he drew her closer. Mary knew that he was watching her intently, but she did not dare to raise her eyes again. Then he continued in a low voice, 'I was wondering, did you . . . mean what you said before, that you might find it dull in Suffolk? I thought, with the house and everything . . . I thought young ladies liked that sort of thing.'

She smiled, despite herself. 'Not *all* young ladies, I think. Or not all of the time.'

'So . . . do you think you might like to come to London, sometimes? Not on your own, I mean, but with a— Or with Mrs Tipton, even, if you could stand her chatter. To see the sights . . . Or there's the Season.' He shrugged, conscious that he was incapable of giving a coherent definition of that annual social whirl. 'It's very . . .

434

fashionable, and there are all sorts of . . . artistic things. You'd like it, I think.'

'Perhaps I might come, if I had friends in London . . . or close by,' she murmured.

'Woolwich is close by. Would you come to see me?'

The question was wonderful and frightening at the same time, and somehow the combination made Mary want to laugh or say something amusing. 'Here? Mightn't that be scandalous? I am certain Drake had his doubts, and Mrs Tipton would be sure to—'

Holland grasped her shoulders, and she forgot the rest of her sentence. 'I don't give a damn about Mrs Tipton, or anyone else, or what they think – only what *you* think.'

The tapping outside was repeated, more urgently this time, but Holland remained as he was, unwilling either to hold Mary more closely or to let her go. 'Tell me.'

She lifted her head and squarely met his gaze. Before she could speak there was a noise on the stair. 'That's Sir William,' Holland whispered. 'Don't blush, now.'

Then she smiled. 'I think,' she began, 'oh, be careful – you weren't to do any bending.'

She *was* blushing rosily by the time Holland straightened up again.

'*Unnecessary* bending,' he corrected, smiling down at her.

435

Author's Note

Although a work of fiction, *The Blackstone Key* is firmly rooted in historical fact. During the last quarter of the eighteenth century, British and French scientists made important contributions to the munitions industries of their respective countries. Antoine Lavoisier's appointment to the Royal Gunpowder and Saltpetre Administration in 1775 led to a dramatic rise in French gunpowder production and experiments to develop a chemical substitute for saltpetre, which France could neither produce nor import in sufficient quantities for military purposes. Because of the East India Company's monopoly of Bengali saltpetre, Britain was more favourably situated, and during the 1780s men such as Richard Watson, Professor of Chemistry at Cambridge, focused on improving the strength of the powder produced. Under the guidance of Colonel William Congreve, the Royal Laboratory at Woolwich undertook a more efficient supervision of production and testing, leading to the government's decision in 1787 to increase its production of gunpowder, rather than relying solely on that which was produced commercially.

When war broke out between France and Britain in

the spring of 1793, however, France had yet to find a reliable substitute for saltpetre. One year later, Lavoisier was executed by the Committee of Public Safety; at his trial his judges informed him that 'The Republic has no need of scientists'. In Britain, the scientific production and testing of gunpowder continued apace, while experiments were conducted at the Woolwich Warren on improved gun carriages and weapons such as Henry Shrapnel's explosive projectiles. Might the French response to British science have been espionage? Perhaps. It is interesting to note that on the night of 13 October 1795 a robbery took place near St Paul's Cathedral. The victim was Count Rumford, an Anglo-American scientist and inventor whose interests included experiments on gunnery and explosives. Rumford himself was not harmed; the thieves took only a large trunk of papers. Writing of the incident the following day he complained, 'What I lament most is the loss of all my Philosophic Papers – the result of whole years of intense study and of innumerable experiments is lost forever.'

Acknowledgements

Few books are produced without help – certainly this one was not. I would particularly like to thank the following for their advice, encouragement, and criticism: Clare Alexander, Joel Eigen, John Ford, Henry Happel, Antonia Hodgson, John Naughton, Mark Perrott, Allen Shapard, Quentin Stafford-Fraser, Sarah Wooldridge, and my parents.

The Counterfeit Guest

Available from Sphere

Spring 1797. The war with France deepens, the Channel Fleet has mutinied . . . and a ruthless traitor lurks within fashionable London society.

Such matters should not concern young Mary Finch, who has recently inherited an unexpected fortune. But her new status brings her little pleasure, and she longs for freedom and adventure.

Mary's restless spirit leads her to a meeting with an elusive spymaster, who offers her an intriguing proposal. With England's security and a friend's safety at risk, Mary arrives at the exotic Champian Hall, determined to uncover its dark secrets. But the knowledge that she seeks is deadly, especially when the hunter becomes the hunted.

Brimming with suspense and drama, *The Counterfeit Guest* is an irresistible historical mystery from the author of the acclaimed *The Blackstone Key*.

The first chapter follows . . .

1

On the Suffolk coast some eight miles east of Woodbridge stood what had once been a priory for women adhering to the Cistercian order. Its appearance had changed over the centuries, and the nuns had long since departed. Yet it was called White Ladies in their memory and, in the spring of 1796, it was to be restored to female rule. A young woman named Mary Finch had inherited both the estate and a considerable fortune, and she had resolved to make her home there.

This resolution could not be enforced immediately. Miss Finch had come to Suffolk under somewhat unusual circumstances, and the lawyers had only recently determined that she was indeed the rightful owner of White Ladies. Various practical matters would also have to be settled before she could take up residence. So, for the time being, she remained at nearby Lindham Hall, as the guest and protégée of its owner, Mrs Tipton.

Lindham Hall was another sphere of feminine influence, a fact to which Cuff, the only masculine member of the household, could testify. Cuff held the offices of coachman and porter, and between Mrs Tipton, Peggy the maid, and Pollock the cook ('them old cats', as he was wont to call them, when he thought no one was listening), he rarely had a moment's peace. Mary Finch also made occasional demands of him, but he did not mind these, somehow. Indeed, sometimes he went so far as volunteering his services, and he joined her in the flower garden on a sunny May afternoon without the least prompting. Observing the slim, straight figure poised on the edge of the lawn, a figure that managed to exude energy even when motionless, he reflected that Miss Mary surely had a way about her.

Mary was deeply engaged in horticultural matters and did not hear him approach. Fashionable ladies, she was convinced, spent a great deal of their time arranging flowers, and she knew little of the art. As a first step in her education she must learn the names of all the likely blooms, and now she repeated, 'Wallflower, wind-flower, cowslip, narcissus, rockfoil,' in the direction of the items in her basket.

'Just so,' agreed Cuff, nodding and touching his hat. 'And that one there?' He pointed at the colourful bed with the toe of his boot.

'Lungwort – what an unpleasant name! Like something witches might use for their spells.' A breeze lifted the curls that had escaped confinement while Mary's attention had been elsewhere, and her smile was similarly mischievous.

Cuff bent and plucked a pale blue flower to add to her collection, and Mary said, 'Forget-me-not. I did not pick any, as they are so small.'

'No, best left where they are, perhaps.' After a moment Cuff added, 'Nothing for him, then, miss?' removing his pipe from between his teeth and frowning, as if its failure to draw had something to do with his question.

444

Mary shook her head, and her voice lost a little of its enthusiasm. 'Not yet.'

The rather complicated logic of Cuff's remark had not confused her. 'Him' referred to a Royal Artillery officer of their acquaintance named Robert Holland. He was part of the unusual circumstances that had first brought Mary to Suffolk and had set in motion what she still privately called her 'Adventure'. Few people were privy to everything that had happened during those strange weeks in October when she had helped to defeat a French spy, and those few had been sworn to secrecy. For his part Cuff knew only that there was a sort of understanding between miss and the captain, and that he, old Cuff, meant to help it along.

The help he provided was of a particular nature. The two young people wished to maintain a correspondence, but they could not do so openly. Holland's letters to Mary, therefore, arrived under cover to Mr Josiah Cuff, and Mary's to Holland were posted by the same J.C. (Mary had also coached him in a likely story should a letter be queried, for she had no confidence in his innate powers of deception.)

'It has been less than a fortnight,' she explained, fretting with her scissors. 'I mean . . . not quite yet.'

'You know best, miss.'

Mary nodded, but she was far from certain that she *did* know best. It was all very difficult. She had not actually seen Holland for more than six months, and their communications in the meantime had been very sparse. In part this was because words did not flow easily from the captain's pen. Indeed, he seemed to hesitate over every line. His efforts had also been restricted, however, by circumstances beyond his control. He held a staff appointment at the regimental headquarters at Woolwich – a place known as the Warren – but in November he had been sent to Gibraltar, ostensibly to oversee an extension to the great siege tunnels. This had not been the only, or even the primary, reason for his employment there, but the epistolary effect had been the same – the mail did not travel very quickly between Gibraltar and Suffolk, and there was always the chance that shipwreck or enemy action might disrupt it altogether.

The character and frequency of Holland's correspondence had naturally affected Mary's. She could hardly answer his cautious reports, in which details of fortress routine featured prominently, with wild displays of emotion. Her letters must mirror his, with accounts of her days at Lindham Hall, or the progress of her legal affairs, or references to the weather. Nor could she reply too promptly. If *he* waited a month between letters then so must she. None of this was the result of indifference or coquetry on her part, but rather a half-understood notion that she must not commit herself any further than she had done. What did she really know of Captain Holland, after all? A correspondence like theirs was not strictly proper – not proper at all, in fact – and people who did improper things often suffered for them, or at least were found out. And being found out, especially whilst she was under Mrs Tipton's authority, was not a pleasant prospect.

Squaring her shoulders and lifting her chin, the latter a particular gesture of decision, Mary told herself not to think about Captain Holland and informed Cuff that she must go inside. He agreed, saying it was just like Peggy to come out for a squint, and then they'd catch it. They parted on those wise words, Mary to the Hall, where she intended to arrange her flowers, and Cuff to the stables to give the harnesses a thorough clean, by which he meant that he was going to have a nap.

Mary pushed the heavy front door closed behind her, kicked off her old boots, and retrieved the neat leather slippers she had left in the passage. She had promised Mrs Tipton to give up ineligible footwear, but with a private exception for gardening, long walks, and any activity that might prove particularly wet or muddy. Others of Mary's station might not have taken such a frugal view, but she could not easily forget a girlhood of genteel poverty and, until very recently, the prospect of a straitened adulthood. Perfectly good shoe leather – or boot leather – oughtn't to be wasted.

Having made the necessary change, she dropped her boots into the large urn that held a collection of walking-sticks, a sword that had allegedly seen action at the Battle of Sedgemoor, and Mrs Tipton's umbrella, and proceeded with her flowers to the kitchen. From there she was ordered to the pantry by Pollock, who suspected that worms and other undesirables were concealed among the blooms, and she wouldn't tolerate none of them crawlies in *her* kitchen. It was from the pantry, therefore, that Mary emerged some time later, clutching two jugs of tastefully arranged spring flowers. One she placed on the sideboard in the entrance hall, and the other she carried into the parlour. This was strictly the second parlour, for the first parlour was grim and uncomfortable, as befits a room preserved for 'best' and, consequently, almost never used.

As Mary crossed the room Mrs Tipton awakened. She had been 'resting her eyes', but now she sought to ward off any suggestion that she had been asleep and might have missed something. She was a small, sharp, imperious old lady, and she blinked at Mary from behind steel-rimmed spectacles. 'Ah, there you are at last,' she cried. 'What have you been doing?'

'Gathering these flowers, ma'am, as you asked. I hope you are pleased with them? The garden is looking lovely in the sunshine.'

'Yes, yes – very pretty. And where is Mr Cuff? He ought to have been helping Peggy to lift the stair carpet, but I expect he has made himself scarce, as he generally does on such occasions.'

'No, ma'am, indeed, he was helping me,' said Mary, loyally, although she had heard something about the carpet project and suspected that it had stimulated his interest in the garden.

Mrs Tipton made a scoffing sound and then declaimed pointedly on Cuff's several shortcomings, all of which threatened to undermine the smooth operation of the household. 'Something will have to be done about it,' she decreed. 'That is how all the trouble started in France, you know.'

'In France, ma'am?' asked Mary, trying not to smile.

'Certainly. Servants getting above themselves, and people unwilling to take a firm hand. And what has been the result? Revolutions, and guillotines, and now this fellow Bonaparte. Well, I shall soon put an end to it. We shall have no *Rights of Man* at Lindham Hall, nor any other nonsense.'

Mary had to bite her lip to maintain her countenance. 'Oh dear.'

'It is a serious matter, and one must regard it as such. Heaven help us if we go the way of the French – the whole country in an uproar and men taking off their breeches.'

Mary knew rather more about the political situation in France, and she attempted to explain. 'I think, ma'am, that you mean—'

'I *mean* men with no breeches,' Mrs Tipton repeated,

her eyes flashing. She disliked being interrupted. '*Sans culottes*, they call themselves.'

'Yes, but they—'

'A perfectly ridiculous practice when it comes to governing a country, but history provides us with many instances of men behaving foolishly, and this is but the latest. In fact . . .' She hesitated as it suddenly occurred to her that this was not the best topic of conversation to pursue. Young persons were impressionable, after all. '. . . your letters have arrived,' she finished.

'My letters?'

'Yes, certainly – on the table.' Mrs Tipton gestured irritably. She also disliked being misheard or misunderstood.

Mary likewise decided to abandon the *sansculottes*, albeit for different reasons. Instead, she gathered the small pile of neatly folded and sealed papers and sat down on the sofa. She was used to her friend's crochets, and she quite enjoyed receiving letters, particularly those that did not engender anxiety. Before she had come to Suffolk a letter had been a rare event. Her circle had consisted of other penurious females, and no one else had had occasion to write to her. Her circle was still small but lately she had begun receiving invitations to dinner parties, and dances, and musical evenings, often from people whom she did not know, but always expressing an earnest desire for her presence. This was what came of being well off, and it was really very charming.

Mary smiled as she glanced at the first message, and Mrs Tipton's own gaze softened into complacency. Almost since Mary's arrival at Lindham Hall Mrs Tipton had entertained an ambition for her – that she should succeed in County society. This ambition might have had something to do with Mrs Tipton's lack of a daughter to mould and influence. On the other hand, she liked to mould and influence most of the people with whom she came into contact. However it had come about, Mary Finch was her particular project, and Mrs Tipton was not displeased with the changes she had wrought during the past seven months. Mary had always been a pretty girl, but pretty in spite of her dowdy, unadorned gowns and ingenuous manner. No one could have mistaken her for anything but a schoolmistress or governess. Yet now her celery-coloured muslin might have been described in the pages of the *Lady's Magazine*, and the colour set off her auburn curls admirably.

That is what a pretty girl needs, mused Mrs Tipton, *a proper setting. And now that those rascally lawyers have consented to turn over her inheritance, who can say what might happen?* It was fortunate that Mary had neither the freckles nor the pale complexion that often accompanied red hair – *no, auburn*, she corrected. And as for the sharp temper . . .

'Well?' she demanded, nodding at the letters in Mary's lap. 'What is the tally?'

'Dinner at Woolthorpe Manor in a fortnight.'

'Yes, very well.'

'A card party at Miss Carmichael's.'

'Negligible, and she will undoubtedly attempt to throw that nephew of hers in your path, which is tiresome. When is it to take place?'

'Saturday.'

Mrs Tipton pursed her lips. 'Do not reply straightaway. Something better may arise.'

'And there is to be a concert at Ickworth Lodge. The countess of Bristol begs we will attend.'

'Hmm. The Herveys are curiosities and not in the best of taste, but a plain refusal might do you harm in other quarters. We must consider how best to respond. What sort of concert?'

Even when she remembered to control her smiles or frowns, Mary's eyes often testified to her state of mind, and now a sense of fun shone through the green depths. '"In the Italian style".'

'Good Lord,' complained Mrs Tipton with a shudder. 'A decent collection of letters, however. What is that thick one?'

'It looks,' said Mary, turning over the wrapper, 'to be from Storey's Court, but I do not think it is Sir William Armitage's hand.'

Mrs Tipton urged her to open it. 'If they are planning a ball you must certainly attend. With Susannah Armitage as good as married there may be some excellent opportunities. There is the carriage to consider, for I do not know that Mr Cuff can drive such a distance . . . his rheumatism, you know, but I daresay something can be contrived.'

'I beg your pardon? Oh, yes,' agreed Mary, absently, as she continued to examine the packet. Was it really a ball? She had received a letter from Sir William quite recently, and he had said nothing about any sort of entertainment. Of course, he might have forgotten. She could almost hear him gaping at Lady Armitage and murmuring, 'A ball, my dear? Here? Ah, certainly, but remind me when it is to occur?'

She smiled. Sir William had proven himself an exceedingly good friend. He had been ever so helpful about her Adventure; it was because of him that Mrs Tipton had never been alarmed or distressed by it. He had managed to charm her, which was no mean feat, and he had not minded her outrageous hints about helping Mary to find her place in society. On the contrary, he had immediately invited Mary to spend Christmas at Storey's Court! Were it not for Sir William she would never have met Susannah and Charlotte, and of course he was Captain Holland's cousin—

451

Captain Holland.

All at once Mary experienced that prickly, shuddery feeling that Peggy said was caused by someone walking across your grave. That was nonsense, but might something have happened to Captain Holland . . . and Sir William had learned of it? Gibraltar was probably a very dangerous place – there were tunnels, after all – and if he *had* received bad news, dear Sir William would certainly write to her straightaway . . .

Her fingers were shaking. Something *had* happened, and she had been bothering about card parties and Italian singers!

'They might send a carriage and servant for you,' mused Mrs Tipton. 'It would be a thoughtful gesture on Sir William's part, and I am sure that if he were reminded . . .'

Mary tore open the seal; the paper inside had a black border. 'He is dead!'

'. . . of our situation. *What* did you say?'

Mary was reading quickly, and now she frowned in confusion. The colour had drained from her face, and she felt stricken and relieved at the same time. 'It is . . . dreadful news . . . Lady Armitage writes, and there is a message from Susannah as well. It was an apoplexy, they believe, and . . . the doctor says he did not suffer.'

'But what *is* it?' demanded Mrs Tipton.

'It is poor Sir William . . . He is dead.'

Virginia R. Knight interviewed Rose Melikan on behalf of Mystery News www.mysterynews.com.

I have enjoyed *The Blackstone Key* and look forward to the remaining two books in the trilogy, *The Counterfeit Guest* in 2009 and *The Mistaken Wife* in 2010.

I'm glad that you enjoyed the story, and thank you for your interest!

While I understand that you have degrees in literature, law and history, what led you from lecturing on British Constitutional History and authoring a biography of a Georgian Lord Chancellor to writing a trilogy of historical mysteries?

The narrative element of history has always appealed to me. As an academic I am trying to communicate information in a way that is both coherent and memorable, and narrative provides an excellent means for this — not to mention that history is full of some of the best stories imaginable. Of course, the weakness of narrative from the historian's point of view is that the facts cannot be altered to make a better story. Sometimes the trail goes cold, or the evidence turns in an unexpected direction, and there is nothing the historian can do about it. That's where the historical novelist has the advantage. The sources still provide a framework, but there is also license to fill in the gaps. In that way the mystery that became The Blackstone Key *began as a bit of a break from my academic work, something fun and a bit less rigorous. In fact, I've found that researching and writing it requires the same level of discipline — as well as being a great deal of fun.*

Have you always enjoyed mysteries?

Yes, in the sense that I enjoy stories with an element of the mysterious, whether that resolves into crime, or espionage, or even the supernatural. I wouldn't say that I'm widely read in the genre, but I am very fond of authors such as Arthur Conan Doyle, Wilkie Collins, Dashiell Hammett, and Dorothy L. Sayers. In my own work I love putting the mystery together, working out all the elements and then deciding what to reveal and when. Perhaps surprisingly, therefore, I'm not one of those readers who consciously try to solve the mystery before the sleuth. Sherlock Holmes knows far more about cigar ash and rare Asian poisons than I do, and for me much of the enjoyment of reading a mystery comes in observing the expert at work.

The promotional material on *The Blackstone Key* offers readers pretty heady comparisons to the gothic sensibility of Charlotte Bronte, the colourful characterization of Charles Dickens, and the plotting panache of Agatha Christie. While I doubt you saw any of those comparisons yourself, who you consider your influences?

At one level I have probably been influenced by most things that I've read; however, it is difficult to see any overt similarities between my stories and the novels of J.R.R. Tolkein or P.G. Wodehouse, two authors whom I greatly admire. I do certainly see the influence of Jane Austen, Daphne Du Maurier, John Buchan, and yes, Charlotte Bronte, but I would like to mention two other authors whose work has been very important to me. The first is Patrick O'Brian and the second is Stanley J. Weyman. O'Brian is perhaps the better known nowadays, but they were both great storytellers, and both created historical worlds that are vivid, accurate, and that perfectly complemented their characters.

You have created some vivid characters in *The Blackstone Key*. I expect some of them to reappear in the two remaining books. Do you have a favourite, beyond your protagonist, Mary Finch?

Do you mean by "favourite" the character that I would most like to meet in real life, or the character that I most enjoy writing? Villains, for instance, can be great fun to write, but I don't know that I would like to meet them outside the pages of a book. Not wanting to give away which of my characters would fall into that category, I'll instead mention Charlotte Armitage. She is rather a trial for her mother, but I think it would be difficult not to like someone of her enthusiasm, good nature, and sense of mischief. She is a little dynamo. She is also great fun to write. Some of her conversations with her cousin seemed to write themselves, they came so easily.

I've known few publishers who are willing to end a successful series at three novels, even if it is planned as a trilogy. Do you plan to end the Mary Finch series with this trilogy, even if it proves very successful?

When the idea for The Blackstone Key *took shape and I came to understand Mary and the other main characters, I thought that I would like to write three stories about them – and this was long before I had any expectation of them being published. I'm now in the midst of* The Mistaken Wife, *and I can foresee the series ending there. I think most series have a natural lifespan, either because the author loses interest or the characters reach the limit of what they can plausibly achieve, and it's a bad idea to re-work tired ground. On the other hand, I do have an idea for a fourth story that I think would offer something new . . . so I guess I'll wait and see.*

If you do end the Finch books with three, given your expertise in Georgian legal and political history, will you pursue other period mysteries?

I think that's quite likely, but can I just put the cat among the pigeons a bit and say that the Georgian is not the only period in which I'm interested?

Some authors I have interviewed are fascinated, if not obsessed, with King Henry II and his family, leading to many novels set in their era, just to be able to continue exploring their stories. They have not only the fascination, but also the familiarity. Do you feel this for the Georgian period, the time of the Regency and the Republicans?

Every historian thinks that their particular period is 'fascinating', but I like the late 18th and early 19th century because politically there is so much happening – Britain loses an empire in North America and gains one in India; political union with Ireland takes place; there are towering, yet eccentric figures like Pitt and Fox; and after having avoided European wars for much of the century, Britain becomes the dominant force against Napoleon. Socially and economically, too, this is an extremely important period for Britain, with the beginning of the Industrial Revolution, the abolition of slavery, and important changes in religious feeling and religious discrimination.

The French Revolutionary and Napoleonic wars are great sources for a novelist. There are the great battles like Trafalgar and Waterloo, and dramatic phases like the Reign of Terror, but throughout the period the political and social atmosphere was highly charged, as a result of the French Revolution. Anyone looking across the English Channel in 1795 would hardly have recognized France. The monarchy was abolished, the